BLOOD AND CURSES
BOOK ONE

OF KINGDOMS AND CURSES

AMY WOODRUFF

This book is a work of fiction. Names, characters, places, and incidents either are products of the author's imagination or are used fictitiously. Any resemblance to actual events or locales or persons, living or dead, is entirely coincidental and not intended by the author.

OF KINGDOMS AND CURSES
Blood and Curses, Book 1

CITY OWL PRESS
www.cityowlpress.com

All rights reserved. Except as permitted under the U.S. Copyright Act of 1976 and applicable international copyright laws, no part of this publication may be reproduced, distributed, transmitted, displayed, stored, scraped, mined, or otherwise used in any form or by any means, whether now known or hereafter devised, including for the training or operation of artificial intelligence or machine learning systems, without the prior written permission of the publisher.

Copyright © 2024 by Amy Woodruff.

Cover Design by MiblArt. All stock photos licensed appropriately.

Page Edges by Painted Wings Publishing Services.

Edited by Danielle DeVor.

For information on subsidiary rights, please contact the publisher at info@cityowlpress.com.

Paperback Edition ISBN: 978-1-64898-469-3

Hardback Edition ISBN: 978-1-64898-496-9

Digital Edition ISBN: 978-1-64898-470-9

For Vance, Kyla, and Meeko

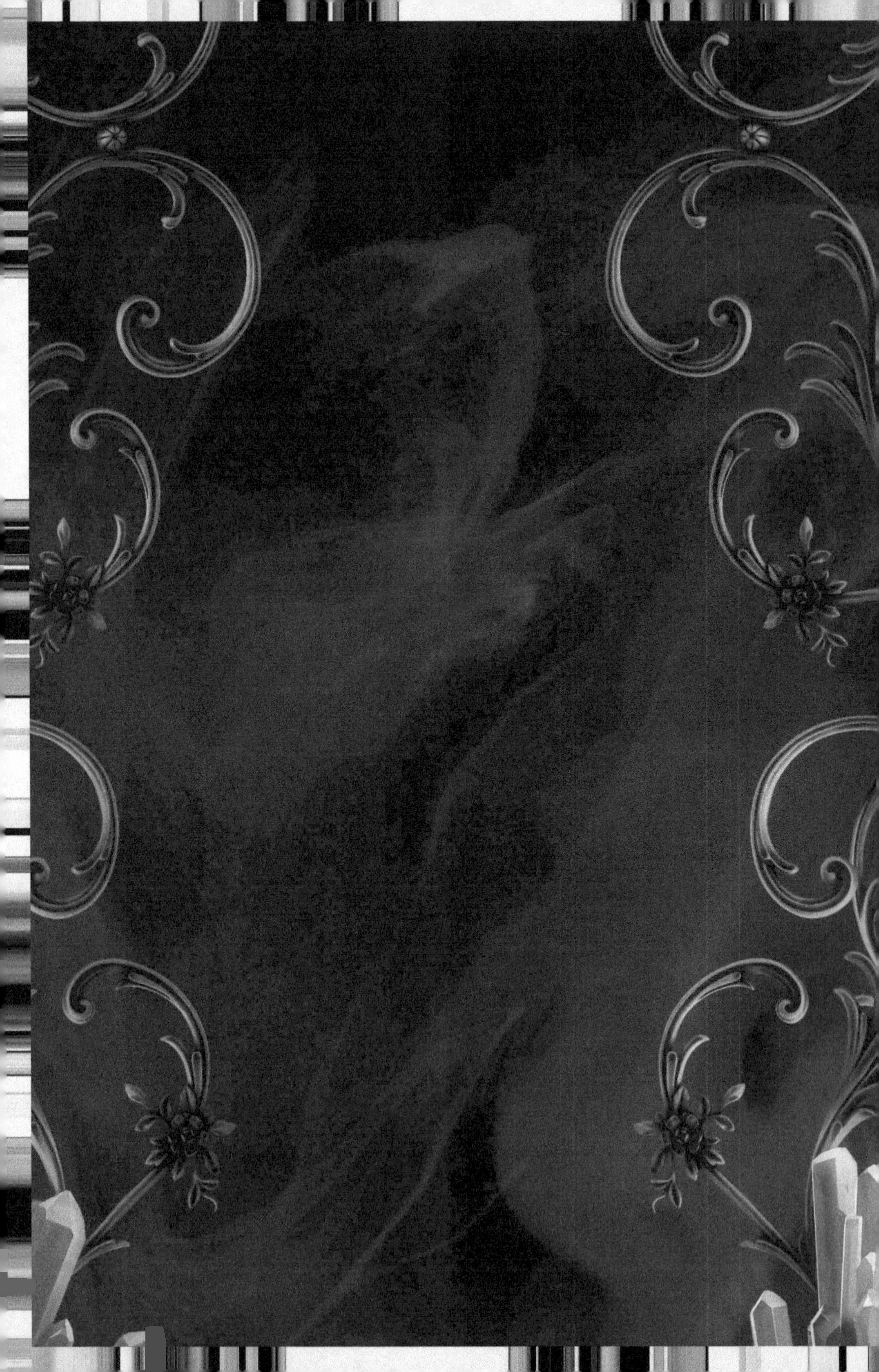

AFTER

CHAPTER ONE

Bridget Adams could separate her life into two distinct parts: Before and After. The simplicity suited her. There was only one problem…she couldn't remember the Before. The After she knew well. In the After, she was the ward to a Witch named Cora, head of the Virgo coven. Under Cora's care, Bridget studied herbs, practiced combat, and learned how to stay silent. In the After, she was one of the few humans living in the Kingdom of Vassuryn.

In the After, she was forced to bury dead bodies in the woods.

Looking down at a half-dug hole, Bridget leaned against her shovel and wiped sweat from her brow. There was no task she hated more. The first time Bridget had seen a Warlock die from magic use; she had actually volunteered for the job. Bile rose in the back of her throat at the memory. She thought she'd come up with a clever plan. The hasty idea had involved her dragging the Warlock to the woods around dusk, so that she could escape at nightfall. But Cora had known better. Within minutes, Bridget had been captured and returned to the coven. Her back still bore the scars of her punishment. Since then, Cora always sent a burly Warlock with her on errands. Once, when he was distracted, she tried to escape again. And again. She never got far.

"I'm not here to watch you sit around and daydream in the woods. Get back to work. I want to make a stop in Bryxton before it gets dark," Dante barked, a snarl on his puffy face. Behind her, he leaned against a tree and sipped from a small, silver flask. Under his breath, he muttered something about being done with kids. With thick arms and a sinister demeanor, Dante was Cora's main henchman. The only thing he liked more than torturing Bridget was ale.

Glaring, she heaved the shovel back into the stiff dirt. Even if she did get lucky one day and finally escape, she didn't know where to go. To the east, the Fae Kingdom of Elyria treated humans even worse than the covens. Although, as the ruling kingdom, Elyrians generally treated all the other species with contempt, according to Cora. To the south, Kastron's border was closed indefinitely to anyone with a coven mark. The Nymphs blamed the covens for their lack of independence. And the human realm was out of the question. The only gate back to Bridget's home was in Elyria, and Cora had made it clear it was impossible to access.

The gate haunted Bridget's dreams. Every night, new scenarios regarding her past plagued her mind. She longed to know about her old life, her *real* life, and how she traveled through the gate and ended up in Cora's care. Bridget's early memories of her seven months in Vassuryn were a blur of confusion, pain, and sorrow. Whenever she tried to remember those first days, her body physically rejected the memories. Vomit escaped her lips, or she passed out. In her possession, though, were two things Bridget believed were from the human realm, and she clung to them like a lifeline. A note and a necklace.

The necklace, an amethyst on a gold chain, never left her neck. Likewise, the note never left her pocket. Wiping her damp and dirty hands on her green top, Bridget pulled out the wrinkled paper. It was ripped down the middle and specks of blood colored the corner.

Your name is Bridget Adams. I'm sorry. He will...

Every day, Bridget cursed whoever tore the note and cut off the rest. It was pathetic. Her name was the only thing of the Before she knew. Sometimes, she would sit in the dark and repeat her name to herself, over and over, to make sure she didn't forget. And sometimes, she crumpled up the note and longed to throw it away because whoever had written it had clearly known what would happen to her when she crossed the gate. It was the same thing that happened to all humans when they crossed into Elyria.

They were cursed.

Bridget pushed her shovel into the dirt a little harder. Cursed. The word taunted her. Each human who crossed the gate was cursed to lose their memories. If she wanted to return to the human realm, it would happen to her again. Not that she cared. She would gladly give up every memory of Vassuryn to go back, even if she had no idea what awaited her there. On her loneliest nights, she liked to believe her dreams were real memories. Some things seemed to repeat—golden brown eyes, neon clothes, dark braids, and buildings that touched the sky. The images were vivid in her dreams, but they faded into fuzz when she awoke. With one last flip of dirt, Bridget finished the hole.

Behind her, Dante grunted, "Finally. It's about time. Hurry up and get it buried so we can leave."

It. Bridget clenched her jaw. She couldn't stomach looking at the dead Witch as she dragged the body toward the deep crevice. If Bridget remembered correctly, her name was Beatrix. The Virgo coven constantly moved camp. Beatrix had been in charge of camouflaging their tents to blend into the forest. However, the large spell always tired her. That morning, Cora had asked Beatrix to perform the spell again, even though the coven hadn't gathered any new herbs, flowers, or dirt that week. With no enhancers and nothing to help channel her magic, it only took a few minutes for Beatrix to bleed from the eyes and fall lifelessly to the ground.

Bridget had seen at least ten Witches and Warlocks fall in the last two months. Each time, Cora repeated her favorite lesson: all magic comes at a price. And lately, the coven had been performing more magic than Bridget could ever remember.

With a sigh, Bridget leaned down and began to push the body into the hole. As she did, her necklace popped out of her shirt and caught hold of the buckle of Beatrix's muddied cloak. Before Bridget could unhook it, the body rolled into the grave, snapping off her necklace in the process. The back of her neck stung as she jumped forward to grab it, but it was too late. Bridget ground her teeth together when she spotted the necklace in the hole, a glimmer of purple and gold in the darkness. Beside her, Dante used the tip of his boot to kick a pile of loose dirt into the grave.

"Stop," Bridget screeched. She scrambled to her feet and pushed him in the chest. "My necklace fell off. It's still down there."

Without a word, Dante grabbed her by the collar and shoved her in the hole.

When Bridget slammed onto Beatrix's lifeless form, she let out a sharp gasp. Searing pain exploded across her back. Through her ringing ears, she heard Dante's faint chuckles. After she caught her breath, Bridget rolled over and grabbed her necklace. The clasp was broken, and she couldn't get it back on. Blinking away the water pooling in her eyes, she shoved the necklace into her pocket and hoped a shop in Bryxton could fix it.

As she grabbed onto a loose root to climb out, a sharp zing went through her temple. Bridget swiped her hand in the air but felt nothing around her. Shaking her head, she grabbed the root again. Without warning, blinding pain crashed through her mind. Screaming, she bent over and braced herself on her knees. The fire burning in her brain left her breathless. Then, for a split-second, she saw a roaring river. When she thought she could take no more, the feeling suddenly subsided. Bridget stayed hunched over, breathing hard as she tried to clear her blurred vision. Throat tightening, she watched drops of blood splatter the dirt in front of her. When she wiped her nose, red stained her black leather gloves.

"What the hell is wrong with you? Elyrian soldiers could be nearby. Are you trying to get us killed?" Dante bellowed.

"Me? You're the one who pushed me down here," Bridget accused. "I must have hit my head the wrong way."

She glanced around the hole in confusion. The excruciating pain had disappeared, but a poking ache wouldn't leave the back of her mind. Hesitantly, she reached for the loose root again and clasped it tightly. When nothing happened, she quickly pulled herself out of the open grave.

As fast as she could, she filled the grave with loose dirt. When she was done, Bridget left a stone marker before Dante forcibly steered her in the direction of Bryxton. On the way, she tried not to feel guilty about her thoughts every time Cora asked her to bury one of the Witches or Warlocks. Because it was not dealing with dead bodies that made her hate the task…it was the reminder the fallen coven members gave her. All magic had a cost. And to break her curse, the price was her life. Humans had unsuccessfully tried for centuries. Magic was ruthless and merciless, and her curse held no loopholes. So with each new grave, Bridget could only see one thing: she would never remember her past life again.

CHAPTER TWO

Bridget watched Dante grin deviously the moment they entered Bryxton. She didn't understand his obsession with the town. It was on the smaller side, though most towns in Vassuryn were, and its few winding streets were lined with four-story rickety wooden buildings. Most had rotting shutters and chipped paint, but the town square looked updated. The small area was full of cobblestones and glass windows, making it by far the liveliest part of the village. There were a few shops and a pub, but Bridget had never been in any. Stopping in front of the pub, Dante wrapped his hand around her wrist.

"I'm going inside the pub for some important supplies. I expect you to be here waiting when I get back. Remember what happened last time you disobeyed me? Do you understand?"

Cringing at the smell of his breath, she leaned her head back and tried to put distance between them. A scar on her calf throbbed in response to his threat, and when she didn't answer, he dug his dirty fingernails deeper into her skin.

"Answer me," he barked.

"I understand," Bridget hissed.

Satisfied, Dante flung her wrist away and entered the pub. As she waited for him, Bridget leaned against an abandoned building and watched two old men argue about nearby Elyrian soldiers. From what she could hear, some were spotted a few miles away in Blackburn. The news made her tense. They would have to get back to camp sooner rather than later. A group of Elyrian soldiers had been ransacking and attacking covens throughout Vassuryn. It was the reason Cora constantly moved their camp. If a few drunks knew soldiers were nearby, Cora also did. She would have the camp locked down and blacked out by sunset.

A small fruit stand outside an apothecary got her attention. Her favorite bright orange fruit gleamed in the sun's dim light. Bridget took a step forward, already planning how she would walk by and subtly snag one as she talked to the vendor, when she made eye contact with a man walking out the pub. He was tall, with straight blond hair and a smirk that looked permanently plastered on his face. It wasn't his looks that caught her attention, he wasn't more handsome than any of the other Warlocks in the coven, but the fact that he looked at *her*. As a human, no Witch or Warlock paid her any attention. She was usually avoided at all costs. Color filled her cheeks when she made eye contact with him. His smirk widened.

Bridget didn't know why, but he looked amused, like there was a secret he enjoyed keeping from her. Without thinking, she took a determined step toward him, but a hand grabbed her by the shoulder. She spun around and came face-to-face with the only other human she knew.

"Where have you been?" Alexia whispered harshly, her cheeks flushed under the shadow of the hood she constantly wore.

Bridget ripped her shoulder from Alexia's grip and glared at her. "Don't blame me. Dante's the one who wanted to stop here. Besides, it's not that late," she said, even though the words were false. The sun hung low in the sky, and if they weren't back to camp by the time it was dark, Cora would throw a fit and likely punish her. Bridget couldn't stand the thought of Alexia bossing her around, though. In the beginning, she had tried to be her friend, but Alexia was never receptive. Most of the time, she gave Bridget the cold shoulder.

"You're late enough that Cora sent me out here looking for you and Dante," Alexia grumbled. "Daydreaming in the forest again?"

Heat crept up Bridget's neck. "At least I have thoughts of my own."

Alexia never did anything without Cora's permission. Bridget doubted she knew how to think without her.

Spinning on her heel, Alexia scoffed and strode in the direction of the camp. When she was out of sight, Bridget turned back to the man outside the pub, but he was gone. Frustration twisted in her chest. Something about the man had seemed familiar, and now she would probably never see him again. Nostrils flaring, Bridget stormed past the fruit stand and grabbed a piece of fruit before anyone noticed. The act was reckless, but she no longer cared about getting caught. Jail sounded better than being back at camp.

Minutes later, Dante exited the pub with a large case of brown bottles. An inkling of disappointment bloomed through her when no one stopped them from leaving the small village. She'd heard of Warlocks dragging thieves all the way to Elyria for a trial. If only she were ever that lucky. She doubted Cora, even as a coven leader, would be able to find her there.

On the short walk to the coven's camp, Bridget glared at the darkening sky and silently yelled at the sun for setting. She wasn't in the mood for another lecture from Cora, but Alexia's presence in town guaranteed the event. The other girl rarely left the Witch's side, and when she did, it usually meant trouble for Bridget.

The camp was quiet as they approached. Wind billowed harshly against the large, circular tents as the surrounding trees whistled eerily. Bridget involuntarily shivered when numerous torches died at once, making the horses whine loudly. She couldn't blame the creatures for being antsy; something in the air made her feel the same way. When a new prickling feeling tugged at the back of her mind, Bridget stretched and rubbed her neck. No matter what she did, the feeling wouldn't subside. She itched to claw it but knew it wouldn't help if it were a pulled muscle. A group of gossiping young Witches around her age gave her a funny look before they retreated into a tent. Bridget hated that her cheeks reddened.

Dante scoffed and headed to his tent without a backwards glance.

Hearing her name called, she turned and spotted one of the older Warlocks waving at her. Bridget walked to where he fixed a horse's shoe. She gave him a small smile, but it wasn't returned. He was usually friendly with her, but he seemed in a tense mood.

"Cora's ordered everyone inside. The prince was spotted outside of Blackburn."

Bridget frowned. She knew little about the royal family, except that they were Fae and very powerful. It was strange to her that the prince would even be Vassuryn, let alone be seen as a threat to their nomadic coven. "I thought we were hiding from the Elyrian soldiers."

The Warlock stood up and threw the broken horseshoe to the ground. "We're not hiding from anyone. If it comes to a fight, we will win. We have the advantage. Elyrian soldiers underestimate our numbers, but believe me, that prince is deadlier than any group of soldiers. Do as Cora says and stay hidden."

With that, he stormed away. Confusion rolled through Bridget. She had always thought it was a group of rogue soldiers that terrorized different covens throughout Vassuryn. However, the Warlock's words made it seem like the attacks were organized by the Fae and Elyria. Bridget's stomach swirled as she contemplated asking Cora about it, but there was no topic Cora avoided more than the royal family.

Bridget took a deep breath before she entered Cora's tent. Dim firelight crackled, lighting the spacious shelter with a warm glow. From the corner, Alexia smirked. Cora sat at a wooden desk. As Bridget approached, she didn't look up from her writing.

"You were almost late," the Witch murmured.

Bridget squared her shoulders. "But I wasn't."

Cora stiffened. She slammed her pen on the table and looked up at Bridget with pursed lips. Fire brewed behind her pale eyes. Just as Bridget began to wonder if she had made a terrible mistake, Cora blinked and stood up.

"If you had dawdled any longer, you would have put the entire coven at risk. Elyrian soldiers are nearby," she stated evenly.

"I thought it was the prince," Bridget blurted, unable to stop herself from calling Cora's bluff.

Cora's face remained impassive, except for a brief flattening of her mouth. "Who told you that?"

"I heard it in town."

Bridget could tell Cora didn't believe her. The Witch silently approached her and stared. Just when Bridget was convinced Cora could hear the stuttering of her heart, the Witch's hand snatched the orange fruit out of her pocket.

"I've told you this is a bad habit." With a tight smile, Cora put the fruit on the desk and pulled out a knife.

"She's lying," Alexia hissed from the corner. "No one in this hellish town even knows what the prince looks like. Someone is spilling secrets."

"And you do? Why is knowing the prince is nearby a secret?" Bridget asked, "It seems like pertinent information."

"Enough," Cora sighed, stepping between the two. "Bridget is right. The news that the prince has been in charge of the soldiers targeting covens throughout Vassuryn shouldn't be a secret."

"So he's been in Vassuryn this whole time?" Bridget asked. Without warning, a throb of pain went through her head. She bit the inside of her cheek to stop herself from reacting. "Why? Doesn't he have better things to do?"

"He hates Witches. That's all you need to know," Cora replied sharply, cutting the fruit, harder and quicker than before.

Something gnawed at Bridget's chest. It was the same feeling she had when she awoke from a vivid dream. The more she thought about the prince, the more it overwhelmed her. "But why? There has to be a reason. You can't be the future leader of the kingdoms and despise almost half the population."

"He was in the human realm for almost three years," Cora interjected, "he knows nothing about Vassuryn, or Kastron, for that matter. He doesn't understand what life is really like outside the walls of his palace."

Cora's venomous words gave Bridget pause. She wasn't sure if it was shock or jealousy that roared in her heart over the fact that he spent so much time in the place she wanted to be. "But I don't understand..." Bridget trailed off, rubbing at her chest.

"He has the power to destroy our way of life and everything we hold dear, and you dare question *why*?" Cora bellowed, slamming the tip of the knife into the desk, "We are your family. We have taken care of you. Do you wish to see us destroyed?"

Bridget silently stared at Cora's wild, frenzied face, afraid of what would come out of her mouth. Every scar on her body cried out and stopped her from moving. Heart pounding, she braced herself for a slap. Instead, surprise washed through her when Cora simply straightened her blouse and turned away.

"Maybe it's a good thing you're so curious about the prince. It will make what's coming next much easier."

Bridget glanced at Alexia for any hint of what Cora meant, but the girl remained stone-faced. When Cora snapped her fingers, Alexia stepped forward.

"Fetch Everly," Cora ordered.

Resisting the urge to roll her eyes at Alexia's immediate obedience, Bridget said, "I didn't realize there was anyone named Everly in the coven."

"She's been in Astraeus, gathering information for us."

Bridget knew little about Elyria's capital city. Like most of the coven, she had never been outside Vassuryn, and Astraeus was located in the heart of the Fae-filled Elyria. To her, it was odd that a Witch resided there.

"Is it normal for Witches to work in Astraeus?"

Cora's lips turned up slightly. "You have much to learn. Only in the country are the species so divided."

Before Bridget could ask more, Alexia returned to the tent. Behind her, a short, curvy Witch grinned widely. Her tan skin glowed in the candlelight, but Bridget's focus was on her clothes. The dark leather ensemble was different from anything she had ever seen. It looked modern and durable. Bridget's only outfit was a pair of tan pants and a billowy green top with way too many grass stains.

Cora greeted the Witch with a warm smile and kissed both her cheeks. "I hope it wasn't too hard to sneak away."

Everly shook her head and stared at Bridget. She shifted uncomfortably, feeling dissected. After a thorough once-over, Everly turned to Cora and asked, "Is she ready?"

"She doesn't have a choice."

Narrowing her eyes, Bridget took a step forward. "Ready for what?"

"Whenever a prince of Elyria turns twenty-one, a tournament is held to find his bride," Cora answered, "the prince ran away before that happened. However, he's back now, and the king has ordered for the tournament to commence."

"What does that have to do with me?" Bridget asked, "Or you? From what you've told me, the royal family seems to only like Fae."

"The Regina Torneamentum involves girls chosen from all the kingdoms. And we want you to enter."

CHAPTER THREE

Bridget gaped at them, unable to come up with one single reason why they would want her, a human, to try to compete to marry the prince. A *Fae*. "Are you crazy?" Bridget sputtered, "I can't enter that. I'm human. And why even have a tournament? Can't he find a girl on his own?"

"It started as a way to preserve magic in the royal family's bloodline after the Cavamynian War, but now it's tradition. The girl with the strongest magical ability wins and marries the prince."

"Supposedly," Everly said under her breath.

Cora sent her a look. "The winner is usually Fae. There are rumors that the winner is always pre-determined."

Bridget shook her head. Of course it was fixed. She doubted it was ever real. "This is a joke, right? Even if they didn't already have a girl picked out, there's no way I could win."

"Are you stupid? It's not about winning," Alexia spat. Bridget clenched her fists and resisted the urge to send her a nasty retort back.

"We need information," Everly explained. "As a contestant, you'll be able to find out what we need."

Bridget's lips twitched in annoyance at her tone. She didn't understand why they thought entering her into the tournament was a good idea. What made them think the king would even accept her as a contestant?

"Are humans even allowed to enter?"

"Not humans from Vassuryn," Cora said, "but you'll be entering as a girl from Andarre."

Bridget raised a brow. "I doubt the king or prince will believe I come from some made up kingdom."

Alexia scoffed. "Andarre is a very real place. It's an island off the coast of Kastron. It was founded by humans fleeing Elyria after the war. You should read a book every once in a while."

A million things flew through Bridget's head, including numerous plans to get away from Cora and find the kingdom she had never heard of. If she weren't so secretly excited, she would've been angry at Cora for keeping the knowledge of such a place from her.

"No ships from Elyria sail there, so it's the perfect back story," Cora added.

Trying not to let Cora's words damper her spirits, Bridget said, "The king can't be that stupid."

"He's already agreed to meet with you," Everly said.

Bridget let out a sharp laugh, still not believing they were serious. "I can't do it. I can hold my own in a fight, but when it comes to magic, I'm useless. I'll be dead within a week."

"No one has died in the tournament," Cora said reassuringly. "As a human, you won't be taken seriously. You'll be able to ask questions and gather information undetected."

"Ask who questions? Like you said, I'm human. No one is going to talk to me."

"The prince will."

Bridget stared at her in disbelief. She had never been more confused. Cora locked down the coven's camp because the prince was nearby. Now she wanted to send her straight to him? And expected him to talk to her? Bridget fiddled with the leather gloves that never left her hands. What would he think when he saw them? Or happened to see what was underneath?

"What could possibly be so important?" Again, Bridget's head pulsed painfully.

Cora paused, then spoke her next words very carefully. "We want to find the other gate to the human realm."

Bridget froze. It was the only thing Cora could have said to get her full attention. "You said there's only one gate to the human realm," Bridget whispered. "You said the Fae guarded it in Astraeus."

"We believe there is another. The prince is proof."

"What do you mean?"

"Everyone knows the poor little prince ran away," Everly said with a fake pout. "His father never would have let him cross the gate. It's guarded day and night. He must have gotten through another way."

Bridget didn't know why, but her mocking the prince sparked a flare of irritation inside her.

"That doesn't sound like proof to me. Besides, what do you want with the human realm?"

"Resources," Cora said. "What we lack here, the human realm has in droves. It's why the king guards the gate the way he does. He doesn't want any of the other kingdoms to have what he does."

Bridget wasn't sure if that was the real reason. It seemed too simple, too convenient. Cora was always scheming. She knew there had to be more to what she wanted, but Bridget was tired of being a pawn. Even if it got her a lashing, Bridget wasn't willing to offer herself to the prince on a whim. "I won't do it."

With a devious smile, Cora said, "If you agree, we'll help you get your memories back."

Bridget's heart stopped. In her wildest dreams, she never expected such an offer from Cora. As much as she wanted to believe her, Bridget knew it was impossible. But there were a lot of things she was discovering today. Bridget looked into her eyes to search for any hint of deceit but could find none. In the corner of her eye, she saw Alexia take a step forward, shocked and intrigued.

"That's not possible," Bridget croaked, afraid of the sudden hope that was building in her heart.

"There are ways. With dark magic, it can be done," Cora said.

Bridget's hope quickly turned into rage. She had heard enough whispers between the Witches and Warlocks to know anything that involved dark magic was nothing good and always ended in death. She felt idiotic; she had briefly forgotten Cora's favorite lesson about magic. "What's the price?"

Before Cora could answer, a frantic Warlock entered the tent. "Cora, Elyrian soldiers were just spotted across the river."

Now that she wasn't solely focused on Cora's words, Bridget heard the restless buzzing outside the tent. The sound of horses galloping away and tents being collapsed made her adrenaline rush. Alexia immediately started gathering everything in sight, and Everly's face drained of color.

"Impossible," Cora whispered, almost to herself. It was the first time Bridget had ever seen her at a loss for words. Bridget hissed when another sharp pain went through her head. Without thinking, she reached up and wiped her nose. When bright red liquid stained her gloves, all three Witches paled.

Suddenly, Cora's eyes darted to Bridget's chest. "Where is your necklace?"

Confused, Bridget pulled the broken jewelry out of her pocket and held it up. "It broke while I was burying Beatrix. What does that have to do—"

"You stupid, stupid girl," Cora roared, grabbing the necklace. Under her breath, she muttered an incantation. The Virgo symbol on the Witch's wrist glowed as the chain mended back together. Seconds later, she shoved it back into Bridget's hands. "Put on the necklace. *Now*."

Too confused to argue, Bridget slipped the necklace around her neck. Immediately, her head stopped aching. She almost doubled over from the sheer relief the action brought her. As shouts echoed from outside, Bridget watched Cora collapse the tent around them and shove a vial of powder into her pocket.

"Everly, meet us in Astraeus in three days," Cora shouted. "Things are moving faster than we expected."

Everly nodded, quickly disappearing into the crowd of the frenzied Virgo coven. Beside Bridget, Cora yelled orders and started an evacuation, just as the clouds in the sky started to swirl and darken. Moments later, a gust of wind almost knocked her to the ground. The swooshing was so loud, she could barely hear Cora screaming at her to get to a horse.

Bridget sprinted toward the frantic horses and grabbed the reins of the closest one she could find. When all the torches and fires surrounding the camp suddenly went out, screams filled the air. As Bridget jumped on her horse, a figure on a hill caught her eye. White eyes glowed brightly beneath a hood. It stared right at her. Suddenly, the hooded figure raised a hand, causing every remaining tent to crumple to the ground. Seconds later, weapons and supplies flew in the air and landed in the river. All around her, various Warlocks and Witches were pushed to the ground by an invisible force. A few feet away, Dante drunkenly scrambled toward the woods, bottles clinking in his hands. Before Bridget could blink, a metal pole flew from the river and sliced him through the chest. She watched in shock as he tumbled to the ground, blood spewing grotesquely from his mouth. On the hill, the mysterious figure stood with a raised fist. She had no time to contemplate the soldier, though, with only one thing on her mind. Run.

The chaos provided Bridget with the perfect opportunity to escape. She kicked her heels into the horse and directed it to the first dark part of the forest she spotted. In the moonlight, the trees of the forest were barely visible, but she didn't care. As long as she got away, any injury would be worth it. When she arrived in an open clearing and saw no one, Bridget's heart soared. She was finally free.

The sound of gallops behind her dampened her short-lived celebration.

Bridget turned her head and saw a hooded figure on a horse chasing her. It looked similar to the one she had seen at the camp. She kicked her heels harder and silently begged her horse to go faster. When she looked again, bright white eyes glowed beneath the hood. It was the one clear sign of a Fae using magic. Somehow, an Elyrian soldier had followed her.

Since her eyes were on the soldier, Bridget didn't notice the fallen tree in front of her. When her horse tried to make the jump, Bridget lost her balance and flew off the horse. She tucked her body before she hit the ground with a painful thud. The world shook as she rolled to a stop. To her left, she saw the hooded figure slow down. Bridget braced herself, expecting the Fae soldier to use magic to drag her forward. Instead, he ran to her. Panicking, she reached into her boot and pulled out a knife. When he got close enough, Bridget threw the dagger as hard as she could at the approaching Fae.

The soldier groaned as the knife pierced his shoulder. Gasping for breath, he fell to his knees. Bridget watched in horror as he calmly pulled it out and rose to his feet. Suddenly, a wall of fire blinded her. Behind her, Cora stepped from the shadows. Eyes black, she muttered a spell, hands outstretched. As blood dripped from her wrists and ears, darkness engulfed the Witch.

On her hands and knees, Bridget tried to scramble away, but ran into Alexia's legs instead. The other girl grabbed the back of her shirt and heaved her off the ground. Before she could protest, she was on the back of a horse. Alexia jumped on in front of her. Behind the fire, the hooded figure held out his hand. A section of the flames sizzled and disappeared, but when he tried to step through, Cora screamed louder. The wall skyrocketed higher, pushing him backward. Satisfied, Cora jumped back on her horse.

"Don't stop for anything. The fire won't hold him long. Follow me," Cora ordered. Alexia nodded. With Bridget in tow, they fled into the night. Unable to stop herself, Bridget looked back at the soldier. The last thing she saw was him staggering through the fire, but soon, he was out of sight.

CHAPTER FOUR

As they rode through the night, all Bridget could focus on was how the soldier had slowed her down and prevented her from getting away. She had been so close…Every so often, disappointment brought tears to her eyes. She desperately hoped Alexia hadn't heard her sniffling.

By the time they reached Terth, exhaustion engulfed her. Sitting on the border of Vassuryn and Elyria, the city was larger than Bridget ever imagined. Buildings reached the sky and glass windows reflected the sun's rays. To her disappointment, Cora stopped them just outside the walls. Bridget admired the architecture and longed to explore the knitted buildings. The skyline appealed to something deep inside her. She couldn't take her eyes away from the mosaic of metal that acted as a divider between the dark green trees of Vassuryn and the looming mountains of Elyria. When Cora sent Alexia into the city for supplies, Bridget burned with jealousy. She tried to sleep, but every time she closed her eyes, the image of the soldier on his knees haunted her.

In the sunlight, Bridget studied Cora. Blood stained the sleeves of her shirt. She had never seen Cora's eyes turn black, or a Witch bleed from the wrists during a spell. A twisting in her stomach prevented her from asking about it, even though it felt like the accusation would roll off her tongue any second. Bridget jumped when a large tube exited the ground and shot through the forest.

"It's called a train," Cora said, following her gaze.

Her bored tone made embarrassment rise up Bridget's spine. She turned away from the city and stared up at the clouds. They seemed to mock her failure. With each day that passed, the realization that she would never get away from Cora cemented itself in her heart.

"Is there any word from the rest of the coven?" Bridget asked, "Is everyone safe?"

"As far as I know, yes. They know where to go next," Cora said, waving her hand. For the past hour, she had been rereading a letter. Whenever Bridget tried to sneak a look, Cora quickly put it away.

Bridget furrowed her brows. While no one in the coven usually spared her a second glance, she was still surprised by Cora's nonchalant attitude. "Shouldn't we join them? What if they need help?"

Cora sighed and stuffed the thick letter in her pocket. "The most important thing right now is getting you to Astraeus."

"Why? Can't we try to look for this other gate on our own? I think joining the tournament is a terrible idea."

"Don't you think I've searched every city in the three kingdoms for even the whisper of a rumor? I have found nothing. Our only chance of finding the gate is the prince."

Bridget pursed her lips. She didn't want to admit it, but the idea of coming face-to-face with the prince terrified her. "If he hates Witches, how do you think he's going to feel about a human?"

Cora smirked and patted her cheek. "You're a pretty girl, Bridget. You'll figure it out."

Cheeks heating at the implication in her words, Bridget recoiled from Cora's grasp.

When Alexia came back with three thick pieces of paper, Cora announced they were taking a train to Astraeus. Within an hour, they were on their way to the station. Due to the rush, Bridget had no time to feel nervous about stepping on a machine that went high speeds. Surprisingly, the atmosphere felt natural and comfortable to her. In their compartment, Bridget leaned against the window and watched the fields pass in a blur.

The majority of the three-hour ride was quiet and bumpy. Whenever they passed a new town or mountain range, Bridget asked about it, but Cora only answered with a hum.

"What happens when we get to Astraeus?" Bridget eventually asked. Alexia, who had been sleeping with her hood pulled around her face, stirred across from her.

"You'll be presented to King Deckard."

"That'll be amusing," Alexia snorted. Bridget glowered at her.

Ignoring both of them, Cora said, "You'll say your name, that you're twenty-one and from Andarre, and then he will accept you in the tournament."

It sounded too simple, too easy. Bridget wasn't sure how she would pull off being from a kingdom she had only learned about yesterday. "After that, what should I do? Just stand there? I bet he'll like that."

"I'm sure he will ask some questions. The key is to stay focused and calm. It's not entering the tournament that is the hard part, but the tasks. You will still need to compete."

"That's helpful," Bridget grumbled, sinking in her seat.

"There's no need to be nervous. You'll be fine. I've trained you well."

Bridget didn't answer. She wasn't nervous. She was annoyed because Cora was sending her in blind. There was no doubt in her mind Cora knew more than she revealed. Bridget glanced up and found Alexia staring at her with an amused grin.

"Care to share what's so funny?"

Alexia shook her head and said nothing.

"You are prepared, but it won't be easy. The tasks are designed to push each contestant to their breaking point, but no one expects you to excel or win. As long as you lay low and don't draw attention to yourself, you'll be able to find out what we need," Cora said.

"And what is that exactly? Because there has to be more to this than finding the location of a gate that probably doesn't exist."

Cora's blue eyes sparked with anger. "Don't question me, girl. The gate is very real."

Bridget wasn't sure if she believed her, but she didn't want to argue. "If a Fae always wins, why do others even bother competing?"

"I said the winner is *usually* Fae. A Witch won the last tournament."

"I wouldn't call it winning," Alexia muttered under her breath. "The Fae girl the king chose died right before the wedding. He was forced to marry the second-best contestant."

Bridget briefly furrowed her brows at the remark, surprised that Alexia knew such information. Rubbing her temples, she pondered the new knowledge that threatened to turn her ideas about Elyria upside down. "So the queen is a Witch? Does that make the prince a Warlock?"

"*Was* a Witch. She died in childbirth many years ago," Cora said. "And no, his powers presented as Fae, but there is a rumor one of his sisters inherited their mother's abilities."

"If that's true, it doesn't make sense why he was in Vassuryn. Why would someone with Witches in their family be in charge of the soldiers harassing covens?"

Cora's eyes flashed menacingly. "The Gemini coven wasn't harassed; they were nearly decimated. Only a few lucky ones survived and recognized who attacked them. Besides, the way those Witches were killed could only be done by a very powerful Fae with a rune. Everyone knows the prince possesses one of the few left in Elyria."

Runes. She could only remember a few times Cora had mentioned the stones used by the Fae to help channel and enhance their magic, and somewhat protect them from its deadly effects. According to her, most had been lost or destroyed along with the Tuathan, the ancestors of the Fae. A rune could only be created by a Tuathan, and only a few of the High Fae remained alive, bound and loyal to the king. Shamans, they were called now. Most were seers or gatekeepers to the other realms. Bridget shivered. At one point, she must have met one.

Swallowing hard, Bridget stared out the window. A hint of darkness still lingered in Cora's eyes, leaving her feeling cold. She didn't want the Witch's rage at the prince to be focused on her.

Cora turned pale and pursed her lips, like she had said too much. Without another word, she hopped out of her seat and exited the compartment. The door rattled loudly behind her. Bridget knew she was probably pacing in the hallway, not daring to leave them too far out of sight. She never did.

After a long moment, Alexia whispered, “There might be more runes out there than you think. In fact—”

“I really don’t care. I don’t plan on getting close enough to any Fae for it to matter,” Bridget said. “Why doesn’t Cora send you to join the tournament? You know more about the Fae and royal family than I do.”

“It should be me. I’m more trustworthy than you. I don’t try to run away every chance I get, or pretend I’ll suddenly remember, or go back to the human realm. I do what Cora tells me to, and I don’t ask questions. It’s why my back and hands are not nearly as scarred as yours.”

Bridget’s entire body flushed. Reflexively, she adjusted the leather gloves on her hands. “Maybe you should. You might learn to think for yourself.”

“There are many girls in this kingdom who would kill for the opportunity you are being given freely,” Alexia chided. “What girl doesn’t want to marry the prince? Who doesn’t wish to break free from the constraints of their ordinary life and become powerful?”

“You think joining the tournament will give me freedom? I’m not free. I never will be.”

The words burned like fire in Bridget’s mouth. She couldn’t believe she had said them aloud, let alone to Alexia, but the longer she stayed in Vassuryn, the truer they became. To her dismay, Alexia began to laugh.

“You know nothing. You appreciate nothing. You always search and dream of more, but when the opportunity for more presents itself, you reject it. You don’t recognize what is right in front of you.”

“And what is right in front of me?” Bridget asked. When Alexia refused to answer, Bridget continued, “At least I *try*. I don’t obey blindly and ignore my own thoughts. I don’t treat things like they don’t matter. Some things do matter.”

“You’re blind,” Alexia said, “and naive. It’s no wonder you never get far.”

Rage rattled Bridget’s bones. She crossed her arms, worried that if her hands were free, she would strangle the girl across for her. Burrowing deeper into her seat, she made a vow to prove Alexia wrong. She would enter the tournament, and make Cora and the coven a distant memory, with or without anyone's help. Surely, when the tournament started, she would be able to get away. She doubted anyone would care if the human wandered off. Getting away from Cora was worth the price of any foolish scheme.

When Cora returned to the compartment, Bridget stated, "I'll do it."

"Do what?" Cora asked calmly. When Bridget made a face, she continued, "If you are going to be around the Fae, you will have to be more careful with your words."

"I'll join the tournament."

Despite Bridget's resolve, the words tasted acidic on her tongue. She knew she never had a choice. A *real* choice. Cora was an expert at making people believe they did their own bidding, not hers. In fact, she half-wondered if Cora had left her alone with Alexia on purpose, knowing the other girl pushed her buttons in a way that made her reckless. But Bridget's decision was made, and she hoped she would stay one step ahead of Cora's plans long enough to escape the tournament and Elyria.

Cora slid next to her. Her gray eyes studied Bridget before she wrapped her arms around her. She knew it was supposed to be a warm embrace, but the Witch felt cold.

"My dear, Bridget," Cora soothed, "I knew I could count on you."

The rest of the train ride was spent in silence. Darkness swirled in the sky when the outline of Astraeus came into view. Even though she had barely slept, Bridget perked up at the announcement of their arrival in the capital city. For a moment, she forgot what the plan was, and instead, felt excited at the prospect of seeing a new place. However, one look at Cora's stern face dampened her spirits.

A strong piney scent hit Bridget's nostrils as they stepped off the train. Sunlight barely peeked over the horizon, giving her a hazy glimpse of green trees and a large stone wall. Mountain peaks loomed like shadows against a navy sky. Nothing prepared her for the number of lights, though; metal and granite buildings, taller than she had ever seen, shined brighter than any star. The sight took her breath away.

Slowly, they followed a crowd through the wide entrance of Astraeus. Two soldiers stood at the grand oval opening but said nothing as people pushed past them. As they entered the city, Cora tugged on Bridget's jacket and pulled the hood tightly over her head. She sent the Witch a puzzled look, but she was ignored with a quick shushing motion.

Silently, Bridget followed the back of Cora's head through crooked and narrow streets. She had thought Terth was impressive, but the capital city of Elyria was even more massive and beautiful. Beneath her feet, a dark material lined the roads, different from the mud and cobblestones she knew in the outskirts of Vassuryn. The sidewalks were full of life, and activity proceeded on every corner. Fae, human-like in every way except for the magic that simmered beneath their skin, bustled around her in a hurry. They, along with various Witches and Warlocks, wore various arrangements of colors, pants, and dresses. Occasionally, Bridget caught a glance of a Nymph or two bustling down the street. Buildings dwarfed her and blocked the sun as she walked. In every window, she spotted glass lights hanging from ceilings, and boxes with black and white moving screens on the walls. She had never seen so many shops, clothes, and food in one place.

"I never knew a place like this existed," Bridget wondered aloud, unable to keep her eyes on one thing.

Cora snapped her fingers and said, "Stay close and don't wander off. Astraeus can be a dangerous place for a human."

In a broader street, numerous signs of varying sizes littered the landscape. Some advertised restaurants or shops, but one stood out to her. The blood red poster announcing the Regina Torneamentum was bigger than the others, brighter even. It looked new, like it had just been hung. Bridget took a step forward to get a closer look at what it said, but a hand pulled her back.

"That poster won't tell you anything you don't already know. Come now. We're late to meet Everly," Cora said.

Bridget swallowed back her annoyance and continued to follow Cora down the street. After a few blocks, she spotted the short Witch that Cora seemed to trust with her life. Everly ran forward and hugged Cora fiercely.

"I'm so glad you weren't caught. When I saw the prince..."

Bridget's eyes darted to Everly. The prince had been at their camp?

"We made it. That's all that matters," Cora said quickly. "Everything is going according to plan."

"Do we get to finally learn about this plan?" Bridget asked, crossing her arms.

The two Witches glared at her.

"Enough of your questioning, Bridget. It's time to go to the palace. It would be wise to practice holding your tongue before we get there."

"I didn't realize we were so short on time. I'll meet you back here tonight, then," Everly said, backing away. "It will look too suspicious if I accompany you."

Bridget was stunned. She didn't expect Cora would take her straight to the palace within minutes of arriving. She hadn't planned or come up with a solid idea about how to sneak away...

"You seem to have something on your mind," Alexia quipped.

Heat flooded Bridget's cheeks at being caught. "I'm just ready to be rid of you."

With that, she stormed past her to follow Cora to the palace.

CHAPTER FIVE

Bridget meticulously analyzed the palace wall, or that's what she assumed they stood in front of. White, thick stone went on for miles, and all she could see behind it was rolling hills and grass. If she listened closely, though, she could hear chatter coming from the other side.

"The palace grounds are expansive and include the Elder Woods. I've heard there's even a lake somewhere beneath the mountain base," Cora said, reading her thoughts. "Apparently, the king rarely lets his subjects leave court, so he provides markets and plenty to do for amusement. The actual palace sits on top of the hill, behind the tree line."

"It's beautiful," Alexia said breathily.

Bridget stared openmouthed, unable to speak due to the sheer size of land that stood in front of her. Escaping the palace might be harder than she thought. And now that she was looking closely, she could see numerous soldiers spread out and pacing on the top of the wall. She wondered if they were there to keep people out…or in.

The entrance to the palace was closed, blocked by a curvy, black metal gate covered in thorny vines. Four muscled guards stood still as statues in front of it. They wore all black and their long-sleeved shirts were formfitting. One stepped forward as Cora approached. From a distance, Bridget watched her hand the female guard a small envelope.

"What is that?" Bridget whispered to Alexia.

The other girl shrugged. "Probably something that gives us permission to enter."

"It looks like a letter," Bridget said, eyeing the wax seal. It was etched with a symbol she didn't recognize.

Alexia opened her mouth to reply but was cut off by the summoning of the guard, who signaled them over with a curt wave. As they approached, Cora mouthed at them to say nothing. The guard eyed her briefly before nodding once. Seconds later, the metal gate creaked open. The sound grated on Bridget's nerves and made her heart tremble in her chest. For a split-second, she was afraid to enter.

With a deep breath, Bridget stepped through the gate. Once she was on the other side, the air seemed different. Heavier, somehow. Numerous gravel walkways split across the grounds, all leading to different destinations. To the right, a small market of various booths and tents stood in a grassy area. Bridget wanted to stop and look, but Cora pushed her forward. They followed the largest path, one that took them upward through the looming trees.

Bridget's legs ached by the time they reached the top of the hill. When the tree line broke, she finally saw it. The palace. It was older than any building she had seen in Astraeus. The stark white stone walls gleamed in the sunlight, and massive windows reflected the rugged image of the mountains surrounding it. Ivy grew from every corner. Bridget wasn't sure how a building could be so beautiful, yet intimidating, at the same time.

The closer they came, the bigger the palace seemed to become to Bridget. When its five story walls began to dwarf her, Cora stopped. The Witch turned and gripped her arm tightly.

"Bridget, things will move quickly from here. Once you're chosen, you most likely won't get to say goodbye. Every five days, take off your necklace at sunset. I'll be able to contact you briefly and help you, if necessary. It'll be my way of checking in. Do you understand?"

Bridget nodded, afraid that if she spoke, she would say that in five days, she planned to be long gone. Her answer seemed to satisfy Cora, though, because the Witch gave her a tight smile and pushed her forward once more. They passed gardens and small alcoves, courtyards and stone walkways, but Cora kept moving. Soon, they stopped in front of an extremely large set of engraved wooden doors. With a closer look, Bridget was able to recognize some Latin symbols, only from peeking inside Cora's tiny spell book a time or two.

Bridget jumped when the doors swung open, revealing a heavyset woman in a lavish green dress. Her brown eyes studied Bridget thoughtfully for a long moment. "Is this her?" She asked Cora.

Cora nodded.

"The king is waiting," the woman stated, grabbing Bridget by the arm.

As she was dragged forward, Bridget looked back at Cora one more time. Catching her eye, the Witch whispered, "Always remember that I thought of you as a daughter. And to bow."

Darkness enveloped Bridget as the doors slammed shut. Once her eyes adjusted, she followed the woman down a long hallway.

Cora's words made Bridget feel sick to her stomach because, for a split-second, warmth entered her heart. She hated that after everything Cora had done to her, she still cared. After all, the Witch had been one of the few constants in the short seven months of life she remembered. Now she had no idea what tomorrow would bring.

The woman stopped right before they turned a corner. With a nod of her head, she wordlessly bade Bridget to keep going and turn right. Reluctantly, Bridget did and entered the largest room she had ever seen. Every inch of the throne room was covered in black and gold marble. Ornate engravings and paintings lined the ceiling. Some looked centuries old, especially a faded one of a dark-haired man with a mustache she had trouble tearing her gaze from. Instead of glass hanging lights, torches lined the walls, giving the room's onyx columns an eerie glow. Bridget's footsteps echoed as she slowly walked toward the solitary figure sitting on a gleaming gold throne. The king didn't look like what she imagined. Instead of being old, scary, and monstrous, he was fairly young. His long white hair contrasted harshly with tan skin and dark, deep-set eyes. Eyes that seemed to dissect her with every step she took.

The king stared at her expectantly as she approached. There was a gleam in his eyes she couldn't quite read. When she got closer, she spotted a black dagger sitting at his hip. It glowed inside the sheath. The handle was obsidian, making her briefly wonder if it was a rune. A few feet from the throne, she performed her best bow. The gesture felt odd.

"I'm—" she began.

"I know who you are. There's no need for false pretenses," the king snapped. Suddenly, his brown eyes glowed white as he stared at her. Bridget braced herself, expecting pain or magic to hit her any second, but nothing happened. After a long moment, the king's eyes returned to normal. His gaze flittered to her necklace. Bridget frowned in confusion.

"Clever," he muttered. Impatiently, he waved a guard over. Bridget hadn't realized anyone else was in the room. "Take her to Orion and get her to sign the contract. After that, gather all the girls in the west courtyard. My son should be arriving soon."

The king stood up and began to walk away, not sparing her a glance.

"That's it?" Bridget blurted before she could stop herself. The second the words were out of her mouth; she knew she had made a mistake.

In the blink of an eye, the king was in front of her. Even though he was only a few inches taller than her, he seemed to tower over her. His irate glare seared her skin. She involuntarily took a step backward.

"That's it? It seems like you've forgotten your place in the grand scheme of things. You're nothing but a pawn in a game you don't understand. A thorn in my side, actually. And right now, with that stone hanging around your neck, you're useless to me," the king hissed menacingly. "And that's not something anyone in this palace wants to be. Remember that next time you think it's wise to speak freely in my presence."

Bridget's heart thundered painfully in her chest as he stormed away. Before she had time to compose herself, a guard dragged her to another room. This one was just to the side of the throne room. A man inside spoke to her, but Bridget, still reeling from the king's words, couldn't hear him over the whooshing in her ears. There was no way she could stay in the palace a second longer. She had to get out. Had to—

Hands clapped in front of her face, snapping her out of her spiraling thoughts.

"Are you listening?" The man asked irritability, waving a thick piece of parchment at her. "To enter the tournament, you'll need to sign this."

"What is that?"

"What do you think?"

Bridget eyed the paper warily. The king had mentioned a contract. She knew the Fae were always very careful and clever with their agreements and promises, but she had never heard of them making people sign anything. Bridget grabbed the paper and tried to read the words, but it was written in Latin. She furrowed her brows.

"What does it say?"

"That you agree to participate in all tasks and stay on the palace grounds until the winner is announced," the man said, rolling his eyes like he had repeated the words too many times before. "The winner is chosen by the prince and announced once all tasks are completed. Also, participants must not harm any member of the royal family."

Bridget had stopped listening when he mentioned being forced to stay on the palace grounds until the end of the tournament. Panic flooded her. That was something she couldn't agree to. And she knew enough about Fae agreements to know that if she signed the contract, there would be major consequences, like death, if she tried to leave. She couldn't stay. She never planned on actually participating. It was only a ruse to get away from Cora…

"How long?" Bridget croaked, "How long does it last?"

Orion sighed. "That's up to the king. The last one took almost a year. He couldn't make up his mind."

"I can't sign that," Bridget said, backing away.

Suddenly, a guard behind her grabbed her and shoved her into a chair.

"Orion, we have strict orders that she doesn't leave this room until it's signed," he stated.

Orion nodded and held out a small needle to her. Bridget's throat tightened. She would have to sign the contract with blood. Briefly, she studied the room's one exit. In her boot, she had two knives. There were three men in the room. She might be able to make it out, but there was no telling what awaited her on the other side of the closed door. Orion's knowing smirk told her it was nothing good.

She was trapped.

Bridget closed her eyes, feeling like she was leaving one prison for another. And this time, she wasn't sure if she would make it out alive. Hand trembling, she grabbed the needle. Wordlessly, she pricked her finger and let a drop fall on the contract. The second it hit the paper; the dot glowed before it absorbed into the paper completely. Forever.

It was done.

"What happens now?" Bridget asked. Regret took over her body.

Orion snatched the contract out of her hand and stuffed it into a drawer. "You'll be escorted to the west courtyard, where the other participants should be waiting. There, the tournament director will explain the rules and tasks."

"Already?"

"Since you decided not to put up a fight, I guess I'll let you be the first to know," Orion winked, "the Regina Torneamentum starts today."

CHAPTER SIX

Orion's words repeated in Bridget's head. The tournament started today. How was that possible? She could have sworn the announcement signs in Astraeus had looked new and the prince was in Vassuryn. Although, according to the king, he was due back soon. She took a deep, calming breath before following another guard out of the room. Everything was moving too fast. Just this morning, she believed she was days away from freedom…Now, she would have to fight against other girls with magical abilities for a prince she didn't care about or know.

At least no one bothered to check her for any weapons.

After a long walk, the guard announced their arrival at the west courtyard. Rose bushes lined the exterior and the scent of various herbs wafted through the air. A gigantic tree stood in the middle, a glittering combination of green, red, and gold leaves. Its gray base was thick and edged with black. Bridget had never seen anything quite like it. A number of Fae mulled around the courtyard, but a group of six girls caught her eye. They stood apart from the crowd in front of a large platform. Some mingled with each other, some stood silent and solemn, but all went quiet as Bridget walked toward them.

Each girl studied her as she approached. Their expressions fluttered between shock and disdain. To Bridget's surprise, one took a step toward her. She had pale skin and slanted eyes. Her black hair flowed down to her waist. Since she bore no coven mark, Bridget guessed she was Fae.

"You're human," she stated, voice wary. "A human has never been allowed to enter the tournament."

Bridget let out a bitter laugh. "Apparently, things change. I'm from Andarre," she lied.

Most of the girls' eyes widened further before they started whispering furiously among themselves. The Fae girl in front of her didn't look like she believed her, though. She stared at Bridget in barely hidden dread.

"What's your name?"

Before Bridget could answer, another girl grabbed her by the arm. "I don't mind humans. You can stand with me," she said, leading her away. She was beautiful, with olive skin and dark eyes. As she looped her arm around hers, Bridget spotted an Aries mark on her wrist.

"Don't mind her. She thinks she's special because she's already friends with the prince," her new companion whispered conspiratorially, holding out a hand, "my name's Quinn."

"Bridget," she replied, quickly shaking the girl's hand.

Quinn led them closer to the tree. A Fae man with a very round waist attempted to climb onto the platform, gaining the attention of everyone in the crowd. All watching slowly shuffled forward. Bridget wondered who all the other people were and why they wanted to listen to the rules. When the man finally made it up, he was out of breath. He stumbled to a tall black pole and cleared his throat. When he began to speak, his voice echoed loudly throughout the courtyard. He introduced himself as the tournament director. Not really listening, Bridget glanced over her shoulder and found the dark-haired Fae girl watching her.

"I thought all the humans in Andarre had special tattoos," Quinn said.

Bridget shrugged, not sure how to answer. She hoped no one else asked her any questions. She knew nothing about Andarre.

"Like any tournament, there will be rules," the man continued. "No one is allowed to use their powers outside of a task, under any circumstances."

"Boring," Quinn quipped, voice colored in disappointment. Bridget felt relieved.

The director cleared his throat again. "There will be four tasks. After each task, a winner will be chosen by the prince based on your display of power and aptitude. The nature of each task will not be revealed until the day of the task."

"This is archaic," a male voice mumbled behind Bridget, speaking with an accent she didn't recognize.

Bridget turned around and saw an extremely good-looking man. He was tall, with cropped, jet-black hair and dark brown skin. He leaned against a stone wall, arms crossed and a look of annoyance on his face. Around her, Bridget noticed she wasn't the only girl stealing glances of him.

"Who's that?" she whispered to Quinn.

Quinn smirked, not having to turn around to know who Bridget was talking about. "He's from Tafari. One of the princes, I believe. I've heard he visits regularly."

"Tafari?"

"Humans," a Nymph scoffed in front of them. The scales on her arms glittered in the sunlight.

"It's a kingdom across the sea and Elyria's oldest ally," Quinn said, giving Bridget a puzzled look.

"Right," Bridget nodded, feigning understanding. She let out a sigh of relief when the Witch turned her attention back to the director.

"You should already be aware you may not leave the palace grounds during the tournament, which will not officially end until the prince announces the final winner after the fourth task. The tournament starts today."

"Why is a human here?" A female voice called out from the crowd. When all eyes swiveled to Bridget at the question, she angrily glared at the back of the woman's head.

"There will be no questions. The prince will arrive shortly. Please proceed to the throne room. Thank you." the director stated and rushed off the platform. The crowd chattered loudly in his wake.

"Already? There are only seven girls here," a blonde Fae complained. "My mother said there were at least thirty girls when she competed."

"And I thought Marin was supposed to be here," the brunette next to her whispered, eyes roaming the emptying courtyard. The blonde shuddered.

"Good riddance. I don't want to be anywhere near her. I get chills every time she speaks."

Bridget watched them curiously as they walked away. She wondered who Marin was and why they seemed so wary of her. Unsure of which way to go, she looked at Quinn for guidance. Everyone seemed to know exactly what to do. Except her.

Quinn's eyes swept over her in puzzlement. "Are those the only clothes you have?"

Bridget's cheeks reddened. She had nothing except the clothes on her back and a pair of knives in her boots. The Virgo coven had lived frugally in the outskirts of Vassuryn. It hadn't bothered her then, but now that she was stuck in the tournament, she felt irritated that Cora hadn't mentioned needing new clothes. Or anything, really, for the tournament.

Bridget fiddled with the edge of her worn out shirt. "Yes, unfortunately."

Quinn nodded. "Once we get to the throne room, we'll be presented to the prince. I'm sure the others left to change. I think we have time to head to the market and find you something new. I'll help you out, just this once."

When the Witch winked playfully, Bridget gave her a grateful smile. Even though she had no desire to catch the prince's attention, she was glad she wouldn't look utterly haggard in front of him.

As Bridget followed Quinn to the courtyard, she wondered how the Witch already knew her way around the palace grounds. She stayed quiet, though, afraid to accidentally push away one of the few people to show her kindness in Elyria, and still unsure whether to trust her.

At the market, Bridget eyed the exit of the palace grounds with longing. Envy overtook as she watched people coming in and out freely. Quinn broke her out of her reverie by tugging her hand and leading her to a tent that sold clothes. She recognized a few items from her short walk through Astraeus. After telling Quinn she trusted whatever she bought her, the Witch held up a short blue dress.

"It'll match your eyes," she said.

Bridget nodded and clutched the dress. It was the first new thing anyone had bought her. Before she could say thank you, a rumble from the other side of the palace wall pierced her ears. It sounded like thunder moving full speed toward the entrance. Many of the market workers jumped in alarm and pulled their tents closed. Even Quinn whipped her head around toward the sound.

Moments later, a group of soldiers on horses came booming through the palace entrance. Dust rapidly filled the air around them, causing Bridget to cough uncontrollably. Through watery eyes, she spotted a carriage enter behind them. Bangs echoed from inside, visibly vibrating the ornate cabin. Before she could ask what was happening, Quinn grabbed her arm and pulled her behind a wooden cart. The Witch put a finger up to her lips in a plea for silence.

"Move!" A tall Fae with dark brown skin bellowed, shoving past soldiers. "Is he spelled in there? If he is, I suggest you release him quickly."

A soldier nodded nervously and pulled out a quartz stone from his pocket. He waved the stone across the carriage doors. With a loud slap, they flew open. Suddenly, the soldier flew backwards and hit a tree. Bridget peeked around the cart to see what, or who, got out.

"Why the hell am I here?" A low voice growled angrily.

All Bridget could see was the back of a man. His hair was light brown, thick, and wavy, and hung right above his broad shoulders. He stood a few inches taller than the other Fae male who ordered his release from the carriage. Bridget found herself wishing he would turn around so she could see his face.

"You know why. Your father is growing impatient," the darker male answered. "You're injured. I guess that explains why you were caught. What happened?"

"It's nothing," the other said with a wave of his hand, "and he's always impatient, especially when it comes to me. Care to explain why I was dragged here all the way from Vassuryn?"

Bridget stopped herself from gasping. Based on his clothing, expensive and regal, she should have already guessed who stood in front of the carriage.

The prince.

"He's ordered the tournament to start today. Before you run off, just know Delphine has entered. You should stay and make sure she knows what she's doing."

"I will, but only for the night. I did ask her not to join," the prince paused briefly, "I was so close."

The hint of devastation in his voice made Bridget's heart sink.

The prince's friend moved toward him with a look of trepidation on his face. "Everyone is saying he's placed a human in the tournament."

A hand pulled on her arm. "Bridget, we need to get back to the palace before they do," Quinn whispered in her ear. Bridget knew she was right, but she couldn't tear herself away from the conversation in front of her, especially since they were now talking about *her*.

After a long moment, the prince replied, "He wouldn't be that stupid."

Bridget tried not to feel stung. It seemed, along with Witches, he disliked humans too.

"You underestimate him," his friend warned.

"Let's go," Quinn hissed, forcibly grabbing her arm. For a small girl, she had a tight grip.

Bridget reluctantly followed her. She spared one last glance at the prince's back. Neither male noticed them sprinting away. When they made it back to the west courtyard, Bridget bent over and tried to catch her breath. Quinn had nearly torn her arm out of its socket dragging her up the hill. To Bridget's envy, the Witch only had faint drops of sweat on her brow.

"There's a bathroom to the right, behind that big bush. Hurry and change. If the prince is already here, they'll start the introductions soon," Quinn said.

"What about you?"

Quinn waved a hand in the air. "Don't worry about me. I'm fine in this."

Bridget glanced at her boots, skirt, and red cloak. It was nice, but the style didn't match the type of dress Quinn had bought her. Before she could ask, Quinn gave her a pointed look and pushed her toward the bathroom. After she changed, Bridget studied herself in the mirror. The blue of the dress did match her eyes, but her red hair looked like it hadn't been brushed in days. She ran fingers through it and tried to smooth it down, but nothing made it look any better. Since the dress was short, her ragged brown boots and gloves looked out of place, but it would have to do. Besides, she didn't know why she cared so much. After she exited the bathroom, Quinn gave her a nod of approval. Despite the uneasy feeling settling in her stomach, Bridget followed her to the throne room.

CHAPTER SEVEN

As they walked, Quinn asked, "Did you get a good look at him?"

A blush involuntarily crept up Bridget's neck. "Not really."

"I saw him from a distance one time. He's handsome," Quinn giggled. The sound made Bridget clench her jaw.

From around the corner, Bridget heard a loud crowd gathering outside the throne room. Her stomach flipped at the thought of so many people watching her be introduced. She wasn't sure how she would convince a bunch of Fae she was from Andarre, especially if they asked questions. Luckily, the crowd didn't seem to notice her as they approached. Before they walked in, they were stopped by the same heavyset woman that had greeted her with Cora.

"You're late. Participants need to wait in the alcove. You'll see the rest of the girls gathered there when you walk in. You'll be introduced one by one. Come forward when you hear your name called," the woman said with an ingenuine smile, adding, "Remember to bow."

The alcove was a hidden corner placed next to the side of the throne room. Heavy velvet curtains fell over the entrance to shield the girls from the crowd. It was small and stifling, especially since a few girls paced nervously. The only one who seemed calm was the Fae girl who had spoken to her earlier. The anxious buzz in the air made her sweat, despite the short dress.

"This is going to be a disaster," Bridget told Quinn. "I didn't realize it would all be so formal...and public."

Having moved next to Bridget, the same Fae girl said, "You'll be okay. Just go out there when you hear your name, and Cade will—"

"We don't need your help, Delphine," Quinn snapped.

Delphine's mouth fell open, stunned by Quinn's quick, harsh remark. Bridget wrung her hands together. For some reason, her chest had tightened at the sound of the prince's name. When she realized Delphine was gazing at her concernedly, Bridget whipped her shaky hands behind her back.

"I understand what to do. Thank you, though."

Delphine frowned in disappointment but moved to the other side of the alcove. When she was out of earshot, Bridget whispered to Quinn, "Why did you do that? She seems nice."

"The first lesson you should learn in this tournament is to trust no one. Everyone here is after the same thing, and it's not friendship," Quinn said.

Bridget nodded, noting that she should also apply the rule to Quinn. She absentmindedly pulled on the ends of her dress, wondering if she should have accepted the gesture from the Witch. Suddenly, the loud chatter around the alcove went quiet. Bridget couldn't see what was happening, but she guessed the king or the prince had arrived. After a few seconds, the tournament director's voice boomed throughout the room, announcing the introductions of each contestant.

One by one, the girls left the alcove—first, Delphine and Alette, the two Fae girls. The audience cheered loudly. Next, Brynley and Quinn, both Witches, were introduced. After that, the two Nymphs, Hai and Ondine, were called. The tournament director said where each girl was from and what kind of magic she possessed. Soon, Bridget was the last girl left in the alcove. Her heart pounded in her chest as she waited for her name.

"You might be surprised by the next participant."

Bridget's head snapped up because it wasn't the director's voice she heard, it was the *king's*. She rushed forward and tried to peek out of the curtain without being seen.

"This year, Andarre decided to send a participant. For years, we've tried to build relations with the isolated island kingdom. It seems that our persistence finally paid off."

A murmur of whispers and spattering applause traveled throughout the large chamber. Through a narrow slit, Bridget spotted the king. He was sitting on the throne, with a smug smile on his face. A black, spiked crown glittered on his head. To his left sat the prince.

Cade.

The name echoed oddly in her head.

Cora and the coven had made him sound terrifying and ruthless, but he was...attractive. Extremely attractive. Handsome, but in a boyish way. The chocolate color of his hair matched his eyes. Her heart stuttered as she studied his high cheekbones and full lips. She couldn't tear her eyes away from him. And even though he wasn't smiling, Bridget thought a grin would suit him. Instead, he glared at his father. For someone who was being introduced to his options for a potential wife, he looked absolutely miserable.

"The tournament can be challenging. I've witnessed it firsthand," the king said, "I'm sure it will be even more difficult for a human. I hope you, like me, are excited to watch how she progresses. In fact, I think this tournament will go down in Elyrian history as one of the best yet. What do you think, Prince Cade?"

The audience cheered, but Cade said nothing. Bridget watched his face drain of color and knuckles turn white as he gripped the arms of his chair. Her stomach knotted. Was he really that opposed to a human?

With a wicked grin on his face, the king nodded at the tournament director. The large man shuffled to a skinny black pole. Nausea rolled over Bridget when the director cleared his throat and said, "Please welcome the next participant, from the Kingdom of Andarre...Bridget."

Before she lost her nerve, Bridget stepped out of the alcove and into the light. The prince's gaze snapped to hers. His eyes widened for a split-second before pure fury overtook his features. Cade sprung up and knocked his chair over with a loud crash. He grabbed his father by the collar and menacingly growled, "What the hell is this?"

Without warning, the scene in front of her exploded. The crowd gasped in horror as guards rushed from all directions to protect the king. As they did, numerous guests were knocked to the ground, including a frazzled Alette. Amid the chaos, Bridget spotted the director jogging to her. The prince yelled at his father, but she couldn't make out what he was saying over the shouts of the guards that tried to separate the two.

"The participants already signed a contract. She can't leave," the king ground out, face purple from the prince's grip.

Bridget froze, chest caving at the fact he wanted her gone that badly. She didn't care. She *didn't* care. Competing wasn't in her original plan, anyway. So why was she feeling so rejected?

The director grabbed her by the arm and dragged her from the throne room. Ears ringing, she barely noticed Quinn walking up to her. Closing her eyes, she tried to make herself go numb. It didn't matter that the prince wanted her gone, she signed the contract and would have to compete. She could do it. She would avoid him at all costs...

"That could have gone better," Quinn said, interrupting her thoughts.

Bridget's throat constricted. "I think he might hate me."

Quinn patted her arm reassuringly. "He was shocked."

Bridget shook her head. She knew it was more than that. The prince was downright furious at her presence. Now, more than ever, she hoped the tournament went by quickly and that she wouldn't run into him again.

Quinn rolled her eyes. "Stop worrying. Come on, don't you want to see your room?"

"We get our own room?" Bridget frowned. She had barely thought about where she would be staying. She was used to sleeping on the floor in whatever private space she could find. As she looked around, she realized most of the girls were already gone.

"There's a whole set of apartments for the participants on the grounds. It's where I've been staying the past few days. Follow me," Quinn said.

Wordlessly, Bridget did. The apartments were on the east end of the palace, with an outside entrance. Unlike the rest of the palace, the floors and walls were wooden and rustic. Inside, a spiral staircase gave visitors access to all three floors. On her way up the stairs, Bridget spotted a kitchen and dining room.

"Most of the girls stay here all day. There's food and a gym. They say we're free to roam the grounds, but every time I've tried to get to the west end, a guard has stopped me," Quinn rambled.

"What's on the west end?" Bridget asked.

"It's where the royal family stays. And a library, I think," Quinn stopped on the third floor and pointed to a room on the right, "that one's free. I'm just on the other side."

"Thank you," Bridget said, slowly creeping toward the room. Hesitantly, she pushed the door open. No one was inside. The small space was nicer than any room she had seen in Vassuryn. A large bed sat in the corner next to a tiny fireplace. Velvet carpet lined the floor and the dark wood walls were scattered with different floral paintings. Red and gold covered every inch of the room. A rectangular foggy window was stationed by the entrance to the washroom, which held a large tub and shower. When Bridget tried to look out at the view, it was too dark to see anything. Disappointed, she stood in the middle of the room, not quite sure what to do. Catching a glimpse of her tangled hair in the mirror, she decided to fill the tub. It was brass and stood above the checkered tile floor. As the hot water rose, the large drain in the middle of the tub caught her eye. She fiddled with her necklace before slipping it off her head. The chain had already been broken once, and she didn't want to risk it falling off again, especially down a swirling drain.

The second the blistering water hit her skin; relaxation buzzed through Bridget's veins. She hoped the bubbles washed away every ounce of humiliation that now seemed permanently tattooed on her skin. The prince hated her. And now she was stuck competing for a chance to *marry* him. Maybe if she never left her room, no one would bother finding her for any of the tasks. Then she would never have to face him again.

Even if he was irritatingly attractive.

When goosebumps rose on her skin, she realized she had soaked in the tub longer than expected, unable to erase the day from her mind. Still, she never knew a bath could be luxurious. Bridget vowed to take one every day just so she could try out all the different smelly soaps.

When she stepped out of the water, exhaustion hit her. She couldn't remember the last time she'd slept for more than an hour. To her surprise, a fluffy robe was sitting outside the washroom. She pulled it on and brushed the knots out of her hair. Then, not bothering to put back on her necklace or clothes, she fell on top of the bed and passed out.

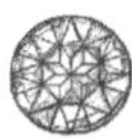

Bridget was floating. She knew she should find it odd, but the sensation felt natural. In fact, she even trusted the sensation to lead her wherever it wanted to take her. It felt like a friend.

She floated down a spiral staircase and into a garden. There, she saw a solid wooden door with multiple rows of black spikes. It looked foreboding. And intimidating. But she traveled to it and then went through it. Now in the dark, she moved down, down, down...

After a moment, she stood before a large stone. At first glance, it looked like any old stone. When she moved closer to it, though, it started to ring. The sound pierced her ears, making her want to turn away, but she kept floating toward it. The moment she touched the stone, her entire body burned. She felt pulled in every direction and couldn't tell which way was up. She needed the feeling to stop, was convinced she would die if didn't...

With a searing gasp, Bridget's eyes popped open. She surged up as her gaze darted around the room. It took her a few moments to recognize her surroundings. She was in her room, she was safe...

Bridget placed a hand on her chest in an attempt to calm her stuttering heart. Panting and covered in sweat, she tried to relax on the bed. She knew it had been a dream, but everything in it had seemed real and familiar. No matter what she did, crystal clear images stayed stuck behind her eyelids. Feeling unsettled, she decided to take a walk to clear her head. Even though she was still in a robe, she quietly slipped out her door and down the staircase, desperate for fresh air. When the cold night wind hit her skin, she regretted not changing. The frigid air stung her bare legs. Just before she turned to go back inside, a side pathway caught her eye. Déjà vu washed over her. Despite herself, she walked toward it.

The narrow alley led her down some steps to a secluded garden. She knew the trees and color of the flowers, and Bridget didn't have to turn her head to know what would be in the right corner.

A wooden door with black spikes.

The second she laid eyes on it, her ears roared. The door was identical to the one in her dream, except this time, it was slightly open. Heart pounding, Bridget crept toward the door. When she looked around the garden and saw no one, she used her fingertips to pry the door open wide enough for her to slip in.

She flinched when it slammed shut behind her. Unlike her dream, the circular stone steps in front of her were lined with torches. Even though her gut screamed at her to turn around, she began to walk down the stairs. Circle after circle, the steps continued. The deeper she went, the colder the air became, until she finally reached the bottom.

A few feet away was a large standing stone. To Bridget's relief, it didn't hum or ring. A man stood in front of it. He turned around as she approached. He was bald, with pointed ears and dark blue tattoos. The ink shimmered in the firelight, like it was made of lazurite. He looked otherworldly.

"You're a Shaman," Bridget whispered.

High Fae. Seer. Gatekeeper. Immortal.

So many names for such powerful beings, when just one would do. *Tuathan*. The man nodded. She wondered if she'd said the word aloud. Fear crept up Bridget's spine, but she remained motionless. As she gazed around the room, she noticed blue crystals circling the standing stone and a thick book that looked like a manifest on a table.

"That's the gate to the human realm, isn't it?" Bridget asked. The man nodded again. Cora had said it was guarded day and night, but only one Fae stood between her and the world where she belonged.

Bridget rushed forward. "I want to cross."

She didn't think of the consequences. It didn't matter that she had signed a contract or would lose her memories again. The human realm was right in front of her, and she wouldn't miss the chance. The Shaman grabbed her hand and led her toward the stone. He muttered another language under his breath, causing the stone and his tattoos to glow. When the humming started, Bridget longed to cover her ears. Suddenly, the Shaman stiffened. His dark irises turned white, and he started to bleed from his nose.

"Bridget, you can't," he said, his voice noticeably lower.

Stunned, she wrenched her hand out his and took a step back. Eyes wide, she yelled, "How do you know my name?"

"If you cross the gate, you'll die," the voice warned.

Bridget frantically looked around, trying to find the source for the Shaman's unexplainable change in demeanor. "The human realm doesn't have magic, right? Maybe once I cross, the contract doesn't matter anymore," she argued. Even to herself, she sounded unconvinced. Despite that, she barely resisted sprinting toward the stone.

The voice turned sympathetic. "It doesn't work that way. There's still magic there, just not in the way you think. It's how we're able to get back."

Bridget bit her lip. She knew he was right. The contract would take her life the moment she touched the stone. She just didn't want to believe it. Blinking away the moisture in her eyes, she remembered the excruciating feeling of crossing in her dream. Her conviction wavered.

"I can't hold him much longer," the Shaman said, looking at something behind her.

Bridget whipped around and saw one of the Fae from the market, the prince's friend. His dark brown eyes were kind as he said, "Come with me. I'll take you back to your room."

He reached out his hand, but she was still torn. Besides her memories, the only thing she wanted was to go back to the human realm. Bridget gazed at the Shaman again. The glow of the rock reflected in his white eyes. At that moment, he wasn't the Shaman, but someone else.

"Who are you?" Bridget asked, almost begging. Her watery eyes spilled with the knowledge that she wouldn't be returning home.

"I'm sorry," the voice replied. It was gravelly and full of pain. As he reached for her, his body abruptly collapsed to the ground. Without thinking, Bridget ran to him and tried to turn him over. The moment she touched him, he grabbed her by the shoulders and rolled her toward the gate, his irises returned to a color as dark as night.

The Shaman's nails dug into her skin. "I have orders."

Bridget grasped on to his forearms and brought her knee up with as much force as she could muster. The Shaman groaned and rolled off her. When she tried to stand up, he lunged for her ankle. Bridget screeched in protest, feeling her body fall toward the gate.

A knife whisked through the air, hitting the Shaman in the shoulder. Bridget had forgotten about the other Fae. Helping her up, he said, "I need to get you out of here. Now."

The Shaman let out a blood-curdling howl as he tried to crawl after them. The Fae helping her reached down and pulled his knife out of the Shaman. Once he did, he bashed the handle into the older man's temple, knocking him out. The glow of the stone dimmed and faded. A piece of hope died in her heart.

Gazing at the Shaman's lifeless body, Bridget asked, "Is he dead?"

"No, but he won't stay unconscious for long. We don't want to be here when he wakes up," he said calmly, pulling her up the stairs. She wheezed, barely able to keep up with his pace.

Once they made it to the top, she breathily asked, "What's your name? How did you know I was down there?"

"It's Finn. I come down this courtyard when I can't sleep. I saw you go inside and decided to follow when I realized the guards were missing," he replied and then furrowed his brow. "Why are you wearing a robe?"

Bridget's cheeks heated. "I fell asleep in it."

"And then decided to keep it on for a midnight stroll?"

"Yes."

They stared at each other for a long moment. Eventually, he let out a short laugh and gave her an incredulous look. With a wave of his hand, he motioned for her to follow him. "The contestant apartments are this way."

They walked in silence until Bridget mustered the nerve to ask, "Who took over the Shaman down there? For a moment, he was…different."

Finn stiffened. "I don't know, but I know you're not from Andarre. You don't have the look. They're known for having large tattoos on the back of their neck and spine."

Bridget froze in her tracks.

"Don't worry. I won't make a public announcement or tell anyone," he added.

“I was told to pretend I was from there,” Bridget admitted carefully, heart still skipping in her chest.

“I figured,” Finn shrugged. “What was it like? Forgetting. Did you have to relearn everything?”

The question took Bridget off guard. No one had ever asked her anything like that. She mulled over her answer for a long time before answering. “No, there were some things that stayed. Like reading and using a fork. Things that are…”

“Muscle memory?”

She nodded, agreeing with the new term. “That’s a good way to put it.”

There was more she wanted to ask him, but they quickly arrived outside the apartments. Finn gave her a dismissive smile and turned away.

“Thank you,” she called out, but he was already gone.

CHAPTER EIGHT

Bridget's eyes burned in protest when a blinding light struck her awake. She had tossed and turned all night, unable to stop the nightmares from plaguing her mind. Eventually, she moved to the floor, hoping the cold wood would relieve her flushed skin. Peeking one eye open, she saw a blurry image of Quinn standing over her. Bridget pulled her blanket over her head and hoped she would get the message to go away.

"Rise and shine," Quinn sang, tugging on the blanket. The tone made Bridget's head pound.

"How did you get in here?" Bridget mumbled, keeping her eyes squeezed shut. Whatever new horror the palace had in store for her could wait. The memory of the gate buzzing and the bloodthirsty snarl of the Shaman made her want to hide in the small room all day. Plus, she had no desire to keep up the pretense of wanting to be in the tournament with the other girls.

"Your door was unlocked," Quinn said and then eyed Bridget's position on the floor. "Long night?"

"You could say that," Bridget sighed, resigning herself to the fact that Quinn wasn't going to leave her alone. She slowly sat up and rubbed the back of her neck. "Is there a task today?"

"No, but it's almost noon. I figured you would want some food. I could practically hear your stomach growling from outside the door," Quinn teased.

At that moment, Bridget's stomach let out a loud groan, making the Witch giggle. She guessed it really had been a while since she ate. Bridget heaved herself off the floor. "Okay, you're right. I'll meet you down there."

After Quinn left the room, Bridget splashed water on her face and braided her hair. While debating whether to wear the blue dress or her raggedy clothes from Vassuryn, she spotted a pile of pants and shirts in the corner of the washroom. Frowning, Bridget inspected the unknown items. She didn't remember seeing the clothes the night before. In the pile was a pair of black pants, a long sleeve red shirt, and a black leather jacket. The outfit looked comfortable, but she would look like a giant fireball in the red top. Bridget groaned and put on the ensemble anyway, including the jacket. It was a little loose and there was a mysterious stain on the right arm, but she liked the feel of the leather.

From the top of the stairs, Bridget heard the other girls chatting loudly in the dining room. She almost ran back to her room, but the churning of her stomach stopped her. Straightening her spine, she made her way to the dining room. There were no chairs, only a large table filled with a variety of food. The smell made Bridget's mouth water.

The blonde Fae, Alette, clicked her tongue at Bridget. "I have to admit, you have some nerve. If the prince reacted to me like he did to you, I wouldn't be able to show my face the rest of the tournament."

"It was a misunderstanding," Delphine argued, giving Bridget a reassuring smile.

"Whatever," Alette muttered, rolling her eyes. She turned to Brynley and started to whisper something but kept her eyes on Bridget.

Bridget glowered at the two as she shoved random food onto her plate. Stuffing a chocolate muffin in her mouth, she walked to where Quinn stood with Hai and Ondine. Bridget smiled, but Quinn's eyes were on her jacket. "Where did you get that?" she asked.

"It was in my room," Bridget shrugged.

Everyone went quiet when a new figure walked into the room. Bridget's stomach dropped. The girl looked so similar to the Shaman she had seen last night. Bridget had to blink and make sure it wasn't him. She had the same pointed ears and iridescent blue tattoos, but her dark hair was cropped short and barely visible on her scalp. Without making a sound, she plucked an apple off the table.

"Marin, what are you doing here?" Alette asked warily.

"What do you think?" Brynley grumbled under her breath.

"You weren't there yesterday. You can't be competing," Alette argued.

Brynley shoved her elbow into the Fae girl's side. "She can do whatever she wants. She's one of *them*, remember?"

Marin stared at them for a long moment. "I was busy," she said, her voice flat. She bit into her apple and chewed slowly.

Bridget understood why Alette seemed peeved she was in the tournament. There was no doubt Marin was more powerful than any girl in the room. None of them stood a chance against a Tuathan. Quinn read her thoughts.

"I've heard she's only half Tuathan," Quinn whispered. "I feel like I need a nap. See you later."

The Witch scurried from the room. Undeserved betrayal washed over Bridget. Quinn was the only reason she had ventured to the dining room. Seconds later, Hai and Ondine turned up their noses at her and moved to a different corner. Bridget stood alone as Marin walked toward her. The girl stopped a few feet away and stared.

"Hi," Bridget said.

"Hello, Bridget," Marin replied. Bridget frowned and wondered how she knew her name. The Shaman girl moved closer, not once blinking. Her dark eyes pierced Bridget's skin.

"You're one of the oldest souls I've ever met," Marin said.

Bridget shuffled her feet, unsure of what to say to such a comment.

Delphine jumped between them. "It's been a while since I've seen you," she said to Marin. "I heard you were away looking for your father. Did you find him?"

Marin's face went blank before she responded, "He wasn't where I expected."

Delphine nodded with a forced, awkward smile on her face. It was the weirdest conversation Bridget had ever been a part of. Across the room, Alette waved a set of tarot cards in the air.

"Did you know these cards have a real rune infused in them? They're an heirloom. My grandmother let me bring them to impress the prince," Alette boasted proudly, pulling the cards out of a velvet sack. "She said they're even more accurate than a Shaman."

"I doubt that," Delphine whispered to Bridget.

She wasn't quiet enough, though, because Alette's eyes darted to her. "Did you say something?"

"No," Delphine replied innocently.

"I only see images. It's random and sometimes they change," Marin announced.

There was a tense moment of silence before Alette cleared her throat and continued, "I've heard the prince trains every afternoon in the field by the Elder Woods. Isn't that right, Delphine?"

"I don't know. That was before...everything," Delphine sighed, irritation forming on her features.

"We should go later and see if he's there. I want to read him a fortune," Alette said. Bridget doubted he was still in Astraeus. When she had spied on him during his arrival, he had told Finn he was only going to stay one night. She didn't want to mention the incident to Alette, though.

"What makes you think he'll talk to you?" Ondine asked.

Alette puffed up her chest. "I'm the only one here who's his type. Before he left, he had a different blonde on his arm every week, and he always hosted these amazing parties in Astraeus. Right, Delphine?"

"Things change," Delphine said. She gave Bridget a sideways glance.

"I doubt it. I heard he wasn't really in the human realm, but in Tafari, drinking and partying with three-boobed harlots the past three years."

"Shut up, Alette," Delphine growled, surprising every girl in the room.

Alette narrowed her eyes but dropped the topic. "Brynley, pick a card," she ordered. She put three cards face down on the table. The Witch contemplated her options before picking the card in the middle.

"You're destined for great things, including one love," Alette gushed.

Bridget rolled her eyes and chewed on a piece of bacon. The fortune sounded generic and made up.

"Does the human have a problem?" Alette sneered. "Don't you want to know your fortune?"

"Not really."

Alette didn't listen. Again, she put three cards face down. This time, she picked up the right one. A black and gold skeleton shimmered in the light. "Looks like you won't make it out of this tournament alive," Alette grinned wickedly. "Shocker."

Nostrils flaring, Bridget charged, ready to slap the smugness off Alette's face. A hand tugged on her arm and stopped her.

"Bridget, have you seen the gym? I'll show you how to work the machines," Delphine said, forcibly dragging her out of the room. She led Bridget to a massive open space. Windows lined the wall, letting natural light flood the room. Large machines with black blocks and mats covered every corner. Fans twirled on the ceiling, creating a calming buzz.

"This is a gym?" Bridget asked.

"The machines help make your muscles stronger," Delphine said, pointing to a particularly intimidating one. "Over there, you can practice combat skills. They added this area to the apartments a few years ago because the tournament can get quite...physical."

Bridget grimaced. Physically, she could hold her own. Against magic, she would fall easily. "Doesn't bode well for me, then."

"Don't worry. I'll help you. Once you get the hang of the machines, it's easy."

Delphine sat down on a machine and showed Bridget how to press her legs against a black metal sheet. She added more weight and then let Bridget try. Her thigh muscles burned with every push. Delphine gave her an approving nod.

"You're strong."

"For a human?"

The bitter words were out of Bridget's mouth before she could stop herself.

"No, for a person," Delphine corrected.

Bridget shot up and wiped her sweaty hands on her pants. For someone close to the prince, she was genuinely kind. She was tempted to question her about Finn and the gate, but instead, Bridget asked, "What ability do you have? Or is it supposed to be a secret?"

Delphine disappeared before her eyes. Bridget waved her hand in front of her, thinking she might have turned invisible.

"Over here."

Bridget whipped around. Delphine, now on the far side of the gym, grinned widely. With a loud pop, she appeared next to Bridget again. Her grin disappeared, though, in a fit of coughs. A drop of blood trickled from the Fae's left ear.

"Does that always happen?" Bridget asked.

"Usually. Sometimes, I bleed from my nose, lose hair, or get sick for a week," Delphine shrugged. "It depends on how far I travel. There's not much Tuathan left in my bloodline and runes are hard to come by, so magic tires me out quickly. Because of that, I try not to travel often. Most Fae would have longer lifespans if they did the same."

"That must be frustrating."

Delphine's cheeks reddened. "I don't care about magic. I want to be a healer. Some Fae have the ability to use magic to heal themselves and others, but it doesn't always work. As you can see, magic takes a toll. We've become too dependent on Vassuryn for their tonics because of it. I want to learn how to do surgery, like in the human realm. Tafari has surgeons too. Maybe I'll go there."

"What is that exactly?" Bridget asked, embarrassed that she couldn't remember or understand what she was talking about.

"I'm sorry. Surgery is where you can open a person up and fix them without using magic at all," Delphine said, her blush deepening. "I think it could be really great for the people here."

"I think so too. I hope you can one day," Bridget agreed. The image of every Witch and Warlock she had seen die and buried in Vassuryn flashed through her head. Would the idea Delphine spoke about have made a difference? She hoped so. As a human, Bridget could see the kingdoms' reliance on magic was a crutch.

"I've already learned a little," Delphine said proudly.

"Delphine!" Alette called from the door, "We're leaving to find the prince and need you to come with us. It'll be weird to walk up to him without a proper introduction."

Delphine's mouth turned down in annoyance. To Bridget, she whispered, "It's not a good idea, but I know she won't leave me alone until I take her. I'll tell you more about Astraeus and the tournament on the way."

"I'm not going," Bridget stated flatly.

"Why not?"

"You saw how he reacted to me yesterday. I don't want to see him unless I absolutely have to."

"See? She doesn't want to come. Let's go," Alette whined, stuffing her tarot cards in her coat pocket. Brynley, Hai, and Ondine all wore begging faces behind her.

"He won't do that again. I promise," Delphine said. When Bridget remained unmoving, she added, "I'm not going unless you come."

A nasty shade of purple overtook Alette's face. Her reaction humored Bridget, so much so that a scheme concocted in her head…and it was worth the price of facing the prince again.

"Fine, but Marin has to come too," Bridget said, reveling in Alette's bulging eyes.

If Alette wanted to meet the prince so badly, Bridget would try her best to make it as memorable as possible.

CHAPTER NINE

Bridget was confident no one in the world talked as much as Alette. The entire walk to the Elder Woods, she rambled incessantly about the prince and what he liked to do before he disappeared. Some stories sounded true, some didn't. But with each new tale, the urge to smack her on the back of the head grew larger. Every once and awhile, Delphine corrected her with the real story. Eventually, Bridget moved to the back of the group to walk with Marin. Her silence was a balm on her nerves. To Bridget's surprise, one of the girls from Kastron joined them.

"I don't know why I came either," Ondine whispered, an embarrassed smile on her face.

"You'll be back in Kastron soon enough," Marin said bluntly.

The smile dropped from the Nymph's face. She moved back beside Hai.

"Is that true?" Bridget asked.

Marin shrugged. "I'm not allowed to elaborate on anything I see. In the past, it's made people go crazy."

Bridget let out a sigh of relief when they reached a large field outside the Elder Woods. It was flat, grassy, and shaded by the pine trees that grew alongside the mountainside. From a distance, Bridget spotted Cade and Finn fighting each other with swords. Surprise rolled over her. From what she'd overheard, the prince wanted to be long gone from the palace as soon as possible. Despite herself, she couldn't tear her eyes away from the sweaty pair, especially Cade. With each swing of his sword, the muscles in his arms bulged and strained against the short sleeves of his black shirt. Tall and toned, he deflected Finn's every blow with ease. She was amazed by how fast he moved, quicker and sharper than any man she'd seen or met in Vassuryn. She swallowed hard and forced herself to look at Finn, hoping to gauge whether or not he would out her for her failed escape attempt. He glanced at her briefly, bur his face remained blank. He walked over and whispered something to Cade, then pointed at the approaching group of girls. When Cade turned around, a loud gasp escaped Bridget's lips. Bruises covered his entire face, and his right eye was almost swollen shut. He cursed and threw his sword to the ground.

"What are you doing here? Is everything okay?" Cade asked Delphine, avoiding eye contact with the rest of the girls.

"Some of the girls wanted to meet you," Delphine said. There was an odd tone in her voice. Bridget couldn't take her eyes off the deep purple mark on his cheek. Her chest prickled when she noticed Delphine wasn't stunned by his appearance. Bridget took a deep breath and pushed the intrusive thought away. She was the last person who had any right to be jealous over Cade, especially when he despised her. Besides, she had a plan to focus on. Well, two plans, actually.

Get as far away from Elyria as possible.

And steal Alette's cards.

There was only one she could achieve today.

Cade ran a hand through his damp hair, making it stick up in the air. "Now's not really a good time."

"I know, but..."

A blonde head pushed her to the side. "I'm Alette. You might know my parents. They own one of the electric companies and absolutely adore your father. They donate to all his charities regularly. My mother actually competed during his tournament. In fact, she almost won."

"Charities? I didn't know he knew the meaning of the word," Finn muttered under his breath. The prince's lips twitched.

When Hai started spewing off her family's history in Kastron, Bridget slowly moved toward Alette. Her plan was stupid and reckless, but her gut told her she knew how to pull it off. The side pocket of her leather jacket was large enough to swipe things in and out quickly.

"Enough about Kastron. It's not like anyone actually wants to visit that sand dune. Did you know I'm excellent at telling fortunes…" Alette began. Bridget took the opportunity to bump her shoulder into the girl's back and grasp the velvet sack sticking out of her pocket.

When Alette stumbled forward, the prince's eyes locked with Bridget's. The jolt of electricity that went through her almost made her lose her breath. Alette glared at her but continued rambling about her tarot cards.

He knew.

Bridget could tell by the way he was looking at her. Heart pounding, she waited for him to expose her. Instead, Cade blinked and turned his attention back to Alette. Throat tightening, Bridget backed away, turned, and mindlessly inspected a bush. After a minute, she felt Cade's eyes on her back and knew she had to abandon step two of her plan.

"The rune has been in our family for generations," Alette said, reaching for her pocket. "I'll show you. Where are they? WHERE ARE THEY?"

Finn flinched at her high-pitched squeal, along with Delphine and Hai.

"Where are what?" Cade asked calmly.

"The tarot cards," Alette hissed. "They were in my pocket and now they're missing."

"Maybe you misplaced them."

"I did not misplace them," Alette spat. She whirled around and pointed a finger at Bridget. "You took them. I know you did."

"Why would I take them? They already told me I was going to die soon," Bridget said blithely. Once more, Cade's intense gaze snapped to hers. Inside her pocket, she felt the outline of the cards and did her best to keep a straight face.

"She's all the way over there, Alette," Delphine argued.

Alette's face turned wild as she glared accusingly at everyone in the field. Eventually, her gaze settled on Marin. "If it wasn't the human, it was you," she snarled. "That freak has been purposefully creeping me out all day."

Alette raised her hand high in the air. Bridget wasn't sure if she was going to hit Marin or search her pockets. But it didn't matter. She was going to stop her either way. Acting on impulse, Bridget reached her hand in her boot. Seconds later, her knife whiffed through the air. It landed perfectly in the grass, leaving a large hole in the sleeve of Alette's coat. A warning. And a message.

"Are you trying to kill me?" Alette wailed, squeezing her arm to her chest. "Did you see that? She just tried to kill me."

"I don't see any blood," Cade said.

Bridget gaped at him, but his face remained unreadable. While Alette cried, he imperceptibly tilted his head. Suddenly, the cards flew out of Bridget's pocket. When they landed a few feet away, Delphine jogged toward them.

"Your cards are on the ground over here. They must have fallen out of your pocket," Delphine said, holding up the velvet sack. Alette rushed over and snatched them from her hand.

"This wasn't an accident. I know she had something to do with it," Alette grunted, face red as she bared her teeth at Bridget.

"It sounds like a misunderstanding to me," Finn said mildly. "We'll take the knife, though, if that makes you feel better. Have a good day, ladies. We have an important meeting to get to."

Bridget watched the prince tuck the knife in his belt and immediately regretted throwing it. She only had two. Now, she was down to one to defend herself. All because she couldn't stand to watch Alette torment Marin, especially over something she did.

Alette rapidly blinked away her tears. "What about your future?" She called, waving the sack at their retreating figures.

"I don't need anyone to tell me my future. It's already been decided," Cade said, not once looking back.

After the incident in the field, Bridget avoided the other contestants, even Quinn and Delphine. She snuck down to eat at odd times and tried to lift weights in the middle of the night. Two days passed in a blur. When she couldn't sleep, her mind churned. The possibility that information about a hidden second gate was somewhere in the palace ate away at her. If she was going to be restricted to the grounds for the foreseeable future, she wanted something to focus on and take her mind off the tournament. The only problem was, she had no idea where to start.

When the need for fresh air overwhelmed her, Bridget visited the small market by the palace entrance. The downhill walk relaxed her body and mind. To her delight, new stalls and tents seemed to be added each day. Even though she had no money to buy anything, she liked watching and hearing the buzz of people bargaining for better deals. As she admired a stand with some juicy apples, a shrill voice rang out behind her.

"Your money's no good here."

Bridget turned and saw a small Nymph girl holding out a gold coin to a particularly nasty looking Fae woman. The little girl put the stationery down and walked away with her head hung. Inwardly fuming, Bridget approached the stall. She tripped and fell against the heavy wood, knocking over several display items.

The ugly Fae snarled at her. "Watch it. You humans are pathetic."

Bridget put her hands up in apology and backed away. Underneath her jacket, she clutched the stationery the young girl wanted. When she found her a few stalls over, she shoved it into the girl's hands without saying anything. The adrenaline in her veins sparked her on. Next, she took an apple, then an embroidered cloth napkin. She didn't need it, but it was pretty.

A familiar face near the end of the market suddenly caught her eye. Bridget froze and studied the blond Warlock that had smirked at her in Bryxton. He stood in front of a green tent and caressed the arm of a man, a flirtatious grin plastered on his face. Impulsively, she crept toward him, unsure whether she wanted to confront him or see if he recognized her.

Once she arrived at his tent, she realized it was an apothecary. Herbs and bottles of potions lined the small shelves and tables. A few moments later, he finished talking to the man and entered the tent, whistling a tune she didn't recognize. She pretended to be reading the ingredients of a red potion as he counted a stack of money.

"You have to pay for that," he stated, not looking up.

Bridget jumped, surprised he noticed her about to slip the potion into her pocket. "I was just looking at it."

He smirked. "I saw you *just looking* at that napkin in your pocket earlier too. Hand it over."

Bridget slammed the vial in his hand. "Are you going to call a guard on me? I don't have any money."

"No, I'm feeling forgiving today," he quipped. He peered at the potion and grimaced in disgust. "Shit. You know this is used for venereal disease, right?"

Blood rushed to Bridget's cheeks as she grabbed the vial out of his hand and threw it on the table. She hadn't been able to read the Latin label. "I've seen you before. In Bryxton," she accused.

"You wouldn't know by looking at it, but that dirty pub in Bryxton has the best mead in Vassuryn," he said nonchalantly, holding out a hand. "Where are my manners? The name's Archer."

"So it was you. Why did it seem like you might know me? And why are you here now?"

"It's quite rude not to introduce yourself back," Archer said, ignoring her questions. "Let me see if I can guess. Is it Anne? Karen? I've run into quite a few Karens in the human realm. It was never a pleasant experience."

"It's Bridget," she said reluctantly, head pounding. "You've been to the human realm?"

"A time or two. Humans are my favorite patrons," Archer said carefully. "They'll pay anything for a few memories."

Bridget's heart stopped. It felt like her deepest, darkest secret had just been said aloud. She didn't know how, but the man in front of knew where she was from. More importantly, he was dangling the one thing she would give anything to have back. But how many times had Cora told her the stories about humans dying from trying to get their memories back? How many people had she seen die because of magic?

"That's impossible," she whispered.

"Is it? I like to experiment. I think I've finally gotten this one right," Archer grinned. He pulled a small glass container out of his pocket. The purple liquid inside swirled and glowed. "Haven't you learned that any magic is possible if you're willing to pay the price? C'est la vie, as the French say."

He placed the potion on the table in front of her. When she didn't move, he scooted it closer.

"You're lying," she said, hands trembling. It took every ounce of her self-control to not grab the vial.

"I'm not. Scout's honor," Archer replied, holding up three fingers. She didn't understand the gesture.

"I don't have anything to give," Bridget said, her throat tightened to the point of pain.

"You could give your hair, teeth, or maybe even a few years of life," he said seriously but then his lips suddenly twitched. "I hear firstborns are popular with some groups, but the *crying...*"

The air whooshed out of Bridget's lungs. He was making fun of her. There was no potion that would give her back what she wanted. Snarling, she stormed out of the tent.

When she was a few stands away, she heard him call out, "You forgot the venereal potion!"

Every person near her took a giant step back with identical stares of horror. Bridget hated that her face turned crimson. Without looking back, she jogged up the hill back to the palace. The entire way, frustrated tears sprang from her eyes.

To her dismay, she came across two people. They stood in the pathway she needed to take to get to the apartments. Bridget stiffened, recognizing the two figures. Delphine's and Cade's furious whispers barely reached her ears. Watching the two of them sent a surge of bitterness through Bridget's chest. And then she immediately chastised herself. She was going crazy. Delphine had been kind to her, and out of all the girls, deserved to be the winner. Unlike her, who *hated* the tournament. Hated that she was stuck in it until she could finally escape to whatever realm would take her. Hated that she didn't even know why she was in Elyria in the first place.

Lost in her thoughts, she stood watching too long, because when Cade rolled his eyes at Delphine, he caught sight of her. Without thinking, Bridget took off running through the grass, hoping there was a back pathway to the palace.

"Bridget!" Delphine called.

Before Bridget could react, Delphine appeared in front of her with a loud pop.

"Have you been crying? What happened?" she asked.

"Nothing. I think I got some dirt in my eye on the way back from the market," Bridget said, furiously rubbing at the appendage.

For a split second, Delphine's eyes went hazy. She suddenly swatted at her head and mumbled something in another language.

"Are you sure?" She eventually asked.

Bridget stared at her incredulously. "I think it's me who should be asking you that. Did you just hit yourself?"

"There was a bug. Look, I understand if you don't want to talk about it, but I'm here if you do," Delphine said kindly. "Actually, I've been looking for you all day."

"Really?" Bridget asked, a spark of fire heating her chest. It hadn't seemed like Delphine cared where she was when she was arguing with the prince. Shamefully, Bridget pursed her lips together.

Delphine's brows furrowed in confusion. "I found out the first task is tomorrow and wanted to let you know."

Guilt filled Bridget's gut. Since arriving at the palace, she had done nothing but screw up. "I'm sorry for snapping at you. Thanks for letting me know. I just...I just want to be alone right now. It's been an odd day."

Delphine nodded and stepped aside. Bridget stormed past her without a backwards glance, unsure and anxious about what tomorrow would bring.

CHAPTER TEN

The walk to the lake was one of the longest in Bridget's life. In a line, the contestants solemnly and silently followed the director to the first task. Bridget's stomach churned as the announcement repeated in her head. Each girl would be placed in a random location in the Elder Woods and then be tested on how well they used their magic and wits to find the finish line. In theory, it didn't sound terrible. She was comfortable in the woods. In Vassuryn, the Virgo coven had spent hours studying forestry and herbs, and they always liked to camp under the shade of the redwoods. Consequently, she knew how to follow the sun and leave markings so she wouldn't get lost. Bridget knew, though, there had to be a catch. She gazed at the tree line of the Elder Woods. Something had to be in there. Once, in Vassuryn, she had seen a Chimera. It had snuck into the Virgo camp to find food. Even emaciated, the beast was formidable. The Chimera's sharp teeth and horns had made even Cora pale. If Bridget remembered right, it took three Warlocks working together to kill it. She could only assume similar monsters roamed Elyria.

By the time they finally arrived at the spectator area for the task, the afternoon sun sizzled the back of Bridget's neck. She was surprised to see so many people buzzing around and making bets. A Fae with a camera snapped pictures.

"Looks like everyone is here today. If you're wondering, the brunette is Elora, and the blonde is Cassia. She's the prince's twin," Quinn whispered. Bridget curiously followed her gaze.

In front of the lake, the royal family sat in large wooden chairs. The king was strategically placed in the center, directly in front of a large black box. It was the first time Bridget had seen them together. None of them were speaking to each other. The youngest sister, Elora, was flirting with a boy around her age. She resembled the king more than the others. Her black hair fell in loose waves as she smiled calculatingly at her target. Cassia, the prince's twin, was her total opposite. Her blonde hair was blinding in the sunlight. She glared at Elora and scoffed.

Elora's dark eyes whipped to her sister. "No one asked for your opinion," she snarled.

Cassia didn't reply. Instead, she sunk down further in her seat and took a long swig from the goblet in her hand. Bridget doubted it was water. Cade sat next to his father. With his eyes squeezed shut, he rested his head in one hand. Bridget wasn't sure if he was concentrating or trying to fall asleep. Faint bruises still covered his face. In his free hand, he tightly clutched an object.

"What's that black box? I keep seeing it," Bridget asked Quinn, forcing herself to tear her eyes off him.

"It's a camera that films the tournament. The footage will be played to the rest of Astraeus later tonight. I'm sure it will just focus on Marin, though," Quinn said. "Look, she's already the center of attention."

Indeed, Marin was surrounded by numerous Fae shouting questions at her, but it didn't look like she enjoyed the onslaught. The Shaman pursed her lips and hunched her shoulders at every new question. Bridget felt a little bad for her. When a woman shoved a camera in Marin's face, the director rushed over.

"Put that thing away. There will be no interviews today," the director bellowed, pushing the man aside. Soon, a guard grabbed the reporter and escorted him away.

Walking over to Marin, Bridget asked, "Does that always happen?"

Marin lifted a shoulder. “I’m the only Tuathan that’s been born this century. I’m used to it.”

Before Bridget could respond, a fluttering in her ear distracted her. She whipped her hand up, ready to swat a fly, but felt nothing. Soon, the feeling encircled her, like a whisper scraping the back of her mind. Confused, she turned and found Elora watching her. The maniacal grin on the princess’s face gave Bridget goosebumps.

A sudden eruption from the king drew the crowd’s attention.

“That’s enough. I’m not going to tolerate any drunken antics today,” the king growled. He snapped a finger and instructed a guard to grab Cassia’s gold goblet. The princess waved it in the air and refused to hand it over.

“If you wanted me sober, then you shouldn’t have forced me to come watch a bunch of girls traipse around in the forest,” Cassia scoffed. “As if that really proves who’s fit to be queen. Don’t you agree, Cade?”

The prince kept his eyes closed and said nothing.

“Neither one of your opinions is needed,” the king replied darkly. He stood up, glowering as he ordered, “Start the task. At this rate, it’ll be nightfall by the time it’s over. The human will most likely slow things down, and I have dinner plans.”

The comment earned a few chuckles from reporters. Bridget ground her teeth together and hoped her expression remained neutral.

Soon, a soldier approached Alette and blindfolded her with a red cloth. When he grabbed her shoulder, they both instantly disappeared. Bridget’s chest tightened. She should have known magic would take her to the forest. Whenever Cora performed a spell on her, it always hurt and left marks. Granted, Bridget knew that had been her intention. Cora was creative with her training and punishments. Still, she nervously wondered if Fae magic would similarly affect her.

One by one, the soldier transported girls into the Elder Woods. Bridget snuck a look at Delphine, who was standing calmly beside her. Her ability was identical to the soldier’s. Bridget envied the Fae. She would be able to pop herself back within moments.

“Good luck,” Delphine said, smiling at Bridget before she also disappeared.

Last, Bridget stood alone as she waited for the soldier to return. Elora caught her eye again and grinned. Before she could react, a blindfold covered her eyes, and then a hand touched her shoulder.

Seconds later, excruciating pain disintegrated her insides as her body was pulled apart and put back together all at once. Bridget screamed in agony as she landed somewhere new. Falling on her knees, she dug her fingers into the dirt beneath her to steady her soul. The faint pop of the Fae leaving barely registered in her mind through the haze of pain. She clumsily tore the blindfold off and stayed on the ground, trying to find the strength to look up.

When she did, her view of the Elder Woods was blurry. Head spinning, Bridget pressed her face in the dirt, ready to stay there forever.

Up, a voice whispered.

Bridget stirred and peeked one eye open. Only trees, dirt, and rocks surrounded her. She laid her dizzy head back down.

Get up, it whispered more urgently. This time, a force pulled on the back of her leather jacket.

Groaning, Bridget pushed herself to her hands and knees. She stayed there for a long moment, breathing hard and refusing to vomit. Eventually, she made it to her feet, her entire body trembling as she did. Bridget studied her surroundings. The trees were so tall, she couldn't see the sun. With no sense of direction, Bridget picked an area that looked nice and stumbled toward it.

Behind her, a stick cracked. Bridget whipped around but spotted no person or animal. She looked away, but the stick cracked again. When Bridget moved toward the sound, a tree branch moved, like it was nodding in approval. She took a few more steps. Further ahead, another branch shook. She was going crazy. Absolutely crazy. The forest was talking to her, and she was listening. She was going to follow the branches through the Elder Woods.

Even in her head, it sounded insane. But with no other options, Bridget started to walk.

Every few minutes, a branch would snap or wave and push her onward. After an hour, she felt confident she was going in the right direction. In fact, she was starting to find the Elder Woods peaceful.

Suddenly, a small body came crashing through a particularly thick area of brush. Bridget automatically reached for the knife hidden inside her boot, relieved they hadn't thought to search her. She wasn't sure if weapons were allowed or not, but it was the only thing she had to defend herself with. Bridget relaxed when she recognized the figure kneeling on the ground. Thick tears rolled down Ondine's face as she clutched her left arm to her chest. When Bridget took a step toward her, the Nymph flinched and crawled away.

"Relax, I'm not going to hurt you. Did someone do that?" Bridget asked, frowning at the oozing gash on Ondine's scaly forearm. It was clean and straight, like it had been done with a sharp object.

"I fell," she replied defensively.

Not believing her, Bridget took another step toward her, but Ondine flinched again and clutched her arm tighter.

"I was just trying to help," Bridget said, raising her palms. When Ondine continued to tremble on the ground, Bridget sighed and waved a short goodbye. If the Nymph didn't want help from her, then there was nothing she could do. When she saw one of the trees shake again, she walked toward it.

After a few minutes, Bridget heard rustling behind her. She spun around and spotted Ondine's face peeking out from behind a tree.

Bridget narrowed her eyes. "Are you following me?"

"No," Ondine squeaked.

"If you're not following me, what are you doing?"

Ondine lowered her eyes. A few tears fell to the ground. "I'm lost."

"And you think I know where I'm going? Don't you have magic you can use?" Bridget asked skeptically.

"Nymphs are shapeshifters. It doesn't do me much good out here, especially since I'm not a very good one. The most I can do are little modifications," Ondine wailed. "And then Hai ditched me to follow Alette."

Bridget could tell Hai had done more than just ditch her, but she kept her mouth shut. Ondine clearly wasn't going to tell her what had happened. She was surprised to hear the other girls had run into each other. Her path through the forest had been quiet and still. Until now.

Bridget studied the shaking Nymph and wondered if she was about to make a mistake.

"Come on," she said, motioning for Ondine to follow.

Ondine eyed the path dubiously. "How do you know that's the right way?"

"I just do," Bridget muttered, not wanting to explain her insane notion of the trees helping her.

When a bird flew by their heads, Ondine jumped. "What was that?" She squealed, wildly flapping her hands.

"Seriously? Have you ever been in a forest?" Bridget asked. A second later, guilt pricked at her chest when she noticed Ondine's shamed face. Kindlier, Bridget asked, "If you know you're not powerful, why join the tournament?"

"My family works for Hai's father. He forced me to join so I could keep an eye on her. I didn't expect it to be like this," Ondine replied quietly, voice breaking. "Everyone told me there would be so many girls and that no one would notice me. They said I wouldn't have to try."

Bridget nodded, recognizing the familiarity in the words. Cora had promised her the same thing. Even though she had agreed to join the tournament as a ruse, Bridget could still sympathize. The contract had thrown a kink in her plans, while the low number of participants had ruined Ondine's. They were both stuck. "It's not what I thought either," Bridget said.

Ondine paused and wiped her face. "I want to go home."

Suddenly, a low growl erupted from behind them. Ondine darted behind Bridget. A creature with giant teeth and matted fur crawled out of the shadows.

"It's a Barghest," Ondine gasped, face pale.

Bridget stared wide-eyed at the beast licking its chops. "How do you get rid of it?"

Ondine's entire body shook as she silently gaped at the massive creature.

"Can't you give yourself claws or something?" Bridget asked. When Ondine remained frozen, Bridget grabbed her arm and dragged her through the trees. The Barghest raced after them. They hadn't gotten far when Ondine tripped over a rock and fell to the ground, nearly pulling Bridget with her. The Nymph made no move to get up.

"Do something!" Bridget screamed.

Suddenly, the Barghest jumped out of the trees and lunged at Bridget. She darted to the right and rolled on the ground. The beast's claws scraped the dirt where she had just been standing. To her left, Ondine lay on the ground, stunned and petrified. With a wet snarl, the Barghest focused its yellow eyes on the motionless Nymph.

Bridget frantically looked around for anything to throw. With the creature's back turned, her knife wouldn't penetrate the spiky, thick fur on its spine enough to do any damage. A few feet away, she found a black rock buried in the dirt. Using all her strength, Bridget threw the rock at the back of the Barghest's head before it reached Ondine. When it hit, the beast whipped around and howled in anger. As it furiously sprinted toward her, the Barghest lifted its forelegs to attack, giving Bridget a perfect target. She reached for her knife and flung it toward the creature's chest.

The Barghest let out a screeching yelp as the knife sliced into its shoulder. It stumbled to the ground and struggled to move. Bridget ran to Ondine and heaved her up.

"Let's go," she shouted, pushing the girl forward. Ondine whimpered but complied.

This time, Bridget didn't look for any shaking trees. She ran as fast as she could, hoping the Barghest wasn't following them. Moments later, she spotted a gap in the forest. Bridget raced toward it, hoping the end was near. Instead, it was something much worse.

Bridget screeched to a halt as she almost stumbled off the edge of a cliff. Loose rocks poked into the soles of her worn-out boots. Down below, the lake sat peacefully. If she squinted, she could see the rest of the girls and royal family waiting at the end of the task. Bridget swallowed hard and dared to look down. Her stomach fell to her feet.

"Look, there's the finish. All we have to do is jump and swim," Ondine squealed happily, pointing to the group of onlookers in the distance. They were so far away and tiny; Bridget couldn't make out their faces. She wanted to scream at Ondine that she couldn't swim, that she currently couldn't even *twitch* a finger, but the words were jammed in her constricting throat. Seconds later, the other girl jumped. Bridget watched as Ondine hit the water and gave herself a fish tail. Soon, she was zipping across the lake.

When Bridget heard a growl behind her, she knew the Barghest hadn't given up completely. She had no more knives, which meant there was only one thing left for her to do. Closing her eyes, Bridget jumped and hoped for the best. She hit the water before she could scream. Body flailing, she tried to find up, air, *anything* that would help stop the burning in her lungs. She kicked hard and hoped she was moving in the right direction. Finally, she broke above the water and gasped for air.

Bridget paddled hard and tried to keep her body upright. Float, kick, float, kick. The motions seemed to keep her afloat. She repeated the mantra in her head over and over. When she finally felt like she was getting the hang of it, her legs seized up, then her arms. Eyes rolling to the back of her head, she sank back into the water. Realizing she had no control over her body, Bridget started to panic. Soon, she fell deeper and deeper. Suddenly, a slice of pain shot through her mind, along with images of a place she had never seen.

She was in a lake, floating on her back. A steady hand lifted her legs. "See, it's not so bad," a voice laughed.

Seconds later, Bridget was back in the lake. She flinched, feeling her legs release. Desperately, she kicked upward, but an invisible hand grasped her ankle. It dragged her down further. Pain pierced her skull once more.

"A doggy paddle is not that impressive," another voice called from shore. There was no bite, only humor.

"It is when an hour ago, she couldn't even float," the voice beside her argued good-naturedly.

Bridget felt her legs and arms gliding through the water, slow and steady. She laughed and lifted her middle finger at both of them.

Her lungs squeezed as she lost air. Bridget's mind felt like it was waging war on itself. Pain shot through her entire body as she lost feeling in her arms and legs. *Sink, swim, sink, swim, sink, swim.* Dual messages exploded all sense inside her brain. At last, Bridget heard a faint scream and an ear-splitting crack. The sound brought her back to her body. Registering that she could move again, Bridget hurriedly swam toward the surface.

The relief of finally having air in her lungs almost made her nauseous. Bridget bobbed in the water, grateful that whatever pulled her under had stopped. To her surprise, she was closer to shore than she expected. The other girls were already done, including Ondine. Bridget saw her wrapped up in a towel next to Hai and glowered at her. Without her, the Nymph would still be stuck in the woods. When she made it to shallow water, no one paid any attention as she approached. Instead, everyone stared anxiously at where the royal family sat. Sparing a glance in that direction, Bridget spotted the king yelling at Cade. Next to them, Elora lay unconscious on the ground.

"Your face," Delphine gasped, wading out into the water to help Bridget to shore.

Bridget reached up and felt blood pouring from her nostrils to her chin. Spitting a glob from her mouth, she wiped her face with the back of her glove. She didn't remember hitting her nose on anything. Her hands trembled as she studied the blood. The cool air mixed with her wet clothes made her shiver, and her leather jacket felt like bricks on her arms. Delphine tried to hand her a towel, but Quinn shoved her to the side and enveloped Bridget in a tight hug.

"Are you okay? You were under the water for a long time," Quinn said.

Teeth chattering, Bridget stuttered, "Something kept pulling me down,"

"Not something, *someone*," Quinn corrected. "Did you feel her inside your head? It's probably why your nose won't stop bleeding."

Bridget furrowed her brows and followed Quinn's gaze to Elora on the ground. At that moment, a guard carefully scooped her up and began carrying her back to the palace. Bridget saw blood streaming from the princess's nose, similar to her own. Further away, the king waved a cracked black stone in the air as he continued to yell at his son. Unresponsive, Cade stared at the lake with crossed arms.

"He saved you," Quinn whispered.

Stunned, Bridget tried to make eye contact with him, but he wouldn't look at her.

"Cade, hurry up and pick a winner so we can get the hell out of here," Cassia snapped.

Without hesitation, Cade replied, "Delphine."

Seconds later, the prince marched back toward the palace, not once looking back. The king let out a loud roar and kicked his chair before he followed him. Wood splinters flew in the air as girls rushed around a red-faced Delphine to congratulate her.

"Shocker," Quinn mumbled irritability.

Bridget shrugged, preoccupied with Cade's retreating figure. When she finally tore her gaze away, she caught Cassia's eye. The princess smirked, having caught her watching him. Bridget's cheeks heated. She hurriedly diverted her attention back to Quinn.

"Are we allowed to leave now? I need to get out of these clothes before I turn permanently blue," Bridget said.

The entire way back to the apartments, she swore she felt Cassia watching her.

CHAPTER ELEVEN

The next day, Bridget sat in the study. It was one of the few rooms in the apartments that was always empty. Its thick armchairs were stiff and uncomfortable, but she didn't mind, finding the silence soothing. All morning, Bridget stared fixedly at the roaring fire against the wall, unable to stop replaying what she saw beneath the water. The more she analyzed the vision, the more convinced she became that it was a memory. A *real* memory. The scents, colors, and voices she had felt too real and tangible. She couldn't close her eyes without seeing it. Her heart vibrated in her chest each it replayed in her mind, like it was reaching for something just out of reach.

And then there was the prince. Cade. Bridget thought of him more often than she wanted to admit. He had saved her, despite the fact that he barely bothered to spare her a glance. She didn't know what to make of him. Absentmindedly, she fiddled with the crumbling paper in her jacket pocket. Her note, the one lifeline she had of her old life, flaked against her fingertips, ruined by the lake's waters. Bitterness surged in her throat. Another thing lost to Elyria. Gritting her teeth, she wadded up the paper and threw it in the fire.

"How are you feeling?"

Bridget jumped at the sound of Delphine's concerned voice. The Fae girl peeked into the room with a shy smile on her face.

"I didn't mean to scare you. Your nosebleed yesterday looked bad, so I wanted to check on you," she said, coming to sit next to Bridget on the couch.

"I'm exhausted, but fine. I usually have trouble sleeping, though," Bridget said, pausing briefly. "Congratulations, by the way."

Delphine shrugged. "I was the safest choice."

"You and the prince have never…" Bridget trailed off, her voice suggestive. After finding Delphine and Cade arguing, the idea hadn't left her head.

"No, gross," Delphine gagged. Seeing Bridget's puzzled look, she laughed. "I mean, he's great, don't get me wrong. But he's like my brother."

"So you've known him a long time?"

"My parents work in the palace, so I've always been around. He was nice enough to let me trail after him and Finn when we were younger, and then got stuck with me."

"He's lucky to have you as a friend," Bridget said, truly meaning it. She hadn't known Delphine long, but truth and honesty laced her every word.

Delphine smiled bashfully. "I try. As the prince, I know it's hard for him to find people he trusts. The king doesn't make things any easier for him either."

"Does he not like humans?" Bridget blurted, still mortified from the contestant introductions.

"Why would you think that?" Delphine asked with a frown.

"Why wouldn't I think that? You saw how he reacted when I was introduced. Since then, he's barely looked at me. But then Quinn said he saved me…" Bridget's face heated when she realized she was ranting. She cleared her throat and stopped before she said anything else stupid. Like that she admired his hair. Delphine gazed at her with a frustrated glower.

"He did save you. And I promise, he didn't react that way when you were introduced because you're human," Delphine replied carefully. "You realize Elora used magic to get inside your head, right?"

Bridget nodded, despite being even more confused by her response. "Quinn told me. She said it's why I had the nosebleed."

"Has that happened before?"

Bridget's nosebleed in Bryxton flashed through her mind. "Maybe. I'm not sure."

Before Delphine could respond, Marin entered the study. Both girls stared at her in surprise as she sat on a couch across from them and opened a book. An awkward silence enveloped the air. After a long moment, Delphine glanced at her watch.

"I have to meet my parents, but we can talk more later. Be careful, Bridget," she warned, squeezing Bridget's gloved hand before leaving.

With just her and Marin in the room, Bridget fiddled with the fabric of the couch, unsure if she should say anything or leave. Just when she had made up her mind to flee the room, Marin spoke.

"What you've been looking for is in the library."

Pulse quickening, Bridget's gaze darted to Marin. A million questions flew through her mind before she finally settled on one conclusion: Marin knew she wanted to find the hidden second gate and go back to the human realm.

"What are you talking about?" Bridget asked.

"The afternoon is usually a good time to visit," Marin said, slamming her book shut. In the blink of an eye, she was gone.

Bridget stilled on the couch as she mulled over the girl's words. How did Marin possibly know what kept her up at night? Had she seen her returning to the human realm? Bridget couldn't shake the notion Marin had. Shamans were called seers for a reason. And to think, Cora was right all along. The answers about another gate *were* inside the palace. Hope sprouted inside Bridget's chest. Unable to subdue it, she went in search of the library.

Besides Marin, the only other person to mention a library to Bridget was Quinn. She remembered the Witch's complaint about not being allowed to enter the west end of the palace. After a long walk through numerous courtyards and corridors, the architecture of the palace began to change. The hallways became narrow and enclosed. Instead of large decorative paintings, all Bridget saw were closed doors. And it was quiet. Not a soul seemed to be around.

When Bridget began to think she had accidentally wandered to an abandoned area, a large arched entrance came into view. Curious, she peeked inside. Her jaw dropped. It was the most spectacular room she had ever seen. Rows upon rows of books towered above her. Shelves seemed to go for ages. Sunlight reflected on the glass vaulted ceiling, causing little rainbows to appear in the air. Even the air felt crisper and cleaner than the rest of the palace.

In awe, Bridget slowly walked inside and studied the breathtaking expanse. When she looked up at the second floor, her eyes widened in shock. A figure paced on a lofted bridge. But not just anyone. Cade. His brown hair was messy as he stared intently at a small black box in his hand.

Seconds later, he spotted her watching him and jumped.

"Shit," Cade exclaimed, dropping the box on the floor with a thud. He closed his eyes and pinched the bridge of his nose.

"I'm sorry, I didn't know anyone was in here," Bridget apologized, her palms sweaty inside her gloves.

With a sigh, Cade picked up the box and placed it in his pocket. With a hint of accusation in his voice, he asked, "What are you doing here?"

Bridget's throat tightened. Had Marin led her into some sort of trap? "Am I not allowed?"

"No, you are," Cade muttered under his breath. "I'll go."

He jumped on a ladder and slid down the side before landing smoothly on the ground. Bridget watched as he strode past her with a clenched jaw. Her chest stung at his obvious determination to avoid her. She swallowed down the urge to call out and thank him for not letting her drown, but since he refused to look at her, she began to doubt he even meant to save her at all.

When he reached the doorway, Cade suddenly stopped. He stood there, stiff and frozen, for a long moment. His white knuckles clenched the door frame.

"What were you looking for?" he asked quietly, not turning around.

Surprised, Bridget blurted, "Books."

Cade's head dropped back at the joke. He turned around, there was a hint of a smile on his face. "What kind of books?"

"History, I guess. Someone told me this place would have what I'm looking for," Bridget replied carefully. She wasn't sure exactly what Marin meant, and if she should mention the Shaman to the prince. Her journey to the library had been fueled by hope. Now, she had no idea what to look for inside the millions of books that lay in front of her.

"There's plenty of long and boring history books in here, but the interesting ones are hidden away," Cade said, motioning for her to follow him.

As he passed her, he eyed her gloved hands for a split-second. Bridget's heart spiked at his nearness, and at the fact that *of course* her gloved hands were the first thing he noticed, and though she was curious about his sudden change in demeanor, she remained still. He had no reason to help her. In fact, he had made it clear that helping her was probably the last thing he ever wanted to do again. Unless there was something in it for him. Based on the calculations that swirled in his eyes, it was the conclusion she was leaning toward.

When Cade noticed she wasn't moving, he turned back around. Rubbing his chin, he said, "The way I see it, you have three options. One, you can look through all these books on your own. Two, you go back to the apartments. Maybe Alette will have a history book that interests you."

The thought left a sour taste in her mouth. She must have made a face because she swore his lips twitched.

"Or..." he continued.

Or she could follow him. Bargain with him. Whatever it was Fae did with humans. There was no way she had time to search through the library on her own. Trying to find the right book might take weeks. Weeks she didn't have. Even though she didn't want to admit it, she needed help almost as much as she needed to find a way back to the human realm. And deep down, she knew couldn't resist the challenge in his unspoken words, the dare hanging in the air to choose option three. So she stubbornly met his gaze and waved him forward. She bristled when he smirked.

Bridget followed him to the back of the library. On the second shelf in the corner, Cade tugged on a light blue book. Once he did, the shelf shot outward an inch, making Bridget jump. He grasped the edge and pulled it open like a door. With a grin, Cade waved her inside.

“Wow,” Bridget breathed as she took in the secret room. A long table with various manuscripts and pages scattered across the top sat in the middle. Shelves of old books lined the wall, some thick and collecting dust. Every inch of the room was covered with maps, journals, or globes. Most objects looked like they hadn’t been touched in years. Gold-lined floor to ceiling windows covered the back wall.

“Most of my family’s dirty little secrets are kept in this room. You can read and borrow what you want,” Cade said, leaning against the edge of the table. He crossed his ankles and preoccupied himself with something on the edge of his sleeve.

“Thank you,” Bridget stuttered, keenly aware that they were alone together in the tiny space. She tried to busy herself with a map, but she didn’t recognize any of the kingdoms on it. After a minute, Cade remained by the table. He fiddled with some papers. She didn’t know why he was still in the room. He usually removed himself from her presence as quickly as possible.

“You’re still here,” Bridget stated, even though she meant it to be a question.

Surprise flickered across his face. “Are you trying to kick me out of my own library?”

“That depends. Will kicking you out get me released from the tournament?”

The words were out of Bridget’s mouth before she could stop them. It was the first thing that had come to her mind. She slammed her lips shut, stunned she’d let slip her desire to leave the tournament to the *one person* it revolved around. She braced herself for a harsh remark or for a stern order to get out. She would’ve received that, or much worse, from Cora.

To her relief, he grinned. “No.”

The amusement in his eyes sparked her on. “Then I guess you can stay.”

She tore her gaze away from his and moved to stand in front of the first bookshelf she could reach. The titles were in languages she couldn’t read.

“I didn’t mean to interrupt you,” Bridget added, fingering a particular dusty leather-bound book.

"You didn't. I just needed somewhere to think," Cade said.

Bridget paused her perusing to steal a glance of him. He was still irritatingly attractive, even with purple bags under his eyes, like he hadn't slept more than a few hours. She wondered if she'd accidentally said the thought aloud because Cade suddenly stood up and met her penetrating stare. Her neck heated as he moved toward her. She hated that every nerve ending in her body flared awake. When he was close enough for her to see the faint freckles on his nose, he reached down and pulled her knife out of his boot.

"Don't tell anyone I gave this back to you," Cade said, putting the heavy silver dagger in her hand. "Where did you learn to throw like that?"

Bridget grasped it tightly, relieved to have one back, and relieved her hands weren't as shaky as her insides felt. "It was the easiest weapon for me to learn," she said, quickly biting down on her tongue. Why couldn't she control her mouth around him? She'd almost mentioned Vassuryn and Cora.

Nodding, Cade said, "It's a skill suited for someone with quick hands." When Bridget sent him a puzzled look, he added, "Alette's cards."

Bridget almost laughed aloud at the memory of Alette's furious, purple face. "How did you know?" She asked curiously. He'd spotted her swiping the cards right away.

"I've seen the trick before," Cade murmured, studying her face. "Is that something else you learned in Andarre?"

When Bridget swallowed hard, he smirked knowingly. His brown eyes dared her to tell him the truth. She raised her chin and let the confession tumble from her lips.

"I'm not from Andarre."

"I know. Every citizen in Andarre has a rune etched into their neck to protect themselves from the effects of magic. It's why they've been able to stay an independent kingdom. They copied the practice from the Shamans. People mistake the markings for tattoos. You can usually spot the purple lines here," he said, rubbing his thumb across the base of her neck. The action sent sparks flying across her skin. Heart pounding, she gazed up at him. He was so close; Bridget could feel his breath on her face. She knew she should pull away. It was the smart thing to do. The *only* thing to do. Especially when he'd already made it clear he disdained humans. But the spicy, citrus scent wafting from him permeated her senses and kept her rooted to the spot. When his fingers brushed her collarbone, her breath hitched.

The sound seemed to wake him up. Cade tore his hand away and moved to the other side of the room. Clearing his throat, he said, "But you know someone from there."

"No, I didn't even know Andarre existed until last week," Bridget confessed, cheeks hot.

"You have one of their runes," he said, brows furrowed. "I saw the amethyst around your neck the first night."

"The necklace is something I've always had. I don't remember where I got it," Bridget said. When she reached up to show him the stone, she couldn't find it around her neck. Frowning, she said, "I usually never take it off..."

Bridget could see the necklace sitting on her nightstand. The first night, she had taken it off to bathe. Since then, every time she tried to put it on, something had stopped her. She couldn't remember what...

"It seems like someone's been messing with your head," Cade said. "When you go back to your room, put it on. That particular rune is known for protecting the wearer from certain magics. Without it, Elora nearly drowned you."

"Why did she do that?"

Cade's eyes darkened. "She likes to cause trouble. Luckily, she's never been good at blocking her thoughts. She won't bother you again, though. My father sent her to Tafari."

"That's surprising. Based on what he's said to me, I think he would enjoy watching the human struggle," Bridget said. His threat about being useless sent shivers down her spine every time she thought about it.

"The tournament is his number one priority right now. Plus, my father and I have an agreement. Her presence jeopardizes that, so he sent her away," Cade said, moving to stand in front of the window. He stared at the skyline of Astraeus for a long moment, the muscles in his back taut and stiff.

"When I was under the water, I think I got a memory back."

The words escaped Bridget's lips, whether to fill the silence or make the idea real, she didn't know. Mainly, she couldn't fight the urge to tell him. Cade whipped around, clearly stunned.

"You already figured out I'm not from Andarre, so I might as well tell you the truth," Bridget continued nervously. "I'm from the human realm. At least, I think. I have no memories, so I must be, but I've been living with a coven in Vassuryn for the last seven months."

Instead of questioning her about Vassuryn or the coven, like she expected, Cade asked, "What did you see in the water?"

"A lake, similar to the one here. It felt so real and familiar. I think I was learning how to swim," Bridget said, her eyes hazy as she recalled the memory. "Do you think Elora managed to reach some dormant part of my brain?"

"It wasn't just Elora in your head. I was there too," Cade confessed quietly. "It was the only way to stop her. I went in and used a quartz to pull her out. Somehow, you managed to grasp on to some of the magic. I thought it cracked because I channeled too much power through it, but it might have been the price of your memory."

Bridget remembered the ear-splitting crack, so loud she heard it beneath the water, and how the king had furiously waved the broken rock in the air. "It was a rune?"

"One of the few we have left. My father was furious," Cade said, with a hint of amusement on his face.

"Did he do that?" Bridget asked, eyeing the faint bruise that marred his cheekbone.

"Last week. I could've gotten it healed but didn't want to give him the satisfaction. All he did for the broken rune was take my vault key. I think he was mad that I used one of his and not my own."

Cade pointed to the outline of a pendant buried beneath his shirt. Bridget paused before asking the one question that haunted her. "Do you think I'll get any more memories back?"

"No, I don't. I'm sorry."

Bridget turned away to hide the devastation that she knew was on her face. Taking a deep breath, she pushed it down. She would not break in front of him.

Cade must have caught it, though, because he softly asked, "So what did you really come looking for? It has to be for more than history books. None of the other contestants have wandered this far."

Bridget knew she had already said too much; knew this was their first real conversation and that she shouldn't trust a Fae, especially one that was the prince. As she studied his steady gaze, though, her heart whispered: *trust*. "I was looking for information about other gates to the human realm."

Cade didn't look surprised. He moved closer to her and said, "Look, I know what happened the other night. Finn told me. I know you want to get back to your life, but you'll die if you leave the palace before the tournament is over."

Bridget ground her teeth together, remembering how close she had come to being free. "I know. It's not for now. I won't try to cross until then."

"Wait, what other information do you need? You've already seen where the gate is," Cade said, eyes laced with confusion.

"Do you really think your father is going to let me cross? I don't know what happened the other night, but Cora said he usually has it guarded day and night."

Cade tensed. "Cora? Is that who took you? Where is she now?"

"Took me?" Bridget repeated, bewildered by the ferocity in his question. "Like I said, I've been with her and the Virgo coven for as long as I can remember, but that doesn't matter now. I don't plan on ever seeing her again."

"She made you enter the tournament, didn't she?"

"Yes, to find this hidden second gate. I went along with it because I thought I could get away before it started. I didn't expect the contract. By then, it was too late to run," Bridget said. "So where is it?"

"I don't know what Cora heard, but there's only one gate."

Bridget narrowed her eyes. "Then how did you travel to the human realm? Or were you really partying with three breasted harlots in Tafari like Alette says?"

Cade sputtered incredulously. "I've never even been to Tafari. I got to the human realm through *the* gate. The one here in the palace."

"Your father let you cross?" Bridget asked disbelievingly.

"No, there was a Shaman, Echnav. He was one of my tutors growing up. He sent me across in the middle of the night before anyone knew I was gone."

"Was he the Shaman guarding the gate the other night?"

"No, he disappeared after I left, but I know someone who can find him. Once we do, he'll send you through the gate. He won't ask for anything."

Bridget wasn't listening. She couldn't get rid of the feeling there was another. "Are you sure?"

"Of course, he—"

"No, about the second gate," Bridget snapped, cutting him off. Cora wasn't a fool. If she thought there was another way to the human realm, it was for a good reason.

"Bridget..."

A loud cracking sound reverberated in the air. The deafening pop made Bridget jump as it echoed through her bones.

"What was that?" Bridget gasped.

"It can't be..." Cade said, face drained of color. He ran to the window and glanced outside. "It sounded like a gunshot."

"A gunshot?" Bridget repeated. The word felt odd on her tongue. Outside the window, the sun hung low in the sky.

"Stay here," Cade ordered, squeezing her arm as he passed her. Bridget's skin burned at the touch. Before he walked out the door, he turned back around. "Come back tomorrow around this time. Tell no one and make sure you aren't followed."

"So this is real?" Bridget blurted. "Why are you even talking to me?"

For a split-second, Cade's face changed, like he'd seen a ghost. He quickly composed himself and nodded. "You may have information about the covens I need. Just be here tomorrow."

Seconds later, he was gone. And even though he'd admitted wanting to talk to her for information, for the first time, Bridget looked forward to tomorrow.

CHAPTER TWELVE

The next morning, the apartments were eerily quiet when Bridget went down for lunch. She felt more confident with her necklace hanging firmly around her neck. It was never coming off again, especially if it meant Cora couldn't contact her with it on. When she entered the dining room, Alette and Brynley whispered furiously in the corner. Hai paced nervously. When Delphine spotted her, she grabbed her arm and dragged her inside.

"Where have you been?" she whispered furiously.

"I was sleeping," Bridget lied. After the library, she had gone straight to her room and put on her necklace, like Cade had asked. Her mind felt a little clearer, but the rune didn't stop the nightmares.

"Something happened. They asked us to wait in here for everyone," Delphine said gravely. "Whatever it is, it's not good."

Another figure entered the room. Quinn raised an eyebrow at the somber scene. "Why does everyone look like the tournament was just canceled?"

"Don't be crass," Hai snapped.

"Excuse me?" Quinn sneered.

"Calm down," Delphine said, stepping between the two. "We were told to wait here and lock the door. She's worried because Ondine hasn't come down yet."

"The door isn't locked. In fact, it's wide open," Quinn stated derisively, grabbing a bread roll from the table.

"Not everyone was here yet," Brynley mumbled, her arms crossed defensively. There was a long moment as they all glanced at each other, unsure of what to do. Even though Ondine was still missing, Bridget could tell most of the girls wanted to lock the door. No one moved, though.

"I'll do it," Bridget sighed. As her hand touched the door, it swung open. She jumped back and automatically took a defensive stance.

The director slipped inside, eyeing Bridget's posture dubiously. He cleared his throat and scratched his collar. "Ladies, I'm afraid I have some bad news."

"Shouldn't we wait for Marin and Ondine?" Bridget asked.

"Marin is busy with another task at the moment," the director replied, exasperated. "However, Ondine has been injured. I can't explain what happened, but she's not doing well. Our healers are doing the best they can. If you wish to visit her, let me know, and I will escort you to the infirmary."

Hai let out a loud cry.

"That's the only explanation we get?" Quinn stated hotly.

Bridget's stomach dropped, thinking of the girl who wanted to go home. While the Nymph had never thanked her for her help during the first task, she didn't wish any ill will on her.

"Yes. If there are no more questions, please proceed back to your rooms for the time being. The palace is perfectly safe, but it's better not to take any chances," the director replied stonily. Before anyone could react, he slipped out of the room. Bridget stared after him. He always seemed to be in a hurry.

Alette grabbed Brynley by the arm and frantically whispered something in her ear. Soon, the two girls rushed away. In the corner, Delphine comforted a sobbing Hai. Bridget gazed at the afternoon light streaming through the windows. The urge to meet Cade in the library overwhelmed her, despite a small part of her thinking he might not show up. Hoping no one noticed her, she slowly backed out of the dining room.

"Where are you going?" Quinn asked, her tone suspicious.

"I need some fresh air."

Bridget sped away before Quinn could stop her. She was almost to the west wing when her heart finally slowed down. Once again, there were no guards in sight. A few times, a maid scurried past her, but none questioned her. She glanced around for any onlookers before she entered the library.

As she tiptoed to the back, Bridget's insides twisted. Most of the night, she had replayed everything said between her and Cade. He knew where she was from and what she wanted and didn't try to have her kicked out of the palace. Or arrested. And just having one person know the truth about her felt like a relief. Their one conversation felt like one of the most normal things to happen to her in Elyria, or Vassuryn. Bridget couldn't recall a single time Cora or Alexia really *talked* to her.

To her surprise, Cade was already waiting for her. Leaning against a shelf, he stared intently at his little black box, looking unfairly handsome in black leather. The only spot of color on him was a dark green undershirt. He looked up as she approached.

"Hi," Cade said with a small smile.

"Hi," Bridget replied, unable to stop herself from grinning. She locked eyes with him, and for a long moment, they stared at each other. The impact of his gaze sent electricity down her spine. Bridget forced her eyes away and pointed to the box in his hand. "What is that? You were looking at it yesterday too."

Cade looked amused but handed over the device. It was heavy and smooth in her hands. She tapped on the sides, but nothing happened. When she was done with her inspection, he slipped the device in his pocket.

"It's a phone. In the human realm, people use it to communicate. It doesn't work here, but I can still turn it on," Cade said, opening the loose shelf. He motioned for her to enter.

A new set of maps lay on the table. This time, Bridget recognized the top one. The geography of the four kingdoms was different than she imagined. Elyria lay between the forest-ridden Vassuryn and coastal Kastron. North of them all, past the mountains, was Cavamyne. Abandoned and destroyed, the once homeland of the Tuathan barely had any landmarks recorded. A large area of land across the sea caught her eye.

"I didn't realize Tafari was so far away," Bridget said, tracing the distant southern kingdom with her finger.

"By ship, it takes a week or two," Cade said. "But Castor travels back and forth from there through the human realm. It's much easier that way. He's the youngest of their four princes. You might have seen him around. He's here helping me with something."

Bridget nodded, remembering the good-looking stranger that mocked the tournament. "Tafari has its own gate?"

"Tafari is more advanced than Elyria. Unlike my father or grandfather, they've actually tried to keep up with the human realm's technology and incorporate it with their own," Cade replied irritably. "We're a few decades behind, thanks to my father's obsession with one Shaman's vision."

Bridget gazed at him, unable to ignore the longing in his eyes. Once again, it looked like he hadn't slept.

"Why did you leave the human realm?" she asked quietly. "Were you happy there?"

After a long pause, Cade said, "I was. As for why I left, it's complicated. I didn't have much of a choice."

Bridget's curiosity pressed her to question him more. Somehow, she refrained and chewed on the inside of her cheek. The openness in his eyes had shuttered closed. She doubted he would answer. Eventually, she asked, "Do you want to go back?"

Cade scratched his neck and flicked a scrap of paper off the table. "Don't you?"

"Of course. I know I'll lose my memories again, but I hope there might be a family…or something, waiting for me," Bridget said.

Beside her, Cade went still.

"I wonder where they think I've been," Bridget continued softly.

"Sometimes I can't sleep because I can't stop imagining different terrible scenarios about how I ended up here."

When she dared to glance at Cade, he looked pained.

"And sometimes I think I don't even want to know anyone from my old life because they let it happen."

The words felt hollow as they escaped her mouth. She had told herself the lie so many times, it felt like the truth. Believing it had become easier than hoping. Bridget cleared her throat, embarrassed by the recklessness that had overtaken her. Secret musings that hid in her heart shouldn't be shared with a prince.

Still, she couldn't help but ask, "How do you get here from the human realm?"

"The same as here," he answered hoarsely. "Once you find the gate, you need a Shaman, and like with most old Fae magic, you have to agree."

Bridget's heart splintered, even though the revelation didn't feel like surprise. She should have known. Alexia's words slashed through her mind like a fiery whip. Maybe she really was blind and naïve. Her throat tightened.

"So I have no one to blame but myself," Bridget said, letting out a sharp laugh. "I can't even retrace my steps to figure out what happened. I don't remember much after crossing. Those first weeks were a blur of confusion, pain, and blood. It was months before I realized I was lost and stuck."

Whether real or imagined, the feel of fingers digging in her side and black eyes lit by flame haunted her dreams. She recoiled when Cade grabbed her right hand, dragging her out of the images. For a second, she had forgotten where she was. Safe, and away from Cora. Not trapped in a dark tent with her, where torment was the only thing that survived.

Cade rubbed his thumb over the leather of her glove. Even through the material, sparks heated her skin.

"Is that when this happened?" he asked, somehow knowing her gloves covered more than skin.

Bridget quickly snatched her hand away. "That came later."

"You can show me," Cade pressed, reaching for her again.

"No, I can't." She moved to stand on the other side of the table.

Wanting to change the subject, Bridget said, "What happened yesterday? There was that weird noise and then this morning, the director told us Ondine was hurt."

Cade blinked and took a moment to process her diversion. "She's dead, from the weapon we heard yesterday. They won't announce it until after the tournament. For now, they'll send her body back to Kaston and tell everyone else she wasn't strong enough to stay in the tournament any longer."

Sorrow swelled in Bridget's gut. Ondine, who only wanted to go home, who barely looked eighteen and had a whole life ahead of her. Marin had told the Nymph she would return to Kastron soon enough. Had she seen the girl lifeless and cold on a train, bound for burial?

"Why cover it up?"

"Guns are from the human realm. They've always been forbidden to import. My father wants it kept quiet until he figures out how it was brought over. As we speak, he has the Shamans pouring over manifests. Our healers don't know what to do with a wound like that. Anywhere else, she probably would've survived."

"Why her? She didn't care about the tournament. She didn't even have enough power to defend herself against the Barghest in the Elder Woods. Are contestants being targeted?"

"I'm not sure, but I have both Finn and Castor trying to help me figure it out." Cade was suddenly in front of her, his gaze determined. "I'm going to help you get back to the human realm. And look for this mysterious second gate. If you think it exists, I believe you."

Stunned, Bridget searched his face and tried to find the catch in his words. It didn't take long before yesterday came rushing back at her. *The covens.* He wanted information about the covens. She'd been so wrapped in...*him*, really, she'd completely forgotten the reason he was speaking to her in the first place.

It was a fact she needed to remember.

And she needed to get a grip on the heat that ran through her veins every time he looked at her.

"So you'll help me go home for information about the covens?" she asked.

Cade's gaze faltered. "Yes."

"I'll tell you anything you want to know," she promised, then quickly averted her gaze. If she was going to control the fire raging in her veins, before it consumed her completely, her focus needed to be on something else. Anything else. She grabbed the maps and suggested they start there. And if anyone were to ask about her stolen glances, she would deny it.

It was dark by the time Bridget left the library. Flushed, she hurried down the hallway, surprised by how fast the hours flew by. She hoped there was still leftover food in the dining room. For some reason, she was craving a waffle.

"I didn't think contestants were allowed to be in this area of the palace," a voice drawled, startling Bridget so much she almost fell to the ground. She whipped around and found Cassia watching her. The blonde princess smirked and leaned against a marble pillar.

"I was reading in the library," Bridget said, trying to keep her voice even. Her throat traitorously bobbed when Cassia narrowed her eyes and stalked forward.

"Is that so? Because I believe I saw my brother go in there a few hours ago," Cassia taunted, "And I haven't seen him since."

Bridget tensed, wondering exactly what she was accusing her of and if she should get ready for a fight. To her surprise, Cassia suddenly burst out laughing. After a few amused chuckles, she swiped at the corner of her eye.

"He really does think he's smarter than everyone else, doesn't he?" Cassia mumbled under her breath.

"Can I go now?" Bridget asked impatiently.

Cassia rolled her eyes. "Come with me," she said, walking away. She didn't check to see if Bridget followed.

Despite the stubborn clench straining her jaw, Bridget did. If Cassia wanted to harm her, she suspected she would've done it by now. The princess seemed straightforward. Cold, but straightforward.

Down the hall, Cassia led her to a dark, windowless room. The floor was bouncy and carpeted. Rigid, waved foam lined the walls. In the corner, long wooden sticks and swords sat in a basket. With no explanation, Cassia picked up a roll of white tape and began wrapping her hands.

"What is this place?" Bridget finally asked.

"It's the perfect room to practice combat skills. My father had this built for Cade, but he doesn't use it anymore." Cassia shrugged.

"That explains the foam, but not why I'm here."

"I overheard my father talking to the director earlier today. The second task is in four days. You'll be tested in hand-to-hand combat," Cassia said. "Obviously, you'll be at a disadvantage. The other girls will be free to use their magic, while they'll make you take off that handy little necklace of yours."

Bridget stared at her and blinked, stunned by the news. She jumped when Cassia threw the tape roll at her and motioned for her to wrap her hands.

"You'll need to play to your strengths," Cassia continued. "You're tall, so you'll have a chance to overpower your opponent once their body weakens from magic use. Your challenge will be staying conscious until that happens. I can help with that."

Sighing, Bridget tossed the tape aside in frustration. "I don't need this. My gloves stay on. Besides, why are you even helping me? I don't know if you noticed, but your sister tried to drown me a few days ago."

"Penance. I need my brother's forgiveness," Cassia replied shortly, walking out to the center of the floor with a thin wooden stick.

Bridget wasn't sure what that had to do with her, but she followed Cassia anyway. Standing in front of her, she could see how much she resembled her twin. Their hair was different, but their brown eyes and bone structure were the same. "What did you do?"

"It doesn't matter now, but he hasn't spoken to me since. Neither has Delphine nor Finn," she added quietly. "We all grew up together, but they took his side. At least Castor still bothers to check in."

"I keep hearing his name. Why is he here and not Tafari?"

Cassia looked puzzled at her curiosity, but still answered, "He's the youngest of four brothers, so there's not much for him to do there, in terms of ruling. I think he's spent more time here and the human realm than his own kingdom. His parents give him the freedom to do what he wants. Not that he does. He's too honorable. It was always Cade that was known as the wild prince."

A flash of annoyance went through Bridget upon hearing Cade's nickname. She wanted to ask more, but Cassia suddenly flung the wooden stick forward and hit the side of Bridget's leg. The tip left a sharp stinging pain in her muscle. When she hissed in protest, Cassia grinned.

"Back when he bothered, this used to be my father's favorite thing to train me with. He said the pain would toughen me up for Fae magic."

"You're the Witch," Bridget concluded, rubbing her thigh. She gazed at Cassia's neck and wrists, trying to find a coven mark.

"Fantastic. I didn't realize that was common knowledge now," Cassia sneered bitterly. "And don't bother looking for my mark. I don't belong to any coven."

This time, when Cassia whipped the stick again, Bridget was ready. She jumped and rolled to the side, successfully avoiding another harsh hit.

"You've already had some training," Cassia said.

Bridget lifted a shoulder, silently thanking Cora for one good thing to leave her with. "A little."

"It's better than nothing. What's your pain tolerance like?"

"I can take pain," Bridget said, reflexively flexing her hands.

"Good. Now go get a stick."

CHAPTER THIRTEEN

The next few days, Bridget did nothing but train with Cassia. She knew she had no chance of winning the second task, or any task, but she didn't want to make a fool of herself. She was determined not to go down without a fight. Plus, training kept her mind off Cade. Bridget's stomach rolled in embarrassment every time she thought of him. Every time she was around him, reason and logic seemed to disappear from her body. Out of all people, she wasn't sure why he was the one that got her to spill secrets, including a notion that there was a hidden second gate to the human realm. And even though he'd offered his help, she couldn't face him until she got better control of herself.

Cade wasn't the only person she was avoiding, though. She hadn't been able to face the other girls after learning the truth about Ondine. Bridget was confident one of them would be able to tell she knew something by looking at her face. Cora always told her she was a terrible liar. So she was back to eating at times when everyone was gone or asleep. Except today. All morning, her stomach had growled fiercely, to the point of pain. Taking a chance, Bridget crept downstairs.

To her dismay, Delphine, Hai, Brynley, and Alette were in the dining room, talking and munching. Their quiet chatter silenced as she approached the table and grabbed a muffin. Wary gazes fell on her, except Delphine's, who smiled at her.

"It's been a while since I've seen you. You look like you've been working hard," she said, eyeing the faint bruises dotting Bridget's arms.

"Right?" Alette retorted dubiously, harshly grabbing Bridget's wrist to get a better look at the marks. "Strange for someone who never seems to be around."

Bridget yanked her arm from Alette's grasp. "What I do and where I go is none of your business," she snapped, piling more food on her plate. She wanted to eat and leave as quickly as possible.

"Touchy," Alette murmured, a satisfied smirk on her face as she lifted her palms.

"Leave her alone, Alette. I've seen her working out late at night," Delphine lied, sneaking a glance at Bridget. "Besides, the director said to lay low until Ondine is better."

Hai, who was trembling in the corner, suddenly let out a small cry. "I've tried so many times, but they still won't let me see her."

Guilt overwhelmed Bridget as she studied Hai's red-rimmed eyes and puffy face. No matter what the king wanted, it didn't seem fair to keep her in the dark about her friend's death. Feeling someone's gaze, Bridget looked up and made eye contact with Delphine. Without having to ask, she could tell the other girl knew about Ondine, too, and was feeling just as remorseful. Delphine imperceptibly shook her head, silently telling her to keep quiet.

"You need to let it go and focus on the second task," Alette advised. "They'll probably announce it when we least expect it. You wouldn't want to miss it because you're stuck in the infirmary, would you?"

"Surely it won't happen until she's better," Brynley interjected. "We all had to sign that paper…"

"You're probably right," Alette said, clearly irritated. A moment later, her blue eyes turned wicked as she stared at Bridget, "Though it's a shame it's little Ondine that's hurt. We all know who the prince wishes would be too weak to finish and be forced to drop out."

Anger bubbled inside Bridget. She was right to avoid the other girls, especially Alette. She doubted the Fae girl would feel any morsel of sadness when she learned about Ondine's death. After throwing her empty plate down on the table, Bridget stormed to the door.

"Looks like I hurt her feelings," Alette sniggered, not bothering to feign a whisper.

Bridget whirled around. "Not at all. But if I stay in this room any longer, the sound of your voice is going to give me a permanent headache," she sneered, before adding, "The second task is tomorrow, by the way."

As Bridget left, the room erupted into chaos. She didn't bother to look back, not even at Delphine, to answer their hysterical accusations. If she had to guess, the news of the second task wasn't a surprise to her.

To calm her nerves, Bridget grabbed her leather jacket and headed to the palace's southern garden. By chance, she had come across the small area after a workout with Cassia. The colorful hibiscus flowers, green trees, and worn stone made her feel peaceful. When she arrived, she was relieved to find it empty. As she paced around some bushes, a flash of purple caught Bridget's eye. Curious, she leaned against one of the garden's stone pillars and slowly peered around it. Below, Quinn sat on her knees in a grassy field. Back toward her, the Witch held something in her hand and gazed at the sky. Squinting, Bridget stood on her toes and tried to get a better look.

Suddenly, a hand grabbed her shoulder.

"Who are you spying on?"

Without thinking, Bridget whipped around and punched her assailant in the face. She gasped and covered her mouth when she realized who stood behind her.

"Ow," Cade sputtered, grabbing his chin.

Heart still racing, Bridget slapped him on the arm and exclaimed, "Why did you do that?"

"Me? I'm not the one that just went full Sarah Connor on an innocent bystander," Cade argued indignantly.

"What?"

"Nevermind," Cade sighed, shaking his head. His gaze turned concerned. "You haven't come back to the library."

Bridget looked back at Quinn, but she had disappeared. Disappointed, she turned to Cade. Her stomach fluttered under the intensity of his stare. His golden-brown eyes scorched into hers, leaving her dizzy. For a split-second, she forgot all the reasons she wanted to avoid him in the first place. When she found her voice, she said, "I found out about the second task. I've been trying to practice."

"That explains the bruises," Cade said, reaching up to trace her swollen cheekbone. When Bridget barely suppressed a shiver, he smirked. "And the right hook. How do you know? I only found out this morning."

Mouth going dry, Bridget reluctantly confessed, "Your sister. Cassia. Believe it or not, she's actually been helping me."

She watched his expression war between shock and anger. "What the hell, Bridget? You can't trust her."

"Well, unlike your other one, she hasn't tried to drown me yet," Bridget retorted dryly. "Besides, I don't have to trust her for her to help me. Do I think it's weird that she is? Yes, but she's your sister. She says she wants your forgiveness."

Rolling his eyes, Cade said, "She doesn't know when to keep her mouth shut."

"Why are you being so hard on her? She seems really remorseful," Bridget said, the annoyance in her voice barely hidden. She was willing to give up everything for the chance to see if she had a family in the human realm, while Cade actively ignored the sister who was trying anything to get his attention.

"If you knew what she did, you would be just as angry," Cade growled.

"Then tell me."

"I can't."

Irritation flared in her chest. Bridget turned away, ready to storm back to the apartments, but Cade's hand gently wrapped around her wrist. His rough fingers barely applied any pressure, but the gesture stopped her in her tracks. When she didn't resist, he pulled her closer. "I don't want to argue about Cassia. Train with her if you want. Is that the only reason you've been avoiding me?"

"Yes," Bridget whispered, hoping he didn't notice the lie or hear her intake of breath.

Cade searched her face for a long moment. Eventually, he hummed low in his throat and nodded, like he didn't quite believe her, but accepted her answer. "Why didn't you ask me?"

"Ask you what?"

"To train you," Cade said, fingers dancing over the skin of her arms. Goosebumps erupted over every inch of her.

"I saw you in the field with Finn, remember? I wouldn't be able to keep up," Bridget replied shakily. She felt her cheeks heat as she imagined training with Cade. Of him sweaty, breathing hard, and pulling her close...

"I think you would hold your own. It would be fun," Cade said, lips tilted at the corners.

Fun. It wasn't a word she associated with Elyria or the tournament. The idea jarred her back to reality. Could training be fun if she was with Cade? It seemed life or death every time she practiced with Cora or Cassia. Deep in her thoughts, Cade's hand on her neck surprised her. When she accidentally flinched, Cade cleared his throat and took a step back. "I have something to show you," he said, pulling her inside to an empty corridor.

"The creepy painting?" Bridget asked, nodding at the wall behind him. A massive portrait featuring a dark-headed woman with a heart in one hand sent chills up her spine.

With furrowed brows, Cade glanced at the art piece. "What? No, I didn't even realize that was there. Actually, you might find that interesting. But more importantly," he said, grabbing a folded piece of paper from his pocket, "you're right about there being another gate. It has to exist."

Bridget's mouth fell open in shock. It had only been a few days since she'd expressed her beliefs about a second gate to him, and he already had proof. If she was being honest, the longer she was away from Cora, the more she'd started to believe that the second gate was the hope of a deranged Witch trying to grasp for any source of power.

"How do you know?"

"My father has been obsessing over the Astraeus gate manifestos for days trying to figure out how a gun got through, which got me thinking... I can't believe I didn't check this before," Cade ranted, quickly unfolding the paper. "The gate is guarded twenty-four hours a day by the Shamans and a select handful of guards. They're the only ones who can let people in or out. This paper is from the month you must have arrived. There's no record of you."

Bridget glanced at the paper and only saw a handful of instances of comings and goings in the month of December. Cargo for each trip was written next to each occurrence. As she scanned, Cade's name caught her eye. It showed him returning on December 25th. Bridget did a double take at his companions: Finn and Cassia. No one, not even Cade, had mentioned the two of them being with him in the human realm. Her name was nowhere to be found, nor were the names of anyone else.

"Before we jump to conclusions, are you sure I wasn't deliberately left off this? Someone could have paid or bargained with a Shaman to leave something off, right?" Bridget asked.

"I've already been in the heads of all the Shamans. None of them have any memory of you."

Bridget's jaw slackened. Was that his power? Reading people's minds? Cora had made it sound deadlier…or maybe there were multiple things he could do.

"Everyone that comes through that gate is required to sign a manifest with blood," he continued. "The tower is lined with runes to ensure that happens, so nothing unwanted comes through. If there's a lie…"

"The price is paid," Bridget finished hoarsely. He was right. She had to come through somewhere else. There was no other option. The proof was in her very hand. "Do you think your father knows?"

"No, he would have already used the other gate to his advantage or destroyed it, like the others," Cade said. "We'll have to do some more digging. Before humans were cursed, there were many gates. There are old journals in the library that might have some more information."

Bridget nodded, mind still reeling. The second gate existed, and she'd come through there. More than ever, she wished she remembered her early days in Astraeus, or Vassuryn, or wherever the gate was located. "Wait, humans weren't always cursed?" Bridget asked, finally processing his words.

"No, according to legend, they were cursed around 500 years ago."

Cade pointed at the painting. "Which is why I thought you would find the meaning behind this painting interesting. It's weird. I always thought this hung in the gallery."

Bridget looked at the portrait closer. Three people were depicted. The dark-haired woman with the heart in her hand stood on a stone in the very middle, looking wild and crazy. On her right, a solemn man with pointed ears carried a glowing sword. On her left, a woman lay dead on the ground, chest open and hollow. Another ice-cold chill ran down her spine.

"What happened?" Bridget asked, eyes glued to the woman in the middle.

Beside her, Cade gazed at the portrait with a weird look on his face. After a few seconds, he quickly shook himself out of his sudden reverie. "I learned the story from Echnav, the Shaman I told you about, but I guess it all started when one of the Tuathan princes fell in love with a human. Back then, there were many gates, so people could cross over to the human realm anytime they wanted."

"Was it a huge scandal?"

"Actually, no. Elyria used to be ruled by humans. Cavamyne was the kingdom where the Fae and Tuathan lived. Believe it or not, the Fae are a result of Tuathans mating with humans. Elyria didn't become home for the Fae until after the Cavamynian War."

Cavamyne, a place often talked about, but never in enough detail. Most people were scared to even whisper the name. All Bridget knew was that the old northern kingdom was abandoned, and that the war destroyed most of the Tuathan. "I don't understand. Why curse humans then?"

"The Cavamynian War was taking place with the Sanguis coven. They had conquered Vassuryn and Kastron and were close to claiming Elyria and Cavamyne. The head Witch of the coven, Vega, offered to marry the Tuathan Prince to end the war."

"I've never heard of the Sanguis coven. I thought they were all named after constellations," Bridget said. "But based on the painting, I'm guessing he said no."

"The coven doesn't exist anymore. The members were a group of rogue Witches and Warlocks brainwashed by the power of blood magic.

They were all banished after the war. And you're right, he said no. As you can see, Vega didn't take the rejection well. She killed the prince's lover and used her blood to create the curse on the humans. There's not much recorded after that. Cavamyne was in ruins, so the Fae moved to Elyria. After the Sanguis were banished, every gate was destroyed. Except one."

"Two," Bridget corrected. The painting drew her attention again. As she stared at the melancholy figures, she couldn't help but think there was more to the story, that it wasn't as simple as a rejected marriage proposal. "What happened to the prince?"

"You know what? I'm not sure. I think the younger brother became king."

When footsteps sounded from the end of the hallway, Cade flinched away from her. The air disappeared from her lungs as reality came crashing down on her. She wasn't supposed to be alone with Cade, let alone talking to him. Suddenly, she was the unwanted human that he was repulsed by on the first night. Chest tightening, she took a step back, noting the look of relief on Cade's face when he realized it was Finn coming down the hallway. Seconds later, he glanced at her and frowned.

"What are you doing?" Cade asked, narrowing his eyes at her retreating figure.

"I need to go," Bridget blurted, rushing away. She hoped her watery eyes were from the wind blowing pollen all over the palace grounds.

CHAPTER FOURTEEN

Bridget sat on her bedroom floor, head resting on her knees. She hadn't moved in hours. The second task would be announced any minute, and she'd done nothing to prepare all day. All she could do was think about Cade and the story and the second gate and how quickly he'd moved away from her...All night, her mind warred with itself, trapping her on the ground as she battled nightmares and nausea. She hated that Cade had begun to make a nightly appearance, standing next to Cora as he bled her dry and muttered spells. For the last hour, she'd been convincing herself to get up and eat. It seemed to be helping; her vision was no longer fuzzy. She would compete in the second task ,and she would let no Fae humiliate her.

A knock sounded from her door. Legs trembling, Bridget slowly walked over to open it, hoping it wasn't Cade. To her relief, Delphine stood on the other side. She was dressed for the task in long pants and a tank top; her long black hair was braided down her back.

With a nervous smile, Delphine said, "We have to be in the southern field by the palace entrance in an hour."

"Thanks, Delphine. I'm ready. I just need to find my shoes." Bridget glanced at her own outfit of pajama pants and a baggy t-shirt; she was nowhere near ready. Even though Delphine looked prepared, Bridget could tell she was anxious from her stiff posture and fidgety hands. After a quick glance around the hallway, Delphine grabbed something from her boot.

"You need to take this. It's a strength enhancer," Delphine whispered, slipping a purple vial into Bridget's hands.

"I thought enhancers weren't allowed," Bridget said, absentmindedly grasping her necklace, even though it was a rune. She was dreading the moment she did, afraid that Cora would immediately know and try to contact her.

"Runes aren't allowed, especially if they protect you from magic. They won't be able to tell if we've taken a potion," Delphine explained. "I guarantee the other girls have taken something similar."

Bridget eyed the vial warily. She knew magic affected humans differently, that nothing given by the Fae was for free, but if Delphine was right, she would need it to keep up with her opponent. "Are you taking one?" Bridget asked.

Delphine grabbed a second vial from her boot and downed it. She let out a short cough as the potion went down. "Trust me," she pleaded, wiping the back of her hand on her mouth.

Taking a deep breath, Bridget raised the vial to her lips and chugged.

With her red hair secured in a high ponytail, Bridget made the long trek to the south end of the palace. She could feel the effects of the potion on her muscles. Her limbs felt lighter and stronger. Her mind seemed hyper-aware of the movements around her, even though she felt naked without her necklace.

The girls and the director were waiting in a circle outside a makeshift fence. Everyone, even Alette, fidgeted nervously. Voices from the crowd inside the rudimentary arena echoed loudly through the hills. Bridget was surprised to see so many people had shown up to watch the task. She tried not to let it shake her. She walked up and stood between Delphine and Quinn.

"Ladies, the second task will test your strength in hand-to-hand combat," the director stated. "As queen, you will be expected to defend Elyria against its enemies. You will be facing highly trained members of the guard. The match will end when someone is pinned or knocked unconscious. The winner will be chosen based on how quickly they can bring down their opponent. Healers will be standing by in case of injury."

When no one asked any questions, the director opened the fence doors and escorted them inside an arena. The wood looked bright and new, like it had just been built. Bright lights from above reflected on the director's bald head. Bridget wondered if they would ever learn his name.

"At least we don't have to fight each other," Brynley whispered as the crowd parted for them to walk to a center stage. Even though she agreed with her, Bridget thought fighting the other girls would be easier. As far as she knew, their lives did not revolve around defense and protection, like the guards.

At the center of the grassy area was a high, square stage. Ropes lined the edges, making it look even more intimidating. The director led them to the right of the stage where a space was reserved for the contestants, next to a large camera. Fae, Witches, and Nymphs crowded around them, each one trying to get a good view. Many were pushed up against the palace's stone wall as they held goblets in their hands. Based on the spicy smell, she guessed wine was being served. Bridget had never seen so many people in the palace. She wondered if the king had opened the gates to anyone in Astraeus to watch the task. Rage bubbled inside her. The tournament was already demeaning enough, now, the girls were forced to be cheap entertainment.

To her left, the royal family sat on another stage close by, their view perfectly in line with the competition. She didn't dare look up. Instead, she turned her back to them and found Quinn. The last time she had seen her, she'd been kneeling in a field. The Witch leaned against the stage and picked at her nails, acting like she didn't have a care in the world.

"I saw you yesterday. Alone by the garden," Bridget said, keeping her voice casual.

"My magic felt off. I needed some alone time to channel some fire," Quinn shrugged.

Bridget nodded, unsure why she was so suspicious. She hadn't seen any fire around, though, which was a staple for the Aries coven magic. "Are you okay now?"

"I'm prepared to take down this stubby little guard with ease, if that's what you mean," she quipped, nodding at the short, muscled Fae that was waiting for her on stage. Apparently, she was going first. With a sly grin, she jumped through the ropes with ease, ready to start.

A hot, enraged voice whispered in her ear, "Why does the prince keep staring at you?"

Bridget turned to meet Alette's hostile glare. She wiped away the spit that had splashed across her cheek with a grimace. "He's not," Bridget replied coolly, even though she had felt his eyes burning holes in her since she had entered the arena.

"He hasn't taken his eyes off you since we walked in," Alette hissed indignantly.

Bridget rolled her eyes. "You need to focus on the task." She didn't want to look at Cade, but it bothered her that Alette was, enough that she noticed where his eyes wandered.

Alette hackled. "It's not me you need to worry about. I doubt you'll make it two seconds."

When Bridget made no reply, Alette scoffed and moved to stand beside Brynley. Seconds later, the director started making a speech, but Bridget wasn't listening. She stared at the stage and silently reviewed every move she had learned with Cassia. Before she made it through her mental checklist, a sharp pain went through her head. Bridget recoiled, but then felt him. *Cade*. His presence wrapped around her skull soothingly.

I can stop this, his voice echoed softly through her mind. Bridget swung her head around and glared at him. So this is what he could do? Whisper things in her head?

Cade stared impassively at the stage. If she didn't hear him in her head, she wouldn't have guessed he was performing magic at all. For the first time, his morganite rune hung on top of his shirt and his hair…

Bridget scowled. The last thing she wanted him to hear were her thoughts. Besides, she wanted to fight. She needed to prove herself.

Get out of my head, she growled. After a brief sting in her right temple, he was gone. She hated that she felt hollow. In his chair, Cade grimaced in irritation.

When Bridget turned back to the director, she caught Cassia's eye. The princess gazed between the two, obviously picking up on their conversation. With a fleeting gaze at Cade, Cassia hopped out of her chair and made her way toward Bridget. The crowd, focused on whatever the director and the king were bantering about, didn't notice her walking through the rowdy expanse. Except the girls. They all stared at the princess with open jaws as she approached Bridget.

"I don't think this conversation applies to any of you," Cassia barked, making them all turn away. She grabbed Bridget's arm. "I saw that exchange. Cade's right, this is ridiculous. You should let him stop it."

Bridget ripped her arm away and snapped, "If you didn't think I could win, why did you help me?"

"Stop thinking about yourself," Cassia chastised. "You may know this whole tournament is bullshit, but the others don't. Do you really want the other girls to risk their life on something we all know is fixed?"

Guilt filled Bridget's chest. Cassia's words confirmed the truth she didn't dare think. She looked around at the other girls. Their eyes were wide, focused, and scared. Only Marin seemed calm. They truly believed every task in the tournament would help prove their worth to the king and prince. They were willing to sacrifice their health and body to prove it, while Bridget was solely determined to prove her worth as a human. She understood Cassia's point but looking at the king's gleeful face, she knew the task was inevitable.

"Even if Cade stops it now, it will happen eventually."

Cassie didn't argue, but a resigned look settled on her face. She knew it too. Her father wouldn't be stopped for long.

"You would have more time to train," Cassia said quietly in one last attempt to convince her. Bridget fought an eye roll, realizing Cade's true intentions. She wondered if he had been talking to Cassia in her head too. A bell rang and Quinn moved to the center of the stage.

"Too late," Bridget said. The short guard generated an invisible shield as Quinn attempted a punch. She turned to Cassia, determination on her face. "I can do this."

Cassia nodded briefly before returning to her seat. When she sat down, the king narrowed his eyes in suspicion, but Cassia said nothing, keeping her focus on the match in front of her. Quinn kicked and punched furiously at a shield, but it seemed to be wavering. The Fae guard's arms shook as blood dripped from his ears. Seconds later, the shield dropped, and the guard collapsed to his knees. Quinn swung her leg around and kicked him hard in the head. When he didn't get back up, cheers erupted. With a grin plastered on her face, Quinn did a small curtsy. She'd barely broken a sweat. Relief swept through Bridget. If all the guards were only able to summon shields, she really would have a chance.

Brynley's match was next. Her opponent had similar magic to Quinn's. Instead of using a large shield, the new guard used shields around her fists to make her punches harder and stronger. She punched Brynley in the face, causing the Witch to stumble briefly. Lip bleeding, Brynley swung back, managing to hit the guard in the ear. Before the guard could react, Brynley let out a roar and jumped on top of her, pushing her to the ground. Holding down her arms, Brynlee head-butted the guard in the face. The guard yelped and struggled but couldn't get up. A bell rang and Brynley hopped up in victory.

Marin stepped on stage. The crowd went silent. When the next soldier turned around and realized who he was fighting, his face went pale. He sprinted over to the director and whispered furiously in his ear.

"Uh, looks like we have a forfeit," the director sputtered and then ran the bell, "Marin wins."

The crowd booed and shouted obscenities at the solider who hurried out of the arena. Marin shrugged and hopped off stage. When Delphine slid under the ropes, she didn't seem as confident as the others. She paced the edges of the stage, waiting for her opponent to make the first move. Bridget snuck a look at Cade. He leaned forward, failing to hide his concern. Faster than she could blink, the guard was in front of Delphine, punching her hard in the face. Bridget heard a crack as she went down and hit the floor with a loud thud. The guard lifted his leg to step on her, but Delphine transported herself to the other side of the stage before the blow hit. Bridget gasped as the guard moved in a blur back to Delphine, this time punching her in the stomach. He was *fast*, and his abilities seemed to be the perfect foil to Delphine's. She moved again. Seconds later, Delphine was on her knees, gasping for breath. Blood trickled from her swollen nose. Bridget saw Cade yell at his father, but the king ignored him.

The guard quickly appeared in front of Delphine again and kneed her in the chin. Delphine fell onto her back. And didn't get up. In horror, Bridget watched as two healers ran onto the stage and grabbed her. People were still cheering and raising their goblets in the air as the healers carried Delphine out of the courtyard. Bridget felt like she was going to vomit. Delphine, one of the kindest people she had ever met, didn't deserve such treatment. Bridget looked at Cade and found him staring back at her with similar distress in his eyes.

The rest of the matches went by in a blur, even Alette's. Bridget no longer cared what happened to the others. When it was finally her turn, the director pulled her arm and pushed her on stage without a word. Last. She was always last. Bridget frantically surveyed the audience, but all she found were jeers and raised glasses. Hours of wine had made the crowd restless. Breathing hard, she looked at Cade. He was out of his chair, fists clenched. She shook her head, signaling to him to sit down. She could do it. No matter what happened, she wouldn't go down without a fight.

More boos erupted from the audience as she stood alone on stage, some even yelled and demanded she take off her gloves. Bridget ignored the chants and focused on the woman crawling through the ropes. She was shorter than Bridget, but her muscles bulged intimidatingly. Grinning with maniacal enthusiasm, she flicked her wrists. Bridget was suddenly hit all over with a bitter smelling liquid. The soldier had elemental abilities. Wine had risen from every goblet in the courtyard and been flung straight toward her. The force of the blow stung her skin. Coughing from the taste, Bridget wiped her eyes. She was drenched in purple. When the audience realized what the soldier had done, laughter erupted.

Glaring at the soldier, Bridget stalked forward, hoping to land a punch. The guard flicked her wrists again, lifting the wine staining her clothes and flinging it back down on her, harder than before. The force sent Bridget tumbling backward. She landed stiffly on her back and gasped as her breath escaped her chest. Laughter erupted again. Bridget closed her eyes and focused on her breathing.

In and out.

All she had to do was outlast the pain.

Bridget pushed herself up and got to her feet. The soldier smirked. After a moment, she held out her arms in mock surrender.

"How about I make it a little easier for you?" The soldier taunted. "No more magic."

The two circled each other before Bridget surged forward, punching her square in the jaw. The audience went quiet as the soldier stumbled back. She stared at Bridget in shock, clearly not expecting to be hit so hard. As blood dribbled from her mouth, the guard jetted forward and grabbed Bridget by the shoulders. Pushing back, Bridget brought her knee up to the soldier's stomach. The action sent them both to the ground. The soldier grabbed Bridget by the hair and punched her hard in the chin. Seeing stars, Bridget lifted her hands and dug her fingers into the other girl's eyes. The soldier screeched and rolled off. Bridget crawled to the other side of the stage. Pressure swelled under her left eye.

Using the ropes, Bridget stood back up. The soldier did the same. Blood laced the woman's teeth and scratch marks covered her eye socket, bright red against pale skin. "Enough," the soldier hissed, holding out a hand. The air suddenly disappeared around Bridget. She fell back to her knees, gasping for breath. Clenching her chest, Bridget tried to crawl forward. The soldier held up her other hand and pushed Bridget backward with a gust of wind. Looking up, Bridget saw the soldier's nose begin to bleed heavily. The Fae's endurance was waning, it wouldn't be long before she collapsed; she just had to hold on until then. Bridget closed her mouth, trying to hold on to the last of her air. She crawled forward again, face purple. The soldier sent another gust of wind, but it was too weak to move her.

As Bridget's vision turned black, the soldier fell to her knees. The Fae doubled over as blood spilled from her face all over the stage. At last, Bridget gasped as air filled her lungs. Her entire body shook with relief. Feeling dizzy, Bridget struggled to stand up, but she was determined to end it. The entire arena was silent. Bridget stood in front of the guard and lifted her leg, ready to give a final blow.

A loud, deafening pop suddenly exploded from outside the palace walls. Screams erupted as the lights went out with a searing pulse. With only moonlight shining in the arena, Bridget could barely see the outlines of people running frantically in every direction for an exit. More pops sounded again, this time from somewhere further. Hysterical shouts and pleas echoed all around her.

Cade. She had to get Cade. Bridget blindly crawled through the ropes. As she hit the ground, she immediately got knocked down by someone running. The palms of her hands stung from the fall. She heaved herself up and moved to where she thought the royal family had been sitting. Bridget had made it a few feet when someone grabbed her from behind. She recognized the touch immediately.

"Cade, what's happening?"

Before he could respond, the sight of Fae flying aimlessly through the air made her jump.

"Get out of my way," the king bellowed irately, eyes and obsidian dagger glowing brightly, "The shots are coming from outside the walls, idiots. This ends tonight."

Again, the king raised the dagger and sent more bystanders into the air as he cleared a path for himself. A group of soldiers trailed closely behind him. Once he was through the gate, Cade's eyes turned white. He lifted his hands before a loud clang echoed throughout the arena. It took Bridget a second to realize he had slammed the front gate shut. With another wave of his hand, dim lights came back on. "He's right about the shots, but whoever cut the lights still has to be inside," Cade said.

Outside the gate, another shot rang out. Cade flicked his wrist, and a gun flew through the air. It landed right in front of him. The weapon was small and oddly shaped. With the lights back on, people began to dart to the palace wall, where they squatted with their heads down. Some still ran around, panic written on the features, unsure of what to do. Even over the chaos, Bridget could hear the king's voice barking orders in the distance. She couldn't see the other girls anywhere.

Quick footsteps sounded from behind her. Bridget whipped around and saw a masked man sprinting out of the crowd toward them, sword raised.

"Watch out," Bridget gasped, tightly grabbing onto Cade's arm to move them both out of the way. She wasn't quick enough for the man's downward motion. The sword pierced through the skin of her forearm and left a stinging, open slice. When the man lifted the weapon again, Cade pushed her behind him and lifted his hand. The motion froze the sword in place. Seconds later, it was flung to the side.

When the masked man realized he was empty-handed, his arms suddenly transformed. Long, bony claws erupted from his fingertips. Under the mask, sharp teeth jutted out. With a snarl, he launched himself at them. Bridget braced for impact, but Cade squeezed his hand into a fist and lifted the man high in the air. With a flick of his wrist, Cade jetted the man into the palace's wall, where he hit with a sickening crack. The man didn't fall to the ground, though, but remained hovered and pressed against the stone.

To her left, another masked man darted toward them, fists raised. Stepping in front of Cade's back, Bridget dug her feet into the ground, ready to lunge, but the man's neck suddenly snapped. He fell to the ground in a lifeless heap.

Beside her, Cade breathed heavily, hand in the air. Slowly, his brown eyes returned to normal. He wiped the blood from his nose before he gently inspected her forearm. "Are you alright?"

She studied the cut. It wasn't as deep as she expected, but it throbbed painfully. Cade ripped a piece of his shirt and wrapped it tightly around the wound. Bridget gaped at him. Since Vassuryn, she'd been curious about his power, especially since the Virgo coven cowered at the thought of him. Not only did he have the ability to enter minds, but he could also manipulate objects around him. He'd expertly fought off two men and barely moved an inch. And now, she couldn't believe someone so extraordinarily powerful tended to her wound. The contrast jarred her senses.

"Thank you," he said, eyes meeting hers in a serious gaze, "but don't ever do that again."

Bridget started to chuckle, but Cade's face remained stony. "Okay," she promised. "Do you think there's more?"

"Outside the walls. I entered that one's head briefly. Only two snuck inside," Cade said, nodding at the wheezing man still propped up against the wall. His morganite rune glowed dimly, proof that he still channeled it for power.

With a high-pitched order, Cassia shoved her way through the crowd. She briefly eyed the dead man lying on the ground. "Is that a Nymph?"

"They're both from Kastron," Cade replied darkly. He leaned down and searched the man but found nothing in his pockets. "I kept the one on the wall alive for questioning."

"Do you think this is about Ondine?" Bridget asked.

"That little Nymph was a nobody in Kastron," Cassia scoffed. "Besides, the ones outside the wall have a gun. This wasn't an impulse retaliation for a dead girl. This must have been planned far in advance."

Cade sighed and rubbed his forehead at her bluntness. "You're right, but I could already tell their memories have been tampered with. We'll have to get Castor to try some spells to reverse it."

"Father won't like that. He thinks Castor is too involved," Cassia said, walking over to Bridget to inspect her arm. "You need a healer."

"She's right, you should go to the infirmary. We'll take him down to the cells to be questioned," Cade said reassuringly.

Bridget hesitated, not wanting to leave, but the trashed arena seemed calm as more guards piled back through the gate. Cassia rolled her eyes and shooed her away with a small wave of her fingers. Begrudgingly, Bridget nodded and spared them one last look before heading to the infirmary.

CHAPTER FIFTEEN

After finding the infirmary, Bridget spent the next several hours next to Delphine's bed. The Fae girl had been in and out of consciousness for hours. Healers came by periodically to perform various spells. With her bruises quickly fading, Delphine already looked better. When Bridget had first arrived, a healer had given her a healing potion too. Seconds later, the cut on her arm had burned and festered. The healer had immediately ordered her to vomit. The agony and sight of her oozing arm made the instruction easy to follow. Afterward, all the healer had done for her was messily stitch the wound on her arm and complain under her breath about humans and magic. Bridget knew the scar would be ugly, but it would match the others on her body.

Behind her, the infirmary was full of people that had been trampled or knocked down during the second task. Healers ran rampant all over the large room, trying to keep up with the demand. When Delphine had first awoken, she'd been shocked by the frenzy until Bridget explained. So far, she hadn't heard a healer mention any gunshot wounds, but she didn't know if that was a good or bad sign. Bridget knew they would keep the dead out of the infirmary. A pit formed in her stomach when she realized she hadn't seen the director or the other girls, either. Next to her, Delphine stirred in the bed.

"Did I pass out again?" she asked hazily, rubbing her eyes.

"The healer said it might do that. On the plus side, your face doesn't look as swollen."

"That means the spell is working." Delphine said, studying the chaotic infirmary. "I should be helping."

"You need rest," Bridget chastised.

"So do you. You look like one of the drunken brawlers that frequent the bars in Astraeus," Delphine argued, warily studying the wine, dirt, and blood that covered Bridget's body.

"I'm fine," Bridget said, waving her hand dismissively. If the roles were reversed, she guessed Delphine wouldn't leave. So she stayed.

After a long moment, Bridget asked, "Why did you join the tournament?"

Delphine had already made it clear that she had no desire to marry Cade, yet she'd signed a binding blood contract. Bridget hadn't been able to figure out the source of her motivation, especially when she had dreams of her own that didn't involve marrying a prince.

"The king is..." Delphine searched for the right words, "Not who he used to be. He threatened my parents, even though they've been loyal to him and have worked in the palace for ages. I think he wanted me to join to ensure Cade would come back, no matter what. He knew he wouldn't leave me bound to a contract forever."

"I'm sorry," Bridget whispered. She wondered if any of the other girls had similar stories. Ondine hadn't wanted to join the tournament either.

"It's not your fault. Plus, I knew Cade didn't want to marry any of the girls that were being chosen. I thought if I joined, he had a safe choice. He could choose me and know that I wouldn't make him follow through with it."

Bridget smiled warmly. After the first task, Delphine had said she was the safe choice. At the time, Bridget hadn't realized how true her words were, thinking she was being modest, but Delphine sacrificed her freedom to ensure Cade kept his. Bridget deeply admired her loyalty. She wasn't sure she would've done the same in Delphine's situation, especially when freedom was one of the things she wanted most.

"You've given up so much…" Bridget said with a hint of disbelief in her voice.

"Only for a little while," Delphine corrected. "After this tournament, things will go back to normal, and I'll be free to live my life the way I want."

While Bridget didn't share her unwavering optimism, it was hard not to be inspired by her relentlessness. "I hope so," Bridget said, surprised by how much she meant her words, for both Delphine and herself.

Delphine's dark eyes lit up with excitement when they shifted to the door. "Finn!" She cried happily.

Bridget turned and saw the Fae warrior. Her neck heated when she remembered how she'd fled the hallway the night before. Cade followed closely behind him. Both males grinned as they approached Delphine.

"Wow," Finn teased as he eyed Delphine's face, "Cade wasn't lying when he said you were pummeled."

"I didn't say *pummeled...*" Cade said defensively. He moved to stand beside Bridget and did a double take at her wild appearance.

Delphine hit Finn on the arm and asked, "I know you've been busy with other things, but a hello now and then between orders would be nice. How long are you here for?"

"Until this whole mess gets sorted out," Finn shrugged. "Deckard needs all the help he can get right now."

Cade gingerly grabbed Bridget's forearm and inspected the new bandage. "Did they give you stitches instead of using a healing spell?"

"The potion they gave me made the cut worse. The healer didn't want to do any further damage, so no more magic for me," Bridget said dismissively. "Although the potion Delphine gave me didn't hurt me."

He opened his mouth to argue, but Delphine stopped him. "She doesn't need you to coddle her," she ribbed, and then her cheeks reddened slightly. "And that was just water, not a real potion. I thought it would help your confidence."

Cade sent her a weary glare.

Finn turned to Bridget and smiled impressively. "I heard you won your match."

Bridget stifled a groan. Due to what had happened afterward, she'd completely forgotten about the match. It seemed minuscule now compared to the current state of the palace. "If the lights hadn't gone out," Bridget grumbled, "I would have."

"I think it still counts."

Looking around, Cade sniffed loudly. His nose wrinkled in disgust. "Bridget, is that you?"

"She's covered in wine and blood," Finn answered dryly, "what do you think?"

"So are half the people in this room," Cade argued indignantly, hands waving.

Delphine sighed. "Cade, her hair is *purple...*"

"Dude, she's standing right next to you," Finn scoffed, giving Cade an unbelieving stare. "I can smell her from here."

"Okay, I get it! I smell," Bridget snapped loudly. Her cheeks burned painfully. She knew she should've already changed, but considering everything, it hadn't been a high priority. The three Fae went silent with identical looks of shame.

"I'll go take a bath," Bridget muttered, overwhelmed by the conversation, anyway. It all seemed so *normal,* she didn't know what to make of it. Why did she, out of all contestants, seem to fit in with them?

"The nurses have nose plugs," Delphine offered kindly.

Bridget shook her head and grabbed her discolored, matted ponytail. "I don't want my hair to stay this color permanently."

"I think it suits you," Cade called out supportively as she headed for the door. Bridget fought the urge to turn around and roll her eyes at him.

"That was lame," Delphine whispered teasingly.

Once out in the hallway, Bridget genuinely laughed for the first time in Elyria.

CHAPTER SIXTEEN

Warm afternoon light shimmered through Bridget's window. She didn't remember falling asleep. It'd been dawn when she made it back to her room. After her bath, she'd spent almost an hour trying to undo the knots in her red hair. Bridget reached up, still able to feel some of them. Dried, sticky wine had done her long locks no favors.

She shakily rose, surprised to hear no buzz of life coming from the apartments. Anxiety pulled at her stomach. She hoped none of the other girls had met the same fate as Ondine. Bridget rubbed her head and tried to reassure herself that Cade would've said in the infirmary if someone had been hurt.

Just as Bridget grabbed a hairbrush, a sharp pain pierced her skull. Once she recognized the presence, she gritted her teeth.

Your necklace is still off, Cade's voice echoed, sounding surprised.

Bridget grabbed her necklace off the nightstand, annoyed that she had forgotten to put it back on.

I told you to stay out of my head, she snapped, trying to think of nothing else but her words. She hoped that was all he could hear or see. Bridget wasn't sure how his abilities worked.

He chuckled, *It's quite nice in here.*

Cade, she growled in warning.

Come to my room. When you get to the library, turn left. I'll leave the door open.

He disappeared with a soft pinch.

Wiping her nose, Bridget tugged her necklace over her head. Suddenly feeling eager and jittery, she quickly put on her boots. She rushed out the door but stopped short when another figure stood in her way. Quinn casually leaned against the balcony railing and nonchalantly picked at her nails. She looked tired, and there was a fading black smudge on her forearm.

When the Witch didn't look up from her ministrations, Bridget warily asked, "Is there a reason you're standing in front of my door?"

"I heard the palace is on lockdown," Quinn said, crossing her arms. "If you're thinking of leaving, I wouldn't. There might be more Kastronians lurking around."

"Really? I haven't heard anything," Bridget replied. If the king hadn't caught them all, she didn't think Cade would be asking her to come to his room. After a long pause, Bridget added, "I want to take a walk. Surely that's fine."

"How many walks have you been on this week? I think I've lost count." Quinn's eyes narrowed.

Bridget's breath quickened. She thought she'd been discreet. There was no way her actions could be deemed suspicious unless the Witch had been watching her closely.

"The tournament's been harder than I thought. I need to keep up my endurance," Bridget said stiffly.

"Right," Quinn nodded. "You did last longer in the arena than I thought you would."

The comment stung. She didn't understand why Quinn was so hostile suddenly. The Witch was the first girl in the tournament to show her kindness. Her change in demeanor was jarring. Bridget gazed at the other closed doors and asked, "Have you seen the other girls? Is everyone okay? Your arm looks like it was hit with some kind of spell."

"Everyone's fine," Quinn said, rolling her eyes. "And you know what they say, magic always comes with a price. I'm surprised you noticed. Aren't you desperate for fresh air?"

Before Bridget could blink, Quinn walked back to her room and slammed the door shut.

For a long moment, Bridget stood in the hallway, confused and unsure what kind of spell would warrant such a mark for payment. The entire walk to the west end of the palace, she contemplated Quinn's attitude change. Did she somehow know she'd been spending time with Cade? During the attack, she hadn't seen her nearby. But that didn't mean Quinn had missed her running for the prince...

The area around the library was empty when Bridget arrived. Out of the corner of her eye, she spotted a door slightly ajar further down the hall. After making her way to it, she hesitantly pushed it open and saw Cade sitting at his desk. He flipped through an old journal. His room was much larger and grander than any of the contestant apartments. The walls were dark blue, and gray marble lined the floor. A large bed was nestled between two fireplaces. Books and papers overwhelmed his broad wooden desk, like he was constantly moving, pacing, and reading. From enjoyment or insomnia, she wasn't sure. From Alette's stories, she had half-expected piles of booze and evidence of wild nights, but his space was neat and cozy. As she entered, Cade looked up and smiled softly. Her stomach fluttered.

"I miss the purple," he said with mock disappointment.

Bridget punched his arm. "Quinn said the palace is on some sort of lockdown. She was practically guarding my room. Is that true?"

"No, I wouldn't have asked you to come all the way here if it was." Frowning, Cade reached up and traced the bruise around her eye. The action sent Bridget's heart racing. She froze, unable to stop herself from glancing up at his lips. Lips now inches away from hers. His thumb, still on her cheek, sent heat rushing through her every vein. After a moment, Cade swallowed hard and turned away.

"Did the man you captured say anything about the attack?" Bridget asked breathily.

"Not yet. My father is with him now. He'll get him to talk," he said. Darkness entered his eyes. He sat down on the edge of the bed and ran a hand through his messy brown hair. It didn't look like he had slept at all. "I've never seen him so rattled," he added.

Bridget sat down beside him but made sure to leave a little space between them. The urge to move closer was overwhelming. "Really?"

"Human weapons have made it into Elyria, and he has no idea how. Then, somehow, the Kastronians get their hands on them. There's no gate there. He's convinced someone is trying to assassinate him for the throne."

She furrowed her brows at the idea. None of the recent events had involved the king. He hadn't even been in the courtyard when the Kastronians came flying at them with swords.

"Am I interrupting?" an accented voice teased from the door. Reflexively, Bridget sprang away from Cade as the prince from Tafari peeked his head in from the hallway. He smirked mischievously; eyebrows raised at the two of them on the bed. To her surprise, Cade seemed unbothered. He grinned at his friend and got up to greet him.

"This is Bridget," Cade said, motioning for her to join them.

"Castor Bardot," the foreign prince said, giving her a dazzling smile. Bridget would've flushed if she wasn't already so…flushed. He was as handsome as she remembered, with dark olive skin and sharp cheekbones. Bridget briefly glanced at his neck and noted the faint Capricorn symbol right above his collarbone.

"It's nice to put a face to the name," Castor added.

Before Bridget could ask him what he meant, Cade interrupted.

"Castor's been helping us figure out what happened to Ondine. Did you find anything?"

"I swept the area where Ondine's body was found with every spell I could think of and still couldn't produce an echo," Castor said. "Whoever did this knew how to cover their tracks, so it was most likely a Witch or Warlock."

"An echo?" Bridget asked.

"It's like a magical video recording," Castor replied casually, riffling through the bag slung across his shoulder.

Cade sent him a look as Bridget mumbled, "I'll pretend to know what that is."

"On a hunch, I collected this." Castor pulled out a rock the size of an apple and handed it to Cade. Bridget leaned forward for a closer look but could see nothing. It looked like a normal rock.

"Now use the blue light," Castor said, handing them a tiny flashlight. Cade waved the light over the rock. Messy, dark symbols appeared all over the surface.

"I hoped I was wrong, but only dark magic could completely erase an echo," Castor said, clearly displeased.

Cade studied the rock for a few more moments before handing it back to Castor. "The Sanguis coven was banished a long time ago."

"That doesn't mean someone hasn't started practicing on their own.".

Cade pinched the bridge of his nose. "Shit."

A chill went down Bridget's spine. She remembered Cade's words about the rogue coven. She knew little about dark magic, but assumed it was performed with sacrifice, suffering, and blood. She imagined what horrors an entire coven dedicated to such practices would produce and came up with images similar to her nightmares.

"My family needs to know about this. I'll need to head back to Tafari to make sure the artifacts belonging to the Sanguis haven't been touched. Have you seen yours lately?"

"We only have one," Cade said. "I saw it last time I was in the vault. It looks like it hasn't been touched in years."

"Good. If the culprit really is trying to revive the Sanguis coven, they won't get far without those. My guess is that they're after yours. I'll travel back to Tafari through the human realm, so I can check on..." Castor stopped and glanced briefly at Bridget, "you know what."

"Subtle," Cade said, rolling his eyes.

Before Castor headed for the door, he turned to Bridget one last time. "I'm sorry you're stuck in this tournament. Come visit Tafari, if you ever have the chance. You'll never want to go back to Manhattan again."

With that, he was gone.

"I don't think I've ever been to a Manhattan," Bridget murmured, puzzled by his words.

"It's a city in the human realm," Cade exhaled, deep in thought about Castor's news.

Bridget studied him. There was still so much she didn't know about him. Everything she'd heard, even in Vassuryn, seemed to contradict the person she was getting to know. Especially his treatment of the covens. Whenever she looked at him, she wondered how he was the same Fae Prince that almost decimated the Geminis and hunted the Virgos. The pieces of him in her head wouldn't fit together, no matter how many times she tried to get them to.

"So you're friends with a Warlock?" Bridget questioned.

"Several, actually," Cade said, a hint of puzzlement in his voice, "I've known Castor almost as long as Finn. Believe it or not, he's the one that helped me get settled in the human realm. I had no idea what to do when I got there. When I tracked him down, he showed me around, helped me find a place to live, and even found me a job when I got bored. Why do you ask?"

"No reason," Bridget mumbled, listening to the excuses coming from her heart. His potential answer to the question that haunted her loomed over her head more and more every day. Not once had he asked her about the covens. And now, they were already past the second task of the tournament. She knew it wouldn't be long before their newly built comradery came crashing down. She didn't want to spend the time she had left with him spewing accusations. So instead, she turned to him and said, "Ondine was killed with a gun. During the second task, it was Kastronians, not Witches, who used them. Are you sure the markings are dark magic?"

"I recognized the symbols from the old journals. And no matter what Castor says, only someone highly trained is capable of using blood magic. A Witch can't just decide to try it out for fun. This has to be bigger than one person going after an artifact."

"You think whoever killed her is working with the Kastronians?"

"Possibly. Too much has happened in the last seven months to be a coincidence," Cade said, voice frustrated. "Like I said, there's no gate in Kastron. Unless the gate you came through is there, which means we need to figure out where it's located as soon as possible. And now my father is going to try to end the tournament as soon as he can. He wants the least amount of people in the palace as possible. I wouldn't be surprised if he announced the third task tomorrow."

Bridget wasn't sure what to say. More than anything, she wanted the tournament to end so she could finally go back to the human realm, but they still hadn't found the second gate. And returning meant forgetting everything again. As she looked at Cade, the inevitability of the curse scared her for the first time.

Cade reached toward his desk and grabbed a very worn, dusty leather-bound book. "This was one of the old king's journals from the Cavamynian War. I haven't read it yet. I'm still working on another one. Take it. Read it. I hope there might be something about the other gate in there."

Cade handed her the journal. It felt old and fragile in her hands. Bridget hadn't thought of finding answers in a journal, although she doubted a king would reveal the exact location of a hidden gate on the very first page. She opened it up and peeked, just in case. She skimmed a bunch of detailed lines about a swim in a river when she spotted the name of the writer. Deckard. The same as Cade's father. Bridget glanced at Cade, who seemed to have spotted the name as well. A subdued look formed on his face.

"What happened?" Bridget asked. "Delphine implied he wasn't always..."

"An asshole?" Cade scoffed, crossing his arms. Pausing, he took a deep breath. "I had a younger brother. Riker."

Bridget tried not to let the shock show on her face.

"When I was around ten, most of my abilities had already manifested," Cade continued quietly, voice tight, "I don't know why, but I'm able to do things no one else in my family can, things my father can only do with his rune. My father expected the same of him. When he couldn't, my father pushed and pushed and pushed. Until it broke him."

"The magic took its toll," Bridget said in a low voice, sorrow deep in her chest. She now understood his resentment of magic and the broken relationship with his father.

"That's why you left," she whispered conclusively.

"I had to," Cade's voice broke. "It was my fault. If I would've..."

"It wasn't your fault," Bridget replied softly, reaching up to stroke his cheek. He turned to her; his brown eyes broken. She swallowed hard, unable to look away from the intensity. Bridget leaned forward and was a breath away from his lips when he suddenly jerked back. Cade cursed and kicked a chair, moving a few feet away from her.

"I'm sorry," Bridget said, her face hot from mortification. She couldn't believe she thought… had tried…Her chest tightened painfully.

Cade grabbed his hair. "It's not you."

Bridget didn't believe him. She grabbed the journal and hurried toward the door. "I'm going to go read this. I'll let you know if it says anything about the gate."

She ran, and he didn't stop her.

CHAPTER SEVENTEEN

The next day, Bridget did everything she could think of to keep her mind off Cade. Her throat and cheeks burned painfully every time she remembered him jerking away from her, clearly not interested. She'd also never been more confused. From the beginning, Bridget had felt their connection, *knew* it was there, but Cade always kept a distance. Maybe it was all in her head, and she saw what she wanted, but his eyes when he'd told her about his brother…

Bridget slammed the old king's journal shut in frustration. She had been trying to read, but the previous day's events kept infiltrating her mind. Also, it was hard to concentrate when the old king rattled on about blood magic, spells, and Cavamyne…the journal was useless. Bridget hadn't come across a single mention of a gate yet. Rubbing her temples, she tried to calm her anxiety. If what Cade had said about the tournament ending quickly was true, she would be able to get away from Elyria soon. Away from Fae, nightmares, Witches, Cade…When she crossed the gate, she would lose her memories again, but perhaps it was a blessing in disguise. There were many things she wanted to forget.

Feeling like she was crawling out of her skin, Bridget decided to take a walk. Fresh air always cleared her head. She put on her leather jacket and threw the hood over her head. She didn't want to interact or talk with anyone, and hoped the hood covered her red hair enough to render her inconspicuous. With a sigh, she made her way down the stairs of the apartments. The outside air was muggy and damp. For a long moment, Bridget stared out at the misting field that led to the market. The drizzling weather seemed to perfectly reflect her mood.

Eventually, her walk led her to where the palace market was set up. Bridget glanced at it briefly, intent on not stopping, but a figure in a green cloak froze her in place. Just inside the palace gate stood Alexia, staring right at her. Stomach dropping, Bridget frantically looked around for Cora. Alexia never strayed far from her. When she didn't spot the Witch anywhere, relief nearly stopped her heart. Warily, Bridget approached Alexia. Her body shook beneath her large jacket. The other girl didn't move. Alexia's hands were clasped delicately in front of her, like she'd expected Bridget to find her all along. Beneath her hood, Alexia smirked.

"What the hell are you doing here?" Bridget hissed.

Alexia scoffed and raised her eyebrows slightly. "What do you think?"

Cora. It was always about Cora for Alexia. Bridget didn't understand her undying devotion to the Witch that had done nothing but manipulate them. "I'm never going back to the coven or Vassuryn. Cora's not worth your loyalty. No matter what you want to believe, she manipulated and tortured us. She's selfish and only cares about how much power she has."

"I owe her a life debt. I will stay with her until that's paid," Alexia replied monotonously, like it was something she had repeated many times before. "And she took care of you in a realm that despises your kind. You owe her some gratitude."

"That's not an excuse," Bridget argued, not believing what she was hearing. Her whole life in Vassuryn centered around manipulation and lies. Nightmares still plagued her. She didn't know how to tell what was real or not anymore. Bridget's chest heaved rapidly as emotion overtook her.

"She wants you to know she's enjoyed watching your progress in the tournament, even if the nightly recordings don't show much of you."

"I don't care."

Alexia eyed her pathetically. "Your emotions control you."

"Don't lecture me. I'm done. Get out."

"Last time I checked, the king is still in charge," Alexia said blithely. "This is an open market."

Bridget's blood boiled. "Tell Cora this necklace is never leaving my neck, and I refuse to speak to her again."

"When this tournament is over, you won't have a choice. She's waiting nearby in the city. You won't get far without her knowing," Alexia drawled pompously, reaffirming Bridget's worst fear. "Unless you've already found the second gate."

"There is no second gate," Bridget lied, hoping the panic on her face did not show. "Cora sent me here for nothing."

"You've never been a good liar, Bridget. What has the prince told you?"

"What makes you think he's even spoken to me?"

Alexia laughed. "I would love to dangle your past right in front of you, but we're running out of time. What do you know about the second gate?"

Bridget's heart squeezed painfully in her chest. *Alexia,* of all people, was another person that seemed to know more about her past than her. She couldn't take it anymore. Damn the consequences, she wanted her memories. Bridget knew what she had to do next.

"I don't know anything about a second gate," Bridget spat. "Now leave."

Alexia nodded, smirking in a way that said she did not believe her. "We'll be in touch," she taunted, turning to leave. Her green cloak billowed in the wind.

Once she was out of sight, Bridget angrily strode toward the apothecary tent, mind set on one thing. Heart pounding wildly, she knew she should stop and think about what she was determined to do, but she was tired of feeling powerless in her own life. When she got to Archer's stand, the sides of the tent were rolled down and closed. Narrowing her eyes, she saw a shadow moving inside. Bridget slammed the flap up and marched toward him.

Archer jumped at her entrance. "Hello to you too," he said, eyes wary.

"I want my memories," Bridget demanded. Without thinking, she grabbed the front of his shirt and pushed him against a table, making his numerous vials clink together. "Name your price."

His hands waved in the air. "First, I might not have what you need," Archer replied nervously, voice strained. "Second, I need to *breathe*."

Noticing his face turning purple, Bridget let go of her grip. With a deep breath, she said, "Last time, you said—"

"I say a lot of things," Archer quipped, straightening out his shirt with a dramatic flourish. "What's changed?"

"Too many things in my life are not adding up," Bridget ranted desperately as she fiddled with her gloves. "I need to know who I am."

"You can do that without your memories."

"I can't," Bridget said, voice cracking. She had been living in the skin of someone else for too long.

"So stubborn," Archer chastised as he clicked his tongue in admonishment. "I might have something." Removing a key from around his neck, he walked over to a tall, locked cabinet in the corner. He rummaged through its contents for a few moments before pulling out a vial of swirling purple liquid. Archer waved it in front of her face. "It's experimental," he warned.

"What's the price?"

"Let's make a deal," Archer grinned, tossing the vial into the air. "You try it, and it works, then we'll discuss payment."

Bridget gritted her teeth. "And if it doesn't?"

Archer's mouth closed abruptly as his eyes moved to something behind her. Bridget whirled around. Cade and Castor stood in the tent. She swallowed a groan as her cheeks reddened against her will. He was the last person she wanted to see today.

Archer placed the vial on the edge of the table, inches away from Bridget.

"Hello, handsome," he drawled, eyes on Castor. The Warlock shifted uncomfortably.

Cade's steely gaze narrowed on Archer. "I'm surprised to see this booth still standing. I thought you had been banned from the palace market."

"What are you doing here?" Bridget asked Castor, confused by his appearance. Last time she had seen him, he was going back to Tafari. She could feel Cade's eyes on her, but she refused to look at him.

"The king won't allow me to cross the gate. We were on our way to look for a ship when we spotted you."

"Can I get you boys anything?" Archer intoned stiffly. "I've got remedies for warts, unwanted toe hair, syphilis..."

Cade glared at him before moving closer to Bridget. "What are you doing in here?"

"I was just looking," Bridget shrugged.

Archer suddenly tried to pinch one of Cade's stray wavy hairs. "Did you bring hairspray with you when you crossed over? Your hair is just... immaculate."

Cade slapped his hand away with furrowed brows.

"You're about to lose your hand," Castor growled.

Bridget rolled her eyes and pushed Cade toward the door. "Let's go," she said. She could see Archer was having way too much fun messing with them. With one last look at Archer's smirking face, she followed Cade and Castor out of the tent. When they got closer to the palace gate, Cade grabbed her by the elbow and stopped her.

"Do you think you could find a ship on your own? We need a minute," he told Castor. The Warlock nodded and left to explore the market. Cade ran a hand through his damp hair before he asked, "What did you take?"

"What?" Bridget said, acting confused.

"You grabbed a vial off the table. What is it?"

Bridget blinked, shocked that he had caught her. She fingered the vial, the key to her memories, in her pocket. "Nothing, just something to help me sleep."

Cade narrowed his brown eyes. "You're lying."

She hated that he was able to see through her so easily. "Why do you keep doing this?" Bridget asked in frustration. In his room, she thought she'd begun to truly know him...that the growing connection she felt hadn't been one-sided. But he had rejected her, with no explanation. She didn't understand why he kept pursuing her and tracking her down in markets.

"Doing what?" Cade asked, exasperatedly.

"This," Bridget hissed, flipping her hand between them. "You ignore every other contestant. You don't offer to stop tasks for them or promise to help them. You said you wanted information about the covens, but not once have you asked me about them. What makes me the exception?"

Anger and regret flashed across his face. Cade glanced around the courtyard and lowered his voice. "Not here."

"Right, we only talk in secret," she scoffed, raising her voice so that it drew the attention of the market patrons. "Are you too embarrassed to be seen with the human?"

Cade visibly flinched at her words. Shaking her head, she turned to go back to the palace.

"That's not it," Cade argued hotly, following her up the hill. When she did not slow down, he pulled at her arm. "Bridget, wait! Stop."

"No, *you* stop," Bridget shouted, rounding on him. "I don't need your pity."

"You don't understand."

"You keep saying that. What don't I understand?" Bridget asked, throat tightening. She could hardly breathe. "You act like you hate me, but then save my life. You ask me to come meet you in secret libraries and tell me all these *things...*" Her voice turned to a whisper as her eyes filled with tears, "But you won't kiss me."

There was a hint of devastation in his eyes. "My father..."

"Stop letting him control you," Bridget snapped, desperate for an answer. "You're more powerful than him. You can fight him. You can—"

"I will," Cade promised, grabbing her arms. "One day, I will. But right now, it's not just about me. There are lives on the line, including yours. Please, trust me."

He was still talking in riddles, and she couldn't bear it any longer. "I'm tired of being a pawn in this stupid game," Bridget murmured brokenly, glancing up at him. She couldn't stop the words spilling from her mouth. "What were you doing in Vassuryn? Why did you do it? I might not have been forced to enter this stupid tournament if Cora hadn't felt threatened."

"Do what?"

"Hunt and kill all those Witches," Bridget replied, her voice hard. Cade's face drained of color. "My coven moved around for months because they were fleeing from you. Did you think we were the Sanguis?"

Bridget pressed her lips together in frustration at her use of 'we.' Even when she knew the truth, Cora's influence still held strong. She was not a

Witch. She was not part of a coven. Bridget repeated the words over and over in her head.

"I wasn't hunting Witches..."

"Then what about all those attacks?" Bridget asked. She wanted to assume Cora had been lying about him killing Witches, but the night she found out she would enter the tournament, her camp had been attacked. She had seen and felt the panic of those around her. Bridget thought of the man that had chased her. For a split-second, she wondered if it had been him...

"I wasn't hunting them because they were Witches," Cade said frantically. "I was..."

He stopped and let out a frustrated shout, fists clenched.

"You were what?" Bridget pushed. "Did you really kill entire covens?"

"No," Cade sputtered, not looking at her, "Not after the first time."

"The first time?"

"I killed one coven, right after I returned," Cade replied, voice deep and impassioned. "I hadn't used magic in over three years, and I just... exploded. I tracked them down because they had stolen something. Most of them had already fled by the time I got there. Blood was everywhere, and I thought..."

"Thought what?"

"It doesn't matter," Cade snapped. He finally faced her. His eyes were haunted. "I did it, and I can't take it back."

Bridget swallowed hard. "What about the others?"

"There were no others. I don't know what Cora told you," Cade said, gently grabbing her chin and lifting her eyes to his, "but I wasn't hunting Witches."

His voice, heavy with implication, shook Bridget to her core. Cade nudged at knowledge deep in her head that was locked away. She could feel it, below the surface, but every time she reached for it, it disappeared. Paralyzing pain ripped through her body. She *knew*, but every understanding, every thought that formed muddled as quickly as it came. Nausea overwhelmed her.

As he held her arms, Cade's wide eyes searched hers desperately. She thought of every conversation she had with him, what his words always seem to imply, and asked the one question that scared her the most. "Do you know who I am?"

Cade stiffened. He closed his eyes, like he could not stand to see her beg. That's when she knew he wouldn't tell her. Still, she pressed. "Please tell me," Bridget implored, vision blurring. "I keep seeing and feeling things I don't understand. I just..."

A loud pop made the two of them jump. "Is everything okay?" Delphine asked concernedly, suddenly appearing on the path before them. Bridget wasn't sure how she'd known where they were. She stepped away from Cade and wiped away a tear that had fallen.

"We need a minute, Delphine," Cade said roughly.

"The king just announced the third task," Delphine replied softly. "We're needed in the library."

"Shit," he muttered. Bridget felt too overwhelmed to move. As Delphine reached them, Cade gently pushed Bridget's lower back to guide her.

Delphine stepped between them. "The three of us can't show up together," she warned.

"I need to go to the bathroom first, anyway," Bridget said, hurrying away from them. She heard Cade start to follow her.

"I'll go with her," Delphine said, footsteps echoing closely behind her own. When Bridget reached the apartment door, she could no longer see Cade behind her. She ran inside and hunched over the stairway railing, breathing deeply.

Delphine placed a hand on her back. "What happened?"

"Nothing. I'm overreacting," Bridget croaked. "What's the third task?"

"It's a test over Elyrian history," Delphine said reluctantly.

Bridget let out a short, hard laugh. "This day could not get any better," she said, already knowing she was going to fail. Cora had told her some history, but she didn't know if she could trust that knowledge. There was only one person she wanted to hear from now. Bridget pulled the vial out of her pocket.

"What is that?" Delphine asked as Bridget popped open the top.

"A calming potion," Bridget lied. Raising the vial to her lips, she downed the liquid in one gulp.

CHAPTER
EIGHTEEN

Bridget was grateful Delphine sensed her mood and didn't ask her any more questions on their way to the library. Disappointment weighed on her soul. She had expected an onslaught of memories the second the potion entered her body, but nothing happened. She was still the same. A human stuck in Elyria with no identity. She had been an idiot for trusting Archer. He'd probably given her some useless concoction as a joke.

When they arrived at the library, the other girls sat at a long table set up between shelves in the front area. The expanse was tense and quiet. A few Fae from the king's court stood around the girls, Finn included. Along with a camera, the royal family, except Elora, sat in their own chairs in front of the oval stained-glass window. The other tasks had been attended by many more onlookers. Bridget wasn't sure if that was because of the palace's current situation, or that no one wanted to watch a bunch of girls take a test.

"You're late," the king stated irritably as the girls found the last two open seats. The intensity of his glare made Bridget's stomach turn. She opened her mouth to reply, but Delphine interjected first.

"I needed to use the bathroom," Delphine said.

The king rolled his eyes. As Bridget sat down, her hands began to shake uncontrollably. She clenched her fists in an attempt to keep them steady. When it didn't work, Bridget stuffed her hands under the table. Across from her, Quinn stared. The Witch sent her a puzzled look. Further down, Bridget heard Alette scoff.

"The human ruins things, like always," she sneered. Seconds later, the pencil in front of Alette flew up and smacked her on the forehead. The Fae girl gasped and glared at Marin in accusation. Only Bridget noticed Cade's lips twisting in suppressed amusement.

"We've wasted enough time," King Deckard barked menacingly. "Director."

At the king's command, the tournament director hurried toward the head of the table with a stack of papers in his hands. Bridget's skin turned clammy. She would fail and the king would probably read her terrible answers to everyone in the room the moment she finished her test. Behind her, Bridget felt Finn lean down. "You don't look so hot," he whispered.

"I'm fine," she said, briefly gazing up to find Cade watching her concernedly. Finn raised an unbelieving eyebrow. Luckily, the director's voice prevented him from asking any more questions.

"You will have sixty minutes to complete a short answer examination on the history of Elyria," the director explained hurriedly as he passed out the test paper. "As queen, you will need to demonstrate extensive knowledge of all aspects of the kingdom. The contestant with the highest score will be declared the winner."

"We have to sit here for sixty minutes?" Cassia spat incredulously.

The king silenced her with a glare. "Did anyone ask you to speak?"

"It won't take that long. I'll see you back in your room with a glass of wine by sunset," Marin announced monotonously. The king groaned. Cassia banged her head against her chair in irritation.

"Next time, keep your visions to yourself."

Bridget's shaky hand grabbed her pencil. When the director set the test in front of her, her eyes blurred. She squinted at the first question. Quinn kicked her under the table. Gritting her teeth in annoyance, Bridget gazed up at her. The Witch mouthed, "You're sweating."

"It's hot in here," Bridget replied, rubbing the back of her soaked neck.

The room was sweltering. She couldn't understand how some of the other girls had on sweaters. Taking a labored breath, Bridget tried to focus on the questions in front of her.

1. When was Elyria founded?

Bridget closed her eyes and rested her head in her hands. She was already stumped by the first question. Cora had trained her on many things, but history wasn't one of them. Bridget resigned herself to the fact she would have to guess.

In 1492, Columbus sailed the ocean blue.

Her eyes popped open at the intrusive thought. Instinctually, Bridget reached up to check for her necklace. The stone still dangled from her neck, but the line kept repeating in her head. The tone sounded musical. Bridget didn't remember ever hearing about someone named Columbus, but she couldn't think of anything else. She slowly wrote it down. Her gloves, soaked from her sweating hands, smeared the writing.

1. Which king enacted a decree that prohibited the use of blood magic?

Bridget thought hard, trying to remember if Cade or Castor had mentioned a name while talking about the Sanguis. Her head pounded.

George Washington

The thought sent a sharp pain down her spine. Bridget tried not to flinch. Breathing deeply through her nose, she wrote down the name. It was better than nothing. Before she could read the next question, her stomach and chest tightened. Nausea rolled over her in waves.

Bridget leaned over a bright blue counter, diligently studying the papers in front of her. Eighties music blasted in the background. She faintly smelled waffles and syrup. Suddenly, the papers were ripped out of her hands from someone behind her.

With an annoyed sigh, Bridget whipped around and tried to grab her homework from Cade. He held it above her head as he sat down on the circular stool beside her. "What the hell is this?" He murmured, frowning as his eyes roamed over the paper.

"It's calculus," she snapped, ripping it from his hand.

"Is that another language?"

The genuine confusion in his voice stopped Bridget from making another snide remark. "It's math," she said. "It's a prerequisite I have to pass..."

On the floor, something warm cradled Bridget's head. Her entire body ached and pulsed in an unsteady rhythm. She had just been studying her math homework. How had she ended up on the ground?

"Bridget, are you okay?" Delphine's voice echoed from somewhere far away.

Cade tried to lift her head up further, ordering, "We need some water."

Bridget strained to open her eyes. The ceiling above her spun in quick circles. She couldn't focus on any of the dark blurs that stood above her or recognize their faces or the gold and white painted walls. "Where am I?" she croaked.

"You're in the library," Cade said. His face, closer than the others, finally came into focus. His golden eyes were filled with worry. Reality hit her like a ton of bricks. Elyria, the library, the third task She was supposed to be taking a test. With a groan, she tried to sit up. Her hand slipped on something thick and slimy. A horrible, sickening smell wafted up to her nose. Bridget gazed in horror at the floor, her shirt, and Cade's arms.

"Did I throw up?" Bridget gasped in mortification. The sight of her vomit made her feel nauseous all over again. "I don't remember throwing up."

"Unfortunately, we do. Shut off the camera. The rest of Elyria can find out the winner tomorrow," the king bellowed in irritation from his chair, "but the task must continue."

Cade ignored him and handed her the glass of water that Finn had found. Bridget slurped it down messily, unable to quench her thirst. Her throat burned with every gulp. When she gave the empty glass back to Finn, she saw Alette run up behind Cade.

Alette's eyes went wide in fake shock. "Oh my goodness," she squeaked, falling to the ground. Brynley hurried over to her and felt her forehead. If it didn't hurt so much to move, Bridget would have rolled her eyes.

"Prince Cade," Brynley urged. "I think Alette needs some help."

"I don't think she wants mine. I'm covered in vomit," Cade replied curtly. He motioned with eyes to Finn to go over there. With a resigned glare, Finn complied. Within seconds, Alette was sitting up and reassuring everyone that she was fine.

"Enough. She either finishes the test or leaves the tournament," King Deckard snarled.

"She's sick," Cade argued, tightening his grip on Bridget's shoulders. Without a word, the king flicked his hand and sent Cade flying back to his seat. The room went quiet when he landed with a loud smack. Cade struggled furiously to move his arms and legs, but the king circled his hand and choked him from afar. Cassia gripped her armrests and gazed at Cade anxiously.

"I can finish," Bridget wheezed, weakly pulling herself up. Delphine helped her to the chair. Once she was seated, the king released Cade. To his credit, he didn't gasp for breath. Instead, he vehemently glowered at his father.

"Good," the king said, "that wasn't so hard."

No one spoke as he returned to his seat. After a long, tense silence, the director cleared his throat and ordered the girls to finish. Bridget struggled to keep her eyes opened. Her stomach clenched painfully, and her head felt like it would explode at any second. After the fifth question, Bridget gave up. She put her pencil down and stared at a question mark on the paper to stay focused and upright.

After a long forty-five minutes, the director announced, "Time's up."

One by one, he gathered the tests. Bridget thought it was over, but he sat down at the head of the table and started to grade each one. She laid her head down on the table and found the cold surface soothing.

Bridget wasn't sure how much time had passed when she heard the king's voice.

"Who won?"

"Marin," the director stated monotonously. He grabbed the papers and left the room in a quick flourish. Cassia groaned in relief and left the room right after him, briefly sparing a glance at Bridget.

"That's no surprise. She's been around longer than any of us. She had an unfair advantage," Alette grumbled.

"That's the second task you've won. I'm impressed," the king said mildly.

Marin stared at him with a blank expression. Bridget didn't know she had been the winner of the second task. Dizziness overwhelmed her before she could think about it too much, though. The other girls remained unmoving; disappointment written on their faces. Except one. Alette snapped out of her chair and stared at Bridget in disgust. "I think the human is going to be sick again."

Bridget couldn't even attempt a weak glare. The king snapped his fingers at the guards beside him.

"Escort her back to her room before she violates anything else," he growled.

Finn tried to help her up, but two Fae guards pushed him aside. Grabbing underneath her shoulders, they dragged her from the library. She barely heard Cade's protests. All she wanted to do was lay in her bed and sleep for a very long time.

A faint knock woke Bridget up. She peered through the one eye she could get open and saw her room. Slightly disturbed that she didn't remember getting there or laying down, she tried to sit up. Her limbs didn't respond, though, even as she heard another knock. Dizziness washed over her, forcing her eyes shut again. Sleep. Sleep was good. There was a loud pop. Rough shaking pulled her from oblivion.

"I'm sorry, but you weren't answering," Delphine said.

Bridget felt a hand on her forehead. "I can't move," she muttered into her pillow.

Delphine turned her over. "Cade's worried. We all are."

The vision she had of Cade in the strangest looking restaurant popped back into her head. It had felt so real… "About my calculus?" Bridget asked hazily, briefly falling back into the memory.

Delphine stiffened. "I don't know what that is, but he wants you to come to his room."

"I can't move," Bridget repeated, breath labored and harsh. If she concentrated hard enough, she was able to move her big toe. It would take her a while to get there.

"Can I take you?" Delphine asked, grabbing her forearm. Bridget nodded and closed her eyes as another wave of nausea overtook her.

"You might feel sick for a second," she added.

Bridget didn't think she could feel much sicker, but as Delphine transported them to Cade's room, she was wrong. All at once, her entire body was ripped apart and then put back together. Excruciating pain rippled through her bones as she screamed in agony and landed on her knees in Cade's bedroom. A pair of strong hands grabbed Bridget's shoulders before her head smacked against the hard stone.

"What the hell?" Cade growled as he picked her up and moved her to the bed. "How is she this much worse?"

"I don't know, but she has a fever."

As Cade palmed her forehead, Bridget's muscles tensed. She grabbed her skull and tried to push away the radiating pain.

"She stole a potion from the apothecary," she heard Cade say to Delphine.

"I saw her take it. It was a calming drought."

She wanted to tell them she had lied, but vomit started to make its way up from her stomach. Bridget covered her mouth, not wanting to spew it everywhere. A hand thrust a bowl in front of her just in time. She heaved painfully as acid burned her throat. When she was done, her body pulsed in relief. The pain in her head dimmed as her body relaxed.

"I feel better," Bridget mumbled, leaning back against a pillow. She slowly opened her eyes. Cade, Delphine, and Finn stared at her.

"You do?" Cade asked skeptically. He held the large bowl of vomit in his hands.

"I think I just needed to get it out of me," Bridget said. Her hands shook as she tried to pull the covers higher, suddenly cold.

Finn wrinkled his nose at the bowl in Cade's hands and gagged. "How are you holding that?"

"That's not helpful, Finn," Delphine grumbled. Glaring, Cade tried to shove the bowl into Finn's hands. The Fae jumped and backed away. Bridget wanted to laugh but let out a hoarse cough instead.

Delphine sat down beside her. "You must have had a bad reaction to the magic."

"I'm fine. I can go back to my room," Bridget muttered unconvincingly. She didn't think she could move if she tried. The bed felt so comfortable and the desire for sleep overwhelmed her senses.

"You're not going anywhere," Cade said sternly, his voice suddenly very far away.

"He's right. You might get sick again."

Bridget snuggled further into the pillow and fell into oblivion.

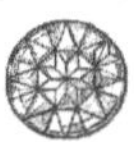

The faint rustling of papers gently woke Bridget. She slowly opened her heavy eyelids. The room was empty, except for Cade who sat at his desk, hunched over a journal. Both fireplaces crackled. Bridget struggled to swallow. Her entire body screamed with soreness and exhaustion. She could also feel a puddle of sweat soaking the sheets around her.

"Cade," she croaked. Her throat protested in agony. At the sound of her voice, Cade whipped around, brown eyes swimming with relief.

"You're awake. How are you feeling?"

Bridget struggled to lift her head to no avail. Dizziness washed over her with each attempted movement. "My head is pounding."

"I had some soup delivered. It might help," Cade said, grabbing a small, steaming bowl. He gently lifted her shoulders and placed her upright. With a grateful smile, Bridget weakly took the soup from his hands. The smell of the broth made her stomach growl loudly. Cade raised an eyebrow and laughed.

Bridget's cheeks heated slightly at the echoing noise reverberating from her stomach. She brought the bowl to her lips and eagerly slurped down the warm liquid. After a few gulps, Bridget said, "Thank you. I've been having the strangest dreams."

"Fevers will do that to you."

"Do you know what calculus is?" Bridget asked.

Cade's eyes went wide. Face paling, he reached for her. Startled, Bridget lost the already weak grip she had on the bowl. It fell forward and spilled directly onto Cade's lap.

"I'm so sorry," Bridget gasped.

"It's okay. Just give me a second to change," Cade said, jumping up. He placed the bowl on his desk and hurried toward the bathroom. At the last second, Cade pulled his phone out of his pocket and threw it on the bed.

As the phone hit the comforter, the screen lit up. Bridget's heart stopped. It was...her. And Cade. His arms were wrapped around her as they stood in front of a giant, multicolored tree. Both of them donned wide grins. As she processed the image, her brain convulsed. Blood poured from her ears as blinding pain shot through her skull. She couldn't control the screams that escaped her mouth. Cade jolted back into the room. The alarm on his face confirmed what she already knew.

"Is this me?" Bridget asked hoarsely, holding up the phone. The movement caused the picture to appear again. Fiery lightning zipped down her spine when she saw her face. Back arched, she fell back onto the bed as blood spurted from her nose. Cade ran to her and ripped off her necklace. His eyes turned white as he held a hand over her face and tried to enter her mind. To do what, Bridget wasn't sure. She felt his presence for a split-second before he was violently thrown out by the sheer force of pressure that squeezed her head.

"What was in that vial?" Cade demanded. His ears now matched her bloodied ones.

"I'm sorry," Bridget apologized weakly, gazing into his distressed eyes. "I wanted to remember."

Cade cursed and picked her up off the bed. Rushing from his room, he flicked his head to pop open the door. With each movement, her skull felt like it was being cracked in two. Every part of her body burned and ached. She had just wanted to remember...

Bridget let out a tiny scream of anguish as they jostled to a stop. She squinted as a door flew open, revealing Cassia.

"I need your help," Cade pleaded.

"We agreed..."

"I don't give a shit about what we agreed to," Cade hissed.

"That's not fair," Bridget whispered, eyes watery.

Bridget screamed as the memory slashed through her head. No more. No more. No more. She wanted to beg, but the words wouldn't come. Fire, agony, and splintering pain destroyed her muscles and bones. And spinning. Every thought, dream, or memory she ever had spun wildly in her mind, leading her toward a darkness that was becoming more and more appealing. Agonizing spasms racked her body. She lost track of time and where she was and who she was with. She wanted it to stop.

"What do you mean, you can't find him?" Cade bellowed. Bridget's eyelids were heavy as she tried to look up. She was in a room she didn't recognize. Delphine and Cade stood at the foot of the bed, Castor between them. The foreign prince held a firm hand on Cade's chest. Cassia and Finn acted like guards beside the bed. Both look worried with crossed arms and tense faces. Bridget opened her mouth to speak, but she couldn't find the strength to form any words.

"Cade, it's the middle of the night," Delphine said. "The market is closed. His tent is gone."

"He can't have gone far," Cade argued furiously.

Castor pushed him back an inch. "Calm down."

Snarling, Cade turned away from them and kicked a dresser. "We need to know exactly what he gave her."

Violent spasms overtook Bridget's body again. Her jaw clenched painfully as the scene around her blurred and shook. A hand turned her onto her side. She wasn't sure how much time had passed before her muscles finally relaxed. Bridget's chest heaved as she struggled to take in air. She felt Cade place a cold cloth on her forehead.

“That’s her third seizure,” Delphine said softly. “Her brain won’t be able to take much more.”

“Castor, you must have some ideas. I’ve heard of this happening in Tafari,” Cassia said.

“I think I can help,” Castor said hesitantly, cracking his knuckles. “I can try a spell. A human has never survived getting their memories back because the price of the curse has always been too high. Their bodies can’t handle it physically, and they have no magic that can help ease the exchange. Nothing equal to give in return. And a Fae has never been willing to…”

“To pay it for them,” Cassia finished in understanding, sharing a look with Cade.

“Do it,” Cade growled. “I’ll pay it.”

Bridget tried to grab him, to tell him *no*, but he pushed her hand away and stood up. Cade and Castor stared at each other, their silent conversation long and tense. She wondered if Cade was in his mind.

“Do you understand?” Castor asked gravely.

“Do it.”

Cassia's gaze shifted anxiously between the two. “Cade…”

Bridget’s muscles started to tense again. A scream escaped her lips, but she tried to fight it. Whatever the price, she didn’t want Cade to pay for her mistake.

“I’ll pay it!” Cade roared. “Just do it!”

At his command, Castor moved over her. Bridget shook her head, trying to tell him to stop, but he ignored her and drizzled a strange smelling herb over her head. His Capricorn mark started to glow as he muttered an incantation.

“Are we sure this is going to work?” Finn asked.

Castor’s incantations grew louder as the lights in the room began to flicker. With each word, an invisible hand squeezed her brain, tighter and tighter. Her vision turned white. When she thought she could take no more, the pressure exploded and dissipated in one large gush. The relief that soared through her body was paralyzing.

A moment passed.

Bridget finally understood, finally *knew*.

"*Cade*," she whispered.

His anguished eyes widened at the recognition in her voice. Blood ran from his nose. She wanted to scream, cry, and kiss him all at the same time. She wanted to hit him and demand to know how he could have possibly let her end up in Elyria. He had *lied* to her and yet, she had never been so relieved to see him.

The more she knew, the more overwhelmed she became.

So she closed her eyes and succumbed to the memories.

BEFORE

CHAPTER NINETEEN

JULY

"I asked for the lemon blueberry pie to be a la mode."

Gritting her teeth, Bridget stared down at the *very* a la mode pie that was being shoved in her face. Her day had already been the shits. First, she had been late to work and chewed out by her asshole manager Paul. How was it her fault the subway malfunctioned and stalled for thirty minutes? Then, her new lawyer had called. In a rush to answer, she had accidentally knocked into a food runner and spilled a pitcher of syrup all over her uniform. Bridget didn't know which was worse, missing the call or the fact that she was now forced to wear an old pair of hot pink leggings and a cheap Hungry Pies shirt for the rest of her shift. Even though the shirt was from the diner's old collection of merch, she was sure Paul would still take it out of her check.

"I know," Bridget said, plastering a fake grin on her face. "That's exactly what I gave you."

"This is not a la mode," the woman sneered.

The rest of her family, a husband and two kids, continued to devour their own slices of pie without a care in the world. They were clearly tourists in their matching 'I Love NY' t-shirts and Statue of Liberty hats.

Most of the customers who visited Hungry Pies were. The 80s themed diner was two stories tall and a block away from the One World Trade Center. The neon colors of the outside walls and large animatronic dancing pie practically screamed 'take my money' to out-of-town visitors.

Bridget pushed the pie back in front of her. Ice cream was starting to pool around the edges of the plate. "Yes, it is."

"A la mode means nothing extra," the woman snarled. "This pie clearly has ice cream and whipped cream on it."

"Lady, a la mode does not mean what you think it means," Bridget snapped.

The woman's nose flared angrily. She slammed her fist down on the neon linoleum table. "I want to speak to someone in charge," she shouted. "I'm lactose intolerant. You could have killed me!"

Bridget grabbed the pie, knowing very well that the woman in front of her was not lactose intolerant. She had ordered mozzarella sticks for an appetizer. She needed the job, though, even if tourists made it a living hell. Paul had already warned her if someone else complained about her again, she would be fired.

"No need," Bridget said with a tight-lipped smile. "I'll get you a new slice for free. I'll remove the mozzarella sticks from your bill too."

The woman glowed smugly as Bridget walked away. She shoved the pie in the trash and took a deep breath to calm down. She closed her eyes and kept repeating to herself that she needed the money, especially if her lawyer had tried to contact her. Bridget knew she shouldn't be getting her hopes up, but he had promised to only call when he had good news, or the next court date was set. A new order pad was suddenly shoved in her hands.

"Marnie threw up all over my office floor. I need you to cover her tables," Paul ordered, his nose wrinkled in disgust.

"But that's downstairs," Bridget argued. She had worked at Hungry Pies for over a year and had always finagled her way into working the second floor. The floor to ceiling windows offered a view of the Woolworth Building, so most patrons requested a table upstairs. The bottom floor was slow and usually occupied by the few regulars the diner acquired.

"No arguments," Paul said. He gave her a hard shove toward the stairs. Glaring, Bridget followed him down. She stopped short when she saw who was sitting in her new section in the back-corner booth. It was one of their regulars each waitress fought over every time he came in. Except her. He always sat downstairs, and she had a strict second floor only policy. Bridget couldn't deny that he was very attractive, especially his thick brown hair and dark eyes that radiated danger and secrets. He looked around her age. She had found herself staring at him from the top floor a time or two, only to chastise herself for doing so. On Wednesday afternoons, he came alone. On Saturdays, though, he almost always had a different girl with him. Bridget inwardly groaned because, of course, it was Saturday, and the girl sitting across from him seemed like a mini version of the woman she had encountered upstairs.

"No fair," Scarlett, her coworker, pouted. "You get the hot guy today."

"I don't want him," Bridget replied, rolling her eyes. "You have the table."

Scarlett eyed Paul, who was now glaring at them. "I like my job," she muttered under her breath as she pulled her dark braids into a bun.

Bridget sighed, knowing if she didn't hurry over to the booth, Paul would start yelling at her from across the room. "That lady up there needs a new lemon blueberry," Bridget told her, tilting her head up at her old section.

"Do I need to spit on it?" Scarlett asked seriously.

"If anyone asks, I told you no," Bridget said, cracking a smile. Rolling her shoulders, Bridget walked over to the booth. The willowy blonde girl crossed her arms and stared at her expectantly. They both already had water and coffee in front of them, which meant one less thing for her to worry about.

"Are you two ready to order?" Bridget asked. Not looking up, she clicked her pen open and focused on the order pad.

"You're not our waitress," the regular said. She lifted her eyes and found him staring at her, disbelief and confusion written on his face.

"I am now," Bridget sighed, trying to ignore his alarmed tone. "Are you ready or what?"

"You work here?"

Annoyed, Bridget crossed her arms. "Do you think I like wearing neon pink leggings?" Instead of her comment shutting him up, like she hoped, he *grinned*.

"Sweetie, stop harassing the poor waitress," the blonde said through gritted teeth. With fake sweetness, she asked, "Do you have a salad?"

"It's pretty basic. Lettuce, a few cherry tomatoes, maybe one crouton."

The blonde shoved her menu into Bridget's stomach. "I'll have that with a balsamic vinaigrette."

"We have ranch," Bridget told her curtly. She was sure her rising blood pressure was turning her face the same color as her hair.

"Whatever," she scoffed, dismissing Bridget with a wave of her hand. She pulled out her phone and began scrolling through a social media app.

Bridget turned back to the man with a tight smile. "And for you... sweetie?"

His tongue moved inside his cheek, clearly amused. "It's Cade. And I'll have the waffles. Thank you"

"I don't care. Sweetie suits you," she said, ripping the menu from his hand and marching toward the kitchen. Ian, the line cook, grabbed the order from her hand. He read the paper and frowned.

"Someone seriously ordered the salad?"

"I tried to warn her," Bridget said, even though she didn't. There were many unappetizing things served at Hungry Pies, but the salad topped the list. She leaned against the bar counter and gazed back at the booth. Moving downstairs had guaranteed her that she wouldn't be getting her regular number of tips today. Briefly, she studied *Cade*. He had on an expensive-looking outfit. And the blonde with him didn't seem like the type to go out with someone who had low financial status. It would be so easy to...

"Don't," Scarlett's stern voice interrupted her internal planning.

"What?"

"I see what you're thinking. He's a regular."

Bridget had worked with Scarlett her entire time at the diner. They had bonded over their mutual hatred of Paul and lack of parents. Eventually, Scarlett had learned about Bridget's secret little habit, a habit she had acquired in her early foster care days. She was a great pickpocket.

Growing up, stealthily taking someone's wallet or watch was the only guaranteed way she would be able to eat. Lately, she enjoyed targeting rude customers. The servers of Manhattan deserved some justice.

"I bet he won't even notice," Bridget replied. "Something is clearly wrong with him if he frequents this place."

Before Scarlett could argue, her order appeared in the window. Bridget grabbed the plates and headed back to the booth. She dropped the food on the sticky table.

"The waffles and the salad," Bridget muttered. She turned away, but was stopped by a nasally, sneering voice.

"There's something wrong with my salad," the blonde stated, using one finger to push the salad away from her.

The man rubbed the back of his neck. "No, there's not," he told Bridget. "The salad is fine."

"There's a hair," the blonde argued snidely.

Bridget gazed down at the flimsy-looking salad. It looked gross, but there was no hair. "I don't see one."

"Well, there is. Take it back, and I want it comped from our bill."

"Don't," Cade said, clearly annoyed. "I'll pay for it."

Bridget rolled her eyes. "Whatever." She snatched up the salad and hurried away. She was ready for her shit day to be over.

After a few moments, the couple's arguing voices started to attract the attention of the entire diner. From her stance by the door, Bridget couldn't hear what they were saying. The blonde ranted and pointed angrily at Cade. He laughed incredulously at something she shouted, causing her to storm out of the diner. The bell above the door rattled sharply at the furious slam. Shaking his head, Cade grabbed his wallet out of his back-right pocket and put money down on the table. As he stood up to leave, Bridget moved into place for her plan. He hadn't been the rude one, but he was the next best thing. And he had annoyed her.

Before he made it to the door, Bridget smacked into him and reached for his back pocket. Usually, when she ran into a patron, they sneered at her and told her to watch where she was going. She was just a lowly, clumsy waitress to them. Not this time. As she stumbled forward, Cade grabbed her by the arms and steadied her.

"Are you okay?" he asked. The real concern in his eyes took her breath away. The orbs looked golden brown in the sunlight. He was so close; she could smell the spicy scent of his cologne. She hated that she didn't want to move.

Bridget nodded and swallowed hard. Embarrassed by her reaction to his closeness, she managed to pull herself away from him and run toward the kitchen. She busied herself at the soda machine until she finally heard the bell indicating he had left. The moment it rang, Bridget walked back to the booth to pick up the money he had left for the check and found a one hundred-dollar bill. She felt torn between anger and shame. Who leaves that much money for a $14.00 ticket? Bridget fingered the outline of his wallet in her pocket. And who takes someone's wallet that tips them that much?

Sighing, she grabbed the money. The next time he came in, she would give the wallet to Marnie and tell her to say she found it in the booth. And she would make sure to never work downstairs again.

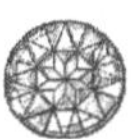

It was sunset when her shift ended. The Manhattan heat suffocated her as she stepped outside Hungry Pies. Bridget's tiny apartment in the Bronx was at least an hour subway ride from the diner. As she turned to go to the station, she saw a large bald man with multiple tattoos watching her from across the street. Her stomach twisted. It was the third day in a row she had seen him. Staying on the other side of the street, she started speed walking toward the subway. He followed. When she came to an intersection, she managed to jump behind a taxi and make it across the street before the light turned red. Bridget felt relieved when she spotted him stuck behind a large tour group at the crosswalk.

She was almost at the station when it was her turn to be stopped by a light. The rush hour traffic that filled the street allowed no openings for her to maneuver across. Her heel bounced up and down impatiently as she waited for the signal to turn green.

Suddenly, a hand grabbed her arm from behind.

Bridget whipped around, her fist raised. When she saw it was the handsome regular from the diner, she wrenched her arm from his grasp. "What the hell?" she gasped. Her eyes darted around for the bald man, but she didn't see him.

"I'm sorry. I didn't mean to scare you," he said, holding up his hands. "I've been trying to get your attention for over two blocks now."

Bridget's mouth fell open. "Why?"

"I wanted to apologize for this morning…" he sighed, running a hand through his hair.

"There's no need," Bridget said with a tight smile. She did not have time for whatever he was trying to pull right now. From the corner of her eye, she saw the light turn green. She hurried across the street. "Have a nice day," she called.

He followed her. "Wait! I'm serious," he said, easily catching up her before she made it to the subway stairs. "I don't want you to think I'm some kind of asshole that—"

"That brings a different girl to the same restaurant every weekend?" Bridget finished blithely, looking behind him for the man following her. She knew he wouldn't be far now. If Cade would leave her alone…

"So you've worked there awhile," he concluded, face drawn in resignation.

"Almost a year now."

"Look…"

"I don't know if this is part of some 12-step program you're in, but I don't need an apology," Bridget snapped, pulling out her hundred-dollar tip. She shoved the bill into his chest. "Or your pity."

Bridget tensed as she spotted the bald man making a beeline for them, eyes dark and focused.

In front of her, Cade gazed around wildly. "What do you keep looking at?"

She only had a few seconds before she was caught. She steeled her nerves, ready for the inevitable. She had avoided the tattooed man's boss long enough.

"You need to leave," Bridget ordered.

Cade's spine straightened. "No."

Bridget stared at him incredulously and pushed him back. "Go."

"No," he argued, standing his ground as she continued to shove him with her entire body.

She pushed against him harder. "Go!"

With a groan, Bridget backed away when the large, tattooed man approached them. He was sweating and breathing heavily. "The little thief finally decided to show her face."

Cade raised an eyebrow at her. "Thief?"

"Boss wants his money," he jeered, cracking his knuckles loudly.

"Tell 'Boss' he's going to have to wait a little longer," Bridget replied bitingly. Marco had been trying to track her down for months for her loan repayment. At one point, she had saved enough to pay him back in full. But then her apartment flooded. And Nylah had needed new shoes.

Marco's lackey took a threatening step forward. "He's tired of waiting."

"Alright, back up," Cade said, positioning himself in front of her. "How much does she owe you?"

"Are you serious?" Bridget grumbled, trying to push him out of the way. She did not need him to swoop in and save her. Cade ignored her and patted around for his wallet. When he felt his back pocket empty, he clenched his jaw in realization. His dark eyes flashed between anger and amusement.

The tattooed man shoved him against the wall. "What were you saying, pretty boy?"

Before Bridget could blink, Cade grabbed the large man and flipped him to the ground with ease. The lackey hit the sidewalk with a crunching thud. He groaned and struggled to breath.

"What the fuck!" Bridget gasped. "How did you do that?"

"Hey!" A man called from a black car across the street. He jumped out of the driver's seat and ran toward them, gun in hand. Of course, he had backup. Knowing they wouldn't have time to outrun him in the subway in front of them, she grabbed Cade's hand.

"C'mon," Bridget yelled, pulling him down the sidewalk.

Together, they weaved through crowds of suited men and tour groups as the lackey called out to them from behind. After destroying a table full of knock-off purses, they passed an empty alley. Cade pulled on her arm. A chain-link fence stood behind the dumpsters.

"There should be another subway entrance on the other side."

Nodding, Bridget sprinted after him as he climbed and hopped over the fence in one move. It took her a few more tries. Cade caught her and pulled her toward the subway stairs she saw in front of them. Before they ran down the steps, the lackey began to climb the fence.

"He certainly moves better than the other one," Cade quipped.

Despite herself, Bridget laughed. They hurried down the stairs and jumped the turnstile to make it onto the waiting train. The doors closed right as the lackey made it to the platform. He banged angrily on the door windows as the train sped away. Everyone on the train seemed unfazed. Bridget leaned over and put her hands on her knees to try to catch her breath. Adrenaline shook her legs.

"How did you learn to do all that?" Bridget heaved. "Are you like a black belt or a wrestler or something?"

"Who were those guys?" he asked curiously, ignoring her question. He didn't seem winded like her. Sure, he was tall and muscular, but she would've never guessed he would be able to take down a man almost twice his size in less than a second. She couldn't believe she'd thought she was in good shape.

"I borrowed some money from their boss about a year ago," Bridget said, plopping down in one of the train seats.

"How much?"

Bridget gazed up at him, unsure why she wanted to justify herself to him. "$2000. I needed a lawyer."

"And they were your best option?"

"You wouldn't understand," Bridget muttered. While she hadn't taken anything, she had still peeked into his wallet. He was clearly well off.

"Try me," he challenged, sitting down beside her.

"My sister is still in foster care," Bridget said quietly after a long moment, surprised at her own honesty. She barely told anyone about Nylah, her younger sister, not by blood, but by bond, and here she was, telling a stranger she just met. "When I turned eighteen, I tried to get custody of her. Obviously, they denied my request, but I've been trying ever since."

Cade's eyes softened. "They know where you work."

"Don't worry, I know how to get them to back off." She gazed down at the small emerald ring on her right hand. Even though she had vowed never to part with it, she knew she had no choice. She tucked her hand under her leg when she noticed Cade's gaze follow hers. An automated voice announced they were close to the next stop.

With a smirk, Cade held out an open hand. Gritting her teeth, Bridget pulled his wallet out of her pocket and placed it in his outstretched palm.

"Are you going to turn me in?"

"No, I haven't had a Saturday like this in a long time," Cade said, a wide grin on his face. Bridget furrowed her brows, wondering what kind of Saturdays he was used to experiencing.

"Cade Morgan," he said, holding out a hand to shake.

"I didn't ask," Bridget replied, keeping her hands to herself. The train rolled to a stop.

His lips twitched in amusement. "We just got chased by the mob through the financial district. I think you owe me your name."

The train doors opened as Bridget scoffed. "Marco is not the *mob...*"

She had been on the subway enough times to know how long the doors stayed open. At the last second, she hopped up and jolted onto the platform as the doors closed behind her. She turned and saw Cade shaking his head at her through the window, a shit-eating grin on his face.

"My name's Bridget," she called as the train pulled away, unsure if he could even hear her. After today, Bridget wondered if he would ever show up at Hungry Pies again.

On Monday, Bridget headed upstairs to start her shift. At two o'clock in the afternoon, the diner was relatively empty. Sunday was her only day off, and she had spent it studying for her calculus exam, not thinking about Cade. Or his hair. Or his smile. When she finally called her lawyer back, he had told her their court date was delayed another sixty days. Again. Her toe still ached from kicking her tiny dresser in frustration. Nylah had already been moved through two foster homes in the past year. Why would they not let her have her? No ten-year-old should have four different families in the span of three years. When she made it to the second floor, a deep voice made her jump.

"Bridget Adams."

She turned and found Cade sitting at a table in the corner. She gritted her teeth at the smug smirk on his face. "Marnie told me your name," he added.

She crossed her arms. "What are you doing here?"

"I'm hungry."

"I mean upstairs," Bridget glared. Even though her stomach fluttered at the sight of him, he felt too dangerous for her to deal with. She had Nylah and school to focus on. It was better for her if he stayed in his usual seat.

"I never realized how great the view was up here," he said, glancing out the window. "I think I found my new favorite table."

"It's a good thing my section is over there," Bridget quipped, nodding her head toward the other side of the room. Cade narrowed his eyes. When he realized she wasn't joking, he stood up and moved to an open table on the left side.

"Even better," he grinned.

She tried not to smile. No good would come of whatever relationship he was trying to pursue. Bridget sighed. "What do you want?"

He must have sensed her discomfort because his smile dropped. "Nothing. I just wanted to make sure you weren't cornered by Marco in a dark alley somewhere after you ditched me."

"I told you I would take care of it."

Cade's gaze moved to the empty ring finger on her right hand. "I'm sorry."

"It wasn't that important," she lied. She straightened up and plastered a smile on her face. "Are you going to order? I was hoping to finish an online quiz during the dead time."

"A quiz about what?"

The genuine interest and attention in his voice made her cave.

"One of the judge's stipulations to get custody of my sister is to show proof that I'm enrolled in college, at least part-time, and making A's. I'm studying engineering."

His brown eyes softened. "Your sister is lucky to have you."

"Thank you," Bridget said, cheeks reddening slightly. She felt too seen under his gaze. "Do you have any siblings?" She asked, noting the sudden, faraway look on his face.

"Two sisters," Cade said, voice rough. "I haven't spoken to them, or any of my family, in almost three years."

"That must be tough." She had not seen Nylah in two weeks and that already felt like torture. She couldn't imagine three years.

"It's easier than you think." Cade said, lips twisting.

Her curiosity was piqued, but she didn't want to push. Instead, she held up her order pad and said, "You know what's easy? Placing an order."

When he laughed, no matter what she kept telling herself, she knew she wouldn't be able to stay away.

CHAPTER TWENTY

AUGUST

"It's a classic."

"Homeward Bound is not a classic," Bridget groaned. She and Cade had been arguing about movies for the past thirty minutes. Sitting across from him at his usual table upstairs, she knew she should be paying attention to the few other customers she had, but she couldn't pull herself away from him. It was becoming a bad habit. "And never admit to anyone else that it made you, a grown man, cry."

"How can you not cry when Shadow comes running over that hill?"

She had cried…when she was eight. She couldn't believe he had never seen the movie until a few months ago. "That still doesn't make it a classic."

Cade shook his head. "What's a classic then, smarty pants?"

"I don't know…" Bridget trailed off, trying to think of a good answer. Growing up, she had never watched many movies. She was lucky if any foster home she joined even had a television. One house had a few VHS tapes; one of them she had watched over and over. She still remembered every word.

"Ever After," Bridget said.

"Isn't that the remake of Cinderella you always talk about?"

"It's not just a remake," Bridget argued. And she did not always talk about it. "It's the best version of a well-known classic tale. The costumes, the music, the prince..."

Cade grinned widely. "So you have a thing for the prince?"

She didn't understand why he looked so smug. "No," she stammered, blushing slightly, "I just—"

"Can I get some more coffee?"

Bridget turned to the older man holding up his empty coffee cup at one of her tables. He stared at her exasperatedly, the newspaper spread out in front of him.

"Duty calls," she muttered. With a sigh, she stood up and grabbed the empty cup. Scarlett was waiting for her as she walked into the kitchen, arms crossed and eyes expectant.

"When are you going to ask him out?"

Bridget fiddled with the coffee machine. "What are you talking about?" she asked, unable to look at her. She didn't have to ask to know which *him* Scarlett was referring to.

"Stop playing dumb," Scarlett scoffed, shoving her playfully. "He comes in here almost every day now."

She tried to ignore the flutter in her chest. Since early July, Cade had started coming into Hungry Pies almost every time she worked, usually during the afternoon lull. At first, she had wondered if he even had a job at all and lived off a trust fund. He certainly dressed like it. Eventually, she caved, asked, and learned that he was some sort of marketing executive at Bardot Industries, a giant tech conglomerate based out of London. Bridget thought it was a little strange, especially since she had to show him how to use an iPad one day, but he had spoken about it enough times for her to believe he was legitimately employed. Even if he tended to spend most afternoons at the diner. When he came in, they talked, laughed, and argued about various things. He even helped her study sometimes. Their routine had become her favorite part of the day. Her tips had been slowly dwindling, but she couldn't bring herself to care. All she had been able to think about lately was his chocolate brown eyes, the way he laughed, and how electricity ripped through her whenever his hand…

Bridget blushed and cleared her throat. "He likes the food."

"Honey, no man likes waffles that much," Scarlett said, eyebrow raised.

"I do," one of the downstairs waiters commented as he stepped in between them to grab an order from the kitchen window.

"Mind your own damn business, Larry," Scarlett snapped. The waiter scurried off.

"It's not like that," Bridget argued weakly. It was true. In all their time together, Cade had never implied he wanted anything more.

"I have eyes. I see the way he looks at you. When was the last time he brought a girl here?"

The Saturday they had met. Not that she was keeping track…

Scarlett seemed to read her thoughts. "Why are you in such denial?"

"Because…I'm me. And I have Nylah to focus on."

Cade was a young, handsome, apparently big-shot executive, and she was an ex-foster kid who could barely afford rent. He could have any girl he wanted. She had *robbed* him and then unloaded her custody drama onto him.

"I don't have time for a boyfriend," Bridget added.

"Everybody has time for a boyfriend. Anyone who says differently is lying to themselves."

Larry rushed past them again. "She's right," he said.

Scarlett glared at him. The coffee maker beeped, so Bridget gathered the steaming cup and sugar packets.

"Just go up there and ask him out for a drink," Scarlett said. "I'll cover for you."

"If you're so convinced he likes me, why hasn't he asked me out then?"

"Because you, Bridget Adams," Scarlett replied, poking her head, "have a big sign plastered to your forehead that says back off."

Bridget rolled her eyes and walked out of the kitchen with the coffee. "I do not."

"I bet you twenty dollars she won't do it," Larry chimed in, holding out a hand to Scarlett.

She eyed him warily for a moment. "You're on," she shrugged, shaking his hand.

Paul lifted his head from his place behind the bar. "I bet fifty."

Bridget stared at them all, both angry and flabbergasted. How long had they been talking about this behind her back? She gritted her teeth.

"I'll do it," she growled. Bridget stormed up the stairs and slammed the old man's coffee on his table. She heard him yell in protest, but she kept walking toward Cade's table. She felt determined until he gazed up at her and smiled. Her false confidence drained from her as she approached him.

"Is everything okay?" Cade asked. She realized her hands were shaking.

"Do you want a drink?" Bridget asked hoarsely. Cade briefly glanced at his water in confusion. She cleared her throat, correcting nervously, "After my shift, do you want to go get a drink?"

Cade froze. Eyes torn, his throat bobbed as he said, "Bridget…"

Bridget blushed furiously. She was never going to listen to Scarlett. Ever again. "Nevermind," she squeaked, throat tightening painfully. She couldn't bear to hear his excuses. All of her insides squeezed into an excruciating knot. "There's a new bar I've been wanting to try, but I can't convince Scarlett to go with me," Bridget rambled. "I'll go by myself."

It was a dumb excuse. She couldn't go by herself. She didn't turn twenty-one until next month.

An awkward silence enveloped them. "I need to get back to work," they both said simultaneously.

"Of course. Have a good day," Bridget mumbled.

She hurried down the stairs and rushed into the employee restroom. Pacing, she tried to calm down. She would not cry. She had vowed a long time ago to never cry over a boy again. Scarlett slammed the door open, concern on her face.

"He said no."

"What the hell…I'm sorry, I really thought…"

"It's fine," Bridget said, hating that her voice cracked. "It's the answer I expected anyway."

Taking a deep breath, she feigned a smile and got back to work. Luckily, Cade was already gone when she came out.

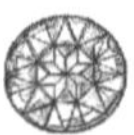

Bridget hadn't wanted to admit she was hurt and embarrassed by Cade's rejection, but she was, and instead of facing him like an adult, she called out sick from work the next day. And the next. She knew she couldn't avoid him forever, but she still needed time to bury every little feeling she had for him. So far, it hadn't been going well. On Sunday, she headed into Hungry Pies. It was usually her day off, but she needed money and knew it was the one day Cade never visited.

"You look good for a sick girl," Scarlett said dryly as she walked in the door. Bridget reached under the register and grabbed an apron.

"Shut up."

"What are you going to do tomorrow?" Scarlett questioned.

Bridget shrugged. "I haven't thought that far ahead yet."

She was most likely going to call out sick again. And then look for a different job.

"You and I both know you can't quit this job," Scarlett said.

"I know," Bridget groaned. Hungry Pies was one of the best tipping restaurants closest to City Hall. She wanted to be near the family court in case she received a last-second call about Nylah. She wouldn't quit, even to avoid Cade. "I can't face him yet."

"You have to."

"I *know*," Bridget repeated irritably, reaching down into her purse to grab her order pad.

"No, I literally mean right now. He just walked in."

At Scarlett's words, Bridget jumped up. She hadn't noticed Larry walking past them with a full tray of food held high in the air. Her head smacked into the tray, sending the contents flying onto the heads of a family of five and Larry to the ground. The entire diner went silent.

"Oh my God," Bridget gasped, covering her mouth. Larry rolled around on the floor, clasping his knee in pain. Two little kids' heads were covered in a chocolate shake. A crumpled piece of pie sat on their father's head. Then, without thinking, she backed up and suddenly ran into Marnie. A bowl of tomato soup emptied itself onto Bridget's neon uniform.

"What the fuck is wrong with you?" Marnie cried, trying to wipe off the few drops of soup that had gotten on her.

"I'm so sorry," Bridget said, frantically looking around at the mess she had made. She spotted Cade by the door. He stared at her, shocked and open-mouthed. The family of five glowered at her. Ian ran from the kitchen and tried to help Larry up.

"Get out," Paul ordered angrily, face bright red.

Scarlett stepped in front of her. "It was an accident."

"Get out!" Paul screamed. When he turned away and began apologizing profusely to the family, Bridget grabbed her purse and ran out the door.

"Bridget!"

She closed her eyes at the sound of Cade's voice, too embarrassed to face him. "Leave me alone," Bridget hissed and strode faster toward the subway.

When she reached the entrance, she stopped at the top of the stairs. Tomato soup dripped messily from her uniform. She probably needed to buy a new shirt before she rode a public train all the way to the Bronx. Not that she had any money to buy a new shirt. Bridget pinched the bridge of her nose and tried not to cry.

Cade touched the back of her arm. "Are you okay?"

"No, I'm not okay," Bridget bellowed, whipping around to glare at him. "Paul just fired me. I needed that job."

"I know," Cade said quietly. "Maybe I can go back in there and talk to him."

Bridget shook her head. "I don't need your help."

She took a deep breath, not wanting to take her anger out on him. If she had been brave and faced him earlier, the incident would have never happened. Besides, Paul hadn't exactly said she was fired. Just 'get out.' She could probably convince him to let her come back tomorrow. Hopefully.

"I will handle Paul," Bridget sighed. "Tomorrow."

"At least let me give you a ride," Cade offered, gazing at her uniform. "My car is parked around the corner."

"I'm not going to let you pay for a taxi all the way out to the Bronx."

"It's not a taxi. It's my car," Cade said. When she stared at him dumbly, he added slowly, "I drove."

"We're in Manhattan," Bridget stated incredulously, still not believing that he drove around the country's most undriveable city. How the hell did he ever find parking spots?

"I know," Cade replied, rolling his eyes. She wondered how many times he had been looked at like he was crazy for driving in the city. He grabbed her by the hand and pulled her down the sidewalk. "Let's go."

Cade stopped in front of a small black Audi. Of course he would have some fancy sports car. He opened the passenger door for her and let her climb in. The inside was covered in black leather and seemed to be kept in pristine condition.

"Why do you have a car?" Bridget questioned as Cade hopped in the driver's seat. Within seconds, the car was on and peeling down Barclay Street. "Holy shit," she breathed at his speed, reflexively grabbing onto her seat.

"It's great, right?" Cade chuckled as he weaved in and out of traffic. "I love driving. Getting my license is one of the first things I did when I—"

"When you what?" Bridget asked after he froze.

"Moved to New York," he finished hesitantly.

Bridget raised a skeptical eyebrow. "Most people go to Times Square."

Cade laughed. "This is much more exciting." He stepped on the gas harder as they turned onto the parkway.

"If you say so," she mumbled. The subway worked just fine for her.

A tense silence enveloped them. Bridget fidgeted with the edge of her shorts as she realized this was the first time they had ever truly been alone together. Her stomach clenched, and her mind raced for something to say.

Cade cleared his throat. "So you're feeling better?"

"What?"

"You haven't shown up to work in almost three days. Paul said you were sick."

"It was just a cold," Bridget said, scratching her neck. She had forgotten she had been avoiding him. Embarrassment washed over her again. What must he think of her now?

"I didn't know you went to the diner on Sundays," Bridget said.

Cade shrugged. "I usually don't, but I thought you might be avoiding me," he said, eyeing her briefly.

Bridget forced out a short laugh. "Why would I be avoiding you?"

His knuckles tightened on the steering wheel. She turned her body to gaze out the window. They sat in heavy silence for the rest of the trip. Once they arrived in the Bronx, Bridget gave him brief directions to her apartment building. Dread settled in her stomach as she realized he would see where she lived. Her building was old and worn down. He probably lived in a fancy building with a concierge.

"You can drop me off here," Bridget said, pointing to the corner of her street.

Cade shook his head and began looking around for an open spot. "No, I'll park and walk you up to your apartment."

"No, drop me off," Bridget ordered. She tried to keep the alarm out of her voice. She had already humiliated herself enough today and did not want him to pity her more.

Cade gazed at her for a long moment, his eyes wounded. "Are you serious?"

"Yes," Bridget whispered, crossing her arms. She didn't know why he looked so hurt. He was the one who rejected her. With his jaw clenched, he stopped the car in front of her building door. Bridget hopped out and slammed the door. She did not look back.

Paul called the following day, begging her to come to work. A charter bus full of teenagers had piled into the diner, and they were swamped. Bridget eagerly agreed, thrilled she wouldn't have to beg for her job back. By late afternoon, Cade hadn't shown up. He didn't show up the next day, either. By Wednesday, Bridget couldn't get rid of the knot in her stomach. She felt hypocritical. It hadn't bothered her when she had been avoiding him, but now...she was starting to be afraid that he would never come to the diner again.

Chewing her lip anxiously, she rushed down the stairs to put in an order for one of her tables. Bridget was handing the paper to Ian when she spotted Cade's messy mop of brown hair. He was sitting in a corner booth, but he wasn't alone. A lanky blond man sat with him. Hair cropped short, the blond looked a few years older than them and wore an expensive-looking suit. Bridget's heart dropped. Was he seriously going to hide in the corner to avoid her? Cade spotted her staring and looked down guiltily. She walked over to their table.

"Hi," she greeted hesitantly.

"I thought the blonde was our waitress," the other man replied, referring to Marnie.

"She is…" Bridget said, voice trailing off confusedly as she tried to read the expression on Cade's face. His eyes seemed to be pleading with her about something. When she furrowed her brows, he sighed and ran a hand through his hair.

"Jake is one of our new account executives," Cade said irritably. "He insisted on seeing where I run off to every day."

Jake laughed at the dark expression on Cade's face. "I'm trying to figure you out, Morgan. You're younger than most of the interns and already have the position I'm working toward."

Seconds later, his dark blue eyes trailed over Bridget, causing Cade to clench his jaw. "I get why you like this place now."

"Are you new to the city?" Bridget asked politely, trying not to feel insulted by Cade's visible annoyance with her.

"Did the accent give me away?" Jake asked, leaning back in his chair with a grin. Now that she had a good look at him, he was cute. He was obviously full of shit, but she could see how the dimples on his cheeks made him endearing to some women.

"Just a little," Bridget said with a small smile. Cade rolled his eyes and stared out the window.

"I moved here from London last month. Have you ever been?"

Marnie walked up to the booth and almost knocked Bridget out of the way. "Are you ready to order?" she asked with a feigned bored expression.

"Yes."

"No."

Their contradicting answers were said in unison. Jake smirked as Cade glowered and ordered them two cheeseburgers.

"I've never been to London. I've never even left New York," Bridget said once Marnie had left. She felt Cade's surprised gaze.

"Then you're the perfect tour guide," Jake grinned, clapping his hands together excitedly. He eyed Cade for a moment before continuing, "Our office is having a gala Friday night. Would you like to go?"

"No, she doesn't want to go to that," Cade replied sharply.

"Who says I don't?" Bridget argued, glaring at him.

"She's feisty," Jake said, brows raised in amusement. "Don't listen to Morgan. He already said he's not going. He doesn't do parties apparently. So what do you say?"

"Sure," Bridget said, blazing satisfaction coursing through her at the sight of Cade's clenched fists.

Jake pulled out his phone and handed it to her. "Put your number in, and I'll text you the details."

"See you Friday," Bridget said with a smile, handing back his phone before she strode off to check her tables. She felt Cade's eyes on her the entire way up the stairs.

About thirty minutes passed before she felt Cade grab her arm from behind. She turned and saw Jake missing from the bottom floor.

"What the hell, Bridget?" Cade hissed. "That guy's a jerk. He's already tried to sleep with half the girls in our office."

"He seemed nice," Bridget argued indignantly. "Besides, he can't be too bad. You had lunch with him."

"Not by choice," Cade said through gritted teeth.

"And why sit downstairs?" Bridget seethed, finally asking the question that had been gnawing at her. "Are you embarrassed to be friends with me?"

"What?" Cade asked incredulously, "No!"

"Is that why you don't want me to go to the gala?" Bridget asked, narrowing her eyes. Her heart started to pound painfully in her chest.

"I don't even want to go to the gala!" Cade bellowed. When he noticed the eyes of the diner on them, he closed his eyes and took a deep breath through his nose. "It's just going to be a bunch of executives kissing each other's asses."

Bridget's phone buzzed. She took it out of her pocket and saw a text from Jake. "Oh, look, he already sent me the details," she replied, waving the phone in his face.

"I can't believe you gave him your number," Cade scowled. "I don't even have your number."

"You never asked," Bridget snapped.

He struggled for a reply. After a moment, he glowered furiously at her. "You're serious about this?"

"Yes."

She had never been more serious about anything in her life. She would go to that party and enjoy every ounce of misery it brought him.

Cade took a step forward and asked hesitantly, "Is this about last week?"

"Get over yourself," Bridget spat. "A cute boy asked me to a party, and I said yes. End of story."

Growling, Cade stormed out of the diner. Bridget stood there frozen, unsure of what she had just done. Now that the moment had passed, she wasn't sure what she had gotten herself into. His reaction to her going to the party had hurt her and made her blind with rage.

Scarlett shook her shoulder. "What the hell was that about?"

"I need your help," Bridget whispered helplessly.

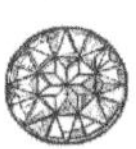

Bridget stood outside the Beekman Hotel, waiting for Jake. She fought the urge to pace. She regretted agreeing to go to the gala. What had she been thinking? Just looking at the outside of the venue, she knew she wouldn't fit in. The dress she was wearing wasn't even hers. She'd borrowed it from Scarlett. It was red, silky, and had a low back. At first, she had refused to wear it. She hated wearing red and felt like it clashed with her hair, but Scarlett had insisted. Also, her friend's shoes were already rubbing blisters on her heels. Plus, she hadn't seen Cade since their fight. Even though she didn't want to admit it, she missed him. Bridget didn't want to piss him off anymore and wanted to flee the hotel before Jake arrived. She had no idea what she was doing outside a fancy hotel waiting for someone she didn't even like.

A black car pulled up. Jake stepped out and gave her a once-over. He was wearing a slim-fitted tux.

"You look great," he said.

Jake held out his arm with a grin. Bridget leaned her head toward him in gratitude and reluctantly took his arm. She let him lead her into the hotel. The building was even more beautiful on the inside. High ceilings, gold fixtures, and antique wooden walls made it feel cozy and sophisticated. They took an elevator to the second floor to a large hall with arched entries. Crystal chandeliers hung from above, and there were floor-to-ceiling windows.

"This hotel is amazing," she breathed. Piano covers of old, popular songs blasted from the speakers as a few people danced in the middle of the room. A few tables and bars lined the walls.

"Do you want a drink?" Jake asked.

She nodded, and he left her standing by the arched doorway. Bridget wrung her hands together, unsure of what to do. People around her were chatting about business and the stock market. When she turned to her left, she suddenly found Cade walking toward her. The sight of him in a suit took her breath away. Instead of traditional black, his tux was dark blue. His eyes softened as he looked at her.

"You look beautiful," Cade said quietly.

"I thought you weren't coming," she whispered, her heart fluttering erratically in her chest.

"I couldn't miss the opportunity to see you in something other than neon," he replied, lips tilting slightly.

She stared at him, wanting to say she was sorry, but unsure where to start.

A bubbling glass appeared in her face. "Champagne?" Jake asked.

Cade scowled at him. "She's only twenty."

Bridget fought the urge to roll her eyes. He knew she had drunk alcohol before. She grabbed the glass from Jake's hand and sipped on it.

"Are you a cop now, Morgan?" Jake asked, downing his glass in one gulp. His eyes darted to a large man with a bellowing laugh across the room. "One sec, that's the VP."

Jake bolted away, leaving them alone once more. After a moment, Cade held out his hand.

"Do you want to dance?" He asked.

Bridget stared at the couples moving gracefully across the dance floor. A song from the 1990s she recognized started playing. "I'm not very good."

With a confident grin, he grabbed her hand and pulled her to the center of the action. "Follow my lead," he said, grabbing her waist.

His fingers seared the bare skin on her lower back and sent electricity up her spine. Cade moved her back and forth across the dance floor. She only stumbled a few times.

"For someone who hates parties," she said breathlessly, "you're good at this."

"Things like this remind me of another life," he said, eyes darkening, "one I'd rather not think about."

She understood. She avoided thinking of her time in foster care at all costs. The only good thing that had come from that time was Nylah. "This is my first dance," Bridget blurted out. Cade's eyes moved to hers in surprise. "I never went to prom or anything. I could never afford the dress."

Cade smiled softly and then suddenly dipped her, so low that her hair brushed the floor. She couldn't help but laugh.

"I'm honored," he murmured.

As he pulled her up, she stumbled into him. They stood chest to chest now, and she could feel his breath fanning her face as she gazed into his eyes. His arms tightened around her waist and if she moved forward a little …

"Stop hogging my date, Morgan," Jake said, placing a hand between them.

Bridget swallowed hard as her cheeks flushed. Cade glowered as Jake grabbed her waist and pulled her with him onto the floor. She sent him an apologetic look as she got led away, overwhelmed by what had almost happened.

After a few awkward dances with Jake, the music stopped so that a few people could make some speeches. When the president of the Manhattan office started talking, she glanced around and saw Cade laughing with a pretty girl with dark brown hair. She couldn't stop the white-hot rage that flowed through her. She suddenly felt very warm.

"I need some air," Bridget muttered to Jake.

She marched away without waiting for an answer. Grabbing a champagne glass, she found an open, empty balcony. She downed the bubbling liquid in one gulp and placed the empty flute on the concrete edge. The warm August air did not help her blistering skin.

The door opened behind her.

"Are you okay?" Cade asked.

Bridget clenched her fists on the railing. She hated that she wasn't surprised he had followed her out here. "Weren't you in the middle of something?" she snapped, unable to stop herself.

"I'm not the one who came here with a date," Cade replied indignantly, striding over to her.

"What was I supposed to do? You rejected me. You—"

She was cut off by his lips pressing fiercely against hers. Electricity filled her veins. Bridget groaned and kissed him back, mouth moving furiously against his. When his tongue entered her mouth, she pulled him closer as he backed her up against the balcony railing. Cade ran his fingers through her hair as he pressed against her. She could feel every hard inch of him. He lifted her leg and started moving his hand lower...

"Am I interrupting?"

The sound of Jake's voice hit her like an ice bucket. With a gasp, she pulled her lips away from Cade. Her legs were practically wrapped around him, and her dress was bunched up around her waist. Jumping up and smoothing out the material of her dress, she ran inside to find the elevator without looking at either of them. She could not believe what she had gotten herself into. She had just thrown herself at Cade on a balcony, in public, while on a date with another man. Not that she liked Jake, but she still felt bad. She pressed frantically on the down button. With a beep, the elevator opened, and she hurried in. Before the doors closed, Cade zipped in and pressed the emergency stop button.

"Why did you do that?" Bridget whispered. She knew he understood she wasn't talking about the elevator.

"I've fought the urge to do that, and more, for weeks now," Cade murmured, tucking her red hair behind her ears.

"I don't understand," Bridget said, her breathing becoming shallow. "You've never…"

"I'm being transferred to the London office," Cade replied softly. Bridget's throat tightened painfully as she tried to focus on his words. "They want me to leave sometime next month. I thought if I stayed away, it would make the move easier. But seeing you tonight, in that dress," he whispered, fingering the thin red straps, "and with Jake, I couldn't stop myself."

Bridget swallowed hard. Her heart broke at his news. She couldn't imagine him being on the other side of the world. In that moment, all she knew was that he was right in front of her, and she wanted him more than anything. No matter that price.

"You're leaving next month, and I have a sister to worry about," Bridget began, knowing her heart would regret her words one day.

"Right," Cade replied, furrowing his brows as he tried to figure out what she was implying.

Bridget moved closer to him and grabbed his lapels. "So why don't we just have…fun?"

"Fun?" Cade repeated. His eyes heated in a way that sent lava rushing to her core.

"Yeah. Fun," Bridget said shakily as his hand grazed her bare back. "We both know this can't last, but we still want to…"

Cade pulled her flush against him. His lips brushed down her neck. "Want to what?"

Her legs shook. "We could make a contract," she sighed breathlessly as she wrapped her fingers in his thick hair.

"No," he hissed, making her heart stop briefly. He quickly cleared his throat and pressed his lips against her pulse. "No contracts," Cade murmured.

"But we agree?" Bridget mumbled, unable to focus on anything but the sensation of his lips on her skin.

She felt him smile against her neck. "Agree to what?"

"Cade..." Bridget growled, pressing herself against him. He lifted his head and kissed her hotly. Her stomach dropped to the floor as her entire body pulsed. She had never wanted anyone more.

It was a long time before they left the elevator.

CHAPTER TWENTY-ONE

SEPTEMBER

"Cade," she groaned warningly. He rolled on top of her and started to nibble on her neck, hand trailing lower and lower. It was late in the morning, and they were lying in his bed in his West Village apartment. She had begun to spend most nights at his place. Not that she was complaining…

"You're going to be late for work," Bridget argued weakly. Despite her protests, she opened her legs further for him as he began to caress her inner thigh.

"Who cares?" Cade murmured against her skin as his head moved downward.

"Oh my god," Bridget breathed as he curled two fingers into her. She felt him grin against her stomach. If he didn't care about work, neither did she. She didn't even have to be there for a few more hours… "Oh my God," Bridget gasped, bolting up. She grabbed her phone off the nightstand. "What's today?"

She clicked on her phone. September 17th.

"Shit," Bridget hissed as she jumped out of bed, "Today is my scheduled visitation with Nylah." She fumbled around the floor for her jeans and t-shirt. Bridget ran into the bathroom, glanced at herself in the mirror, and frantically tried to brush the tangles from her red hair. "I can't be late."

"You're fine," Cade called, "it's only 8:30."

"Do I look like a mess?" Bridget asked, hurrying out of the bathroom. She had no time for makeup, and she was pretty sure the back of her hair was still knotted.

Cade smiled softly. "No."

"You're full of shit," Bridget said, rolling her eyes. She leaned down and kissed him quickly, laughing when he tried to hold on to her a little longer.

Bridget rushed down the stairs and hopped on the subway to the Lower East Side. She couldn't believe she had been too wrapped up in Cade to notice the time or date. She had been lucky that Nylah's new foster parents had agreed to let her have some time with her at all. Bridget didn't like her new caregiver, but she was glad Nylah was out of a group home. For now. They lived in an old high-rise apartment building right next to the river. Graffiti lined the outside walls, and rickety A/C units hung out every window. She trekked up the stairs to the tenth floor. The door flew open the second she knocked.

"Happy birthday!" Nylah squealed. She jumped up and tightly wrapped her arms around Bridget's neck.

"Hey, you," Bridget said, blinking rapidly. She would *not* cry. Nylah pulled back and presented her with a large, hand-drawn card. Her dark spiral curls bounced as she grinned excitedly.

"It's beautiful," Bridget smiled. In all honesty, she could not tell if it was supposed to be her or a dog on the cover. Art school was not in her future. Regardless, Bridget would still hang it on her mini fridge.

Nylah glowed proudly. "I worked on it all week."

"I can tell. Are you ready to go?"

"She needs to be back by 11:00," a short, heavy-set woman called impatiently from the couch. She stared aimlessly at the television as she munched on a bag of chips. Bridget gritted her teeth and grabbed Nylah's hand.

"Sure thing, Brenda."

They grabbed bagel sandwiches for breakfast before heading to the local park. They had been on a years-long mission to find the best bagels in New York, but, so far, had not chosen a winner. Bridget preferred sweet, while Nylah preferred salty. As they sat on a bench, Bridget toyed with the ends of Nylah's hair that were sticking up wildly.

"Has no one been helping with your hair?" She frowned, trying to smooth down the black hair bunched into two buns. Nylah shrugged, still munching on her bagel.

"How was your first day of school?"

"Pretty boring. My new teacher is a bitch," Nylah said bluntly.

Bridget popped her lightly on the arm. "Nylah."

"She is!" Nylah argued indignantly. "She doesn't care if anyone gets bullied during lunch."

"Is that happening to you?" Bridget asked, brows furrowed in concern.

Nylah tossed her bagel wrapper into the trash and crossed her arms. "No, but one of my friends keeps getting picked on because of the food she brings."

Bridget sighed. Kids hadn't changed much since she was in school. She remembered one girl crying every day during lunch because she always had kimchi.

"I know school can be tough," Bridget said quietly, "but focus on your grades. Good grades mean—"

"Freedom," Nylah finished, rolling her eyes exasperatedly, "I know."

Bridget had seen too many foster kids drop out of high school and disappear. She had almost been one of them. She had vowed a long time ago to never let that happen to Nylah. Yet the little girl still seemed anxious. "It won't last forever," Bridget said encouragingly.

Nylah's eyes moved to her neck. "What's that?"

Bridget looked down and gasped. A small purple bruise was forming right above her collarbone. She was going to kill Cade. Of all days… "I burned myself," she mumbled, swiping at her hair so that it covered her neck.

"With what?" Nylah asked skeptically.

"A curling iron."

"You don't curl your hair," Nylah argued. She grabbed Bridget's straight red hair and pushed it out of the way so she could get a better look. She gazed at Bridget deviously. "Is that a hickey?"

"How do you know what a hickey is?" Bridget gasped, shoving her away.

"I'm ten, not stupid."

Her cheeks reddening, Bridget crossed her arms defensively. "You shouldn't know about any of that stuff yet," she griped.

"Blame the Internet," Nylah said. "So is he your boyfriend?"

"I don't know," Bridget muttered honestly. She spent most of her time with him, and he certainly acted like her boyfriend, but he was about to move. She was afraid that if she labeled him in any way, it would be much harder to get over him when he left. Nylah reached over and pinched her arm. Hard. Bridget glared at her.

"Ow! What was that for?"

"You obviously like him. What's the problem?"

"It's complicated."

"Uncomplicate it. You should bring him here to meet me," Nylah said, batting her eyes.

"No," Bridget said sharply. Boyfriends—not that she really ever had any—and Nylah were two things Bridget was not willing to mix. Especially if they were about to leave for the other side of the world.

"Why not?"

"He's leaving soon."

Nylah stuck out her bottom lip. "I still want to meet him."

"Maybe," Bridget reluctantly mumbled, rolling her eyes. Nylah knew she couldn't resist that puppy dog look.

Nylah suddenly grabbed her hand. "You deserve to be happy," she whispered. She was more intelligent than any ten-year-old had the right to be. Bridget wrapped her arm around her and kissed her on the forehead.

"I am happy," she murmured, content to enjoy a simple morning with her sister.

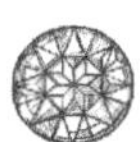

"How's your knee, Larry?" Bridget asked as she walked into Hungry Pies. The balding waiter was still fumbling around on crutches, even though she had seen him sprint toward the toilets the other day. He constantly complained about his IBS.

"The ladies dig the crutches," he wheezed, pushing up his thick glasses. "Plus, I always get a good seat on the subway. Even the grandmas get up for me."

Bridget nodded slowly, unsure of what to say.

"Happy birthday!" Scarlett shrieked as she flew out of the kitchen. "Which bar are we hitting up tonight? Don't give me that look. Taking a shot on your twenty-first birthday is a rite of passage."

"I've never heard that, but you know the best ones better than me," Bridget said. After leaving Nylah, she wasn't in the mood to celebrate anymore. All she wanted to do was go home, sleep, and forget it was her birthday. It was usually just another day for her.

"Girl, don't get me started," Scarlett uttered in excitement. She whipped out her phone and began scrolling through an app. "I need to go find you a crown and a birthday sash so we can get some free drinks."

"It's your birthday?"

Bridget turned and found Cade staring at her, eyes stormy and confused. Scarlett gave her a look that told her she was in trouble. Pursing her lips together, she grabbed Cade's arm and dragged him outside.

"You didn't think to even mention it to me?"

"I didn't think it was that important," Bridget said, suddenly feeling guilty.

"Why would it not be important?"

"I don't know, Cade," Bridget argued indignantly, throwing her hands in the air. "Maybe because you could leave at any second. I didn't want to say anything because I didn't want to make you feel like you had to stay or do something for me."

"That's ridiculous," he said, brown eyes gleaming with ire. "Did you really think I wouldn't care?"

She had been too afraid to find out. For her, their agreement to stay casual was getting harder by the day. Bridget was doing everything she could to maintain some semblance of control. "We agreed..."

"I don't give a shit about what we agreed to."

"That's not fair," Bridget whispered, eyes watery.

Regret flashed across his face. "You're right," he sighed. "I need to go. I have some errands to run."

"You just got here."

The words sounded pathetic out of her mouth.

"I'll see you later," he said. Cade kissed her forehead and then quickly strode down the street. She wanted to call out to him but was frozen in place, paralyzed by the truth she didn't want to share. Her chest burned and shook with every breath. Every barrier she had placed up to protect herself was slowly crumbling. Bridget knew she had no one to blame but herself. As the sidewalk buzzed around her, she watched the back of Cade's head until he was out of sight.

The rest of her shift flew by in a staggering blur. Before she knew it, she was in an East Village cocktail bar with the rest of the Hungry Pies staff. Forced into a sash and crown, Bridget quickly moved the group up to the front of the line. As they crowded around the bar, she sent Cade a text with their location.

"Birthday girl gets to pick the shots," Scarlett said enthusiastically.

"Nothing with tequila," Larry shouted over the music.

Scarlett shoved him, causing him to wobble on his crutches. "Shut up, Larry. No one asked you what you wanted."

Bridget glanced at her phone and saw no new notifications. Swallowing hard, she shoved the device back in her purse, determined not to look at it for the rest of the night. "Four tequila shots, please," she called out to the bartender. Larry groaned.

Marnie held up the big shot in her hand. "Should we sing?"

"Definitely not," Bridget said.

Scarlett wrapped her arm around Bridget's shoulders. "Later then, when you're too drunk to protest."

Bridget sniggered and clinked her glass with the others. Then she threw her head back and downed the burning liquid in one gulp. Scarlett and Marnie cheered.

"They grow up so fast," Scarlett said, feigning anguish. "I'll get us another round."

The later it got, the more the crowd pushed them against the bar. Marnie elbowed Larry in the stomach. "For the last time, Larry, six inches needs to be between us at all times," she hissed threateningly.

As Scarlett tried to get the bartender's attention, arms wrapped around Bridget's waist. "You shouldn't let random strangers grab you in a bar," a voice murmured in her ear.

Bridget elbowed Cade lightly and then turned around. "I could tell it was you."

Relief flooded through her to see Cade smiling. His face faltered imperceptibly as he spotted the crown on her head. Feeling self-conscious, Bridget reached up to take it off.

"Keep it on," Cade said, grabbing her hand and lowering it, "it suits you."

Bridget tightened her arms around his waist and gazed up at him. "I'm sorry," she said, still unsure if she was apologizing for keeping her birthday a secret or for pretending she was fine with their casual agreement. Playing with the ends of her hair, Cade leaned forward and gave her a soft peck on the lips.

"As cute as you two are, I'm tired of watching you swap spit," Scarlett quipped. She handed Bridget a drink and then shoved another one into Cade's chest. "It's about time you showed up. The next round is on you."

"Yes, ma'am."

Only a little bit of tequila spilled onto his shirt. Bridget laughed as they took another shot. After a few more drinks, the stuffy air of the small bar felt sweltering. Marnie and Scarlett shared an oversized armchair, laughing about something Bridget couldn't hear. At the same time, Larry stood in line for the bathroom. Cade pulled on her elbow.

"Do you want to get some air?" He asked.

She nodded and followed him out the door. The sidewalk was loud and crowded. About a block away, they found a park. Cade pulled her to a bench and sat down. The loud voices of people bar hopping and club music became a faint murmur.

"Why didn't you tell me?" He asked, faintly pulling on the edge of the sash.

Bridget took a long moment to answer. The words felt stuck in her throat.

"I know I'm the one who suggested…fun," Bridget muttered. The word felt acidic on her tongue, "But I wake up every morning afraid it's the day you're going to say you're leaving. I thought if there were some parts of me I kept to myself, it would be that much easier to pull myself together when it happens."

She looked down at her hands. The heat of his gaze made her stomach clench.

"I have something for you," Cade said suddenly.

"You didn't have to…" Bridget protested weakly as he pulled a small black bag out of his pocket and handed it to her.

She opened the cloth package and dumped the contents into her palm. She froze, hand shaking slightly. Her emerald ring, the one she had sold to pay her debts to Marco, glistened in the moonlight. "How did you find this?" she asked hoarsely.

"Did you know there are thirteen pawn shops within walking distance of Hungry Pies?" Cade said, lips tilting upward slightly. "And at least thirty-five south of Central Park?"

"I don't understand," Bridget whispered. "I went back a few days later, and it was already gone."

She had gone back to beg for some kind of payment plan, anything to get it back, and had been heartbroken to find out it was already sold. She clasped the ring tightly in her hand.

"It's my mother's ring," she admitted, voice breaking. "I can't even remember what she looked like, but I remember this being on her hand the day she died. I took it before anyone noticed it was gone."

"I started searching for it after I left the diner that day. I could tell it was important, no matter what you kept saying. I've had it all this time. I just didn't know how to give it to you," Cade said, reaching up to wipe away the tear from her cheek she didn't know had fallen. "I know we agreed to fun, but it was never about that for me either."

Bridget swallowed hard, heart pounding in her chest. "So this is real?"

"It's always been real," Cade said. He took the ring and placed it on her right hand.

"But you're leaving..."

"I'm staying. I told them earlier today."

Bridget's gaze snapped to his in surprise. Happiness soared through her, leaving her breathless and dizzy. She couldn't stop the smile that formed on her face. "Were they mad?" she asked, even though she didn't really care. He was staying, and that's all that mattered.

"It doesn't matter," Cade said, gazing at her intently. "I'm not going anywhere."

His thumb grazed her cheek before he leaned in and kissed her. In that moment, it didn't matter that they were sitting on a dirty park bench in the middle of Manhattan or that she was wearing a tacky plastic crown. She had never felt happier.

CHAPTER

TWENTY-TWO

OCTOBER

Bridget spat her toothpaste into the sink. "Are you sure this isn't too soon?" she asked, glancing at Cade's reflection in the bathroom mirror.

He had just gotten back from his daily morning run. His dark hair was damp, and his red face glistened with sweat. She hadn't realized how avid a runner he was until she moved in with him. He sometimes ran twice a day. Bridget had tried to go with him one morning, but she hadn't been able to keep up.

"Asking that question for the fifth time will not change my answer." Cade grinned and shook his wet hair at her. Tiny sweat droplets slapped against her raised hand.

"Gross," she said, even though she didn't mind seeing him all hot and sweaty.

"You're already here most nights," Cade said, reaching to turn on the shower, "plus, this place is closer to Nylah and work. I think it's a win for everyone."

"How is it a win for you?"

With a devious smirk, Cade suddenly pulled her against him. She squealed and struggled to escape his wet and stinky grasp.

"Enough," she laughed, wrinkling her nose, "you really do reek."

Cade chuckled and released her. Sending him a playful glare, she walked to the kitchen to make some coffee. As she started the machine, there was a knock at the door. With a confused frown, she went to answer it. A tall man with dark skin and a shaved head stood before her. He was wearing the strangest clothes. The pants were black, thick, and form-fitting. His top was leathery and dark gray, with a large hood that hung around his back and neck. His face faltered slightly as he gazed at her.

"I'm sorry. I must have the wrong apartment," he said, quickly turning away.

"Are you looking for Cade?" she asked hesitantly, stopping him in his tracks. He pivoted and eyed her warily.

"Is he here?"

"He's in the shower," Bridget said. Then, when he continued to stare and offer no explanation, she clumsily asked, "Is he expecting you?"

"No, I'm an old friend from home," he said tentatively. Bridget couldn't help but gape at him. Cade never talked about his family or where he was from. Based on what she did know, she thought they must be shady people or dead. He visibly stiffened whenever she brought them up. Still hearing the shower running, she inwardly debated what to do next.

"Come on in," she eventually said, unsure if she was making the right decision. She held out a hand, "I'm Bridget."

"Finn," he replied, following her inside. He circled the living room and kitchen, dark eyes scanning the walls and windows. Finally, he stopped in front of a picture they had just put on the wall a few days ago. Finn studied it intently.

"Do you live here too?" he asked.

"It's pretty recent," Bridget said, feeling awkward by his perusal of the room. "That was the day we visited Coney Island. Can you believe I've lived in New York my whole life and had never visited?"

He blinked at her like he had no idea what she was talking about.

After a long moment, she furrowed her brows at him. "So, where are you from?"

"What are you doing here?"

Bridget turned and saw Cade standing outside the bedroom door. He was staring at Finn like he had just seen a ghost. His face was paler than Bridget had ever seen it.

"It's been a long time," Finn said with a small smile. He walked over to Cade and hesitantly squeezed his shoulder. "It's good to see you."

"Is…everything okay?" Cade asked tensely.

Finn nodded. "For the most part."

There was a long, heavy silence as they gazed at each other. Both looked wary of each other, especially Cade. She wondered if she had made a mistake by letting Finn inside. They obviously needed to work something out. Wanting to give them space, Bridget blurted, "I'll be right back."

She ran into the bedroom and closed the door. Bridget groaned as she looked at the time. She would be late for work if she didn't leave in the next five minutes. She threw on her uniform and pulled up her hair. She was about to open the door when she heard their muted voices. They seemed to be arguing. Hesitating, she leaned against the door and tried to listen.

"If I'm not back with you by tomorrow, he'll send someone else," Finn argued calmly.

"Let him try," Cade growled. "Plus, there are over five million people in this city. There's no guarantee that…"

"I found you within a matter of days."

"Because you know me. I told you what I was doing when I left," Cade said. "Anyone else he sends won't know where to start."

Finn let out a long, frustrated sigh. "No, but the next person he sends won't hesitate to do what needs to be done *when* you're found. Not if. When. And now that you've got—"

"Leave her out of this," Cade snapped.

Alarmed and confused, Bridget swung the bedroom door open. Both men froze and stopped talking at her sudden appearance. All three stared awkwardly at each other.

"I need to head to work," Bridget told them. "Are you two going to be okay?"

"We're fine," Cade replied with a tight smile. "I'll take the day off and show Finn around the city. It's his first time in New York."

Bridget nodded. She wasn't sure if she believed him, but she trusted him. She gave him a quick peck on the cheek and left.

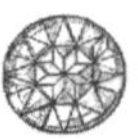

Anxiety coursed through Bridget her entire shift. She had never seen Cade so tense and alarmed. Plus, what she had overheard kept repeating in her head. Cade's past had always been a mystery, but it now seemed to be catching up with him. She wondered what that meant for her. But it was *Cade*. She only hoped he would tell her what was happening sooner rather than later. Around lunchtime, she walked out of the kitchen and spotted Cade and Finn sitting in her section. Their demeanors were the exact opposite of when she had last seen them. They were talking animatedly and laughing about something. Finn now wore jeans and a button-down top. Frowning in confusion, Bridget walked over to them.

"I didn't expect to see you in here today," Bridget said.

"Cade wanted to show me where you worked," Finn said. "I'm sorry if I startled you this morning."

"It's no big deal," Bridget replied, mind still reeling from their sudden change in disposition. She was relieved, but still had a ton of questions. "Are you going to be staying long?"

"Cade mentioned a guest bedroom..." Finn trailed off and glanced at Cade with uncertainty.

"Is that okay?" Cade asked her.

Bridget quickly nodded. "Yeah, of course," she said. If Cade was bringing someone from his past into their lives, she wanted to support him. Even if it would be a little crowded in the apartment.

Scarlett walked over and bumped her hip. "Who do we have here?" She asked curiously, eyeing Finn.

"This is Finn," Bridget said, realizing too late that she never got his last name. The male in question nodded politely.

"We've been friends since we were kids," Cade explained. "He's in town visiting."

"That's perfect. There's a Halloween party tomorrow," Scarlett shrieked excitedly. "It's official. You're coming."

"Will he be there?" Finn asked. He was gazing at Ian through the small kitchen window.

Scarlett raised an eyebrow. "He will be if I tell him to," she stated intensely. Finn blinked at her, unsure if she was serious or not.

"Don't scare the poor boy on his first day in the big city," Cade laughed. Finn glared and threw a wadded-up straw wrapper at him.

"Where would we even find costumes this late?" Bridget asked, even though a party did sound fun. It was the day before Halloween. Every costume store in the city was probably sold out.

"Just go online and get overnight delivery," Scarlett sighed. She grabbed Bridget's phone from her back pocket and thrust it into her hands. Clapping her hands together, she snapped, "Pronto!"

"Is she always that bossy?" Finn asked as she walked away.

She and Cade answered in unison, "Yes."

Bridget sat down next to Cade and began scrolling through a costume website. She started naming off options. "Sexy nurse, sexy nun, sexy fairy…"

Finn choked on the water he had been sipping.

"Are you okay?" Bridget asked.

"I think you should go with that one," he sputtered out hoarsely.

She felt Cade kick him under the table. "Why don't we dress up as something together?" He asked, grinning at her.

"I didn't realize you were so cheesy," Bridget teased.

"*Charming*, not cheesy."

"My mistake," Bridget said, flicking him lightly on the arm. He laughed and flicked her right back. Then, when she noticed Finn watching them with a strange look on his face, she went back to scrolling.

After a few minutes, she gasped. "I found the perfect costume," she squealed. Cade tried to grab the phone from her, but she jumped up and ran to the kitchen to show Scarlett her idea.

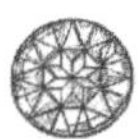

"You know, when I told you to pick out our costumes," Cade said, "I thought you would choose something sexy, like a pirate or a vampire."

They had entered a wild, crammed costume party in the West Village. Strobe lights danced along the walls as dance music blared on the speakers. She was surprised by the number of people crammed into one room. Bridget spotted Finn, Scarlett, and Ian weaving through the crowd, searching for drinks.

"This is totally sexy," Bridget argued, waving at their costumes. She rolled her lips together to stop herself from grinning.

"Really?" Cade replied with a tight-lipped, unbelieving smile. "Bob Ross is sexy to you?"

"The wig is so eye-catching," she choked out, but giggles still escaped her lips. When Cade had walked out of the bedroom in the tight jeans, wig, and fake beard, she and Finn had practically fallen to the floor in laughter. She was his tree. Her costume was a tight black bodysuit with artificial leaves glued to it. She had definitely given herself the easier outfit.

"It's not that funny," Cade said, but he was laughing too.

"We've already gotten so many compliments."

Almost everyone had stopped them on the sidewalk outside the venue to comment on their costumes. The bouncer had even snapped a picture of them when they arrived. Bridget watched Finn, dressed as a knight, and Ian start dancing.

"Is everything okay with Finn?" she asked suddenly. Cade still hadn't mentioned the initial animosity between them. "I heard you arguing this morning."

The smile slowly faded from his face. "What did you hear?"

Bridget hesitated, suddenly afraid to hear his answer. "It sounded like someone is looking for you."

"My father," Cade admitted after a long pause, jaw clenched. "He wants me to come home."

"Will you?" Bridget whispered, her breathing becoming shallow. Panic twisted her stomach.

"No," Cade said, swiping a thumb across her cheek. "Neither will Finn.

He's going to stay and help." Before she could ask him what he meant, Cade added, "I'll go get us some drinks."

She watched him disappear into the crowd. A sinking feeling that all was not right overwhelmed her. As she people-watched and waited for Cade, a hand tapped her shoulder.

She turned and found a short man dressed in a superhero costume ready to yell in her ear. "I'm sorry to bother you, but I'm one of the club's social media managers. Would you mind if we posted the picture of you and your date on our page? We're compiling a list of the best costumes."

Bridget shrugged. "Sure."

"Great! Can I get your names?"

Cade didn't have any form of social media and usually made sure all her posts were private when she posted a picture. She guessed it was the nature of working for a large tech company. He probably saw the ugly side of the Internet daily. Bridget hesitated, unsure if he wanted his name *and* picture on a public website. When the man continued to stare expectantly, she hesitantly said, "Cade Morgan and Bridget Adams."

After jotting the names down on his phone, the man quickly strode away. Her eyes darted around the crowded room, looking for Cade, Finn, or Scarlett. Instead, her gaze landed on a bizarre-looking man in the corner. He was bald and had blue tattoos covering the majority of his skin. His yellow robes looked like something out of an anime show she had once seen, and it seemed like he had prosthetics on his ears to make them pointy. What caught her attention, though, was his stillness. He stood frozen among the loud, celebratory crowd. He didn't seem to blink as he stared intently at something. Bridget followed his eyeline. She tensed. He stared at Cade, who had his back turned as he ordered from the bar.

Bridget strode toward him, ignoring the arguments in her head that she was being paranoid. Something about the stare irked her. The man seemed predatory, almost possessive. She remembered overhearing Finn say that Cade's father would send others after him. If the man was one of those people, she wanted to find out and give Cade enough time to get away. He didn't move as she approached.

"Can I help you with something?" Bridget asked hostilely as she positioned herself in front of him.

The man let out a feral hiss. “Out of my way, you pathetic human,” he grunted, pushing her aside.

He moved across the room to another corner. Bridget froze, unsure of how to react to such a comment. She soon spotted Cade weaving through the crowd toward her with Finn and Ian. With a smile, he handed her one of the drinks in his hands.

“A man keeps watching you,” Bridget said. Like he could hear them, the man in the corner narrowed his eyes as he watched her speak to Cade. His dark eyes gave her chills.

“What?” Cade asked, head swiveling. “Where?”

Bridget nodded her head toward the corner. “The bald one,” she said, causing Cade and Finn to visibly stiffen. “He called me a pathetic human.”

Cade’s throat bobbed as he looked at Finn, who nodded. He grabbed her hand and pulled her across the room toward the stranger. She faintly heard Finn tell Ian to stay put. A large group of giggling girls screaming about Jell-O shots darted in front of them. The man was gone when they moved out of the way.

“Which way did he go?” Cade shouted heatedly over the music, gripping her hand tighter.

“I think to the right,” Finn said.

Bridget followed them to a hidden side exit door. Inside, an old metal stairway vibrated to the beat of the club music. They were five floors up. She heard the echo of footsteps rushing down the stairs below them. A brief flash of yellow appeared through the holey, grated steps.

“What’s going on?” Bridget asked Cade as they sprinted downward. “Do you know him?”

He didn’t answer. When they reached the bottom of the stairs, Finn kicked the exit door open. The alley in front of them was empty, quiet, and damp. Cade ripped off his wig and took a defensive stance in front of her. When Finn pulled out a large knife from his boot, Bridget's eyes went wide.

A screeching bellow erupted from behind a parked car. The strange man jumped over the hood and launched himself at Finn. A long, thin sword was gripped tightly in his right hand. A fucking sword. In the middle of Manhattan. It sliced through the air with a low whistle.

Stunned, Bridget watched Finn block the heavy blow with his knife. Cade let go of her hand and charged toward the man.

A few months ago, she had seen Cade take down the largest man she had ever seen with ease, but whoever Finn and Cade were fighting now seemed to be just as strong and quick as they were. It was like watching a boxing match at super speed, except for the knife and sword that kept clanking together.

Suddenly, the man twisted to the left and kicked Finn square in the chest. With a gasping breath, he clutched the front of his shirt and staggered backward. The man's eyes locked on her. He bolted toward her; sword raised high above his head.

Before she could react, Cade jumped in front of her. The sword came down on his raised forearm. Drops of blood splattered through the air, but Cade still grabbed the man by the throat and threw him to the ground. The man caught himself and quickly rolled back to his feet. He crouched low as Cade and Finn began to circle to him.

As the man turned his back to her, Bridget spotted a small sack of powder tied to his belt. The dust moved and glistened unnaturally. The man tensed and reached for the powder when Cade began to move toward him. Without thinking, Bridget launched herself onto the strange man's back. She clawed her fingernails into his cheeks and whipped his head back.

She barely registered Cade and Finn's stunned faces before the man howled and rammed her into the alley's brick wall. Pain exploded from the back of her skull. Seeing stars, she let go and fell to the ground. To her surprise, the man turned and sprinted down the street. Finn quickly followed. Cade rushed to her and picked her up off the ground.

"What the hell were you thinking? Are you okay?"

Bridget nodded and rapidly blinked in an attempt to clear her head. She held up the small sack she had swiped from the man's belt on her way to the ground. "I think he was trying to throw this at you."

Cade eyed it in recognition but didn't explain. He grabbed the powder from her and stuffed it in his pocket. "I need you to go home. Once you're there, lock all the doors and windows," he said, eyes darting around the alley in the direction Finn went.

"No," Bridget said stubbornly. Her hands shook from adrenaline, but she didn't want to leave his side. The cut on his arm oozed blood.

"Please."

The slight tone of desperation in his voice stopped her from arguing further. Throat tight, she nodded and watched him run after Finn. Shivering from much more than the cold October air, she pulled out her phone and called a taxi. Their apartment was only a few blocks away, but the night seemed more menacing than it had been yesterday.

When she got home, she locked everything in sight, just like Cade had told her, and sat on the couch. Her knee bobbed up and down anxiously. When minutes ticked by and they still hadn't shown up, Bridget began to pace.

She rubbed the back of her head and felt the early formation of a large knot. The whole night reminded her of a dream. She was beginning to see why Cade never talked about his family. They were obviously very dangerous and very powerful. She couldn't get over the sword, though. Who the hell sends someone with a *sword* to fetch their son? It was the 21st century. Guns were more accessible than medieval weapons. Plus, the outfit...the whole situation seemed so bizarre.

Two hours passed before she heard a noise outside the apartment door. She stiffened, recognizing the sound of a screwdriver. There was no peephole, so she pressed her ear up against the cold metal. When she heard Cade's muffled voice, she flung the door open. Finn was measuring the frame with his hands. Cade knelt on the ground as he fiddled with a box and screwdriver. Both looked sweaty and exhausted.

Bridget stared at them expectantly. "What happened?"

"We took care of it," Finn said resignedly. Cade still didn't look at her. Instead, his focus remained on the small box in front of him.

"What does that mean?" Bridget asked, annoyance seeping into her voice. She crossed her arms and eyed Cade. There was new blood spatter on his collar, and his wound remained untouched. "You probably need to go to the hospital."

"I'm fine," Cade said, standing up to face her. His face was weary and guarded. "We bought some thread. Finn will stitch me up, but we need to get this put on before anything else happens."

Bridget studied the device in Cade's hands. "Is that a doorbell camera?"

"It's just a precaution."

"You need to explain. Now."

"I will. I promise. But this hallway is not the time or place."

Finn shuffled uncomfortably as his eyes darted between the two. "I'll need some warm water and a towel for his stitches," he suggested tentatively. "Can you get that ready for me?"

Bridget gritted her teeth together. "Sure," she replied. She shut the door a little too hard and had the overwhelming feeling that things were about to change.

CHAPTER

TWENTY-THREE

NOVEMBER

The month of November passed by in a blur. Finn was still staying in their extra bedroom. While the apartment was large for Manhattan, the days after Halloween had made the space feel like a shoebox. The awkwardness quickly faded, though, and the three of them soon developed a comfortable routine. Finn was neat as a pin and rarely seemed to sleep. One night, she had caught him standing like a sentinel in front of the living room window. He blamed it on a late-night coffee.

Cade had explained the incident on Halloween, in his own enigmatic way. Bridget could tell there was still more he was holding back. She knew he thought he was protecting her, but she was getting more frustrated by the day. Since the fight, Cade's workout routine had turned exhaustive; he and Finn would spend hours in the gym almost every day. There were even a few times he had dragged her with him and made her take a few kickboxing classes.

He also seemed to be obsessed with getting out of the city. They had been going on trips every weekend: the Hamptons, Newport, Atlantic City... Bridget was thankful because their weekend in Newport was the first time she had been out of state. On an unseasonably warm day, Cade had even taught her to swim, but she wasn't blind to his increasing paranoia. It was present, even now. Cade walked ahead of her with Nylah through Central Park. Even though he laughed at something her sister said, Bridget noticed the way his eyes kept scanning the greenery around them. Behind her, Finn and Ian walked hand in hand.

"You're crazy if you think ketchup belongs on a hot dog," Nylah argued, wrinkling her nose at the street food Cade was stuffing into his mouth.

"I think you're crazy. Ketchup tastes good with everything."

"It doesn't taste good with ice cream."

"Have you tried it?" Cade asked.

Nylah stopped walking, uncertainty crossing her face. "No."

"Then you can't say it doesn't taste good with ice cream."

Bridget rolled her lips together as she tried not to laugh at their childish argument.

"So you're telling me," Nylah said with crossed arms and a raised brow, "that you've actually put ketchup on ice cream?"

"That's not the point..."

"He's never tried it either," Bridget called out from behind them. Cade turned and gave her an exasperated glare.

Nylah eyed him speculatively and asked, "How much will you pay me to try it?"

At that moment, Cade's cell phone rang. He pulled it out of his pocket and frowned at the number on the screen. As he answered it, Bridget wrapped her arm around Nylah's shoulders and pulled her further down the concrete path.

"You're incorrigible," Bridget playfully chastised, rubbing the top of the girl's head.

Nylah giggled. "I saw an opportunity and had to take it."

When Bridget heard Cade's voice begin to rise, she directed Nylah toward the playground in front of them and waited for Finn and Ian to catch up with her.

"What's that about?" Finn asked warily as he gazed at Cade.

Bridget shrugged and watched Cade hang up the phone. He ran his fingers through his hair and walked over to them with a grim look on his face.

"That was Bardot security. My office was just broken into."

"Are you serious? Was anything taken?"

"I'm not sure. They want me to come in and look at the security tapes."

Cade and Finn shared a knowing look, and even though he tried to seem nonchalant, tension radiated from his shoulders. Bridget wanted to go with him, but knew it wasn't going to be a quick trip. She glanced at the time on her phone. "Brenda wants Nylah back in an hour," she said, "can we drop her off first?"

"We'll take her," Finn offered, gesturing between himself and Ian.

Bridget bit her lip as her eyes darted between the couple and Nylah on the slide. "Are you sure?"

"Yeah, it's no problem," Ian smiled. He cupped his hands around his mouth and turned to the playground. "Hey Nylah," he shouted, "do you want to go grab some frozen hot chocolate?"

Nylah squealed loudly and jumped from the top of the playground. Bridget tried not to cringe at the reckless move. The young girl sprinted over to them. The poof on her knitted hat bobbed wildly. Even though winter approached, she had been asking to try frozen hot chocolate for weeks.

"I thought you would never ask," Nylah cried dramatically. Pushing herself between Finn and Ian, she looped her arms through theirs and gazed at Bridget with a beaming grin.

"You were just complaining about how cold you were," Bridget chided, trying to ignore the guilt bubbling in her stomach. She hated cutting their time together short and knew Brenda would send her a nasty message later for not bringing Nylah back herself.

"A girl's allowed to change her mind."

Bridget shook her head incredulously before wrapping Nylah up in a tight hug. "Be good. I'll see you soon."

Nylah nodded and then bounced out of her arms to hug Cade. Even though he seemed surprised by the gesture, a soft smile crossed his face. The two of them watched Finn and Ian lead Nylah away until they were out of sight.

Cade didn't say much on their short subway ride to the Bardot building. Bridget grabbed his hand. Stress leaked from every inch of him. He faintly squeezed her hand in acknowledgment, but his brown eyes remained stormy. She wondered if there was something important he was keeping in his office.

A large security guard greeted them as they walked through the building's spinning glass door. "I'm sorry about all this, Mr. Morgan. Thanks for coming down on such short notice."

"How did someone even get up to that floor?" Cade asked irritably. "The elevator requires a key card."

"He had one. It wasn't until I glanced at the monitors and saw your office trashed that I realized something had happened."

The guard was clearly embarrassed by the mishap, but Cade continued to glower at him. He led them to the side and opened a hidden office door. Four large screens showed multiple angles of various areas around the building. He clicked a remote and pulled up the lobby footage from two hours ago. The screen showed a tall blond man in a baseball cap walking slowly to the elevator, keycard in hand. Either he was lucky or aware of the cameras because his back stayed turned to every possible angle.

"How long was he here?" Cade asked as the guard switched the film to his office floor.

"About twenty minutes."

This time, the man's jacket collar covered the majority of his face. He walked straight for Cade's office and fiddled with the door. Within seconds, he had it open. He riffled through each nook and cranny he found. Eventually, papers and drawers scattered on the floor. The man kicked Cade's desk and strode out the door.

"That's enough," Cade said. "We'll head upstairs and see if anything is missing."

"Did you recognize that man?" Bridget asked once they were alone in the elevator. She had watched his reaction more than the actual tape, but Cade had given nothing away.

"No, but he did a good job of hiding his face."

Cade's office was located on the thirtieth floor. The elevator beep echoed throughout the empty space as the door opened. The white floors and glass walls of each office always gave her an eerie shiver. The design seemed otherworldly. The first time she had visited, she had seen why Cade always preferred to work at home or elsewhere. Bridget furrowed her brows at the sight of his metal door handle.

"It's melted," she gasped. The lock looked completely disintegrated. She thought it was odd. She hadn't noticed any kind of tool in the man's hand. Bridget hesitantly reached out to touch the damage.

Cade gently grabbed her hand away. "Don't touch it." He stepped in front of her and pushed the glass door open with his shoulder.

His office looked more trashed than it had on the video. Every item from his bookshelf had been knocked to the ground, and his plushy leather chair was turned over. Cade started to pick up and riffle through the various papers on the ground. Bridget spun around, eyes dancing across every misplaced item. The most valuable items in the room, like Cade's laptop, phone, and tablet, sat untouched on his desk.

"I don't understand, all your electronics are still here. What could he have been looking for?"

Cade let out a sigh and tossed some papers into a trash can. "Luckily, something that isn't here."

"Like what?"

When he didn't reply, Bridget snapped. "Enough. I am sick and tired of all your half-explanations. This was your family, wasn't it?"

"I'm not sure," Cade replied quietly, his entire body still. "I already told you I didn't recognize the man in the video."

"So there are more people looking for you?" Bridget asked incredulously. He said nothing. When she saw something akin to panic rising in his eyes, she moved toward him and grabbed his hands. "Please, tell me what's going on," she pleaded.

"I need you to trust me."

"I do, but are things like this going to keep happening? They obviously know where you are."

Cade said nothing.

"I can't help you if I don't understand what's going on," Bridget continued. "What if you had been here? What if they had found us in the park with Nylah?"

"I won't let anything happen to her," Cade growled, "or you."

"You can't guarantee that, Cade," Bridget cried. "Maybe you should go see him. I can come with you and..."

"No. That's not an option."

Bridget stared at him unbelievingly. "Why not?"

When he kept his lips tightly sealed again, Bridget irately ground her teeth together. Fed up, she stormed toward the door.

"Don't," Cade pleaded, grabbing her hand, "I have a plan."

"A plan? What do you mean?"

Cade took a deep breath. A long moment passed before he answered, "We run."

Bridget gaped at him. His suggestion was the last thing she'd been expecting to hear. No matter how much her heart flipped at the words, it wasn't possible. Too many things tied her to Manhattan. Eventually, Bridget sputtered, "We can't. *I* can't. Nylah..."

"We take her with us," Cade said, grabbing her arms.

Bridget couldn't feel her legs. Couldn't believe that she was actually *considering* his plan. "This is crazy," she muttered, shaking her head.

"I already have everything ready to go," Cade argued. "Passports and IDs with new names, even for Nylah. I have a friend in London that will help."

"How long have you been planning this?" Bridget asked, feeling like she was in a dream. Or a nightmare. That's what she kept telling herself to feel about the scenario. But besides Nylah, Cade was the only person she wasn't willing to lose. And a life with him and Nylah seemed too perfect to pass up.

A look of guilt crossed Cade's face. "Since Halloween."

"And you didn't think to mention it?" Bridget squeaked, anger resurfacing.

"I'm sorry. I wasn't sure if it would come down to this. But it has."

"We would never make it out of the country with Nylah," Bridget said, mind reeling as she imagined how they would actually accomplish leaving. "My visitations with her are only two hours long. Except..."

Bridget froze. It seemed almost too good to be true.

"Except what?"

"Christmas Eve. The court said I'm allowed to have her the entire night," Bridget whispered. The one night of the year she was allowed to have Nylah for more than two hours was a mere twenty-six days away. That day, they would have enough time to get to the airport before Brenda sent anyone looking for them. Her heart thundered in her chest. The idea of leaving with Cade suddenly became real to her. And it wasn't the word 'no' on the tip of her tongue.

"Then that's when we go," Cade said. "We'll lay low until then."

"That's when we go," Bridget repeated, giving him a shaky smile and officially sealing her fate.

CHAPTER
TWENTY-FOUR

DECEMBER

It was Christmas Eve, and Hungry Pies was a madhouse. Since the start of her shift, Bridget had been running at full speed. Customers were piling in steadily as they got ready for various holiday activities around the city. The windows of the second floor were frozen and glossy from the icy weather bombarding Manhattan. The afternoon sun was a mere crack in the thick, dark clouds. But, unlike her coworkers, Bridget welcomed the rush. It was a welcome distraction from the knot forming in her stomach. After her shift, Bridget would pick up Nylah, meet Cade at his office, and leave the city she called home. For good. Her hands shook involuntarily.

Bridget's rising anxiety sent a wave of nausea through her. There was nothing she wanted more than to be with Cade and Nylah. Nothing. But there were so many things that could go wrong. So many things that she would miss.

"Excuse me, I still don't have my refill," a nasally voice called, interrupting her thoughts. Bridget turned and found a glowering, large man holding out a neon glass.

"I'm sorry, one second," Bridget quickly apologized.

She grabbed the cup and sprinted off to the soda machine. Once there, she noticed someone new sitting at one of her tables. Technically, her shift was over, but she figured she had time for one more customer. She didn't want to leave. Not yet. Her throat tightened as she listened to the buzz of the second floor. Bridget closed her eyes and tried to push the feelings down. She couldn't believe she was getting emotional over the annoying little diner she claimed to hate.

Bridget hurriedly delivered the refill and then walked over to her new table. The man sitting there wore a black baseball cap and sunglasses. The collar of his dark blue coat was pulled up high around his face. A slender nose and blond hair were his only visible features.

"What can I get you?" Bridget asked politely. His appearance was puzzling, but she had seen weirder things on the streets of Manhattan. At that moment, "Hungry Eyes" by Eric Carmen started playing loudly. A few customers clapped and started singing along. She cringed. Of course, that song would be one of her last memories of the diner.

"Not a fan?"

At the question, Bridget looked down and found the man watching her closely. "Excuse me?" She asked, too lost in her thoughts to catch his meaning.

"You flinched when the song started," he explained, humor in his voice.

"It plays every hour," Bridget shrugged, trying to sound nonchalant. She took a deep breath and tried to focus. Only a few more hours until she was with Cade and Nylah. Then she would feel more settled.

"Have you worked here long?"

Bridget stiffened. It was an innocent question, and there was no reason for her to feel suspicious. But his tone and the way she could feel his eyes searing into her from beneath his sunglasses set off an alarm in her head. Since November, she had been on high alert. Cade's paranoia had been rubbing off on her.

"We're swamped right now. If you're not ready to order, I can come back in a few minutes," Bridget replied, fighting to keep her voice even.

A tense silence enveloped them before the man finally said, "Water."

Heart pounding, Bridget nodded and ran back to the kitchen. She felt like she was going crazy. He was a regular guy. Nothing more...

"Your shift was over ten minutes ago," Scarlett chastised from behind her. Bridget jumped and raised a hand to her chest.

"You scared me."

Scarlett eyed her warily. "Aren't you supposed to pick up Nylah soon?"

"This place is a mess," Bridget half-heartedly argued.

"This place is always a mess. We can survive Christmas Eve without you," Scarlett said. "Go be with your man and sister."

Bridget studied the girl in front of her. Since her first day at the diner, Scarlett had always been kind and supportive. She had always included her and made her laugh. Bridget would miss her dearly. Scarlett was one of the few people she considered a true friend in her life. She regretted that she could not properly say goodbye.

"You're a great friend. You know that?" Bridget croaked. She blinked away the moisture forming in her eyes.

Scarlett rolled her eyes, but Bridget could see the faint blush on her dark cheeks. "Why do the holidays always make people so sappy?"

"I mean it."

"I know," Scarlett said. She wrapped her arms around Bridget and brought her in for a tight hug. "You're not too bad yourself. Now go."

Bridget knew she was right. It was time. She reluctantly let go of her friend and grabbed her purse from her locker. Scarlett followed her out of the kitchen.

"Everyone is taken care of right now," Bridget said, putting on her black leather jacket. "But the guy at table four needs a water."

Scarlett looked past her and frowned. "What guy?" she asked. Bridget spun around and saw the table was empty.

"Nevermind," Bridget mumbled. She wasn't sure if the creepy guy suddenly disappearing was a good sign or not. Scarlett shooed her down the stairs. At the door, she gazed around the diner one more time. Memories replayed in her head. After a long moment, Bridget walked out of Hungry Pies for the last time.

The plan was in motion when she set foot on the sidewalk. Bridget repeated each step in her head as she walked to the subway. Go home. Grab the bags. Pick up Nylah. Meet Cade. After that, she would follow

Cade's lead. Before she walked down the subway stairs, she sent Cade a text asking if he was still at his office.

Cade hadn't answered her when she arrived in the West Village. Trying to quell her rising worry, she sent him another text. He usually responded to her messages quickly.

Once she made it to their building, Bridget ran up the stairs and into their apartment. She changed out of her uniform and put on her red sweater, black leather jacket, and jeans. The outfit was one of the few left in the closet. She had packed last night. Bridget's few possessions, along with her and Nylah's new identification, sat in a large black suitcase in the living room. She glanced at her phone as she walked out of the bedroom—no new notifications. Bridget glanced up and jumped when she spotted a figure standing in front of the suitcase.

"You scared me," she gasped. Her voice came out harsher than expected. Bridget wasn't sure how many more jump scares her heart could take. With his arms crossed, Finn stared at her with trepidation. She didn't have to ask to know why he looked unhappy. "I thought you'd be at the office with Cade."

"He told me what you're planning to do," Finn stated.

"Look..." Bridget trailed off, searching for the right words. Cade had told her Finn would disapprove of the plan but would eventually come to terms with it. By the tone of his voice, she guessed that hadn't happened yet. She wondered when Cade had told him.

Finn took a step toward her. "You need to let him go."

"What do you mean?" Bridget asked, her heart stuttering at his words. His words were the one possibility she had been unable to bring herself to face or allow as an option.

"He's needed elsewhere," Finn said, dark eyes severe and heavy as he gazed at her. "And he won't leave you, not unless you tell him to."

"You want him to go back to the place he hates most?" Bridget asked, still trying to deny the inevitable truth in Finn's words. "Have you been trying to convince him to leave this entire time?"

The look on his face told her yes. She tried not to feel betrayed.

"I'm sorry, Bridget. I like you. I do," Finn replied, face turning to stone. "But he's a part of something bigger than you realize. He should have left months ago. Instead, he's only been delaying the inevitable. There's no other way. He needs to go back."

"You make it sound like he could never come back," Bridget whispered jaggedly.

"If you love him, you'll let him go," Finn argued, "before it's too late."

The finality in his statements scared her. She knew Cade's family was not ordinary, that something incomprehensible from his past haunted and followed him. Bridget saw it in his eyes every day. But she also knew she wouldn't be able to tell him to leave. Her heart was tied to his, for better or worse.

"It's his choice," Bridget croaked and ran out of the apartment. When she found Cade, they would come back for the suitcase.

She hopped back on the subway and rode to Nylah's neighborhood. Bridget knew Finn thought what he asked her to do was right, and maybe it was. His family obviously needed him for something. As much as it scared her and made her chest ache, she decided to give Cade the option to go home before they left for the airport.

Bridget's swirling thoughts made the ride to Nylah's apartment go by quickly. Before she knew it, she was knocking on the scratched-up door. After a long moment, Brenda finally answered the door with a scowl.

"I'm here to pick up Nylah," Bridget said. She plastered a polite smile on her face to hide her apparent nerves.

"She's still packing," Brenda snapped irritably. Bridget impatiently pushed past the short woman without waiting for an invitation and strode toward Nylah's bedroom. She slammed the door shut to drown out the indignant protests. Nylah was busy shoving a pair of purple pants into a backpack and raised a curious brow at her sister.

"Hey punk, are you ready?" Bridget asked, grinning weakly.

Nylah grabbed a long-sleeved shirt off the floor. She wrinkled her nose at it and tossed it aside. "Almost," the girl replied happily. When she moved to zip up the backpack, Bridget stopped her and peeked inside. She frowned. There was only one outfit packed.

"Are you sure you don't need to pack more?"

"For one night?"

Bridget couldn't look her little sister in the eye. She hated lying to her, but she was afraid Brenda would overhear if she explained the situation in the tiny bedroom. Bridget shoved more clothes in the bag and a pair of tennis shoes. "Let's take these, just in case."

"You're acting weird," Nylah said. The girl eyed her speculatively.

"No, I'm not," Bridget lied. She pulled out a puffy coat from the closet and handed it to Nylah.

"What's going on?"

"Nothing," Bridget replied sharply. "Let's go."

Nylah sighed and walked over to her window. On the bottom ledge sat a small black rock that reflected a rainbow of colors in the sunlight. Nylah picked it up and carefully placed it in her coat pocket.

"A rock, really?" Bridget sighed.

"Cade gave it to me," Nylah argued indignantly. "He told me it was important and to take good care of it."

Bridget furrowed her brows, unable to remember such an occurrence. "When did he give you that?"

"A few weekends ago," Nylah shrugged. "You were in the bathroom."

Brenda glared at Bridget as they left the apartment. She resisted the urge to flip the woman off. Outside, she rechecked her phone. There was still no text back from Cade. Bridget hit the dial button. After a few rings, it went to voicemail. A wave of worry washed over her. It was unlike him not to answer her.

"He's not answering," Bridget said, chewing on her bottom lip.

Nylah rolled her eyes and pulled her toward the subway. "Why are you freaking out? He's probably still at work."

Bridget hoped she was right, but something felt off about the situation. The entire day had felt off. Dread bubbled in her stomach the whole way to the Bardot building. It was a little past 5:00 p.m. when they arrived at the skyscraper. Men and women sped out the front doors, clearly ready for the approaching holiday. Relief soared through Bridget when she spotted Cade's car parked out front. She pulled Nylah through the revolving glass door and walked to the front desk. The security guard saw her approaching and pulled out a sign-in sheet.

"We're here to see Cade Morgan," Bridget stated. She grabbed the clipboard and filled in her name.

"I recognize you from the break-in," the guard replied. "You're his girlfriend, right?" Bridget nodded and handed him back his pen. Then, as he gave her the guest key card for the elevator, he said, "You're not his first visitor today."

Bridget stiffened. Dread returned to her system. "What?"

The guard glanced at the sign-in sheet and pointed at a name written in elegant cursive. "Someone named Cassia."

"Right. Cassia," Bridget murmured numbly, pretending to know the name. She knew there had been a reason for Cade's silence. "Can we?" she asked, eyeing the elevator. The guard nodded. He looked pleased, like he had helped her in some way. Bridget swiped the key card and pushed the button for Cade's floor. The moment the elevator doors closed, she let out a giant breath.

"Who's Cassia?" Nylah asked.

"I'm not sure," Bridget said tensely. The elevator beeped ominously. She grabbed the girl's hand and ordered, "Stay close to me."

Cade's floor was relatively empty. A few workers glanced their way as they walked down the hall, but no one approached them. Bridget didn't spot Cade anywhere. In his office, a slender blonde girl sat in his chair. She had her eyes closed and feet propped up on his desk.

"I already told the other assistant I don't need a...coffee," she snapped impatiently, stumbling over her last word. Without opening her eyes, she waved a dismissive hand at them.

"I'm not an assistant," Bridget replied through clenched teeth. At her words, the blonde perked up and stared at her with annoyance. The girl's brown eyes moved from Bridget and the photograph sitting on Cade's desk.

"You're the lover," Cassia concluded. Her lips turned up at the corners in an amused smile.

Bridget's nostrils flared at her choice of words. "And who the hell are you?"

"I'm his sister," Cassia replied hostilely. She slowly dragged her feet off the desk and stood up. Once the words were said, Bridget immediately saw the resemblance. Cassia and Cade had the same eyes and the same high cheekbones.

"The twin," Bridget said. She gazed around the room for any sign of Cade but found none. She fought the urge to check her phone.

Cassia stopped in surprise. "He's told you about me," she said. Her eyes moved to Nylah. "And who's this?"

"My sister," Bridget replied, moving slightly to block her view of Nylah. Cassia didn't miss the gesture. She saw a flash of hesitation run through the blonde's eyes.

"What do you know?" Cassia asked curiously.

"Enough," Bridget snapped. Her heart pounded in her chest. Where the hell was Cade?

"I doubt that," Cassia snorted. She threw her hands up in the air and glanced around the room. "If you were hoping to find him, he's not here."

"I have eyes."

The blonde's eyes narrowed. "Do you know where he is?"

"Yes," Bridget lied. She felt Nylah pull on her coat sleeve, but she ignored her.

"Take me to him," Cassia ordered. She was now inches from her. Almost the same height, they stood toe to toe. Realizing Cassia didn't know Cade's location, Bridget formulated a plan in her head. Grand Central Station was always a nightmare on Christmas Eve. First, she would lead the blonde to the busy terminal and lose her in the crowd. After that, Bridget hoped she would have enough time to find Cade and get to the airport. The plan didn't mean she had to play nice, though; his sister's haughty demeanor was getting on her nerves.

"Have you ever heard of the word 'please'?"

Flames danced behind Cassia's eyes. "Please," she hissed angrily through a curled upper lip.

Bridget smirked and opened the office door for Cassia. The blonde turned up her nose and strode past her. There were no words of gratitude. Nylah gazed up at Bridget with confusion. Bridget raised a finger to her lips in a shushing motion and silently mouthed that she had a plan.

The three girls rode the elevator in tense silence. After a few minutes, they were out of the Bardot building and on the icy Manhattan sidewalk. Cassia gazed at her expectantly. Bridget moved to lead her to the subway, but the sight of a man stopped her. The same one from the diner, just a block away from them now. She recognized the coat and hat. The man leaned against a brick building and watched them closely.

Bridget turned to Cassia, accusation on her tongue, but the blonde followed her stare with a clueless, furrowed brow. There was no recognition in her brown eyes. Adrenaline buzzed under Bridget's skin. She had to find Cade and get Nylah somewhere safe. Two people now stood in her way. Bridget reached into her purse and fingered a key ring. A reckless idea formed in her head. Even though she didn't have a license, Cade had given her a spare car key for emergencies. Without a doubt, she knew her current situation fit the bill. She could lose the creep in the car and drop Cassia off at a random location. She would figure out how to get her out of the vehicle when the time came.

"I've got a better idea," Bridget said. She pulled out her keys and waved them at Cade's parked car. Nylah's eyes widened in horror. The young girl followed Bridget to the car and pulled on her hand.

"What are you doing?" Nylah whispered incredulously.

"Trust me."

Cassia approached the vehicle warily. She stopped a foot away and acted afraid to come any closer. Bridget sighed and leaned against the driver's side door. She donned a fake grin and hoped it hid her nervousness.

"Are you going to get in?"

Cassia opened the passenger door and skeptically studied the interior. "This will take us to Cade?"

Bridget forced herself to keep a fake smile on her face. "Yes."

With a deep breath, Cassia awkwardly climbed inside the car. After a bit of maneuvering, she finally sat down. She tucked her hands underneath her thighs and sat still as a statue. It was one of the strangest things Bridget had ever seen.

Nylah tapped on Cassia's shoulder from the backseat. "Seatbelt," she quipped as she buckled her own in one quick snap.

Cassia glared but mimicked the action. "I'm not a child."

"Could've fooled me," Bridget mumbled under her breath. Now that she was sitting in the driver's seat, she regretted her decision. Her hands shook as she pressed the start button. Bridget glanced at her phone, hoping there was a message from Cade telling her to stop, but the screen was blank. Suppressing a frustrated groan, she looked up. In the rearview mirror, she saw the creepy man striding toward the car. There was no time to second guess. On a whim, Bridget typed in Newark on her phone's GPS and handed the device to Nylah. Heart pounding, she eased out of Cade's parking spot and slowly started driving down the narrow Manhattan street. Even though the car moved at a snail's pace, Cassia hastily grabbed the door handle.

"Have you never been in a car before?" Nylah asked, skeptically eyeing Cassia's white knuckles.

"Of course, I have," Cassia argued. She whipped her hand off the door and crossed her arms. A tense silence enveloped the car. They were almost to the Holland Tunnel when holiday traffic brought them to a standstill. Cassia groaned and banged her head against the seat.

"How long is this going to take?" Cassia asked.

Nylah waved the phone in the air. "GPS says thirty minutes."

"Are you kidding me?" Cassia grumbled. "I don't have time for this."

Bridget's hands ached from her tight grip on the steering wheel. The complaint didn't help her unstable control of the violent emotions that warred inside her. She pursed her lips together and glared at the blonde beside her. "What are you even doing here?"

Cassia scoffed, "That's none of your business."

"It *is* my business," Bridget hissed. Then, finally, traffic started to move. The car went dark as they entered the tunnel.

Cassia rolled her eyes. "I think you're overestimating your importance in the grand scheme of things."

Bridget was tempted to throw her out of the moving vehicle. "You don't even know me."

Cassia let out a long, hollow laugh. "Do you think you're in love? You know nothing about Cade or who he really is."

Anger turned Bridget's vision red. "Wanna bet?"

There was a long pause. "Seriously, what do you know?"

A blue car weaving in and out of traffic caught Bridget's eye in the rearview mirror. The familiarity of the driver sent her stomach swooping to the floor. "Shut up," she whispered, still not quite believing the sight behind her.

"Excuse me?" Cassia sneered.

"Shut up," Bridget shouted. "I think someone is following us."

Bridget took a random exit as they exited the tunnel. The ramp sent them onto a new highway going south. She tried to speed up, but the car slid slightly on a hidden layer of ice.

"Nylah, did he take the exit?" Bridget asked nervously, hoping her mind was playing tricks on her. She hadn't counted on the man having access to a car.

"Yes."

"Shit," Bridget muttered. Panic buzzed through her veins. Why the hell had she thought she'd be able to pull this off? She tried to speed up again, but the steering wheel shook in protest.

"Do something!" Cassia yelled. She was turned around in her seat, trying to get a better look at the driver.

"I'm trying," Bridget argued. The ice and holiday traffic were making it impossible to switch lanes. Not that Bridget knew how.

"Can't this machine go any faster?" Cassia bellowed.

Bridget would have sent her a nasty look if she hadn't been too afraid to take her eyes off the road. "There are laws."

"It's because she doesn't have a license," Nylah explained matter-of-factly.

Cassia's eyes moved frantically between the two sisters. "What does that mean?"

Nylah sent her an unbelieving stare. "She doesn't know how to drive."

"Are you insane?" Cassia shrieked, grabbing onto the seat. "Pull over! Let me out of this death trap."

"We're on a highway," Bridget seethed. New York was one of the most walkable cities in the world. It wasn't her fault she never got a license. The sound of the phone ringing made all three girls jump.

"Bridget, it's Cade," Nylah exclaimed.

"It's about damn time," Bridget sighed and closed her eyes briefly. She wanted to be angry, but all she felt was relief coursing through her. If he was calling, that meant he was safe. When Nylah tried to hand her the phone, Bridget swatted it away with her shoulder. There was no way she could talk and drive at the same time. "I can't. You answer."

"Where have you been?" Nylah shouted into the phone. "We're literally in a bad Vin Diesel movie right now."

"You lied," Cassia concluded, glaring at her. "Where the hell are we going then?"

"Newark."

"New what?"

The blue car changed lanes. He was now only one car behind them.

"He's catching up to us," Nylah screeched. At that, the young girl cringed at the loud voice coming from the other end of the phone. "She can't talk. She's driving." There was a short pause. "Why are you getting mad at me? I told her it was a stupid plan."

Bridget glared at her sister through the rearview mirror. She had done no such thing. Suddenly, Cassia pulled on her arm.

"Pull over," the blonde demanded.

Bridget tried to elbow her off, but Cassia grabbed the steering and pulled hard. The car's back end hooked to the right. Instinctually, Bridget slammed on the brake. The action sent the car flying through the air. Her world became a blur of tosses, turns, and crunching metal. Eventually, the chaos stopped. Bridget could feel herself hanging upside down. Ears ringing, she tried to survey the damage through blurry eyes. Everything hurt, and she could feel blood dripping from a cut on her forehead.

"Nylah," she croaked. No response came from the back seat. Bridget tried to undo her seatbelt, but it was stuck. Beside her, Cassia swung forward and tried to grab something from her boot.

"Why the hell did you do that?" Bridget roared. She twisted her body enough to see Nylah in the back. The young girl hung limply from her seatbelt. Bridget called her name again, hoping it would cause her to stir, but Nylah didn't respond. To the right, a flash of silver caught her eye. Large blade in hand, Cassia cut herself out of her seatbelt. She plopped to the ground with a hard thud. Glass crunched as Cassia maneuvered herself to the back seat.

"Is she okay?" Bridget asked, but Cassia ignored her as she cut Nylah from her binds. She caught the girl and dragged her toward the shattered window. Bridget pulled on her seatbelt again, but it would not come loose.

"Is that who was following us?" Cassia suddenly asked, eyes on a figure approaching the vehicle. Her face went pale.

Bridget turned and saw the man from the diner walking toward them. "Do you know him?"

"Where's Cade?" Cassia asked.

"I don't know," Bridget replied angrily, wondering why Cassia hadn't cut her seatbelt yet. The man was getting closer. She spotted her phone on the roof and grabbed it. The front was shattered. "Shit, I can't see my screen."

Cassia ripped the device from her hand and began to drag Nylah out the window. Seconds later, she grabbed a stray pen from Cade's center console. After pulling a small piece of paper out of her pocket, she began to scribble something.

"What are you doing?" Bridget bellowed, horror overwhelming her. Cassia was going to take Nylah and leave her here. She ripped the paper out of Cassia's hands. Barely glancing at the words, she stuffed the scrap in her pant pocket.

"He's a Warlock," Cassia said, throwing a small pouch at her. "This might help."

Bridget stared at her. "What does that even mean?" She flailed her body, trying anything to move. Swinging her arms out, she tried to grab Cassia. "You can't take her," Bridget shouted fiercely. "She needs a doctor."

"I'm sorry," Cassia whispered. For a second, Bridget thought she saw genuine remorse cross her face, but Cassia heaved Nylah over her shoulder and took off down the street.

Bridget screamed at her retreating figure, so hard and intense it felt like her throat was being stabbed. Her chest throbbed painfully. Cassia had taken her sister. She didn't even know if she was okay. Tears spattered Bridget's nose and the roof of the car. A loud bang sent her heart into a frenzy. The man was attempting to open the crushed car door. Bridget grabbed the pouch from Cassia and stuffed it in her other pocket.

Light blinded her as the door wrenched open. Bridget tried to punch him, but he flashed a small pocketknife at her. She watched in terror and confusion as he cut her free from the seatbelt. Once she hit the ground, she tried to dart past him, but the man grabbed her by the hair and heaved her up.

"We don't have much time," he said, dragging her thrashing body toward a car. "I need you to agree to cross the gate."

"I'm not going anywhere with you, psycho," Bridget shouted, having no idea what he was talking about. Did he mean an airport gate? She tried to reach up and scratch his face but to no avail. Onlookers gasped and held up their phones as they recorded the pair. Bridget wanted to yell at them and call them cowards for not helping her. Faintly, she heard the sound of sirens coming closer.

"That's not very nice," he chastised when she tried to scratch him again. He held down her arms. "All you need to do is say yes."

"Take me to Cade, and then I'll agree," Bridget bargained and hoped he would take the bait. Cade would protect her and probably take down the psycho in one punch.

The man paused. "I guarantee that if you cross the gate, he will come for you."

"What the fuck are you talking about? Do you mean the airport?"

He said nothing. Airports meant crowds. There was no way he'd be able to drag her to one of the gates without causing attention. She could lose him there, find the police, and call Cade. "Fine. I'll go."

"I need a yes."

"Yes," she hissed. The man opened the car door and stuffed her in the back. Then, before she could crawl out the other side, he blew a powder in her face. Bridget sneezed once before passing out.

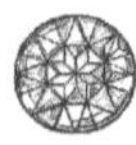

Darkness surrounded her. Woozily, Bridget reached up and tugged on the blindfold on her face. The action was difficult. Her hands were tied together. From the feel of the leather touching her face, she deduced she was in a car. Somewhere in front of her, a door slammed.

"Where have you been?" A voice asked impatiently.

"It took me some time to lose the cops," the man said. "Are you sure he doesn't have any powers here? I swear I feel a tickling in my head."

"You're being paranoid."

Bridget tugged on the blindfold again. Finally, she managed to move it slightly above one eyelid. Shadowy trees and stones loomed around the car. Dim light peeked through the clouds, so she guessed it was dawn. Terror enveloped her as she thought about Cade and Nylah. She wondered if Cassia had found him and hoped Nylah was alright. Behind her, the rear window was foggy. She could barely distinguish the man from the diner and a small woman with a cloak wrapped around her head through the haze.

"Did she agree?" The woman asked.

"Yes."

The woman nodded and dragged a body toward a large stone. A circle of torches gave the rock an eerie glow. Each flame burned brighter when the woman started speaking. After a minute, Bridget could have sworn the stone began to vibrate. Her kidnapper visibly stiffened at the sight of the body.

"Who's that?"

"Why do you care?" The woman chuckled before raising a large knife in the air. Bridget screamed as she watched her plunge the blade into the body's chest. Simultaneously, the man and woman whipped their heads around.

"Somebody's awake. Bring her over here. It's time," the woman ordered.

Bridget scrambled for the door and hastily pulled on the latch. The man grabbed her ankle before she could escape. Despite her kicks to his face, he managed to wrap his arm around her middle and pull her out of the car. In another language, the old woman spoke again. Seconds later, she swiped a finger on the soaked knife and used the blood to draw symbols on the stone. Trying not to gag, Bridget reached into her pocket for the tiny bag hidden there. As she lifted it, the man pulled it out of her hand easily. He raised a brow at her before tossing it aside. The closer they got to the stone, the harder Bridget kicked and screeched. She flinched when the stone began to glow and buzz. The noise reverberated through her bones. Instinct urged her to run. *Nothing good,* her soul screamed. Touching it would bring nothing good.

"Don't worry," the woman cooed, "soon, you won't even remember your own name."

Bridget screamed louder. Inches away from the stone, dread filled her veins. She thought of Nylah and her contagious laughter. She thought of Cade. She couldn't remember the last thing she said to him. Couldn't remember if she had kissed him goodbye that morning.

Couldn't remember—

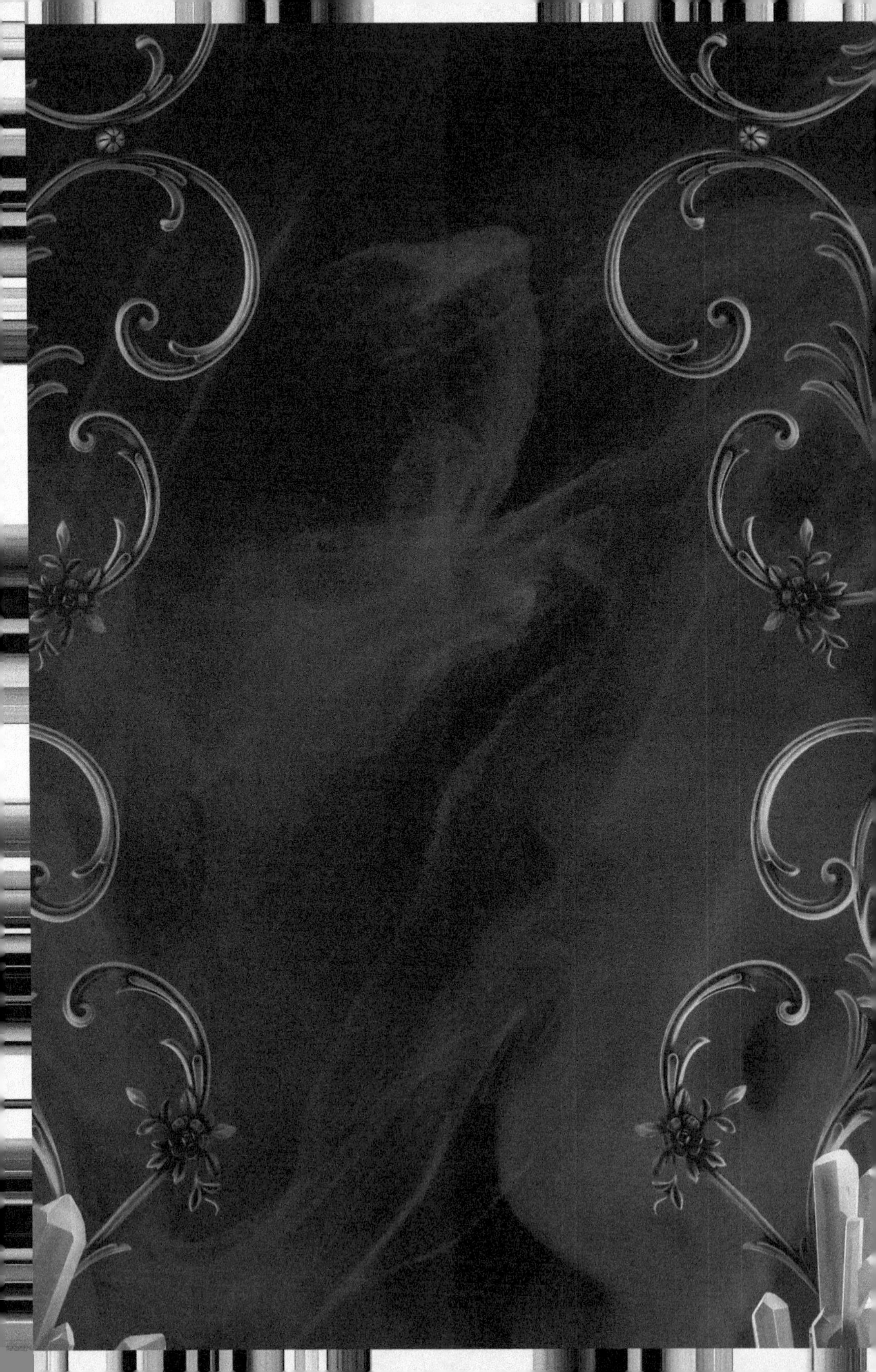

Now

CHAPTER
TWENTY-FIVE

Bridget Adams opened her eyes.

Above her, Cade's face radiated distress and concern. He reached out his hand, but Bridget swatted it away. She frantically twisted around him. There was only one person she wanted to see. Sitting up, she narrowed her eyes at Cassia's pale, retreating figure in the corner. Then, without thinking, Bridget flung herself off the bed and sprung at her.

"Where the hell is she, you bitch?" Bridget screamed violently. Just before her fists could make contact, arms wrapped around her waist and pulled her backward. Bridget thrashed and waved her hands wildly in the air, determined to make Cassia bleed. She snarled when Castor stepped in front of a wide-eyed, frozen Cassia, blocking her view.

"Where is she?" Bridget howled. If anything had happened to Nylah, Cassia was dead.

"She's fine. Nylah's fine. I promise," Cade whispered in her ear.

He repeated the words, again and again, until she understood. When the roaring in her ears finally subsided, Bridget closed her eyes and took a breath.

Nylah was safe. Nylah was okay.

But she was not.

Bridget fell to her knees.

Seven months.

She'd been in Vassuryn and Elyria for *seven* months. She'd been tortured, branded, and hunted in a world that was not her own. She'd seen death, up close, *caused* death, and been separated from the two people she cared about most.

And one of those people had become entirely different in her head.

A prince.

A Fae Prince.

Daring to look up, she found everyone gazing at her warily. From the beginning, they had all known who she was. Anger, betrayal, and devastation warred inside her. What must they think of her? After a moment, she realized Cade was on his knees beside her. She stared at him and tried to fit the two parts of him she knew together. As the new version of him molded in her head, hysteria bubbled up inside her. A giggle escaped her lips.

Delphine and Finn turned to Cade with furrowed brows.

Cade was a *prince*. Everyone in the room had a magical ability, except for her. She had been forced to enter a tournament to compete to marry her own boyfriend. And if she wanted to go home, she would lose her memories again.

Laughter exploded from her chest. She couldn't stop it. The longer it went on, the more her abdomen clenched painfully, the more her body shook uncontrollably.

If she had not lived the past seven months as she had, she would have believed it all to be a dream.

"Why is she laughing?" Finn whispered.

Delphine reached out a hand and said, "I think she's in shock."

Cade motioned for her to step back. "Give her some space."

Bridget's chest heaved. Without warning, hysteria turned to sorrow. She clasped Cade's arm tightly. Two versions of herself now existed. And both wanted him. As two lives replayed in her head, his presence was the only thing that connected them. A real, constant anchor she could tangibly grasp to steady herself. She knew, no matter what, she was safe with him. But she was angry. So angry that she could hardly stand to look at him. She couldn't help but think that if he had been honest with her from the beginning, maybe things would have been different. That together, they could have prevented her from ending up in Elyria lost, scarred, and without her sister. A place where nightmares were a reality.

A place where she would be forced to lose herself again.

Tears blurred her vision.

Faintly, she heard a door close. Bridget's head darted up. The room was empty now, except for Cade. He reached up and wiped away the tears escaping her eyes. His touch brought comfort, and a harsh reminder that yesterday, he had refused to tell her the truth. She flinched away from him. Even though she didn't think it was possible, her heart ached even more at the pain that slashed across his face.

Time. She needed time.

"I thought your family was in the mob," Bridget laughed, sounding choked, "or assassins. Or in some creepy cult."

Elyria was the last thing she imagined.

"I'm sorry," Cade said, voice low and full of pain.

A memory sparked inside her. Bridget turned to face him.

"It was you that night," she said. He had spoken the exact words to her through the mouth of a Shaman. She should have known it had been him with Finn in front of the gate, taking over the Shaman for a brief moment to stop her from going through.

Cade nodded. "My father was trying to prove how easy it was to get to you. I think he was the one influencing you to keep your necklace off too."

Her vision of the gate had not been a dream, but a trap. And she fell for it without hesitation.

"And in Vassuryn," Bridget said, realization dawning on her. In her head, she replayed the night the Virgo coven was attacked. With her memories, she would have recognized the hooded rider in an instant. She knew his body and movements as much as her own. Bridget's stomach twisted as Cade's words that day before came back to her.

He hadn't been hunting Witches.

He had been hunting *her*.

Cora had constantly moved the coven to keep Cade from finding them, finding *her*, not because there was a more significant threat. And the

Witch had succeeded until an accident caused Bridget to take off her necklace. Her headache and nosebleed hadn't been from a fall, but by Cade. He'd been inside her head, trying to find her. And he did.

Until she stabbed him.

"I almost killed you," Bridget breathed, horror-struck.

Cade shook his head. Lips tilting up slightly, he said, "You didn't know. I wasn't expecting a knife, but I was impressed with your aim."

Bridget closed her eyes. The softness in his voice killed her. Cade had been inches from her, and still, Cora had claimed her. Bridget refused to let herself blame her lack of memories. She should've realized she was being manipulated, that the constant moving and hiding wasn't normal. She should have done something more to get away. If she had, her and Cade might not be stuck in the tournament.

"It was you in the forest too. During the first task," Bridget murmured, rubbing her eyes.

Trees couldn't talk. Cade had been helping her, even then.

"Why didn't you tell me?" Bridget asked. She wanted the words to sound harsh, but she couldn't find the strength in her heart, especially when he was already looking at her with such guilt and anguish.

"My father threatened to kill you, and then he promised that if I stayed away, he would let you cross the gate at the end of the tournament. He knew that was my plan all along. Find you and send you back."

Bridget's throat tightened as tiny puzzle pieces fell into place: Cade's initial aversion to her, the sneaking around, the way Cora knew she would be able to get the location of the second gate from him. Somehow, the Witch had known who she was. She was certain. Cora never did anything out of the goodness of her heart. Still, Cora hadn't been the one to originally kidnap her.

"Where were you?" Bridget asked hoarsely.

Cade knew what she meant without asking. "My father didn't trust Cassia to get me back. He sent a group of soldiers behind her through the gate. I spent the day trying to outrun them. When I finally did, it was too late."

Tears continued to flow down Bridget's face. She wished she could go back in time and start that day over. She wished they had decided to run earlier. She wished she had known everything from the beginning.

"I never stopped looking for you," Cade said fiercely. He grabbed her face and caressed his fingers over her hair. "I know you probably wish you'd never met me, but you have to know that. *Believe* that. Every second of those seven months, I was searching. Following every whisper, every thought. I never would have given up."

"I know you did," Bridget croaked. The intensity of his words and the fire in his stare made her crumble. "What happened to Nylah?"

"After the call got cut off, I panicked. I went back to our apartment to find Finn. We searched for hours. Eventually, the police tracked me down. The accident had caused quite a stir on the news. They wanted answers, and eventually, they showed me the footage." Cade's throat bobbed. "I knew then where you were headed."

"It was around dawn when I crossed, I think," Bridget mused as she recounted the events. She recoiled, remembering the body, the knife, and all the blood. She hadn't even seen the face of the person who'd been sacrificed to open the gate.

"Around that time, I found Cassia sitting outside the apartment door with Nylah. They were bruised up, but fine," Cade seethed, "I wanted to kill her for what she'd done, for leaving you like that, but Cassia claimed she knew who took you."

Bridget's eyes snapped to his in surprise. "She knew?"

"Not exactly. She had caught a glimpse of the man's coven tattoo. The Gemini," Cade said. Bridget's stomach dropped. The coven he admitted to killing. A coven she didn't even remember knowing. Somehow, after her arrival, Cora had become her captor. And given her the rune to keep Cade from finding her.

"After that, I took Nylah to the hospital and made sure nothing was broken. Castor checked on her two months ago. He said she was still living with Brenda."

"That's what he was talking about the other day," Bridget said, relief coursing through her. As long as Nylah was safe and far away from Elyria, a small sliver of happiness could reside in her heart. After a pause, Bridget asked, "Where does she think I am?"

A look of trepidation crossed Cade's face.

"You told her?" Bridget sputtered.

"How else was I supposed to explain you suddenly disappearing? Actually, she took it really well."

"Of course, she did. She's ten," Bridget fumed, "she thinks Hogwarts is real."

Bridget pursed her lips as a wave of nausea rolled through her abdomen. She'd been gone almost eight months. Nylah would be eleven now.

"I didn't know what else to do, Bridget. You were missing, and I was going crazy. I was desperate to get back here and find you, but I knew you would want her safe first."

The words hit her like a ton of bricks. Him taking care of Nylah probably set him back hours and guaranteed Cora finding her before him. "You're right. No matter what happened to me, I'm glad you took care of her. If you hadn't, I don't think I'd be able to forgive you," Bridget took a deep breath, before daring to look up at him, "I would be lying if I said just looking at you didn't hurt right now. Do I know everything now?"

Cade grasped her hands tightly. His deep, golden-brown eyes were steady and clear. "Yes, I swear. Yes."

Bridget took the truth in his words and applied it to every broken crevice in her chest.

"I spent so many nights coming up with elaborate reasons for why I ended up in Elyria," Bridget admitted softly, "Never in my wildest dreams did I think it was my own fault. Even if I didn't know what it meant, I agreed to cross the gate. I said yes."

"This is not your fault. It's mine. I should've told you everything. If I had, things might've been different."

Bridget shook her head. "I'm not sure I would have believed you."

She knew she still wouldn't if she hadn't already seen it with her own eyes and lived through the pain of Cora molding her. Even though she didn't want to admit it, being forced into Elyria was perhaps the only way she ever would have believed.

"I did this to you. I couldn't let you go, even when I knew should. You have every right to hate me," Cade said brokenly.

"Cade…" Bridget said, not knowing how to explain that no matter what happened, she could never hate him. The thought alone sent her heart twisting.

"And what I'm about to say is probably the most selfish thing I could say at this moment and probably the last thing you want to hear," Cade said. He sat down beside her and gently grabbed her cheek.

"I love you."

Bridget's heart stopped. Deep down, she always knew, but the words had never been said between them. In a way, the three simple words didn't seem like enough, at least to her. Before, she would have been elated to hear Cade's confession. Now, when she knew what was to come, the words felt both like a gift and a curse.

"I love you," Cade repeated with a small smile. "Every day for the last seven months, I've regretted not saying it to you earlier, and that you crossed the gate without knowing. That you suffered because of me without knowing."

Devastation crossed his face. He took a deep breath and continued.

"I think I've loved you since the first moment I saw you."

Bridget let out a short, hard laugh, trying to ignore the water pooling in her eyes. "When I harassed you and then stole your wallet?"

"Before that."

"What are you talking about?"

"A few months before we met, I saw you," Cade confessed quietly. "I know now it was the day you lost your first custody appeal for Nylah."

All Bridget could do stare at him in shock. He had never said…

"I was walking around on my lunch break, debating whether or not it was time to go back to Elyria," Cade said, his brown eyes glazed over. "It had been almost two years. I knew it was only a matter of time before my father would come after me, and I wanted to return on my terms. Then I saw you. You were crouched outside the courthouse, saying goodbye to Nylah, when a guy in a suit snapped at you to hurry up. You glared at him, but let Nylah go. You looked so devastated."

Bridget's heart crumbled at the memory. Hearing that she had not been granted custody of Nylah had been the worst news of her life. She had never felt more hopeless or alone. She couldn't believe Cade had been there.

"I was about to go over there, but you suddenly fell on the steps. The lawyer helped you up. After he walked away, you had the biggest smile on your face. I was confused, but then I saw it in your hand. His wallet," Cade grinned, but it did not quite reach his eyes. "I laughed, harder than I had in months. You were gone before I crossed the street. I kept coming back to that area, hoping to see you. I told myself I only wanted to meet you, just once. After a few weeks, I noticed a diner nearby."

Bridget stilled, heart pounding erratically in her chest. There was only one diner he could be talking about.

"The bottom floor had a perfect view of the courthouse," Cade mused humorously, reading her thoughts. "I would sit in there and hope to catch a glimpse of you. After a few months, I convinced myself it was hopeless. I called Castor and told him I would cross the gate with him in September. Imagine my surprise when..."

"I was upstairs the entire time," Bridget finished hoarsely. More tears streamed down her face. They could've had so much more time together.

"I couldn't stay away. I kept coming back," Cade remarked sadly. "So you see, if anyone is to blame for what has happened to you, it's me."

Bridget couldn't, though; their meeting felt inevitable. In the diner, she'd been drawn to him also. She'd been the one to push for more. Her hands shook. Even after everything, she wouldn't change a thing. She would choose him—every time. She opened her mouth to tell him so, but the words got caught in her throat. Held back by the anger and fear still flowing through her veins. Held back by reality. There was another person she would choose. And when she did, she would lose him again. Perhaps forever.

She leaned forward and kissed him softly. She hoped it said enough.

After a long moment, she pulled away and took a deep breath. "I remember who took me. It was Archer."

"What?"

"Archer, the Warlock from the market, was the one who took me," Bridget said. "He got me to agree to cross and then blew a powder in my face. It knocked me out. Before I knew it, I was in front of this massive stone. A woman was there. She was old, but there was something familiar about her. She killed someone and performed blood magic."

A myriad of emotions washed over Cade's face. Rage seemed to be taking over. "Only a powerful Witch could use blood magic to cross."

"I don't remember much after that. I only knew my name because of a note I found in my pocket."

"A note?"

"Cassia. I think she tried to write about you, but I ripped it from her hand before she could. It was destroyed in the lake. And then I don't know how I went from Archer to Cora," Bridget pondered. "But I do remember pain and incantations. I think they were using blood magic to find something in my dormant memories. Either the curse was too strong, or I never knew the object in the first place."

"I found the Gemini coven within days of arriving," Cade growled, glancing down at her gloved hands. "There was blood everywhere. I knew you had been there because I found your jacket. You know the rest of the story."

"My hands came later," Bridget said, following his gaze. She leaned her head against the stone wall behind her and murmured, "Deep down, I think I always knew you were out there. I never submitted to Cora, not in the way she wanted. I tried to escape so many times. When I defied her, she would punish me."

Nausea washed over her as she decided to show him. Swallowing hard, she reached for the glove on her left hand. Bridget's whole body shook as she pulled it off. Webbed scarring covered the back of her hand.

"After I tried to escape the first time, Cora branded me with the Virgo mark. One night, I had this vivid dream of a colorful restaurant. Without thinking, I stuck my hand in the closest fire and tried to burn the mark off. It worked."

Bridget slowly took off her right glove. "The next day, Cora cut the Virgo mark into my right hand. After that, I knew she would continue until there was no more open flesh. I stopped trying to get rid of it after that. I wear the gloves because I don't want the reminder that I belong to her. At least, I think that's what she was trying to prove. I hate to look at it."

Cade seemed to be shaking too. Briefly, he ran his fingertips over the empty knuckle on her right ring finger. The loss of her mother's ring cut to her soul. She didn't remember losing it, but she could picture it buried deep in some forest in Vassuryn, lost forever. Suddenly, every object in the room began to vibrate and shift. Bridget turned and found his eyes bright white. She placed a hand on his arm. Within seconds, the glow faded, and the room stilled.

"Where is she?" He hissed.

"I don't know."

"Don't protect her."

"I'm not. I don't know where she is," Bridget argued weakly. She hated that a part of her didn't want to watch Cora die.

The room swayed as the weight of seven long months hit her. With each breath, weakness overwhelmed her as her two lives struggled to merge. She wondered how long it would take her to feel normal again. "I'm so tired, Cade."

Cade stroked her cheek. "I know."

"I have to go back," Bridget croaked. No matter how much she wanted to be with Cade, she couldn't leave Nylah alone. By the way he flinched, she could tell Cade expected and dreaded the statement.

"I know," he repeated.

Needing to regain her composure, she asked, "Can I please have a minute alone?"

Pain flitted across his face, but he nodded and stood up. Once he was gone from the room, the dam that had been holding back her emotions broke. Cries exploded from her chest.

Bridget closed her eyes and sobbed for all she had lost and would continue to lose.

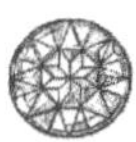

She didn't know how much time had passed when she managed to pick herself off the floor. Bridget didn't recognize the room she was in and hoped she was near a familiar hall. Eyes puffy, she stumbled to the door. When she wrenched it open, she found Cade, Finn, and Delphine sitting on the floor.

"It's late," she said, a little shocked, "you didn't have to wait."

Delphine hopped up and grabbed her arm. "Are you okay?"

"I just needed some time to process…everything."

"Don't worry, we'll find Archer before morning. Castor already started searching. His locator spells are hard to beat," Finn said.

Cade heaved himself off the ground. He looked as tired as she felt, and his voice was hollow as he said, "You need to sleep."

"He's right. It was a big spell," Delphine said. "Your brain needs to heal. I can take you back."

Bridget's eyes darted to Cade. Part of her wanted to stay with him, but Delphine grabbed her hand and transported them back to the apartments before she could protest. Once they arrived, Bridget caught herself against the hallway wall. The magic didn't feel as harsh the third time, but dizziness radiated through her. Delphine gazed at her apologetically.

"I'm sorry."

"It's not your fault. Doing that always makes me dizzy. At least this time it didn't hurt too bad."

"No, not that…I'm sorry for lying to you," Delphine said. "From the beginning, I told him to tell you. I didn't think it was right, especially when he kept asking me to watch and help you. I don't know if he told you that."

Bridget stiffened. "I know you're very loyal to him. You don't have to apologize."

Delphine grabbed her arm. "No, I do. No matter what he thought was best, I should have told you. Maybe if I had, you wouldn't have risked your life and taken that potion. I don't care who you are to him. You're my friend, even if you don't forgive me."

Biting on the inside of her cheek, Bridget said, "Even if you had, I would have taken the potion. It was inevitable. There's nothing to forgive."

Before she could blink, Delphine enveloped her in a tight hug. Bridget's vision became blurry as she thought of the last person to hug her similarly. Scarlett. The two girls were vastly different, but both held special places in her heart.

"Thank you," Bridget whispered. She hoped Delphine knew it was for more than the apology.

Inside her room, the once cozy space felt large and empty. With every movement, her skin crawled harshly against the cold air. Even though she knew it had been seven months, the memory of waking up in the West Village felt fresh. Bridget took a bath and tried to sleep, but the aching in her chest wouldn't subside.

Eventually, she tip-toed to Delphine's room and knocked on the door.

Her friend looked alarmed at the sight of her. "Is everything okay?"

"I'm sorry," Bridget mumbled guiltily, "but will you take me back to Cade's room?"

Delphine blinked a few times before nodding. "Of course."

Seconds later, they stood in front of Cade's door. Blood trickled from Delphine's ears. Bridget doubled over and took several moments to catch her breath. Her stomach clenched painfully.

"Goodnight, Bridget," Delphine said before disappearing in a quick snap.

Long after she was gone, Bridget stared at Cade's door, nerves quaking in her abdomen. She didn't know why. She'd been alone with Cade plenty of times before, even in Elyria, but things felt different. *She* felt different. Just as she had gathered enough nerve to knock, the door swung open. Bridget jumped when Cade almost ran into her.

When he saw it was her, he alertly eyed the hallway around her. After a moment, he pulled her inside the room. "What's wrong?"

Her cheeks heated involuntarily. "I just...my room felt empty. Before I knew what I was doing, I asked Delphine to bring me back, but if you were going somewhere..."

Before she could finish her rambling, Cade interjected, "I was actually going to your room. I didn't want you to go to sleep without this."

He showed her his palm, where her amethyst necklace glistened in the firelight. She had forgotten he'd ripped it off after she'd taken the potion.

"May I?" he asked, undoing the clasp.

Wordlessly, she nodded and turned around. She shivered at the sensation of his rough fingertips gliding across the sensitive skin of her neck, and his breath on her ear sent her pulse skyrocketing as he slowly hooked the gold chain. After he had finished, his hands remained on her shoulders, where he traced the thin straps of her pajamas. Heat surged all the way to her toes.

Bridget stumbled forward, trying to create some distance between them before she jumped him right then and there. It's what she would've done seven months ago, back in their apartment.

But it had been *seven* months, and Bridget, the lost human from Vassuryn, was still figuring out how to be Bridget from Manhattan again.

"I should go..."

"Stay."

Their simultaneous statements contradicted each other.

Stay. It was the exact thing she was hoping and dreading he'd say. Because even though every inch of her wanted nothing more than to stay close to him, she needed time to meld herself into one whole person again. She finally *remembered*, though, and as she looked at him, longing from two lives swelled through her. For his eyes on her, his touch, the spicy scent that was so very Cade...The very longing that had sent her back to his room in the first place.

Bridget's stomach swooped. "I'll stay."

When he nodded, she thought he looked a little relieved. An awkward silence enveloped them as they walked over to the bed. Bridget stared at it, suddenly unsure if she could make herself lie down.

"I haven't been able to sleep in a bed since..." she admitted, then sighed, "actually, I haven't been able to sleep at all."

"We can go to the floor."

"No, I want to try," Bridget insisted. "Part of me still feels like I slept in our apartment last night."

Slowly, Bridget pulled back the comforter and crawled into the bed. Cade mimicked her movements. She rolled onto her side to face him. For a long moment, they stared at each other.

"I missed you," Bridget whispered. There had been a hole in her heart for the last seven months. But, as she looked at Cade, it started to fill. Emotion wracked her bones. She reached out and traced the new lines under his eyes. Her chest ached at the fact that she hadn't been the only one suffering.

"You're here," Cade said, a hint of wonderment in his voice, "I don't want to sleep but..."

Bridget nodded. "I understand."

Lying next to him, she finally felt peace. It was the last thing she expected to feel in Elyria. After her body relaxed, Bridget shimmied closer to him and rested her head on his chest. She reveled in his warmth, then realized she had forgotten an important question.

"What did you have to pay?"

Cade's lips brushed her forehead. "It doesn't matter now."

Too tired to argue, Bridget drifted to sleep.

CHAPTER TWENTY-SIX

Bridget woke up from her first dreamless sleep in seven months. Face down, she burrowed deeper into her pillow. The sensation of fingers lightly tracing her back made her shiver. Realizing Cade was examining the thin scars there, she stilled.

"Are these from Cora as well?" he asked, sensing she was awake.

"Yes," Bridget replied, remembering the night Cora had whipped her for sneaking away from the coven in the middle of the night. The wounds had taken months to heal and still burned if she strained her back muscles. Bridget turned over and pulled up her shirt. She pointed to a long scar on the right side of her stomach. "I think this is from blood magic."

Cade studied the mark for a long time. "Do you remember the incantations? Or what exactly they did?"

Bridget shook her head. His hand on the bare skin of her stomach left her breathless. When his fingers moved from drawing circles around the scar to further down, heat pooled in her belly. Face heating, Bridget cleared her throat and pulled her shirt down. Cade narrowed his eyes but pulled his hand away.

"Is this against the rules? Me being in your bedroom?"

"Probably," Cade shrugged, a small smirk on his face. "This

tournament is different, though. It hasn't followed any of the normal traditions."

"What do you mean?"

"First, there's not nearly enough girls. My father wanted to start the tournament the second you arrived, so I wouldn't have the chance to sneak you away in the middle of the night. And there's you. Apparently from Andarre. Everyone knows that's a lie, but they're too scared to confront my father about it."

"No wonder Alette is so angry all the time," Bridget mused. "Apparently, she trained for the tasks for years. She swears she's your perfect match."

"Good for her, but she's not who my father wants me to pick," Cade replied blithely.

"Me?" Bridget joked, but Cade didn't look amused. She sighed, "Marin."

"He's obsessed with keeping control over the gate and is convinced peace in Elyria is hanging on by a thread. Marin is the answer to our dwindling power, apparently," Cade grumbled. "He's let too many prophecies get to his head."

"Strangely enough, he's right," Bridget said. Cade sent her an incredulous look.

"It's why I'm here," she admitted. "Cora wants the location of the other gate. She was convinced you would tell me where it is."

"I would if I could. Why does she want to know?"

"Vassuryn's economy is in shambles. I think she also wants the Virgo coven to take over the others. She thinks the human realm will have more resources for them to use to their advantage."

Cade shook his head and pinched the bridge of his nose. "The human realm doesn't have what she needs."

"She thinks it does."

"That can't be what this is all about. Besides, she can't use the gate without a Shaman. Unless she knows blood magic."

"I've seen her do dark spells, but nothing like the woman in the forest did," Bridget said, shivering, but she was beginning to learn there were many things she didn't know about Cora.

"Whatever she did the night I found you was powerful enough to keep me contained. I was hurt, but that wasn't an ordinary spell. It doesn't make sense," Cade said. They went quiet as they contemplated.

"The coven's camp moved once a week. All along, it was to keep you from finding me... but what if you weren't the only person Cora was running from?"

Cade's eyes glazed over as he calculated the possibility. At some point in time, she had moved from Archer to Cora's custody. Bridget was starting to believe that Cora was never supposed to be her captor.

"Do you know how to find her?" Cade asked.

By the tone of his voice, Bridget could tell he didn't want a pleasant chat about her lovely time in Vassuryn.

"There was another human living with the Virgo coven. Alexia. She basically worships the ground Cora walks on," Bridget said, rolling her eyes. "I saw her at the market the other day. When I first arrived, Cora told me to take off my necklace every five days so she could contact me. I never did. Alexia said she's been watching me on the recordings."

Cade tensed. "A Witch shouldn't be able to do that."

Puzzled by the alarm in his voice, Bridget reached up to take off her necklace.

"Not now," Cade said, placing his hand over hers. "Later."

His fingers wrapped around her gloved palm. "You don't have to wear these, you know."

Bridget's throat constricted. She trusted him, but it would be a while before she felt comfortable showing anyone else the scars. Cade raised her arm and brushed his lips against the inside of her wrist. Heart racing, she watched him make a trail up to her elbow before he wrapped an arm around her waist and pulled her closer. Bridget leaned forward and was a hair's breadth away from his lips when a knock came from the door. When it opened, Cade closed his eyes and groaned.

Finn jumped back and whipped his hands over his eyes. "Please tell me you have clothes on," he sputtered.

"Unfortunately," Cade muttered. Bridget elbowed him in the ribs. Finn peeked through his fingers before shutting the door.

"We found Archer. We placed him in one of the old cells in the south wing. Castor is with him now."

Simultaneously, Bridget and Cade hopped out of bed. It wasn't until the cold stone hit the bottom of her feet that she remembered her pajamas and lack of shoes. Face reddening, Bridget tried to pull her thin shorts further down on her thighs.

"Has he said anything?" Cade asked.

"Nothing of importance. He won't shut up about being hungry."

Bridget suppressed a groan. She had a feeling getting a straight answer out of Archer wouldn't be easy. "I don't have any shoes. Or appropriate clothing for anything outside of this bedroom."

Cade and Finn shared a quick glance. The latter nodded and said, "I'll wait outside."

Once the door closed, Bridget asked, "What was that about?"

"Finn was around you in the human realm enough to know how stubborn you are about being self-sufficient," Cade replied with a wry grin as he led her toward a closet. "He thinks you're about to yell at me."

"Don't commoners get beheaded for that?"

Cade shot her an exasperated glare. "Don't tempt me. When you first arrived, Delphine noticed you didn't have clothes or money, so I had this delivered." He opened the closet and revealed rows of various pants and shirts. A few pairs of shoes were neatly lined up on the floor. "She's been helping me deliver whatever you needed."

Bridget eyed the clothes appreciatively. She was glad to finally know where the outfits had come from and that she had something to wear. In New York, she would've been angry. She hated it when Cade bought her things, especially if there was nothing equal she could give him in return. Now, her heart softened knowing that he had been trying to help her from her first day in the palace.

"I'm not mad. Being the only human in the competition has been hard enough. I can't imagine how much worse Alette would have been if I had been stuck in that stupid stained shirt and cape."

As she grabbed a new outfit, Bridget decided she was definitely burning the shirt from Cora the moment she returned to her room. Once she was dressed, Finn walked her to the south wing. Since Cade suspected the king had someone following him, he left a few minutes after them. The south wing was old and desolate. Instead of marble and dark gold fixtures, crumbling stones and vines lined the walls. Burning torches illuminated each damp, dark hallway, like an old, abandoned relic frozen in time.

"This wing was the original palace. About 300 years ago, the royal family wanted something more modern and started to build around it," Finn said.

"Why not take it down and start new somewhere else?"

"Places that have seen powerful magic are hard to destroy. Especially if they're made of stone," Finn's hand brushed the mossy wall. Tiny sparks flew up. "Magic is imbued in these walls."

Bridget mimicked his action but felt nothing on her fingertips. "Could it be channeled?"

"Theoretically, but only by someone very powerful. I doubt anyone but a Tuathan could, and they disappeared long ago." After a long pause, he asked, "So do you hold it against me?"

Bridget swallowed hard. The memory of Finn asking her to leave Cade flashed through her head. "No, I understand now why you tried to stop me. I should have listened. But…"

"You love him."

She went silent. The answer was probably written on her face, but it was a truth she couldn't afford to confirm or deny. Eventually, a narrow, winding staircase led them down to a sizable room with three separate barred enclosures. Inside, Castor leaned against the wall, arms crossed, a sour look on his face. Archer sat in the middle cell. A wide grin appeared on his face at the sight of her.

"I'm glad to see you're still in the land of the living," Archer remarked jovially.

Standing face-to-face with the person who dragged her through the gate, rage exploded inside Bridget. She poured every ounce of emotion coursing through her veins into the accusing glare she gave him. Archer's eyes widened in shock.

"It worked. You actually remember."

"Why do you look surprised?"

"Breaking curses isn't an easy business," Archer shrugged. He crept forward in the cell, intently studying her the entire way. "But it's not really broken, is it?" he concluded. His gaze shifted to someone behind her. "What did you pay?"

Bridget whipped around. Cade stood in the doorway. He glowered at Archer. She had never seen such hatred and rage in his eyes. For the first time, she saw the deadly prince he was always rumored to be.

Mouth going dry, she turned back to the smirking man in the cell and asked, "Why wait until now to try to kill me?"

"No one wants you dead," Archer said. "It was a test. And it looks like loverboy passed."

Cade stalked forward menacingly. "What the hell are you talking about?"

"It's not my plan," Archer replied, his hands up in the air. "I'm just the unwilling lackey."

"Unwilling?" Bridget scoffed. "You didn't hesitate to hand over a potion that should have killed me."

"I didn't hand it over. You stole it."

Bridget pursed her lips together in frustration. For a Warlock, he sure talked and picked his words carefully like a Fae.

Castor sighed wearily and joined her and Cade in front of the cell. "Who do you work for? Blood magic is dangerous for Warlock to get wrapped up in," he said. Bridget's ears perked at the accent she finally recognized. British.

"I'm going to need a nicer tone and some incentives," Archer quipped.

Finn growled from his position by the door. "The incentive is your life."

"You haven't been stuck with crazy pants for the last year," Archer countered sharply. "I need a guarantee she won't come after me."

Bridget furrowed her brows. "Cora?"

"I wish."

"If you didn't want to kill her, why try to give Bridget her memories back? A potion that strong is basically a death sentence to a human," Cade stated stormily.

"It wasn't about the memories. She wanted to see how far you would go to protect her," Archer paused. "And I think she was bored."

Castor pinched the bridge of his nose. "Who is she?"

Archer remained quiet.

"I was doing you a courtesy by asking in the first place," Cade murmured. "I can get inside your head and search for the answer any time I want. I promise it's relatively painless."

The grave tone of Cade's voice contradicted his words. Archer went pale and still. After a moment, he plastered a shaky grin on his face.

"I don't see any runes," he laughed. "Plus, she just got her memories back. I don't think you want to scare—"

Archer's eyes suddenly rolled back in his head. Screaming, he fell to the stone floor. Seconds later, dark red blood oozed from his eyes and ears. Bridget winced, unable to tear her eyes away from Cade's onslaught. He'd been in her head plenty of times, but it was never excruciating or unbearable, like it seemed to be for Archer. After a minute, Cade released him. Archer gasped for air and frantically clutched the metal bars in front of him. The Warlock's entire body visibly shook.

Cade's mouth fell open. "It's Quinn."

"The woman at the gate was old," Bridget argued.

Her heart didn't want to believe that one of her few friends in Elyria was the one behind so much suffering, but she'd long suspected the Witch was hiding something. Especially after the second task, when a black mark appeared on her skin.

"She uses a glamor spell," Archer sputtered hoarsely. "She's not from a Tuathan line. Blood magic takes a toll on her."

"What does she want?" Cade asked.

"I'm not entirely sure," Archer coughed, wiping blood from his face. When they all glared at him, he raised his hands defensively. "I swear. It's not like we've spent the past year singing kumbaya around a campfire and sharing life stories."

"Is kumbaya a real word?" Finn whispered to Castor.

"If you had to take a guess," Cade said. When he leaned forward, Archer flinched.

"She's after a stone. That's all I know."

"Witches can't draw power from stones, only elements," Castor refuted.

Cade rubbed the back of his neck and stared at the ceiling contemplatively. "I don't think she's after power. Could it be a curse?"

"What does a stone have to do with a curse?" Bridget asked.

"A Shaman, or Tuathan, needs two things to create a curse: an anchor and blood. You need both to break one, along with the original location where the curse was cast," Castor explained.

"Most people don't know or can find all three," Archer interjected, earning him a silencing glare from Cade.

Bridget pondered over the new knowledge. "So the anchor is usually a stone? Or a rune?"

"A powerful one. Like the obsidian in my father's dagger. Or my morganite pendant," Cade replied.

"I see that under your shirt now," Archer muttered.

"Knowing which stone she wants will help us understand what she's after. Since Shamans are few and far between, a new curse hasn't been created for years," Castor said, eyeing Archer.

"Like I said, I need incentives," Archer remarked casually, even though his hands still shook.

"Pathetic," Finn scoffed.

Archer narrowed his eyes. "Not all of us can afford to be honorable."

"You know nothing about me."

Cade stepped in front of Archer and blocked his view of Finn. "Enough with the bickering. What do you want?"

"I want out of this cell."

"I thought you wanted to be protected from Quinn," Bridget challenged dully. Her head was starting to ache from the continuous back and forth.

"Exactly. I'm a sitting duck here. She could come traipsing down the stairs at any second."

"This wing is abandoned," Finn replied through gritted teeth.

Archer let out a sharp laugh. "Is that supposed to make me feel better?"

"Let's go," Cade said. He grabbed Bridget's hand and pulled her toward the stairs. When they all stared at him in shock, he shrugged nonchalantly.

"We already have the advantage. Quinn doesn't know we're aware of her duplicity, and she's bound by blood to the palace. We'll watch and figure out what she's planning. We don't need him."

Castor rolled his lips together and looked like he wanted to argue; he cast one last hesitant glance at Archer and followed Finn to the door.

"You think it will be that easy?" Archer retorted humorously. When his statement was ignored, he gripped the bars of his cell. "You're playing with fire. She used to be an Aries, after all. Don't say I didn't warn you."

His voice echoed the entire way up the stairs. Bridget wondered how much truth was in his words. So far, Quinn had fooled them all. Who was to say she wasn't already anticipating them catching Archer?

"You're going to let him off that easily?" Finn asked heatedly, locking the wooden door to the cells.

"I was inside his head. He's desperate to get away from her," Cade said, leading the group out of the south wing. "He'll talk by tomorrow. Besides, there's only one thing she could be after."

Castor nodded. "The Bloodstone. It's the only Sanguis artifact that's here."

"That doesn't sound ominous at all," Bridget muttered under her breath.

"It still doesn't explain why Bridget's here. Why drag her into this?" Finn asked tensely.

The group went quiet. Bridget wasn't sure what Cade was thinking, but in her mind, there was only one answer. Leverage.

"Do we confront her?" she asked.

"Not yet. Whatever she's planning, she can't do it until the end of the tournament and the Bloodstone is well protected," Cade replied, squeezing her hand. "We can stop her before she even knows we're on to her."

Bridget clenched her jaw. "Quinn has been one step ahead this entire time. Are you sure feigning ignorance is a good idea?"

"I'll take over guard duty by the apartments and make sure she doesn't try anything else," Finn grunted reluctantly. "Besides, that gives me a good excuse to not have to watch the jabber mouth downstairs. Sorry Castor."

Castor glared at him.

When they reached the center courtyard, the glimmering gray and black tree Bridget once admired seemed dull and droopy.

Frowning, Bridget studied their drawn faces. "She brought the guns into Elyria, didn't she? She killed Ondine."

"Based on what I saw in his head, yes," Cade said. Bridget stopped him when they were a few paces behind Finn and Castor.

"Why didn't you ask him about the second gate?" she whispered. When Cade looked surprised by the question, she tried not to feel irritated that the thought hadn't even crossed his mind. Bridget opened her mouth to retort but was stopped by two guards entering the courtyard. Cade tensed and stepped away from her. At that same moment, her stomach growled loudly.

"Go eat something," Cade ordered, lips twisting in subdued amusement at the sound. "We'll talk more after that."

"But…"

When more guards appeared, Bridget knew she didn't have time to argue. Reluctantly, she walked away from Cade and toward the apartments.

CHAPTER TWENTY-SEVEN

To Bridget's disappointment, the dining room wasn't empty. The moment she opened the large doors, curious stares shot her way. It took Bridget a second to realize why the girls eyed her. To her, the third task felt like a lifetime ago. It was hard to believe that only one day had passed since she vomited her guts up in the library; so much had happened since then. She was no longer the same girl. Literally. Plus, during the task, Cade had openly argued with his father over the state of her well-being in front of everyone. Bridget was sure the other girls would want to know why.

She had no answers for them. At least, not ones she could share.

As Alette and Brynley burned holes in the back of her head, Bridget let out a sigh of relief that Quinn was nowhere in sight. With her memories freshly ingrained in her head, she wasn't sure she could pretend to know nothing about the Witch. Her entire body throbbed like an open wound. Bridget was afraid one wrong word or action would send her into an emotional spiral she couldn't control. The only things keeping her together were Cade, and the promise that he would help her get back to Nylah and the human realm.

As long as she focused on that, she would be okay.

Nothing else mattered.

Nothing else could matter.

Not even the fact that Cade would have to promise to marry one of the girls in the room for her to be free.

The realization knocked the breath from her lungs.

Clenching her fists, she strode to the long center table and violently swiped two muffins off a silver platter. Bridget raised one to her lips, but she couldn't force herself to take a bite. She suddenly wasn't hungry.

"What a shame," Alette's voice drawled snidely, "all of us were hoping you'd be too sick to continue on with the tournament."

"I'm sorry to disappoint you," Bridget snapped.

. Bridget rolled her lips together tightly in regret, suddenly afraid that she would let her past with Cade accidentally spill from her lips. If she was going to convince people she still had no memories, she would have to do better at keeping her mouth shut. To her luck, Alette rolled her eyes and whispered something to Brynley.

Hai shyly approached her. "Are you feeling any better?"

"I think I was just really nervous," Bridget said. She hoped the lie sounded more convincing than it did in her head.

Hai tentatively patted her arm. "At least there's only one more task left."

In the corner, Marin whispered, "As far as we know."

The entire room went still. Bridget heard Alette and Brynley gulp. When she walked in, she hadn't even noticed Marin. The Shaman studied her curiously.

"It looks like I need to start getting ready," Marin said, quickly leaving the room.

"I get chills every time she does that," Brynley said, shuddering dramatically.

The entire tournament, the other girls had been wary and afraid of Marin's prophetic tendencies. Some, like Alette, seemed jealous of her power. Before, Bridget had felt a kinship with her. They were both outsiders. Or so she thought. Now, as she watched Marin's retreating figure, a profound resentment seeped into Bridget's bones and blinded her vision. Deep down, she knew Cade would have to pick Marin to end the tournament. And she would have to watch it happen. In her head, she played out the event. Her chest burned hotly.

There had to be another way. There had—

A hand touched her arm.

Bridget flinched. To her right, Hai gazed at her in confusion. It took her a moment to remember she was in the dining room. She put a hand on her chest in an attempt to calm her heart. Feeling something sticky in her hand, Bridget looked down. A chocolate muffin was smashed and torn to bits on her fingertips.

"Have you seen Delphine?" Bridget asked hoarsely. She needed to get out of the apartments before she went crazy and smashed something else. Or accidentally called Cade her boyfriend.

Alette's nasally voice drawled from the other side of the table. "Are you coming, Hai? I've suddenly lost my appetite."

Bridget clenched her jaw and fought the urge to snap back at her. Hai's face faltered slightly. After giving Bridget a helpless, apologetic shrug, she followed Alette and Brynley out of the dining hall.

Bridget stood alone. The side window gave her a perfect view of the mountains and Astraeus. Her chest tightened as she looked at the city. Really looked. Now that she had her memories, all of Elyria seemed different, including the capital. It was obvious now that Astraeus was a city stuck between two worlds. The buildings were a blend of modernity and tradition, and much of the human realm was in the bones of the city. Electricity flowed freely, but no cars zoomed through the streets. Buildings rivaling skyscrapers nestled together outside the palace wall, but cobblestones and tented markets lined the corners. It was like Cade's ancestors had chosen only what they liked from the human realm to bring to Elyria. And made sure only the Fae benefitted. Vassuryn was full of run-down wooden buildings and dirt roads. She wondered if Kastron was the same.

"She lives."

Bridget stiffened at the sound of the voice. Heart pounding, she slowly turned to face Quinn. The Witch stood in the middle of the dining room's doorway with a smirk painted on her face. Bridget cleared her throat and struggled to find her voice.

"I must have eaten something bad," she said, "I'm feeling better now, though. I need to find Delphine."

Bridget tried to walk past her, but Quinn flung the heavy doors closed. The click of the lock echoed loudly in the large room.

"So Archer couldn't keep his mouth shut," Quinn drawled in a bored tone. The Witch stalked toward Bridget and began to circle her.

"I don't know what you're talking about."

Doing her best to keep a straight face, Bridget twisted her ankle around in her boot to find her dagger. Dread twisted her insides when she realized it was still in her room, in the boots she had taken off before asking Delphine to take her to Cade...

"It's not nice to lie, Bridget," Quinn chastised, clicking her tongue. "I thought we were closer than that."

When Quinn placed herself inches away from her face, Bridget glared at her. The girl's brown eyes were dark and stormy as she studied Bridget intently. After a long moment, Quinn's lips twisted. She let out a hard, short laugh. She flicked the amethyst stone around Bridget's neck.

"I guess I can't be too mad at Archer," Quinn said. "Not all of us have fancy stones to keep the prince out of our head."

"What do you want?" Bridget hissed, stepping away to put distance between them.

Quinn rolled her eyes and walked to the banquet table. "Why ask a question you already know the answer to?" she asked, biting into a muffin.

Bridget ripped the pastry from her hand and threw it across the room, earning her a look of annoyance from the Witch. While Cade had guessed right about Quinn wanting the Bloodstone, there was still so much more she wanted to know.

"Why did you bring me here? Why do this to me?"

"It's complicated," Quinn replied with a taunting smile.

Rage exploded inside Bridget's chest. Seeing red, she grabbed a glass plate from the table and tried to smash it on Quinn's head. The Witch dodged the blow and stumbled backward.

"What was that for? I think you're taking your anger out on the wrong person."

Bridget disagreed. The girl in front of her deserved every bit of malice currently coursing through her veins. Quinn had kidnapped her, tortured her, pretended to be her friend, and murdered Ondine. Screw Cade's plan. Whatever else she was planning, Bridget wanted to know. Immediately. Growling, she launched herself at Quinn and smacked her down on the table. Glass crunched underneath the Witch's back.

"You could be sitting up in your room right now," Quinn croaked, "without a care in the world."

Suddenly, Quinn grabbed Bridget's neck and squeezed hard. Bridget gasped for breath and tried to peel her fingers away. In a quick move, Quinn rolled them over and battered Bridget's head down on the wood. Glass shards stung and pricked her neck.

Quinn sneered. "But Cade couldn't stay away, could he?"

Vision blurring, Bridget reached her hand out and tried to find anything on the table to use as a weapon. She grabbed the first smooth thing she felt. Recognizing the shape of a fork, Bridget whipped her arm up and dug the silver prongs into Quinn's shoulder. The Witch screeched and loosened her grip. Bridget violently pushed her away and stood up, breathing heavily.

With a vicious stare, Quinn bared her teeth and removed the fork. Blood squirted from the wound. "Isn't that why you're here in the first place?" she continued venomously. "Aren't you mad?"

Hearing her try to push the blame on Cade made Bridget snap. Their relationship wasn't defined by his actions alone. With a growl, she grabbed a velvet chair and threw it at Quinn, who laughed when it missed and landed on the table, snapping it in half. When Quinn began muttering in Latin, Bridget rushed forward to tackle her. Suddenly, the blood dripping from Quinn's shoulder turned black and seared a symbol into the witch's skin. When her eyes darkened, Quinn flicked a hand and froze Bridget's legs. With no more feeling in her lower extremities, Bridget tumbled to the ground. Above her, Quinn smirked and dug one foot into her chest.

"Granted, I did push. Especially when he was doing too good of a job ignoring you. I shot Ondine to make him scared enough to seek you out. Turns out, I didn't even need to. You managed that on your own. Men are so predictable. Did you even make him grovel when you got your memories back?"

Bridget gasped when Quinn pressed her boot down harder on her sternum. Any second, her chest would crack. When she couldn't push the girl's foot off, she panicked. Bridget reached for the stone around her neck, hoping Cade would be able to hear her thoughts without it.

Quinn bent down and shoved Bridget's hand away. "Don't bother. He won't make it here in time," she said. "Ondine was good for one thing, though. Her blood gave me enough power to influence some weak-minded Kastronians to attack during the second task. That, I did for fun."

The movement eased the pressure on her chest, but Bridget still couldn't feel her legs. "What do you want?" she croaked. She wondered if this was it, that maybe Quinn had planned to use her for blood magic after all.

"I'm not going to kill you," Quinn cooed. "This is just the beginning."

Suddenly, Quinn's dark hair turned white and stringy. More onyx symbols like the one on her shoulder began to appear all over her arms. The tan skin on her face became dull and sunken. Bridget's eyes went wide. Within seconds, Quinn was a wraith of herself.

"I wasn't always like this, you know. I blame your boyfriend. He's the reason I got into this mess in the first place," Quinn said bitterly.

Bridget reached up to slap Quinn's face, but the black lines flowing from the witch's eyes surged brighter. She flicked her wrist, freezing Bridget's hands against the hard stone beneath her.

"What the hell are you talking about?" Bridget squirmed and tried to move any body part.

Quinn pressed her lips against Bridget's ear. "Let all your little friends know it's only a matter of time until I get the Bloodstone," she whispered threateningly. When Quinn pulled back, she yanked Bridget's necklace off. "Thanks for this," she smirked, dangling the stone in the air, "I can't have loverboy tracking me down."

The doors of the dining room burst open, sending wooden splinters flying through the room. Bridget felt her arms and legs tingle as Quinn's body returned to its glamoured state. Without warning, the Witch sprinted toward the window. A loud crash sounded as she shattered the glass with her elbow and jumped out.

Sword in hand, Finn rushed into the room. He kneeled beside Bridget and helped her sit up. Her arms and legs tingled, like they had been asleep for a very long time. Fire reverberated through her limbs with each movement.

"Please tell me that it wasn't Quinn who just jumped out the window," Finn said.

Bridget shakily pointed at the window. "There's a steep ledge on that side of the building. The rocks look sharp."

"What the hell?" Finn muttered, sprinting to the gaping glass. "I don't know how she landed without breaking anything, but it looks like she's heading for the front gate."

"She can't leave the palace grounds. We all signed blood contracts," Bridget coughed.

Doubt crept into Finn's eyes. With a deep breath, he braced himself. "The Elder Woods still have plenty of places to hide. I haven't made a jump like this in years. Wish me luck."

Before Bridget could stop him, he leapt out the window after Quinn.

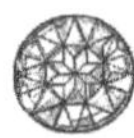

"How the hell did this happen?" Cade hissed, staring intently as Delphine picked out tiny glass pieces from the back of Bridget's neck.

She was grateful her fight with Quinn had left her relatively unscathed, except for a large, swollen bruise underneath her lower hairline. When Delphine picked out the last tiny shard, Cade ran a hand through his messy hair and started to pace.

"She must have been planning an escape route for a while," Finn said, leaning against the fireplace mantel in Cade's room. "She was fast. And disappeared too quickly."

Even seconds behind her, Finn had lost track of Quinn in the narrow, crooked streets of Astraeus. Despite the tournament still happening, she had left the palace grounds. And survived. Bridget flinched when Delphine poured some kind of liquid on her neck.

"Do you have any ideas?" Cade asked Castor. The Warlock, deep in thought, rubbed his chin.

"All the contestants signed a blood contract. She must have found a loophole," Castor replied.

"Does this mean any contestant can leave?" Bridget asked, not daring to look at Cade. She was afraid to see his reaction to the hope now flickering in her chest. Perhaps they wouldn't be forced to finish the tournament after all…Out of the corner of her eye, she saw Cade stiffen. Even though the heat of his gaze burned her cheek, she didn't turn. With a curious glance in Cade's direction, Castor stepped forward.

"Before we jump to any conclusions, we should figure out if there even is a loophole," he said. "This is a centuries-old tournament."

"Could she have used blood magic?" Delphine asked. "Or gotten away with not signing the contract?"

"I hate to say it, but the clown in the dungeon might know what is going on," Finn grunted.

Bridget stood up and moved toward the door. "Why don't I just try walking out of the palace?"

"No."

The barely restrained fury in Cade's voice made Bridget sit back down on the bed.

"I'm a contestant. I'll do it," Delphine said.

"No one is going to do anything," Castor stated firmly. "Let's find the contracts and check the wording."

All eyes moved to Cade, who stood deep in thought in front of the fireplace. "We need to keep this from my father for as long as possible," he eventually said. "If he thinks there's any possibility I can leave the palace grounds with Bridget, he'll try to have her killed. The contracts are in his scribe's office. He'll be suspicious if he finds out I went in there."

"What are you suggesting?" Castor asked.

When Cade's wary gaze flickered to her, Bridget knew exactly what he planned to do.

"Are you sure you can trust her?" Bridget asked through gritted teeth.

She hadn't seen Cassia since attacking her, nor did she want to. Even though it had been seven months since the car accident, the memory of watching her drag an unconscious Nylah away still felt fresh in Bridget's mind. It was an action she might not be able to forgive. Ever. Even if deep down, she knew it was for Nylah's safety.

"Bridget has a point," Finn said, "Cassia is…unpredictable."

"Not the word I would have used," Bridget muttered under her breath.

Cade's lips twitched.

"She helped Bridget with the second task. She'll help us now. She wants back in everyone's good graces, especially Cade's," Castor argued.

By the way Castor forced his face to remain passive, Bridget wondered if there was a history there.

"I hate to say it, but it has to be her. She can grab the contracts without being noticed," Cade said.

Delphine stood up and rolled her shoulders. "That's my cue. I'll be right back." With a pop, she disappeared.

Cade took a seat next to Bridget on the edge of the bed. She fought the urge to lean against him. Instead, she asked, "What are we going to do about the Bloodstone?"

"It's safe in the vault."

"Quinn said it was only a matter of time," Bridget argued, narrowing her eyes. "She also said it was your fault she became part of the Sanguis coven."

Her earlier frustration with him for not asking Archer about the second gate came roaring back. And though she didn't want to admit it, Quinn's choice of words struck a chord. There was still so much about Cade's past she didn't know. The entire tournament, Cade's reputation had been a hot topic among the contestants, especially Alette. Now, Bridget couldn't help but wonder how much of it was true.

"I swear, I'd never met her before this tournament," Cade replied heatedly. "And the Sanguis coven has been in another realm for over 500 years. She hasn't been forced or manipulated into anything. Whatever she's doing, she's doing it alone."

A loud pop interrupted their tense stare down.

"Cassia agreed to help. She's on her way there now," Delphine announced. Noticing the new strained atmosphere of the room, she gazed warily between Bridget and Cade. Finn shrugged and handed her a glass of wine.

"If we've learned anything, it's that she isn't wasting any time. We should get the Bloodstone before she does," Bridget said.

Cade huffed angrily and stood up. By the way he pinched the bridge of his nose, she knew he agreed with her, but the stubborn set of his jaw kept him from saying the words.

After a long moment, Castor asked, "What's the problem?"

"The vault requires a key. Only two exist. One for the king and one for the queen, but my father never trusted my mother," Cade said wryly. "He gave me the second key on my sixteenth birthday but took it back the day I used the quartz to save Bridget in the lake. I'm sure he's guarding both like a hawk."

"I don't understand. I've seen the vault and there is no door. Can't we just sneak in?" Delphine asked.

"The vault is protected by embedded ancient runes that are cursed to detect and destroy any hint of magic. Any Fae, Witch, Shaman, or Nymph that enters without a key, dies," Cade answered gravely.

Bridget stilled. His carefully chosen words revealed the idea that he didn't want to suggest. Finn and Delphine shared a look that told her they understood too. She felt Castor's eyes on her.

"What happens if a human enters?" he asked.

The bedroom door sprung open, making the entire group jump.

"I've got your bloody contracts," Cassia said, waving the papers in the air. "Why was getting these so important?"

Cade ripped the contracts from her hand and began skimming through each one.

"You're welcome," Cassia sneered. Rolling her eyes, she grabbed the wine from Delphine's hand and downed it.

"One of the contestants successfully left the palace grounds," Cade said. His eyes glazed over as he focused on the words in front of him. Seconds later, he handed a few contracts to Castor and Finn.

"That's impossible. Which one?"

"Quinn," Delphine replied.

Cassia raised a brow at Bridget, as if daring her to speak. Stubbornly, Bridget crossed her arms and refused to acknowledge her.

"This is absolute gibberish. I don't think this dialect hasn't been used for centuries," Finn said.

"That's probably how long it's been since blood contracts were used for the tournament," Cade said.

"Really? Why now?" Bridget asked him. She moved to his side and studied the papers over his shoulder. The ancient and foreign words looked like scribbles on the page.

"By forcing you to the grounds, he guaranteed my participation," Cade said. Her heart skipped a beat when his brown eyes met hers. Despite still being frustrated with him, Bridget leaned her chin against his shoulder and gave him a soft smile. Out of the corner of her eye, she saw Cassia make a gagging face.

Castor slammed the papers down on Cade's desk in frustration. "I can't find any loopholes. It's pretty straightforward."

"And Quinn definitely signed hers," Finn said, face scrunched in disgust. He gingerly held up a contract that had a large amount of blood smeared across the bottom. Cassia walked over to Castor and took the contracts from him. She spent the next few minutes reading over each one.

"It's pretty obvious," Cassia scoffed. When everyone glared at her, she rolled her eyes and shoved a parchment into Bridget's hands. "Here's yours. Did you even bother to read this?"

"I'm sorry, but the New York public school system didn't have any classes in ancient Latin."

"Leave her alone. I didn't read it either," Delphine said.

Cassia narrowed her eyes. "I hope you're joking. As a Fae, you should know better."

Anger ripped through Bridget at her patronizing tone. She took a determined step toward Cassia, but Cade's hand on her shoulder held her back.

"Are you here to help or not?" Castor asked quietly. Cassia eyed him for a long moment before she dropped the snarl on her face.

"The contract states the tournament ends *when* a winner is chosen by the prince. It doesn't say he has to wait to pick, just that it won't be announced until after the fourth task," Cassia said. "When blood contracts were still used for the tournament, I don't think our ancestors knew any of the contestants beforehand. Most likely, they didn't decide who would win until the end. Announcement or not, Cade chose the moment Bridget was introduced. We all know that. No matter who our father wanted him to pick, magic can't be fooled. The tournament was over before it even started."

There was a long pause as the group digested Cassia's words. Bridget locked eyes with Cade and felt her heart being torn in half. She was free and could finally leave Elyria to find Nylah. It was what she wanted to do…had to do. But now that leaving was actually possible, a huge knot of dread settled in her stomach. Going back to the human realm meant forgetting everything. Again. Delphine, Finn, Nylah, Cade…And there, she knew there would be no spell that would restore the loss. No loophole. No price that could be paid. Going back also meant facing the possibility that Cade couldn't, or wouldn't, follow. Once, she had asked him if he wanted to go back to the human realm. He hadn't given her a straight answer. When her vision refocused, she saw her own pain reflected on his face. She wondered if his thoughts were the same as hers.

"That's nice," Castor stated impatiently, "but if we want to keep this development from your father, we need to get the Bloodstone before Quinn. There's no guarantee she doesn't have a human stashed somewhere to enter the vault for her."

Bridget took a deep breath to steady herself. There was still much to be done before she would be able to go back, including finding the second gate. She still had time to talk with Cade and figure out the best way to get back to Nylah. Together. There was no reason for her to fall apart. She stuffed down her anxiety and gazed at Castor's stressed form. The king kept him trapped in Elyria and, like her, he seemed determined to get home.

"I can do it. I'll get the Bloodstone," Bridget said, desperate to have something to focus and fixate on.

Cassia let out a loud laugh. When she realized no one else had joined her, her eyes went wide at their serious faces. "She's not joking?"

"Does it look like anyone in this room is in the mood for a joke right now?" Finn asked, sipping on wine.

Turning to Cade, Cassia asked, "Why aren't you saying anything?"

"Because he knows I'm the only one in this room who can enter the vault. Is it here in the palace?"

"No, it's located at the base of Mount Lugh," Cade said.

"Which also happens to be on the grounds of the high commander's residence. He won't let a human onto his property," Cassia sputtered.

"He wouldn't say no to Cade. He can sneak me in," Bridget argued.

"I can't go," Cade said, voice low and tight. Puzzled, Bridget frowned at him. He lowered his eyes and crossed his arms. "It will be too suspicious if I leave the palace. Plus, someone needs to distract my father."

"What if we don't have to deal with the high commander at all?" Delphine remarked. "I'll take Bridget and make sure we land close enough to the vault not to be detected."

"There will still be guards," Finn warned.

"I'll go too," Castor said. "If we're spotted, I'll be able to alter the memories of anyone we may come across."

"Tonight?" Bridget asked, turning to Cade for his opinion. He stared into the roaring fire for a long moment.

"I guess it's time to finally have dinner with my father," Cade said, with a bitter, wry smile on his face.

Knowing it was the last thing he wanted to do, Bridget squeezed his hand. Worry sprouted in her abdomen. Since being in Elyria, the king had shown her nothing but ruthless determination. She didn't think Cade even knew his main goal. Whatever it was, he was willing to sacrifice his own children's happiness for it. If it came to a fight, Cade was powerful, but she knew the obsidian in the king's dagger made him equally so.

"This plan is ridiculous. You'll be lucky not to get caught," Cassia muttered.

Delphine glared at her. "No one asked you. If you're going to shoot down every plan, then get out."

With a dramatic eye roll, Cassia stormed from the room. The slam of the door sent a stab of pain through Bridget's head. She rubbed her temples.

Castor stared at the closed door. Eventually, he said, "I know you don't like her, but she did help. If we're doing this tonight, I'm going to need a few plants from the forest for some spells."

Whatever Cade's reply was, Bridget didn't hear. Agony exploded underneath her skull as the room disappeared. She fell to her knees and screamed.

CHAPTER TWENTY-EIGHT

Distantly, Bridget felt hands wrap around her wrists before a blurry vision of Cora appeared. The Witch leaned over a table and gripped something Bridget couldn't see.

"It's about time you finally took your necklace off. I told you to make yourself available every five days. Do you know how much power this spell requires? How many times I've wasted resources trying it?" Cora snarled.

"You should have taken the hint. I told Alexia I never wanted to speak to you again," Bridget grunted, trying to manage the sensation of her brain being split in two. "Besides, you led me to the one person who wants to keep me away from you the most. What did you expect?"

A light tap knocked at the base of Bridget's skull. The gentle motion almost felt soothing. She briefly wondered if it was Cade trying to get in.

"You're right. That was a miscalculation on my part. But you're here now. That's all I care about. I knew it was only a matter of time before you would come back to me," Cora cooed. The Witch gave her a simpering smile but made no move toward her.

"Don't. I remember everything. I know *everything*. Whatever you wanted from me, you're never going to get it."

Face paling, Cora went deadly still. "That's impossible. Listen to me, Bridget, I—"

A lick of fire shot down Bridget's spinal cord. Unable to withstand the burn, she closed her eyes and leaned into the pressure that now incessantly pulled at her. Seconds later, Cade's presence entered her mind. Bridget gasped at the immediate relief. Pain no longer singed behind her eyelids, but whether it disappeared from Cade blocking it or absorbing it, she didn't know.

"You must be Cora," Cade said from Bridget's mouth. She no longer had control of her body and could only watch what would happen between him and Cora. As she viewed the room through Cade's eyes, horror filled her gut. Blood was everywhere. The windows, the walls, the floor. And on the table, Alexia lay motionless, Cora's fingers dug deep in her abdomen.

"Your Highness," Cora replied, nodding her head slightly. Her arms vibrated as the veins there turned black underneath her skin. Bridget couldn't believe what she was seeing.

Blood magic.

Cora was using blood magic. A hum of agreement from Cade echoed in her head.

"I'm glad we get the chance to speak before I find you and kill you," Cade stated, voice low and threatening. Bridget shivered at the tone.

"Kill me?" Cora asked, forcing a laugh. "Whatever for?"

"Feigning ignorance will not save you. There's nothing you could say that would persuade me to change my mind. If you want a swift death, you'll answer my questions. What does Quinn want with the Bloodstone?"

"I know nothing about her plans, I swear. Bridget was like a daughter to me. I took care of her and saved her from that horrible Witch."

Despite the plea, the Witch dug her fingers deeper into Alexia's side. The action broke whatever barrier Cade had created and sent a wave of scalding pain into Bridget's mind. She screamed, even as Cade quickly pushed it away. Cora's eyes turned completely black as veins eerily hollowed out her face.

"Release her mind. *Now*."

Dust and loose paint chips crumbled from the walls at Cade's words.

"I have information," Cora croaked, entire body shaking violently. "Valuable information. I know things that are pertinent to both of you."

Even though Cora's grip on Bridget's mind has loosened, her vision turned dark. She didn't think she would be able to stay conscious much longer and tried to silently relay the message to Cade.

"You're lying. Release her," Cade roared.

Suddenly, Cora's hands flew up in the air. The room twisted and bent as Bridget's soul was swept back to her body. Before she fully returned, Cora gripped her consciousness once more. Visions flashed through her head. Bridget saw Cade, but he was different than she'd ever seen him. His hair was long and pulled back. He stood in front of a large stone with a glowing sword held high in his hand. A foreign language flowed from his mouth. The vision changed and showed a dark forest illuminated by a full moon. A large creature, black and dripping with a thick substance, growled and leapt toward her. With a gasp, she shoved Cora away and plunged into darkness.

Breathing hard, Bridget's eyes popped open. Cade lay on the ground next to her. He held her head and, like her, struggled for breath. Blood from his ears dripped to his cheeks and chin. She clutched his arms and leaned forward to rest her head against his chest.

"Cade...That animal. Or maybe a monster. Did you see that?"

Cade gently grasped her chin and raised her gaze. After wiping the blood from her nose, he asked, "No, what are you talking about? Are you okay?'

Bridget closed her eyes and gripped him tighter. Without a doubt, the image of the beast would be permanently ingrained in her nightmares.

"What the hell just happened?" Finn demanded. He handed Cade a towel and Bridget a glass of water.

"That was risky. You had no idea who was pulling at her," Castor half-heartedly chastised.

"It was the Witch that held Bridget captive for months. She was using blood magic. It wasn't clean, or traditional, but it looked effective," Cade said, giving Castor a pointed look.

"I was afraid you were going to say that. One Witch was bad enough, but now two? They must be working together."

Bridget chugged a large gulp of water. The liquid burned her scratchy throat. “Do you think she was telling the truth?” she asked Cade, referring to Cora’s bargaining words.

“I think she would say anything to save herself.”

“Are we sure going to the vault tonight is a good idea?” Delphine asked. “It’s already late afternoon. After what her mind has been through the past few days, I think Bridget needs rest.”

“I’m fine. Besides, we don’t have a choice,” Bridget said, more worried about Cade than herself. He looked drained and knew his father would take notice of the bags under his eyes.

Castor stepped forward and helped Cade off the ground. “These Witches didn’t learn blood magic on their own. The Sanguis must have found a way to enter the realm. It’s vital the Bloodstone remains in our possession.”

Cade grunted in agreement. He grabbed Bridget under the shoulders and helped her to the bed. There were only a few hours until sunset. Her limbs ached. Rest. They all needed rest. Once they agreed about where to meet, Castor, Finn, and Delphine left the room. Alone, Bridget rolled over to face Cade. He laid on his back and stared contemplatively at the ceiling.

“Do you think Alexia is dead?”

“I’m not sure. It depends on how many times Cora has done that to her. The body can only take so much.”

Bridget’s heart sank. Even though Alexia got on her last nerve, it was horrifying to see anyone be used or suffer like that. Seeing Cora perform blood magic had shaken her to the core. She mused over her months in Vassuryn and wondered if every Witch and Warlock she had buried had not died from overuse of magic, but from being used by Cora. Bridget opened her mouth to ask Cade about the possibility, but he was already asleep.

Though Cade hadn’t stirred in the past hour, Bridget restlessly tossed and turned. She couldn’t get the strange images she’d seen out of her head. Every time she closed her eyes, she saw the large, beast-like creature springing toward her. To get her mind off it, she riffled through the old king's journal. Bridget read each page twice to understand the riddled passages. The journal read more like a textbook than someone's personal account of their life.

When she saw the word 'Bloodstone' on a page, her heart stopped. Bridget quickly skimmed over the passage but was interrupted by a faint grunt. She whipped around. On the bed, Cade stiffened. When he twitched and muttered again, she ran over to shake him awake. The moment her hands touched his chest, his eyes popped open. With a gasping breath, he looked around the room frantically before he settled his gaze on Bridget.

"It's okay. Everything's okay." She pushed back the damp hair that clung to his forehead. He squeezed her forearm before he sat up and rubbed his eyes.

"Were you having a nightmare?"

"It's nothing," Cade said dismissively. Noticing the journal in her hand, he asked, "Have you been reading the entire time?"

"I couldn't sleep."

Cade hummed in response. He ran a hand through his hair, still looking troubled by his dream.

"It's almost sunset," Bridget said, rubbing a hand down his back. "Everyone will be back soon. Will I know the Bloodstone when I see it?"

"You will. It's the only item in there that's not actually a stone."

Bridget paused her ministrations. "I'm officially confused."

"It's an enchanted hollow quartz," Cade replied, taking her hand and kissing the palm. "The blood of one of the most powerful Tuathan lies inside. A single drop can completely fuel even the largest of spells."

"I see now why Quinn wants it," Bridget said, realizing why it was such a valued artifact among the Sanguis. She gazed thoughtfully at the journal in her hand and thought about what she had read. "The journal said something strange. I was beginning to think..."

Cade's bedroom sprung open. Bridget gritted her teeth when Cassia walked in, no knock or anything.

"Sorry to interrupt," Cassia drawled, no remorse in her voice. "But I need to speak to Bridget."

Cade and Bridget's eyes flickered to each other in confusion. "Delphine and Castor will be here any moment."

"It won't take long."

Cade grabbed Bridget's hands and helped her off the bed. "I guess it's time for me to meet my father. Don't talk to her if you don't want to."

Her breath hitched when she realized she wouldn't see him again before heading to the vault. Cade cupped her cheek. His eyes swam with worry. When he opened his mouth, probably to give her some sort of warning, Bridget stopped him.

"I'll be okay. I promise. I steal stuff all the time. How hard can it be?"

Cade played with the ends of her red hair before he kissed her hard and deep. Bridget flushed, feeling the kiss all the way down to her toes. She wished he hadn't fallen asleep earlier and instead…

He pulled away too soon. With one last peck on her cheek, Cade left. He gave a warning glare to Cassia before he shut the door.

"What do you want?"

Cassia tossed her a small vial that she fumbled to catch.

"That's a tonic that should help alleviate some of the pain in your head. I just made it."

Bridget eyed it speculatively but couldn't find anything suspicious about the liquid. Not that she knew what to look for, in any case. "I'm surprised it's not poison. Not that you would tell me if it was. Besides, I can't take this. The last potion I took nearly killed me."

"I've never wanted to kill you."

"You kidnapped my sister and left me bleeding and trapped in a crashed car. Archer was able to take me because of you. You basically left me for dead."

"I could tell he was a Warlock and knew he probably needed you alive to bargain with Cade," Cassia argued, lips thinning. "I made a split-second decision. It worked out, though. You're here. You remember."

Bridget scoffed. "That's a pretty pathetic defense."

"You don't understand. Witches and Warlocks have the advantage in the human realm. There are enough resources there for them to be able to perform minor spells. If it came down to a fight, I wouldn't have been able to win." Cassia clenched her jaw and avoided Bridget's eyes, like it was hard for her to admit the shortcoming.

"But you're also a Witch..."

Cassia took a deep breath and walked to the window. Keeping her back to Bridget, her next words came out rushed. "I'm not powerful. I'm sure you've heard enough taunting from my father to realize that. I don't even have a coven."

"You don't need powerful magical abilities to win a fight. You showed me that."

When Cassia turned around, there were tears in her eyes. Bridget's mouth fell open.

"I'm sorry," Cassia choked out, clearly struggling. "When my father asked me to find Cade, I was ecstatic. I thought it meant he finally trusted me, despite my lack of power. I've been his biggest disappointment my whole life. The powerful Fae King with the pathetic Witch daughter. I was determined to be the one to finally bring my brother back and restore our family."

"He didn't trust you, though..." Bridget said, remembering Cade telling her about the soldiers that hunted him the day Cassia appeared in Manhattan.

"I know. But I still hoped I could be the one to get it done...and I was."

"But it cost you Cade," Bridget stated, nodding her head in understanding. To please her father, she'd lost her relationship with her twin. Since then, she'd been trying to earn back Cade's trust, which included helping Bridget with the second task to prove she was sorry.

"He's my twin. We'll always be connected. One day, our relationship will be as it once was."

Her tone radiated hope. Bridget rolled her lips together, hating that she understood Cassia. Like her, she would do anything to keep her sibling in her life. Throat tight, she stuffed the vial in her pocket.

"Thank you," Bridget said.

"I still think it's a stupid plan, but good luck," Cassia said, moving toward the door. "I'll keep an eye on Cade tonight. My father won't reveal anything too dastardly if I'm there."

Bridget nodded and watched her leave.

CHAPTER TWENTY-NINE

In front of Cade's fireplace, Bridget gripped Delphine's right hand. She hoped her sweaty palms weren't noticeable through her thin gloves. Any second, they would vanish and appear at the base of Mount Lugh. Bridget had traveled with Delphine before, but the sensation of being ripped apart and glued back together in the span of seconds made her queasy. She wasn't looking forward to the trip. With a brief glance at Castor's calm form, she wondered if it was only her affected by the magic. Probably. Nothing seemed to be easy for humans in Elyria.

When Delphine closed her eyes, Bridget braced herself. After a long moment, nothing happened. Her friend's hand trembled.

Standing on her left, Castor noticed and frowned. "What's wrong?"

"I've never done this with more than two people," Delphine replied sheepishly, cheeks reddening.

"Are you serious? If this is too much…" Bridget said, trying to let go of Delphine's hand, but the Fae girl's grip stayed strong.

"If I don't try, I'll never know, right?"

Castor's lips titled up in admiration. "The malachite you're wearing will help, even if it's not a rune. You can do this."

Delphine took a deep breath and closed her eyes again. This time, Bridget didn't have time to brace herself. Her stomach swooped painfully as she was sliced to pieces and rebuilt. When cold air hit her face, she fell to her knees and gasped for breath. The damp grass beneath her soaked her gloves and pants. Once the nausea subsided, she lifted her eyes and spotted Delphine on the ground in a similar position. Blood dripped from her nose as Castor tried to help her up.

"Delphine, are you okay?" Bridget asked, legs shaking as she stood. Getting a head rush, she tilted to the side and saw black spots. After this, she was going to need at least three days of sleep.

Delphine muttered a reply Bridget couldn't quite hear. The malachite around her neck glowed softly. Bridget leaned against a tree and studied their surroundings. An orchard grew at the base of the mountain. Numerous trees in perfect lines all bore a different fruit. To her right, a large metal fence blocked her view of Astraeus. According to Castor, the high commander lived across town and separately from the royal family, in case an assassination attempt took out the entire palace. Behind her, soft grass turned to dirt and hard stone. Bridget looked up. Standing so close to Mount Lugh, she could no longer see its looming white peak.

"Do you need to stay here?" Castor asked Delphine.

"I can keep going."

Bridget gazed around in confusion, not seeing anything remotely close to a vault. She opened her mouth to ask Castor, but he stopped her and pointed up.

"We have to do a little climbing to get to the vault."

About fifty feet up, a jagged ledge glowed with firelight. Bridget's heart thudded in her chest. The vault lay higher than a comfortable climb. The only thing that calmed her nerves was that the mountainside was not smooth. She began to formulate a rough path in her head that included large stones and crevices that looked sturdy enough to grab.

"Why didn't we land up there?"

"I told her to bring us here," Castor replied. "There are guards stationed up there. I knew both of you would be vulnerable after we landed. They would have easily overpowered us."

Bridget palmed the mountain's dark stone. The cloth gloves on her hands slipped and skittered across the surface. If she had known they would be climbing, she would have worn her leather gloves. She swallowed hard as she realized she wouldn't be able to climb with her hands covered. Hesitantly, Bridget pulled the gloves off. Even though it was dark, she knew Delphine and Castor would be able to see the scars in the moonlight.

When Bridget found a crevice for her foot, she began to climb. Beside her, Castor and Delphine did the same. She felt their eyes gaze at her hands, but to her relief, they said nothing. Out of all three of them, Castor was the best climber. He was quick and nimble and scaled the mountainside with ease. Bridget's arms protested as she followed him, doing her best to keep up. Delphine struggled a few feet below them.

About halfway up, Bridget spotted Astraeus over the metal wall. In the distance, the palace glowed brighter than anything else in the city. She wondered what Cade was doing at that very moment.

A faint siren made Bridget jump. Rocks slid out of the hole where her foot was positioned. She sighed in relief when they didn't hit Delphine beneath her. Seconds later, a large number of soldiers exited the high commander's property. The palace lights flickered on and off ominously.

"What do you think is going on?" Bridget asked, even though the pit in her stomach told her she already knew. Whatever was happening, it had to do with Cade and his father.

"Nothing good," Castor called from above, just as the palace lights surged again. "We need to hurry."

Within a few minutes, he reached the bottom of the ledge. Once he heaved himself over, Bridget heard shouts and a scuffle. The guards. She looked down and made eye contact with Delphine. The girl's eyes were wide.

"Hurry!"

With adrenaline buzzing through her veins, Bridget climbed quickly. Her fingers scraped harshly against the stone with each new grip. When she thought her body would collapse from exhaustion, she reached the ledge. Bridget dug her fingers into the ground and clumsily pulled herself over.

Four soldiers guarded the vault. Three lay unconscious on the ground as Castor wrestled the other. Bridget ran over and jumped on the back of the guard, who stumbled backward in surprise. Hands free, Castor pulled out a powder and blew it in the guard's face. Within seconds, he passed out and fell to the ground, taking Bridget with him. She let out a strangled gasp as the weight of the man smothered her. Castor quickly pulled him off and helped her to her feet. When she heard a strained grunt, Bridget turned and saw Delphine slowly coming over the ledge.

"I never want to do that again," she said, hands coming to rest on her knees. Bridget wholeheartedly agreed. Blood covered her fingertips and her body ached with every movement.

Castor toed one of the guards on the ground. "They won't stay unconscious for long. You'll need to be quick."

Bridget nodded and spared one last glance at the palace. The lights were no longer flickering, but that didn't mean whatever was happening inside had stopped. Tentatively, she approached the vault. The entrance was a large, jagged crack in the mountainside. It looked unnatural, like someone had furiously blasted through the stone. Inside, darkness loomed.

A clicking noise illuminated a spot in the black. Behind her, Castor held out a flashlight. With a grateful smile, she took the tool and toed the entrance to the vault. For a split-second, fear froze the blood in her veins. What if they had been wrong about humans being able to enter? But she had no time for doubts. Gritting her teeth in determination, Bridget stepped into the shadowy cave.

Nothing happened.

She heard Delphine sigh in relief. Without looking back, Bridget ventured into darkness. The flashlight allowed her little visibility. All she could see was damp granite and dirt. After a few minutes, when she had walked for so long, she thought she might be in the wrong cave, a light appeared.

The tunnel expanded and turned into a large, illuminated cavern. Bridget stared in awe at the amount of glistening, breath-taking crystals and stones that were shelved and lined throughout the expansive space. Some were in their original form; others were molded into jewelry or weapons.

Bridget wandered each row, looking for Cade's description of the Bloodstone, but found nothing. Eventually, she came across a darker corner, hidden and purposefully unnoticeable. In it, an old armoire sat dusty and untouched. Bridget hesitantly unclicked the latch and slowly pulled the doors open. Loud creaks echoed throughout the cavern.

Inside, there was a shelf big enough for four items. A space on the far right was empty, for a stone already missing. To the left, two crystals Bridget didn't recognize sat shimmering. And in the middle was a clear quartz that glowed with blood.

Bridget quickly snatched the Bloodstone and shoved it in her pocket. Within seconds, the armoire doors snapped shut, almost taking her fingers with it. The cavern's stone walls wailed and vibrated. Heart pounding, Bridget sprinted toward the exit. The further she went, the more the cave shook. When she reached the tunnel, she almost lost her footing from the violent movement.

Twice, the mountain flung her against the granite wall as she ran. Bridget could feel the bruises already forming on her arms as her lungs pinched and burned. Finally, Castor and Delphine's alarmed faces came into view. Bridget pushed her legs harder and jumped out of the vault toward them. Both of their hands kept her from falling all the way to the ground. She gasped for breath in their arms. Now that she was outside the cave, the mountain was still and calm.

"What the hell happened?" Castor asked.

"There must be more guarding the vault than we think," Bridget croaked out, still trying to catch her breath. "The walls started shaking when I removed the Bloodstone from the armoire."

Bridget pulled the Bloodstone out of her pocket and showed it to Castor and Delphine. Both studied the artifact warily and didn't reach out to touch it. Their hesitation puzzled Bridget. It felt like an ordinary rock in her hand. Shrugging, she stuffed it back into her leather jacket.

"I've already restructured the guards' memories," Castor said. "We should get back to the palace before they wake up. Delphine, you'll need to drop us just outside the east wall. Finn is waiting for us there."

He held out his hand, and when Delphine grabbed it, a faint blush colored her cheeks. Bridget pretended not to see and took her other hand. Delphine took a deep breath and whizzed them away to the palace walls. This time, Bridget felt more nausea than pain. The world blurred around her as she fell to her knees. Again. She hoped this was the last time she would have to travel with Delphine for a while.

"Are you okay?" Finn asked, helping her off the ground. "Did it work? Did you get it?"

"We got it," Bridget said, the Bloodstone heavy in her pocket. "What happened here? We saw lights flickering and a bunch of soldiers rushing toward here. Is Cade alright?"

Finn frowned. "I haven't seen him. I wasn't allowed in the dining room. Since then, it's been quiet. I think he would've contacted me if something was wrong."

Bridget's throat tightened into a knot.

"Delphine needs to rest. Her nose won't stop bleeding," Castor stated, holding up a stumbling Delphine. Not only was blood steadily streaming from her nose, but from her ears as well. Bridget's stomach dropped at the sight of her. She gazed at the tall palace walls.

"Please tell me we don't have to do more climbing."

Finn shook his head and pulled her forward. "No, there's a hidden door a few feet ahead. Cade and I found it when we were kids. I'm not sure the king even knows it's here."

Bridget had a feeling the king knew more than they thought he did. Finn stopped in front of a brick that was darker than the rest of the glistening white stone and pressed on it. An outline of a small doorway appeared in the wall. Finn leaned against it and opened it like a door. Castor and Delphine went through first. Bridget was about to follow when a figure jumped at her from the shadows and grabbed the hood of her jacket. She didn't have time to scream before Finn had the intruder pinned to the ground, sword at their throat.

"Alexia?" Bridget gasped. The girl lay pathetically on the ground with her hands in the air. Blood trickled from her mouth. Even in the moonlight, dark maroon stains were visible on the middle of her cloak.

"Please, I need your help," Alexia wheezed.

"Do you know this person?" Finn asked.

"Unfortunately," Bridget said, pressing against Finn's arm to silently tell him to put his sword away. She crouched down and opened Alexia's cloak. Underneath, the girl's tunic was covered in fresh blood. She couldn't see the wounds, but the flowing liquid told her the cuts were fresh.

"Cora used me for a spell," Alexia grunted. "When I woke up, I ran. I knew I had to get away. I didn't know where else to go."

Alexia winced in pain when Bridget closed the cloak over her stomach. She had never gotten along with the only other human she knew in Elyria, but she knew what it was like to want to get away from Cora. And Alexia was clearly suffering. Bridget admired the determination and strength it must have taken to find her and the palace walls.

"If I help you, will you go running back to Cora when you're healed?" Bridget asked.

"No. That Witch has used me enough. I will not let her use me anymore."

Bridget looked for any hint of deceit in the girl's dark eyes but could find none. After a long moment, she turned to Finn for his opinion.

"I can carry her to one of the spare bedrooms near Cade's room. He'll be able to look in her head and see if she's lying."

Bridget nodded and stepped aside. When Finn picked Alexia up, she wailed and stiffened in pain. He shushed her before walking her through the wall. By the time they were inside the palace, Alexia was unconscious.

"That didn't take long," Bridget said.

"What did that Witch do to her?" Finn asked. The garden around them was empty. Castor and Delphine hadn't waited for them, not that Bridget could blame them. Delphine was in rough shape.

"Blood magic."

They walked in silence the rest of the way, dodging any guards that came across their path. The palace was quieter than usual. She'd half-expected to see the soldiers from the high commander's property patrolling the halls. Near Cade's room, Finn stopped in front of a door. Before they could walk in, a hand clasped Bridget's mouth from behind. She jumped for a split-second before she recognized the person's touch and scent. Whipping around, she hugged Cade tightly. Bridget pulled back to scan him over. No cuts or bruises marred his face, only large bags weighed under his eyes. He made a shushing motion with his finger and ushered them inside.

"Is that Alexia?" Cade asked, not letting go of her as they watched Finn place Alexia on the bed.

"She was waiting for me outside the palace. I don't know for how long. She said she needed help."

"We were hoping you would be able to see if she was lying or not," Finn said, frowning at the blood that covered his tunic.

Cade watched Alexia contemplatively. "If I go in her head now, she might be too weak to survive the process. We don't know how much blood she's lost. Your face is bruised, and your gloves are missing. What happened?"

His thumb brushed over her bare hand, making her shiver. There was a proud twinkle in his concerned gaze. She had forgotten about taking her gloves off. Now that she was aware of the missing coverings, the air on her skin felt foreign, but right at the same time.

"I couldn't climb in my gloves and the vault tried to fight back when I grabbed the Bloodstone. What should I do with it?"

When Bridget reached into her pocket, Cade stopped her. "Keep it, for now. No one knows we have it. If my father does suspect anything, he'll assume it's on me. Besides, you need to wash up and rest."

"So do you," Bridget argued, thumbing the purple under his eyes. "What happened here?"

Cade hesitated; his brown eyes torn.

"What did he do?" Finn asked.

"Nothing I didn't expect," Cade said. "He brought in one of his Shamans to try to show me what he believes is coming."

Bridget studied his tense posture. "And what is that?"

"What a Shaman sees is always changing. It's why their visions are only supposed to be taken with a grain of salt, not obsessed over, like my father's been doing. I only saw flashes. And what I saw is…impossible."

Despite his words, the haunted look in his eyes didn't disappear.

"What about the lights? And all those soldiers?" Bridget asked.

"The Shaman had to enter my head to show me the visions. When he was done, he tried to stay and search for more. That was probably my father's plan all along. Figure out what secrets I'm keeping. I fought him off, but it caused the lights to flicker, and the soldiers came as precaution."

Exhaustion hit Bridget like a freight train. She closed her eyes and leaned against Cade's chest. Even though she wanted to know what he had seen, she didn't think she could stay upright much longer. He placed a steadying hand on her lower back.

"You two get some rest," Finn said. "I'll stay with Alexia and then we can keep switching until she wakes up."

CHAPTER THIRTY

The next day, Alexia remained unconscious, still and silent. The only sign of life she gave was a brief fluttering of eyelids when Delphine changed her bandages. The puncture wounds in Alexia's abdomen bled profusely. And wouldn't stop. They all wondered if Cora was keeping them open for a reason, whether with blood magic or a poisoned blade. Anxious for answers, Bridget sat with Cade as they took their turn watching over Alexia. On the floor, she continued to read through the old king's journal. Beside her, Cade meticulously sketched an image that looked like old ruins. Bridget didn't recognize the sight, but something about it seemed oddly familiar.

"Have you heard anything about the fourth task?" she asked, breaking the comfortable silence.

Cade shook his head and continued to draw. The first three tasks of the tournament had happened in rapid-fire succession. Bridget found the sudden lull odd. Plus, her and Delphine hadn't heard a whisper from the other remaining contestants about the state of the dining room.

Bridget snapped the journal shut and stood up. Thick beads of sweat rolled down her back in the stuffy, small room. She shrugged off her leather jacket and tossed it in the corner. "Has anyone been to check on our friend in the dungeon?" Bridget asked, fanning herself with the heavy book.

"Castor and Finn have both been down there with food and water," Cade answered absentmindedly. He frowned at something he drew and hurriedly scratched it out.

A flame of impatience sparked in Bridget. "Now that we have the Bloodstone, can we finally ask him?"

"Ask him what?"

"About the second gate."

Cade crumpled up the parchment in his hand. "Is it not in the journal?"

"The king that wrote this journal didn't want whatever he wrote down to be easily understood," Bridget said, throwing the book down on her jacket. "I don't understand half the references or locations."

"Tell me something it says, and I'll try to help."

"Why does it matter? It says nothing about another gate. It mentions Cavamyne, which I would like to eventually hear more about, and the original court on almost every page," Bridget ranted. She paused and took a deep breath. The heat had brought an uncomfortable flush to her cheeks. Glancing down at the journal, she finally decided to voice a theory that had been forming in the back of her mind. One that was daring her to hope.

"It does mention the Bloodstone. And a curse."

Cade rubbed the back of his neck. "A Shaman wouldn't have used the Bloodstone as an anchor for a curse. It's too valuable."

"Not even for one really powerful? One that would affect hundreds of lives for years to come?"

"What are you getting at?

"I think the Bloodstone could be the anchor for the curse on the humans," Bridget said. Excitement buzzed in her veins. If she could cross the gate, be reunited with Nylah, and still remember...It was a hope threatening to blossom in her heart. But deep down, she was afraid the mere mention of the thought would jinx the possibility.

"Even if it is, that curse requires the blood of someone who had been dead for over 500 years. I told you the story," Cade said. Weariness overcame his features, like it was a subject he had already pondered over far too much.

"Like the contracts for the tournament, there could be a loophole."

"There's not. Don't you think I've tried to figure out a way to get around the curse? It's impossible. It can't be broken," Cade snapped, eyes flashing with unrestrained frustration.

Bridget closed her eyes, trying to block out his words. The idea had already rooted itself deep in her soul, and she wasn't ready to let go of it. "Why are you so adamant that I'm wrong? We could try—"

The door creaked open.

"I'm here to take a shift," Delphine said, poking her head in. When she noticed their tense postures, she hesitated. "Or I can come back..."

Needing to get out of the suffocating room, Bridget strode past her without a word. The cool air of the hallway calmed her racing heart.

Behind her, Cade muttered to Delphine, "Keep an eye on the jacket. We'll be right back."

A flash of guilt filled Bridget's gut. The Bloodstone. She paused, internally debating if she should go back for it. One glance at Cade's taut expression, though, kept her legs moving forward. Delphine wouldn't let anything happen to it.

They entered his room in tense silence. Bridget darted straight for the sink and poured herself a glass of water.

"We need to talk," Cade said, confirming what Bridget already knew. Her heart sank to her stomach.

She wasn't ready.

She wasn't ready to have vocalized what she knew was coming. Leaving. Forgetting. Becoming a stranger in her own mind again. The fear that her heart wouldn't recognize Cade a second time and that her connection to Nylah would be different with no memories...

How was she supposed to find the strength to step through the gate? The longer she stayed in Elyria, the more intangible the inevitable became in her head.

She didn't want to talk about it. Talking about it would make the future real. The future where she was completely erased again.

"Those are words a girl never wants to hear," Bridget quipped in a last-ditch effort to avoid the subject, but the words came out hoarse and hollow. Cade didn't laugh. He pushed a lock of loose hair behind her ear.

"The curse on humans can't be broken. Vega made sure of that a long time ago," he said.

"But…"

"Okay, let's say you're right. How long are you willing to spend trying to break it? What if it takes years to find a loophole?"

"I can't leave Nylah alone that long," Bridget said, the words nearly stifled by the selfish and cruel desire that a part of her did want to stay and fight for the possibility. But she couldn't imagine going back to find a grown-up Nylah...

"I know," Cade said. Pausing, he took a deep breath and grabbed her hands. "What about me? In five years, what am I doing?"

His future was clear in her mind. She didn't even have to think twice. Since regaining her memories and finding out his true identity, there was nothing she believed more. "You're king," Bridget whispered, afraid the admission would send his father flying into the room.

Based on his expression, she didn't think it was the answer Cade wanted to hear. He looked down at their hands and swallowed hard. "Is that right?" he asked with bitter resignation.

"There's so much you could do for Elyria. You can make it better. You're smart, you're *good…*"

"My father is not going to let go of his power. It's all he has left."

"You're stronger than him. You said that you would fight him one day," Bridget argued. "You can now. I'm free and with the contracts voided, the tournament—"

"Are you free?" Cade challenged fiercely. "You're still here. You want to go back to New York."

It wasn't a question, but Bridget still shakily answered, "Yes."

"And then what?"

"I don't know," Bridget stuttered. She hadn't been able to bring herself to imagine anything past leaving Elyria.

"If I'm king, where does that leave you?"

While Cade's future was obvious and clear in her mind, hers presented itself on a blank canvas. All her life, nothing seemed permanent. Not even where she lived. One year, she had moved foster homes five times. Since then, Bridget had learned to live day by day. Only looking at tomorrow. Tomorrow was the only thing that was certain. Nylah had changed that somewhat. Fighting for custody of her foster sister had given Bridget a clear path to follow, at least for a few years.

Until Cade, she had never had to confront the future. And now it was coming at her faster than she expected. Even at the start of their relationship, she hadn't thought of where things would lead to or imagined any consequences—she only knew that she wanted him. No matter the cost. Bridget's throat filled with a bitter bile. The thought had been so very Fae. And it was costing her more than she thought possible.

"Maybe when Nylah turns eighteen, you come and get us," Bridget suggested. The idea sounded pathetic and unfair the moment the words were out of her mouth.

"And make you lose everything again? Make Nylah lose everything? Do you really think it's safe for her here?"

"I don't know," Bridget wailed, tears filling her eyes. She could barely breathe as her mind swirled to come up with any solution. "If you're king, it will be. Things will be different."

"What if Elyria is never safe?" Cade snarled, pulling out the crumpled sketch from his pocket. His shoulders slumped as he glared at it.

"What did you see yesterday?" Bridget asked. She tried to grab the drawing, but Cade threw it in the fireplace, where it dissolved in seconds.

"It doesn't matter. There's only one way this ends."

"No," Bridget choked, frantically shaking her head. Tears blurred her vision.

"When you were taken, I made a promise to myself that when the time came, I would let you go," Cade said, voice raspy as he tried to brush away her tears. "I didn't before and look where it got you. You're going to go back to the human realm to be with Nylah. You'll have the life that you want…And I'll stay here."

"No," Bridget repeated as a sob wracked through her. The painful lump in her throat prevented her from saying that it wasn't the life she wanted if he wasn't there.

Or maybe she did say the words aloud, because Cade roughly replied, "I can't come after you this time."

"Why not?" Bridget cried.

Cade shut his eyes. A brief tremble shook his body. "It was the price I had to pay to save you," he answered hoarsely. "To get your memories back, I had to give up my ability to cross the gate."

The air left Bridget's lungs. She was falling and could see no end in sight. Heart clenching painfully, she gaped at him, unable to form a rational thought in her head. It was her fault. All her fault...

Her legs wobbled. The room spun. In fact, Bridget was surprised she still stood upright.

Because of her stupid decision to drink Archer's potion, Cade would never be able to return to the human realm.

She was going to be sick.

Bridget was about to voice the concern when a loud thump and a plea for help echoed from the next room. Cade cleared his throat and tightened his grip on her.

"Was that Delphine?"

Frantically, they ran to the next room, where Cade pushed the ajar door open. Delphine lay on the floor, hands and feet bound with a black rope that twisted and tightened with each movement. Red welts marred her pale skin.

"What the hell happened?" Cade asked, kneeling down to free her, but the moment he touched the ropes, they burrowed deeper into Delphine's skin.

"No, don't. We need Castor. She spelled them somehow," Delphine cried. "I've never seen magic like that."

Cade's eyes glowed white as he called for Castor.

"Alexia used magic? She's human," Bridget said. "I *know* that she is."

"Not Alexia. *Me*. Or someone disguised as me, but with horrible, pitch-black eyes," Delphine shuddered. "Before I could scream, these ropes materialized and threw me to the ground. Seconds later, whoever it was and Alexia disappeared in a cloud of smoke."

"Could it have been a Nymph?" Bridget asked.

"Castor's on his way," Cade said as his eyes returned to their normal color. "It can't be a Nymph. Their eyes don't turn black when they transform. Besides, I don't think there's been a Nymph born this century powerful enough to do a full body transformation."

Bile rose in Bridget's throat. "Cora. It has to be her. Quinn wouldn't have taken Alexia with her."

Her eyes darted to the corner of the room, panic and fury igniting like wildfire in her chest. "No, no, no," Bridget breathed, falling to her knees as she desperately patted her jacket. "This can't be happening."

"Please tell me it's only the journal that's missing," Cade uttered tersely.

Dread filled her stomach as she picked up the leathery item. Even though she already knew what she would find, she checked the pocket anyway.

"And..." Bridget trailed, guilt overwhelming her as she held up the jacket toward Cade.

"Fuck," Cade roared, kicking the bed with enough force to splinter the wooden frame.

In frustration, Bridget slammed her jacket into the stone wall. She had been so hot, so distracted by her own worries that she had completely forgotten about the relic in her pocket. Had left the room without a second thought about it. Had, once again, made a rash decision based around her emotions.

And completely fucked everything up.

She squeezed her eyes shut, willing the tears to retreat into her skull.

"I understand taking the Bloodstone, but why the journal?" Delphine asked.

"Cora's been after one thing this entire time," Bridget said. "The location of the other gate must be in there. Cade...would she be able to use the Bloodstone to open it?"

His silence told her yes.

Her heart sank. If Cora used it to open the gate, she was never going to forgive herself. Especially when she'd already cost Cade the ability to cross the gate and return to the place she knew he wanted to be. The place she wanted him to be also. "So what do we do?" Bridget asked.

Cade's eyes darkened. "Once Castor gets here and frees Delphine, we get to visit our least favorite person."

CHAPTER THIRTY-ONE

Bridget stared at the back of Cade's head as they walked down the spiral steps to where Archer was held captive. He hadn't looked at her since Castor had cut Delphine's binds. She hoped that if he felt her eyes on him long enough, he would finally turn around, but he stubbornly kept his gaze on the path in front of them. White hot anger buzzed through her veins. At herself, for leaving the Bloodstone in the room with Alexia. And with him, for not telling her about the price to save her sooner.

Anger was the only thing keeping her afloat, upright, and sane.

If she decided to feel anything else, she was sure she would collapse into a pile of rubble on the floor.

Cade would never be able to return to the human realm.

The Bloodstone was missing.

All because of her.

She couldn't afford to have reality hit her until one of those things were fixed. So down they went, with insane hope that *Archer* would be willing to work with them and tell them what she couldn't discern from the journal.

The moment they entered the dark, damp room, Archer hopped up and smirked triumphantly. Bridget was momentarily startled by his appearance. Despite his current boastful aura, his face was tired and haggard. His time in the cell wasn't doing him any favors.

"I heard Quinn escaped," he crowed. "Can I get an apology?"

Finn glowered at him. "If you want to get out of here, I would shut your mouth and listen."

Archer raised a brow at the proposition and studied Cade's tense stance. "I'm officially intrigued."

"We need the location of the second gate," Bridget said, hoping he would cut to the chase and just tell them. She could tell no one, especially Cade, was in the mood for his games. Castor also looked one thread away from breaking.

"You don't remember?" Archer asked Bridget, his voice taunting.

Bridget glared at him. "Obviously not."

"Tell us or I rip your mind to shreds trying to find it," Cade hissed impatiently. In the blink of an eye, he was inches from Archer's cell. The Warlock took a nervous step back.

Archer chuckled and raised his palms. "Let's make a deal."

"Rip his mind to shreds," Castor growled.

"And I thought we had bonded," Archer chastised, clicking his tongue. Castor took a threatening step forward, but stopped when Cade raised a hand.

"What could you possibly want?" Cade asked. "Quinn is gone. She didn't even bother killing you before she left."

Archer paused, taking a moment to gaze at their tired faces. Even Delphine, the most optimistic of them all, stood quietly in the corner. "I'll take you to the gate," he stated resignedly, but Bridget knew better.

"What's the catch?" She asked.

Lips twisting, he replied, "You let me cross when we get there."

"*You* want to go to the human realm?"

"Don't you?"

Her nostrils flared at his quick response. Archer didn't know what she had just learned about Cade, but the response felt like a slap in the face. She must have flinched because Cade laid a steadying hand on her back. She leaned into the touch, relieved to feel him again.

"Why should we believe you want to leave Elyria?" Finn asked.

"There's nothing left for me here," Archer answered dully. For the first time, Bridget heard sincerity. Everyone was quiet as they waited for Cade's decision.

After a long moment, Cade sighed. "I have a feeling I'm going to regret this. Open his cell."

Finn stepped forward and pulled a pair of keys out of his pocket. When Archer's cell door squeaked open, he rolled his eyes at the Warlock who stretched dramatically. "Wipe that stupid smirk off your face."

"When do we leave?" Archer asked enthusiastically. He reached out to shake Cade's hand but was promptly ignored.

"Where exactly are we going?" Bridget asked.

Archer grinned deviously. "Cavamyne."

Of course. Cavamyne. The one kingdom in Elyria that had the most lore and mystery surrounding it. A kingdom with so much dark history, even the Fae didn't dare travel to it anymore. They should have realized the second gate was located there sooner.

"I was hoping you wouldn't say that," Finn mumbled under his breath. "Why can't we ever go somewhere pleasant? Like a tropical island? I miss Pina Coladas."

"How long does it take to get there?" Delphine asked. "Are there even any roads? I heard most passages were destroyed shortly after the war."

Cade rubbed his forehead. "The only way to get there is by horseback over the mountain. I've seen old maps in the library, but I doubt they're still accurate. I'm guessing it'll take at least a day."

"I know a few shortcuts," Archer said.

Castor rolled his eyes. "Of course, you do."

"Cora already has a few hours on us," Bridget whispered to Cade, urging him with her eyes they needed to hurry. If Cora used the Bloodstone to cross the gate before they got there, she doubted they would be able to find her again.

Cade rolled his lips together, looking torn. "It's going to be noticeable if I'm gone too long. And I don't want my father finding out you can leave."

"It's good you already have the perfect distraction then," Castor said, stepping forward, "Me."

"What do you mean?" Delphine asked.

"It's time I finally go home. The king has kept me from crossing the gate long enough," Castor stated tiredly. "He won't like one of the Tafari Princes causing a scene. I'll give him a big enough headache to not even notice you're gone."

Delphine looked like she wanted to argue.

"Thank you," Cade replied with a grateful smile, briefly squeezing Castor's shoulder.

"You already know I'm coming with you," Finn said. "Besides, someone needs to keep an eye on the clown."

Archer pretended to look affronted. "Clown?" He mouthed, shaking his head.

"Me too. We're ready to go when you are," Delphine said.

Cade smiled, but it didn't reach his eyes. "I'll get the horses ready."

With that, he walked up the stairs without another word. The slam of the wooden door made Bridget flinch.

"Trouble in paradise?" Archer whispered as Finn bound his hands with old metal cuffs.

"Mind your own business," Bridget hissed, trying to ignore the swirling knots in her stomach.

In the stables, everyone was quiet as they readied their horses. The sun, low on the horizon, made the saddles barely visible. Bridget squinted as she tightened the straps. She chuckled to herself, finding it funny how easily she was able to do it on her own. Before Elyria, the only horses she had ever seen were the ones pulling carriages in Central Park. Even then, she had never gotten close enough to touch one, let alone ride one.

As Bridget rubbed her horse's forehead, she sensed Cade behind her. He had changed into a long black cloak and looked unbearably handsome. His hair was slicked back, and his morganite pendant proudly dangled around his neck, no longer hidden. Her breath hitched. Wordlessly, he handed her a thick pair of gloves.

"I thought you said I didn't have to wear them," Bridget mumbled, suddenly feeling self-conscious at the sight of her bare hands.

Cade smirked and grabbed her fingers. When he pressed a kiss to the palm of her hand, butterflies erupted in her stomach. "It will be cold going over the mountain pass."

Bridget's cheeks heated. When she thought he would walk away, he moved closer. His arm brushed against hers. Fiddling with the straps of her saddle, he went silent again.

"Do you think your father will fall for Castor's stunt?" Bridget asked. She wanted to reach out and touch him, the heat from his arm wasn't enough, but she clumsily slid on the gloves instead.

He paused thoughtfully. "No, but it will buy us time."

"You're not mad at me?" she blurted. She didn't want to break the peace between them now, but she couldn't stand not knowing what he was thinking.

A flicker of surprise lit up his face. He reached forward and lightly thumbed the pulse in her neck. Before goosebumps had the chance to erupt on her skin, his lips were on hers, hot and insistent. His fingers dug into her back, making her flush all the way to her toes.

When she clutched the material of his shirt to pull him closer, all her anger dissolved. In that moment, it didn't matter if she was in Elyria, or New York, or that fate seemed to be insistently pulling them in opposite directions. She was with Cade.

And that was enough.

Hours later, or seconds later, Bridget wasn't sure, he pulled away. His fingers traced the edge of her cheekbone.

"You're not the only who left that room," he said.

The words didn't ease all the guilt permanently lodged in her chest, but they were enough to dull the emotion's spike in her heart. Bridget rested her chin against his chest and took a moment to catch her breath. "What if I'm wrong? What if it was Quinn that took Alexia and the Bloodstone? And we're going to Cavamyne for nothing?"

"Is that what you think?" Cade asked quietly.

His calm voice soothed her swirling mind. No, it wasn't what she thought. Alexia was loyal to Cora alone, and Cora wanted to find the second gate. To either wreak havoc on the human realm, or truly help the covens, Bridget wasn't sure. And Quinn probably didn't even know Alexia existed. After a moment, she shook her head. "No, that's where they'll go."

"Cora won't hand over the Bloodstone without a fight," Cade said. There was both worry and warning in his voice.

"I don't want to kill her," Bridget said, and it wasn't until she said the words aloud that she realized she meant them. The truth made her feel shameful and twisted, but she couldn't bear to have Cora's blood on her hands. And if there was one thing she'd learned in Elyria, it was how much hatred and magic could twist a person up and destroy them from the inside out.

Cade ran his hand down her braided hair, making her shiver. "Then we won't," he promised.

"And when we get there, I don't want to go back yet. I need…a little more time."

Time to heal. Time to fix everything she had screwed up. Time to…let him go.

Even if it seemed impossible.

Bridget closed her eyes and leaned forward, wanting nothing more than to feel close to him, when a whine of a horse interrupted her movement. To the right, Archer hopped around with one foot stuck in a stirrup. Finn followed him, trying his best to grab him and free him. Despite everything, watching the two of them struggle made her giggle.

"You're going to let Archer have his own horse?" she asked.

"No, he's riding with Finn," Cade said, grinning mischievously. The sight took her breath away. It had been a while since she had seen his face light up, had seen him truly smile, like he had so many times in that upstairs corner booth in Hungry Pies. And now that he was, she couldn't tear her eyes away from him.

She didn't know what was going to happen when she finally crossed the gate and went back home, but she did know Fae magic. It was magic that loved deals and bargains. So, deep in her heart, she desperately hoped she got the chance to pick one thing from Elyria to remember, just one, because she never wanted to forget the way he was looking at her right now.

A laugh broke free from her throat. "Interesting. If something happens between them, are you sure that's who you want around you for the rest of your life?"

Cade laughed and lightly flicked her nose. And even though she didn't need it, he helped her onto her horse. Bridget rolled her eyes when he was able to effortlessly hop on top of his. Soon, they were all riding into the night, heading for Cavamyne.

CHAPTER
THIRTY-TWO

The journey to Cavamyne was much more daunting than Bridget expected. Since there was no clear road, she tediously followed Cade through every crooked trail and narrow stream in the uninhabited forests surrounding Astraeus. The looming pine trees blocked the light of the moon, and Bridget's chest twisted every time she thought she lost sight of Cade. The darkness was thick and whispered unintelligible things every time she daringly glanced into it. Bridget knew her mind was playing tricks on her, but she couldn't stop shivers from crawling up her spine.

Once they made it to the Balor Mountains, Archer and Finn took the lead. By then, the sun shone brightly in the sky, making the rocky terrain easier to navigate. A few times, Bridget's horse struggled on the steep incline and almost sent her flying backwards. She hoped that Archer was leading them the right way and not to a trap. The stiffness of Cade's shoulders told Bridget he thought the same. He kept his eyes fixed on Archer over the entire mountain pass.

Even though it was early afternoon, the sky muted and darkened as they entered Cavamyne. Swirling gray clouds hovered as far as the eye could see and a barren landscape provided no color or distraction. The land, full of dirt and hollow trees, was lifeless. Light snow fell on her jacket.

In front of her, Delphine sighed impatiently. "Are we close?"

"Patience is a virtue," Archer sang, clicking his tongue obnoxiously.

"For a Warlock, you make a lot of human realm references," Bridget grumbled, mostly to herself, as she thought of the various phrases he had taunted her with when she had no memories. She was far enough back she didn't think he would hear her, but Archer tensed.

The deeper into Cavamyne they traveled, the smokier the air became. Bridget coughed as her watery eyes studied the land around her. Large, rolling hills surrounded them. When she imagined grass, trees, and life on each hump, Cavamyne turned quite beautiful in her head. Only true horror could turn such a place into a wasteland.

Bridget rolled her neck to get rid of the chills that had suddenly overtaken her.

"Are you okay?" Cade asked. She hadn't noticed him move beside her.

"I'm ready to stand on my own two feet again," Bridget said, waving him off. It was the truth. Her ass had numbed halfway up the mountain. She was sure she was going to fall straight to the ground when it was time to get off her horse.

It wasn't long before they came to an expanse of towering ruins. The decrepit stone building seemed to be the only thing left standing in Cavamyne. Even though the structure's roof was missing, it loomed over six stories high. Gaping holes replaced large windows, and vines suffocated any beauty the stones once held.

"Is this…" Bridget's voice trailed, unable to take her eyes off the ruins. Her heart stuttered as a jerking shudder tore through her.

Delphine nodded, just as entranced. "The old Tuathan palace."

"It looks like it was beautiful." When Bridget finally tore her eyes away, she found Cade watching her closely.

"I've heard it was even grander than the one in Tafari. Or even Versailles," Archer said with a slight grin. It faltered when everyone ignored him.

When Cade hopped off his horse, Bridget eagerly did the same. She was proud her legs only wobbled slightly when they hit the ground.

Without warning, a wave of exhaustion hit her. They had barely stopped all day. Around them, there was no sign of Cora. Or any other person.

The click of handcuffs brought her out of her reverie.

"Is this really necessary?" Archer grumbled as Finn tightened the silver circles around his wrists.

"Yes," Finn replied coolly. Bridget was impressed. The entire trip, he had remained unfazed by Archer's constant jabbering.

Cade flicked his head, causing Archer to stumble forward like he was being pushed by an invisible hand. "Is the gate inside?"

"Was that necessary? I could have fallen on my face," Archer said. When Cade glared at him, he continued, "The gate is in the back. It lies in the middle of what's left of the ceremonial courtyard."

Bridget didn't know what a ceremonial courtyard was, but the words gave her goosebumps. Cade must have noticed because he grabbed her hand to lead her inside the ruined palace. What must have been a thick metal door was missing. The rest followed them through the entrance. Bridget heard Finn remove his sword from its sheath.

It was quiet as they walked. Everyone's breath echoed throughout the ruins. When Delphine turned on a flashlight, creatures hidden in the darkness appeared. Bridget flinched and grabbed Cade's hand tighter when a rat scurried by her ankle. The walls and floors were stained, and most of the furniture was either missing or left in tatters. Portraits hung on the walls, but dust or mud prevented Bridget from seeing what was painted.

When they entered a room that looked like it might have been a kitchen, a series of creaks echoed above them.

"What was that?" Delphine asked before the wooden beams above them came crashing down.

Bridget didn't have time to scream before Cade wrapped his arm around her waist and pulled her out of the way. He squeezed her tightly as dust and splinters exploded around them.

Heart pounding, Bridget frantically studied the wreckage. To the side, Delphine was pressed against the wall, having barely missed one of the beams. Finn and Archer were on the ground, trapped underneath two large pieces of wood as they bickered with each other about the best way to get free. Bridget sighed in relief.

"Something's tickling my ankle. Please don't tell me it's a rabid racoon," Archer moaned as he waved his foot off the ground.

Cade rolled his eyes, and with a flick of his hands, the beams flew off them. "It's a weed, you idiot," he growled.

Bridget stopped listening when she noticed a glow coming from a small doorway. Without thinking, she walked toward it. She somehow knew it would lead her to the gate. She faintly heard Cade call her name but kept going. When she stepped through the doorway, her stomach dropped.

About fifty feet in front of her was a large outdoor throne room. Two stone chairs sat above a pitted, circular floor. It was almost stage-like in its design. Rows and rows of torches lit the area and illuminated a flat stone that was positioned directly in the middle.

To Bridget's horror, on the stone lay a trembling, unconscious Alexia. Above her stood Cora. One of her hands dug into Alexia's side, the other grasped the Bloodstone. Black veins protruded from her arms, neck, and face. Her lips moved frantically as she recited a spell under her breath, over and over again. She didn't stop, even when she met Bridget's eyes. The Witch's chest heaved with every breath.

Magic was in the air. Bridget could almost see it. Taste it. The wind howled as power radiated from Cora in waves. Part of Bridget was too scared to move any closer, confident the sheer force of what came out of Cora would knock her to the ground. The stone, though, didn't vibrate or glow like she had seen in the past, like she would expect it to if Cora was trying to open the gate. It remained still under Alexia's body.

When Bridget sensed Cade behind her, she slowly moved forward. Cora stared at them the entire way down. It was the first time Bridget had seen her in person since getting her memories back. She expected to feel more, but all she could see was the shell of a woman who kept her life from her. She would be tortured no more.

Stopping a few feet away from the gate, Bridget grabbed Cade's arm. As she gazed at the stone, a sharp pain went through her chest. For a few seconds, it was hard to breathe. Beside her, Cade's muscles tensed simultaneously.

"Hello, Bridget," Cora said with a pained smile. She didn't seem surprised to see her. In fact, Bridget thought she saw the barest flicker of relief in her eyes.

"What the hell are you doing?" Bridget asked, flinching slightly when the torches suddenly glowed brighter.

Cora let out a shaky, unamused cackle. "As you can see, the Bloodstone isn't working."

Gripping the Bloodstone tighter in her left hand, the Witch mumbled another spell. Again, the stone remained motionless. Bridget swore the ground rumbled. Cora's refusal to give up on the spell was manifesting itself as an outward explosion.

"Didn't the Sanguis teach you how to use it?" Cade asked. Stepping in front of Bridget, he reached out a hand toward Cora, but it was flung backward by an opaque shield. He tried again but got the same result.

"Unlike Quinn, I've had no teacher," Cora said, baring her teeth at him in a snarl. "Everything I've accomplished, I figured out how to do on my own. It hasn't been easy."

Bridget's hackles rose at the prideful tone in her voice. She didn't see much to be proud of. She clearly didn't know how to use the Bloodstone, and it was killing her. "Why? What do you want?"

Cora hissed as more black veins formed under her eyes. "This wasn't always the plan. I was supposed to find you and look after you."

"For Quinn?"

"I saved you from Quinn," Cora gasped, barely able to speak. "But when I learned that it was the prince that was looking for you…My plans changed."

The thundering of footsteps coming from the old palace ruins made Cora grimace and stop her rant. Bridget cursed under her breath as Delphine and Finn, who dragged a reluctant Archer, made their way to the pit.

"If you hold on much longer, you'll kill yourself and Alexia," Cade said.

"Don't tell me what I can do, boy," Cora growled as another pulse of magic vibrated the barrier around her. "You don't understand how much power is running through my veins right now."

"Who wanted to find me?" Bridget asked, desperate for answers before Cora pushed herself too far. She tried to step forward, but Cade held out his arm to stop her.

Cora briefly closed her eyes. "If you would have just loved me, Bridget. With your influence over the future king, we could have done great things together. As a family, we could have changed the foundations of Elyria and brought power and prosperity to the covens..."

"I had a family, and you kept me from them. You tortured me," Bridget shouted, unable to stop her voice from cracking. Tears filled her eyes as she remembered all the times she tried to get away, didn't submit to Cora, or failed to understand the world she was thrown into. All Cora had given her was pain.

"I made you stronger and prepared you for what's to come. Remember that."

Hysteria bubbled up in Bridget's stomach. Eventually, she would cross the gate and forget about Cora forever. She would look down at her hands and not remember the occurrence of each scar. Or know why there was a coven symbol, a zodiac symbol, burned into her skin.

Whatever Cora thought she did was really for nothing.

Bridget didn't know whether to laugh, scream, or cry. The only thing to come was more pain and forgetting. And based on the way the texture of Cora's skin on her arms turned flaky, Bridget was close to believing she would never know *why*.

Squeezing the Bloodstone, Cora screamed the spell at the top of her lungs. Flames shot out of each torch, but the stone remained still.

"Why isn't it working?" Cora groaned, blood flowing freely from the corners of her eyes.

"Because you're not a true Sanguis."

Even though she recognized the voice, Bridget still jumped. Out of the shadows, Quinn appeared between the two stone thrones.

CHAPTER THIRTY-THREE

Quinn crossed her arms and leaned against the smaller one.

"You followed us," Cade stated.

"Not exactly. I knew you'd end up here eventually," Quinn shrugged, fixing her eyes on Bridget. "Because you do want to go back, right? Isn't a little sister missing you?"

"Shut up," Bridget snarled.

Quinn jumped into the pit and moved toward Cora and the gate. Finn raised his sword and pushed Archer and Delphine behind him.

"Back away, Quinn," Cora said threateningly, but her trembling body looked like it was about to collapse. Once and for all.

"Let go of the Bloodstone before it kills us all," Quinn replied in a bored tone.

"Not before I open the gate. Permanently," Cora choked out before another pulse of magic expanded the swirling barrier around her.

"That's not what the Bloodstone is used for," Quinn tittered knowingly as a sly smirk painted her lips. "You're all in way over your head."

"Who's been your teacher?" Cade asked. He grasped the back of Bridget's coat and pulled her back toward him. The movement was subtle, but Quinn's eyes narrowed at the gesture.

"Someone who's been around longer than you can imagine," Quinn said, turning to glare at the Bloodstone. "That thing has become the bane of my existence."

Bridget scoffed incredulously. "Then why do you want it?"

"I don't. She does. And I've been waiting a long time to finally get my hands on it. All I wanted was a simple trade. Bridget for the Bloodstone." Quinn fingered the barrier around Cora and hissed when it burned her. She shook her hand and continued, "But before I could get in contact with the prince, Cora took matters into her own hands. Someone couldn't keep their mouth shut about who you were."

Archer took a step back as Quinn eyed him, annoyance and rage etched on her features.

"And then Cora went to the king," Cade concluded.

"Bridget for the location of the second gate, but he's not a man of his word," Cora seethed, eyes now fully black. Bridget wondered how she was still aware of what was going on at all.

"I could've told you that," Finn muttered.

"You almost ruined everything," Quinn spat at Cora. "Even if I had to join that horrid tournament, it worked out."

Cora sneered at her but made no move to drop the unstable spell.

"How so? You fled the palace after I got my memories back," Bridget stated hostilely.

Quinn laughed. "You still can't see the big picture. Cade couldn't stay away from you. I knew it was only a matter of time before the stone presented itself. Here. In the place I need it most."

Bridget's nostrils flared in anger. When her fists clenched together, Cade placed a steadying hand on her lower back.

"What do you want with the Bloodstone?" he asked.

"The same thing almost everyone here wants," Quinn replied as she slowly pulled a small gun from her back pocket. "To open the gate to another realm."

Everyone, even Cora, tensed as Quinn swirled the gun around her middle finger. But Bridget kept her eyes fixed on the Witch in front of her as she tried to decipher her words. Quinn didn't need the Bloodstone to travel to the human realm. She had already been there on her own. From the back seat of a car, Bridget had watched Quinn drive a knife into a stranger's heart to cross back into Elyria...into Cavamyne.

Bridget's heart skipped a beat. The journal.

The journal, with all its riddles and mumblings, told the story of a war, one that was so devastating it nearly decimated an entire population and changed the entirety of Elyria. A war that only ended because of the last-minute creation of a curse.

When she had seen the words Bloodstone and curse written together on the same page, Bridget had assumed the old king was referring to the curse on the humans. Every book Cade had shown her told the same story. The human girl was killed, the curse was enacted, the crown prince disappeared, the war ended...

But she had been wrong.

So wrong.

Bridget now understood why the last few pages of the journal were so confusing to her.

Because there was not one curse, but *two*.

One created by Vega, the other by the Tuathan.

Banished is the word Cade had used. The word that every history, journal, or record used. But Bridget had never asked what that banishment entailed. She had never stopped to think how such a large, powerful coven was so confidently driven away, never to return again...

Quinn grinned at her tauntingly.

"You're not after the human realm..." Bridget dared to utter.

"Ding ding ding," Quinn sang. "Judging by both your faces, I think you have it figured out."

Bridget whipped her head up to gaze at Cade. All the color drained from his face. She knew his next words would confirm the conclusion that was already dangerously swirling in her gut.

"She wants to open the gate to Iegorus," he said.

"Is that even possible?" Delphine gasped.

Finn shook his head. "They were banished, not cursed."

"Banished with a curse. Your ancestors wanted to make sure the Sanguis never returned again," Quinn said nonchalantly. "It happened right here, you know? Seconds after the curse on the humans was created. You'll never guess who was used to bind it."

"How do you know all this?" Cade asked.

Quinn shrugged. "Like I said, my master has been around for a very long time."

"Breaking that curse will unleash a power that will kill us all," Cade roared, eyes turning white as he geared himself for the fight Bridget could see coming. The morganite around his neck glowed as he began to channel his power.

"Good," Quinn stated coolly. "I don't want to be around for what she has planned."

For a split-second, Bridget saw a flicker of real emotion in her eyes. Fear. Whatever Quinn knew, she was ready to die before experiencing it. For something she apparently worked so hard to achieve, she didn't want it. A brief flash of the monster Bridget had seen in her vision entered her mind. Shivers involuntarily went down her spine.

The click of a gun made her stomach swoop.

"Put the gun down," Cade ordered menacingly. When he tried to step in front of her, Bridget grabbed his arm and pulled him back. She knew there wasn't much she could do, but her heart couldn't take him being that close to the gun. Behind her, she felt Finn shift and slowly move to the right.

Wondering why Cade didn't use his abilities to make Quinn drop the gun, the gem around Quinn's neck caught her eye. Bridget swallowed hard. Her necklace on Quinn glimmered in the firelight. The amethyst rune once protected her. Now it mocked her. Cade wouldn't be able to enter her mind...

He wouldn't be able to fling the gun from her hands. Or stop her from pulling the trigger.

And neither Finn nor Delphine would be fast enough with their abilities to surprise her.

By Quinn's calm demeanor, Bridget had a feeling she knew this. Had planned for it.

To her left, Cora struggled to maintain control of her spell and the

Bloodstone. But to Bridget's surprise, Cora's attention was no longer on the gate, but on *her*. She stared at Bridget, torn and anxious.

The barrier flickered, and the stone pit rumbled again. Bridget was sure the spell would destabilize any second. She saw Cade's eyes flicker between Cora and Quinn as he calculated which one would become the first threat.

Unbothered, Quinn studied the barrel of the gun and said, "As you know, all curses can be broken with a few special ingredients. And I finally have all three here. The Bloodstone, the original site of the curse..."

"And?" Bridget blurted.

Blood. All curses need blood, or a life, to be bound. Bridget knew that much. Her stomach churned. Maybe the curse needed a human. There had to be a reason her fate felt so deeply tied to the Bloodstone.

There had to be a reason why she was brought to Elyria.

It couldn't all be for nothing.

But when Quinn raised the gun, it was not pointed at her.

"The most important ingredient of all," Quinn declared, eyes on Cade, "him."

Panic.

Blinding, horrific panic.

That's all Bridget knew when she spotted Quinn's finger pulling the trigger.

Without thinking, she lunged forward.

A terrible, shrill scream pierced the air.

For a second, Bridget thought it might have come from her mouth as she fell to the ground. But as she took a gasping breath, she realized it was *Cora*.

Then the world exploded.

A blinding light cracked through the air like lightning as the barrier around Cora imploded. Even as Cade pressed a hand to the hole in her abdomen and covered her with his body, Bridget felt heat and wind whip agonizingly across her face. Through the brightness, she saw Finn fly through the air and hit a stone pillar. Delphine and Archer braced themselves against the wall of the stone pit, ducked and covered. Cade mouthed something to her, but she couldn't hear him.

Cora pulled her hand out of Alexia's abdomen and pointed it at Quinn. Tentacles of black smoke erupted from her outstretched fingers and darted straight at Quinn's chest. The younger Witch tried to dodge it, but she wasn't quick enough. When the smoke hit Quinn's arm, both Witches flew backwards with a harrowing screech.

The Bloodstone hit the ground with a soft clink. The gun fell a few feet to Quinn's right.

Ears ringing, Bridget turned her attention back to Cade. Above her, he repeated her name over and over. She tried to speak, but the burning in her side prevented her from doing so. All she could do was cough and gasp for breath. Cade cursed and pressed his hands down harder on where she was bleeding. His hands shook.

"You promised me," Cade croaked, trying, and failing, to sound angry.

Bridget's laugh came out choked, remembering the last time she had jumped in front of him. "I lied," she muttered, attempting a smile. Cade shook his head and pressed a bruising kiss to her lips.

An agonized howl made them both recoil. In the far corner, Quinn scrambled up. Except she no longer looked like the girl Bridget knew. A Witch with gray hair, sunken skin, and black eyes stood before them. She was covered in blood and from bicep down, her left arm was missing.

Hyperventilating, Quinn surged forward and grabbed the Bloodstone off the ground. Seconds later, she stumbled into the darkness.

"She's getting away," Bridget gasped, flailing her arms in an attempt to sit up. She banged her head against the rocky ground and groaned in frustration when she failed. The pain wasn't subsiding. If anything, it seemed to worsen with every breath.

"I don't care if she has the Bloodstone. I'm not leaving you," Cade replied vehemently. The sight of Quinn without a hand was haunting. Bridget wasn't sure the blood loss would even let her get far. She glanced around and spotted the top of Cora's head sticking out from behind the center stone. Now that the Witch was no longer trying to perform a spell with the Bloodstone, the torches had dimmed to a flicker. Next to the thrones, Finn stirred and let out a quiet groan of pain.

Archer, still in cuffs, crawled over to them as Cade ripped off a piece of his cloak to press against her wound.

"Holy shit, that doesn't look good," he breathed, gazing at the red liquid that wouldn't stop oozing from Bridget's side. When Cade glared at him, he held up his hands in innocence, "Didn't mean to state the obvious. I'll check on Finn."

He wobbled over to Finn. A large gash strung across the Fae warrior's forehead, and his arm looked excruciatingly twisted. Hands bound; Archer wouldn't be much help.

"Delphine?" Cade called; his voice hoarse. Bridget watched horror blossom on his face as the hand that had been checking for the exit wound on her back came back clean.

Bridget wiggled her body, thinking she would somehow be able to feel exactly where the bullet lay inside her.

It didn't work.

Delphine slowly hobbled over to them. One side of her face was red and bruised from being pressed up against the stone wall. She swallowed hard as she studied the bullet hole.

"Someone needs to check on Alexia," Bridget said. She couldn't remember the last time she had seen her move. Cade looked annoyed, but Delphine complied.

"She's lost a lot of blood, but I think she's okay…" Delphine murmured. She took off her coat and wrapped it around Alexia's middle.

"Delphine," Cade growled, ordering her back. "I think the bullet is somewhere still inside Bridget."

Bridget's eyelids suddenly felt very heavy. When she tried to close them, Cade shook her hard. Even though she would've done the same thing, Bridget sent him a dirty look.

Delphine knelt beside her and gingerly pulled the ripped parts of Cade's cloak away. The cold air stung Bridget's raw flesh. Cade watched Delphine with bated breath. She tried to stay straight-faced, but the worried crease between Delphine's eyes didn't lie.

It would take more than a few stitches to fix the wound.

Too busy panicking, Bridget didn't hear Delphine's words of warning. Before she could blink, Delphine stuck a finger in the bullet hole and began to dig.

Blazing fire licked Bridget's side. She couldn't control the scream that left her mouth, nor stop the way instinct told her to fight back. Cade held down her shoulders, whispering words she didn't understand, until Delphine was done.

Her dark eyes flickered anxiously. "I can't find the bullet. The wound is too deep. I only know how to do a basic stitch, and I…"

Bridget didn't need Cade's powers to read the unspoken words in Delphine's mind. As a human, there was no guarantee any Fae magic or potion would heal her. The last time she tried, the wound had worsened. She knew Cade wouldn't risk it again. She needed surgery. Human realm surgery. The bullet needed to come out, and she would continue bleeding without any stitching or cauterization soon.

Despite the pain wracking through her body, she wanted to throw up.

"I'm sorry," Delphine whispered, eyes watery. Bridget wasn't sure who she was apologizing to the most, her or Cade.

Bridget gazed at Cade, expecting him to do anything other than agree, to think of another way, *anything*...but as he stared at the blood seeping across her belly and staining his hands, ashen and defeated…

She knew what he had already decided.

"No," Bridget croaked, panic rapidly turning to hysteria. "No! I'm not ready to go yet. It's not time."

Despite wanting to get back to Nylah, how could she leave now? She wasn't ready to forget. They were still supposed to talk, think of a plan, figure out some way she could find him again…

She wasn't ready.

It was too soon.

"Can't you just…fly the bullet out?" Bridget asked Cade, even though she knew it was a dumb question. She had seen enough television to know that pulling a penetrating object out of a body usually made it worse. Bridget wasn't surprised when Cade and Delphine shared a look that told her it was too risky.

Delphine grabbed Bridget's hand and softly said, "I know you believe I can somehow fix this, Bridget, but I can't. Bullet or not, you're going to bleed out."

"Just try," Bridget pleaded, vision blurring.

They both ignored her. Cade's throat bobbed as he gazed between the gate and Bridget. "We'll need a Shaman," he told Delphine roughly, coughing slightly. "Marin, actually. You'll need to travel back to Astraeus and get her. I don't trust the others."

"Cade, please," Bridget begged. She reached up and squeezed his hand that was resting on her shoulder. He closed his eyes, causing tears to roll down his face.

"I've never traveled that far before," Delphine replied warily. "And to do it again with another person..."

"We're running out of time," Cade growled, blinking rapidly. He ripped the Morganite pendant from his neck and shoved it into Delphine's hands. "Take this."

Delphine hesitated, looking shocked at the heirloom in her hands.

"Go!" Cade roared.

Within seconds, she was gone.

As Archer and Finn stumbled toward them, Bridget stared up at Cade. Unable to look away, her heart shattered to pieces. She wanted to memorize every detail of his face in a desperate hope that she would somehow remember the color of his eyes or the exact shape of his lips. Details that Bridget couldn't imagine forgetting, but somehow had before.

"I love you," she whispered as the knot in her throat became unbearable.

She was selfish. So very selfish.

Cade let out a small laugh that sounded torn between devastation and joy. "Now you tell me."

Bridget didn't know when the tears started to freely flow down her face.

Archer sat a hunched-over Finn down next to them. He cradled his arm to his chest. Somehow, Archer had patched up the cut on his forehead. "I'll cross the gate with her and make sure she gets to the hospital," Finn vowed to Cade.

"And remind me of everything," Bridget said, suddenly feeling a spark of hope that she *would* see Cade again one day. "You have to."

Finn looked wary and shared a look with Cade.

"Bridget..." Cade sighed.

"Nylah knows," Bridget reminded him, "she won't let me forget."

"She's only ten, remember? You won't believe her," Cade replied, a twisted, ironic smile forming on his lips.

Bridget shook her head stubbornly. "She's eleven now. It'll be different."

Cade looked like he didn't believe her. Bridget briefly shut her eyes. She was tired. And cold. She wondered when Delphine would be back with Marin.

Bridget tried to sit up when she recognized a silver key being pulled out of Cade's pocket.

"You still have that?"

"Wishful thinking," Cade muttered bitterly as he handed their old apartment key over to Finn. "When you get back to New York, there's a bag in the apartment. You'll need—"

A loud pop echoed throughout the outside court. Bridget saw Delphine first. Ears bleeding and eyes rolled back in her head, she crumpled to the ground.

"Delphine!" Finn gasped.

But it was who stood behind her fallen body that made Bridget's stomach drop.

Eyes glowing white and holding Marin around the neck in the air was the king.

CHAPTER
THIRTY-FOUR

"You're a bigger disappointment every day," the king sneered, tightening his grip on Marin's neck. "Did you really think you could fool me, boy?"

Cade jumped to his feet and crouched in a protective stance over Bridget. "I showed your Shaman nothing," he hissed. In turn, he started to channel his own power. Bridget's heart dropped when she noticed his morganite still around Delphine's neck.

His father's obsidian dagger glowed in its sheath. She wasn't sure if Cade would outlast him without the pendant. Bridget struggled to sit up. The movement knocked the breath out of her.

"Your mind might be out of reach for me, but your sister's isn't. It was all too easy to get inside her head and see what you've been trying to hide."

Bridget inwardly seethed. Of course, even if she didn't try to, Cassia still betrayed them.

"Let go of Marin. Bridget's dying. She needs to send her to the human realm. No matter what happens now, you still get what you want."

Cade's words made the king tighten his grip on Marin further. "And why should I let her?"

Eyes returning to their normal color, Cade lowered his raised hands. "Please."

The king stared at him for a moment before he burst into laughter. "She's done nothing but distract you. You saw what her being here causes. Let her die."

Cade roared and surged forward. With a flick of his wrist, he sent one of the stone boulders that had come loose during Cora's spell flying straight at his father. The king whipped out his dagger and easily cracked the boulder into pebbles. The action sent Marin tumbling to the ground, where she began to cough uncontrollably.

The air fizzled with pure, raw power as Cade and his father continued to hurl magic at each other, both trying to overtake the other's mind. Bridget had never seen anything like it. Cade moved so fast; she could barely keep her eyes on him. Each strike sounded like thunder.

Next to her, Archer and Finn crawled forward and dragged an unconscious Delphine out of the way. Finn held her as Archer used a potion to try to revive her.

"You were ruthless once," the king snarled at Cade, "and worthy of your lineage."

Bridget wished her knife was nearby to throw at him. Too busy seething, she failed to notice Marin coming up behind her. The girl grabbed her under the shoulders and started to drag her toward the gate.

"What are you doing?" Bridget asked, halfway fighting against her. Every time she moved, it felt like her insides shifted.

"Trust me," Marin whispered. She gently placed Bridget against the center stone and began to back away. But right behind her, the king was close, and getting closer, as Cade began to overpower him.

"Marin, no," Bridget yelled, but it was too late. The king violently grabbed the back of Marin's neck and pressed his dagger against her side. The action made Cade stop his assault.

"Are you going to waste your time fighting me, or do you want to save her?" He snarled, flicking his head toward Bridget. Blood dripped from his nose. "I don't think she'll last much longer. I'm willing to make a deal."

Bridget wanted to argue, but she couldn't deny his words. Her entire body had numbed. Despite that, she shook her head and silently told Cade to continue. He bared his teeth and moved to strike his father again, but the king pressed the dagger harder into Marin's side.

"Kill me and I kill the Shaman," he threatened with a wild look on his face. "You won't find another to get Bridget across the gate in time."

Cade studied him intently. Blood poured from the side of his mouth. "You won't. There's only a few Shamans left, and even fewer loyal to you,"

The king scoffed and pressed the dagger into Marin's side. She gasped as it slowly inched inward.

"Stop," Cade spat. "What do you want?"

Soft moaning caught Bridget's attention. Beside her, a decrepit Cora dragged herself forward. She looked nothing like the woman Bridget had known. Her skin was flaky, discolored, and pale, and her eyes were an unrecognizable black and red.

Cora reached a hand forward. It barely hovered above the ground. She moaned something again that Bridget didn't understand. When she waved her hand in the air again, Bridget realized she was trying to hand her something. She opened her palm. Cora dropped her emerald ring in her hand. Her mother's ring.

Bridget quickly grasped it and pulled her hand back in shock. Body broken and burned, Cora stared up at her and tried to mumble something again, but no words came. Seconds later, the light died from her eyes. She went still.

Swallowing hard, Bridget put the ring on and gently closed Cora's eyes. For a split-second, she looked peaceful, like she was sleeping. As she stared at her, Bridget didn't know whether she felt grief or relief.

"I don't appreciate your tone," the king growled, drawing Bridget's attention back. "All I've ever done is try to keep Elyria from falling apart and make sure you have a kingdom to inherit. Despite everything I've shown you, you still doubt me. You still doubt that I'm doing what's best."

"You see what you want to see. The future's not set."

"It is. I've seen it. You've seen it. And it starts today," his father declared furiously, gripping Marin tightly. "I'll send your precious human through the gate, if I have your word that you'll finish the tournament, marry, and stabilize the Fae's position on the throne once and for all."

"Marry Marin, you mean." Power sizzled from Cade's fingertips.

"I don't give a shit anymore. Dwindle our family's power. So be it. The Shamans aren't long for this world anyway," the king grunted. "Your bride is your choice. I'll even give you until the spring solstice."

Bridget gazed at Cade. For once, she didn't know what he was thinking. Eyes determined and steely, he flicked his head at Finn and pointed him toward her.

The king held up a hand and froze Finn in place. "I need your word."

Bridget shook, whether from his words or the blood loss, she didn't know. A Fae's word was as good as a binding contract. She held her breath and waited for Cade's answer.

Cade didn't look at Bridget as he said, "You have my word I'll marry by the next spring solstice."

Bridget closed her eyes and let the inevitable wash over her. Even if she had expected it, the words ripped her heart to shreds. "Cade…" she whispered, just as black spots entered her vision.

Finn had almost reached her when the king stopped him in his tracks again. "No," he ordered.

Cade's demeanor cracked. He gazed anxiously between his father and Finn. "You just said—"

"Bridget can cross," the king grinned maniacally, and then looked right at Archer, "with him."

All eyes went to Archer, still crouched beside Delphine. Handcuffs still circled his wrists and for the first time, he looked lost for words. "Me?"

Archer. She was going to have to trust Archer to help her find Nylah in the human realm.

She was screwed.

The king chuckled at the horrified look on Cade's face. "Finn's injured, and you wouldn't want your best friend to be trapped on the other side, would you?"

"What do you mean?" Cade blurted, looking panicked.

"The second she crosses; I'm destroying this gate. And there are no more Shamans left willing to sneak you or your friends across the one in Astraeus. Echnav is gone. The Warlock goes with her. That's my offer," the king jeered. "He is your prisoner, right? Banishment seems a fine punishment for whatever his crimes are."

"No, he can't be trusted," Cade ranted, trying to dart to Bridget. "He's the one that brought her in the first place. There's no guarantee that—"

Distracted, Cade was vulnerable to his father's attack. With an invisible hand, the king bound Cade in place and choked him. Cade violently jerked against the force. The king drew his dagger out of Marin and pushed her toward the gate.

"Start the process," he ordered. With a snap of his fingers, the handcuffs around Archer's wrists broke in two.

"No, he can't take her. He doesn't know—" Cade hoarsely argued, fighting against the binds as hard as he could, but his father flexed his hand inward and snapped an opaque shield over his mouth. Bridget saw his mouth moving, but no sound came out.

Marin staggered forward and placed her hands against the center stone. Her blue tattoos began to brighten and shimmer. When Archer stepped forward and picked her up, Bridget kept her eyes on Cade. The devastation there brought her more pain than any gunshot wound.

"I've fallen in love with you twice now," Bridget told him. "I'll do it a third time. Even more if I have to."

The king stepped forward and blocked her view of him.

"This kingdom is better off without you. You only bring death."

Bridget wanted to glare at him, argue, fight back, anything...but the strength to hold up her head was rapidly leaving her. She closed her eyes and rested it against Archer's shoulder. She didn't want her last view of Elyria to be the king, red-faced and seething. When it was time, she would fight for one last glance of Cade.

Minutes passed, and they continued to wait. Marin kept muttering words under her breath as she braced herself against the stone, but no movement or vibration came. Bridget wasn't sure how much time had passed when she finally mumbled, "What's taking so long?"

"I have to get the timing right," Marin whispered, only for Bridget to hear. She mustered enough strength to lift her head and ask what the hell she was talking about when the stone finally began to move.

At the same time, Finn snuck forward and placed Cade's morganite pendant around his neck. Seconds later, Cade wrenched his head free.

"Marin, what the hell are you doing? Send her through now!" Cade bellowed, getting an arm free. "She's dying!"

"Stop!" The king barked, face red as he tried to subdue his son.

The stone wailed and shook. Archer took a step forward. Vision fading, Bridget tried to glance at Cade one last time. She saw him screaming and fighting, he was mouthing something…it might have been 'I love you.'

Archer touched the stone and sent them through the gate.

As he did, Bridget's heart stopped.

EPILOGUE

Fire roared through her. Gasping for breath, Bridget tried to breathe through the pain. Every breath she took threatened to make her chest explode. When she opened her eyes, a light blinded her. Wetness drenched her face. It took her a few moments to realize the lights belonged to an ambulance and that the wetness was rain falling from the sky.

The EMT flashed another light in her eye and checked her pupil. Above her, dark trees loomed. She closed her eyes again. It was not fire that brought her back, but electricity. In a haze, she spotted Archer standing behind an AED, tired and out of breath.

Bridget's eyes popped open again as realization hit her.

She was back in the human realm.

And she *remembered*.

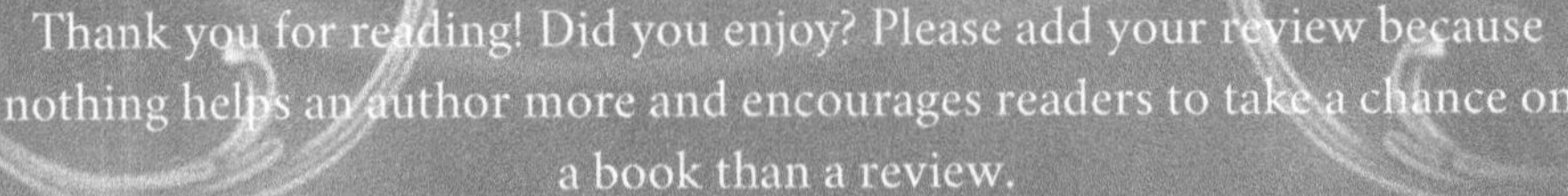

Thank you for reading! Did you enjoy? Please add your review because nothing helps an author more and encourages readers to take a chance on a book than a review.

And don't miss more in the *Blood and Curses* series from Amy Woodruff available now!

Then read THE OTHER SIDE OF THE MIRROR by City Owl Author, Dana Evyn. Turn the page for a sneak peek!

Also be sure to sign up for the City Owl Press newsletter to receive notice of all book releases!

SNEAK PEEK OF THE OTHER SIDE OF THE MIRROR

BY: DANA EVYN

The smoke was everywhere, curling around a framed picture of our family like it would strangle them with those dark tendrils. Just as it was trying to do to us now. The fire had spread too fast, moving too quickly to be real, as though the blaze was a living creature bent on destroying us. I took a deep breath, then coughed harshly as the smoke scorched my throat.

Covering my nose and mouth with my sleeve, I started to move down the hallway toward the back door…but my mother grabbed my wrist, pulling me to a stop. The gold that encircled the pupils of her hazel eyes glowed in the light of the flames as she wordlessly dragged me in the other direction, her other hand clenched around my brother's.

Tobias's eyes were wide as he took in the flames engulfing our home. "We need to help Dad—"

"No." My mother pulled us away from the closest exit and into our living room. "This way."

I struggled as I realized where she was taking us, but her hand was like a steel vise around my wrist. "There's no way out from here, we need to—"

"Trust me," my mother gasped hoarsely as she led us toward the oversized mirror on the back wall. It gleamed strangely in the firelight—the glass rippling curiously.

A trick of the heat?

"This is the only way out," she continued. "You need to get to Quinn's…"

She coughed fitfully, a harsh, choked sound, and I knew if we stayed here another minute, the fire would be the least of our problems. The black smoke seared down my throat, as my eyes streamed tears.

"Mom, you need to tell us what's going on," I croaked. "Who *was* that—"

I didn't have a chance to finish my thought before she placed her hand on my chest and pushed me toward the mirror. Stumbling backwards, I reached behind me, grabbing onto the metal frame of the mirror, screaming as the brass rosettes trailing along the edge of the glass burned into the palm of my hand.

Tobias sucked in a breath as he took in the angry burn. "Eva—"

"You need to go, *now*," my mother choked out, her voice breaking. "Your dad and I will hold him off." She put a hand on my shoulder, squeezing Tobias's hand in the other. "Eyes up, stout hearts. Remember, the only way out is through."

The familiar refrain sounded frighteningly like a goodbye. From a glance, I could tell Tobias heard it too.

A sob lodged in my throat, and I choked on it.

"Come with us, Mom," Tobias pleaded, as confused as I was as he glanced at the undulating mirror. "Don't...you don't have to leave us."

She only looked at him sadly, then at me. "I love you."

For the rest of my life, I would regret not saying those three words back to her in that moment.

Then the door on the other side of the room was kicked open with a crash. A hooded figure stalked forward, barely visible through the smoke. My mother ran at him with a battle cry.

A blinding light flashed through the space, cutting through the din like lightning. My mother started screaming as the glow surrounded her, an endless keening howl as the brightness illuminated the man in the doorway.

Frozen with shock and pain, my eyes locked with his through the haze of the heat, his pale eyes flashing in the strange light as blood dripped from his sword.

His lips curved in a terrifying, soulless smile. "Finally."

My brother took a step toward our mom. But something bright slammed into my chest, and I fell back toward the mirror in an endless instant. All I could think was that I needed to get to Quinn's house, somewhere safe, somewhere I could get help—

But the solid glass wasn't there.

I screamed as I fell into the nothingness, my eyes closing as I welcomed the darkness.

Don't stop now. Keep reading with your copy of THE OTHER SIDE OF THE MIRROR

And find more from Amy Woodruff at
www.awoodruff.com

Don't miss the next book in the *Blood and Curses series* and find more from Amy Woodruff at www.awoodruff.com

Until then, discover THE OTHER SIDE OF THE MIRROR by City Owl Author, Dana Evyn!

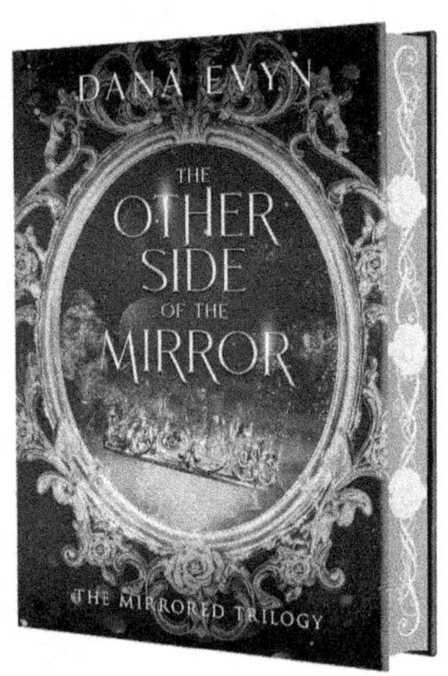

All her life, Eala Duir, a young college professor, has skirted the edges of a fantasy world.

Visions of folk stories coming alive in hearth flames and vivid daydreams where carousel horses ride off to battle, drove Eala to pursue an academic life specializing in tales of the Fae.

When a cryptic message in her grandmother's will sends her to Ireland, Eala clashes with Sionnach Loho, an attractive, enigmatic local expert on folklore. After witnessing Eala's encounter with a ghost girl at an allegedly haunted castle, Sionnach reveals his own ties to the Fae realm. He insists Eala's ability to connect with the supernatural proves she's been sent to partner with him and fulfill a centuries-old otherworldly quest ordained by the mighty Finnbheara, King of the Connacht Fae.

As folktales and faeries collide with Eala's reality, she must decide whether to embrace the fantastic or flee back to the safe and predictable life she thought she always wanted.

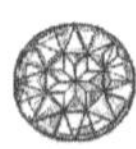

Please sign up for the City Owl Press newsletter at cityowlpress.com for chances to win special subscriber-only contests and giveaways as well as receiving information on upcoming releases and special excerpts.

All reviews are **welcome** and **appreciated**. Please consider leaving one on your favorite social media and book buying sites.

For books in the world of romance and speculative fiction that embody Innovation, Creativity, and Affordability, check out City Owl Press at www.cityowlpress.com.

ACKNOWLEDGMENTS

First, I would like to thank my Savior for blessing me with the ability to write and bring this story to conception. Thank you to my husband Vance, for believing in me from the very beginning and always encouraging me. I love you. Thank you to my mom and dad for always supporting me and helping me. I couldn't have done this without you, either. My besties and my book club girls: you've all made me feel so loved and encouraged through this entire process. I am so lucky to have such amazing friends.

Thanks to everyone on my publishing team, especially my editor, Danielle DeVor, for deciding to take a chance on my book and giving me the opportunity to send it out to the world. City Owl Press, you made a dream come true and have been so wonderful to me. Thank you for everything. Thank you to all my friends on TikTok and Instagram who have been so supportive and always hype up every post. I am so eternally grateful.

There are so many people I'm sure I'm missing that have made this journey possible, if I did, I'm sorry. Finally, thank you to my readers! My book and this journey would be nothing without you. You're the reason I write, and I will be forever grateful you decided to take the trip into the little world I created. Thank you!!

About the Author

AMY WOODRUFF is an author, librarian, and storyteller. Born and raised in Texas, Amy graduated from Texas A&M with a degree in Telecommunication Media Studies. She later obtained a Master's in Library Media and currently works as an elementary librarian in Dallas, where she lives with her husband and twin dogs. Amy has always been passionate about telling stories and writing. She can't wait to share all the adventures living in her mind with readers.

www.awoodruff.com

instagram.com/amywoodruffauthor
tiktok.com/@amywoodruffauthor

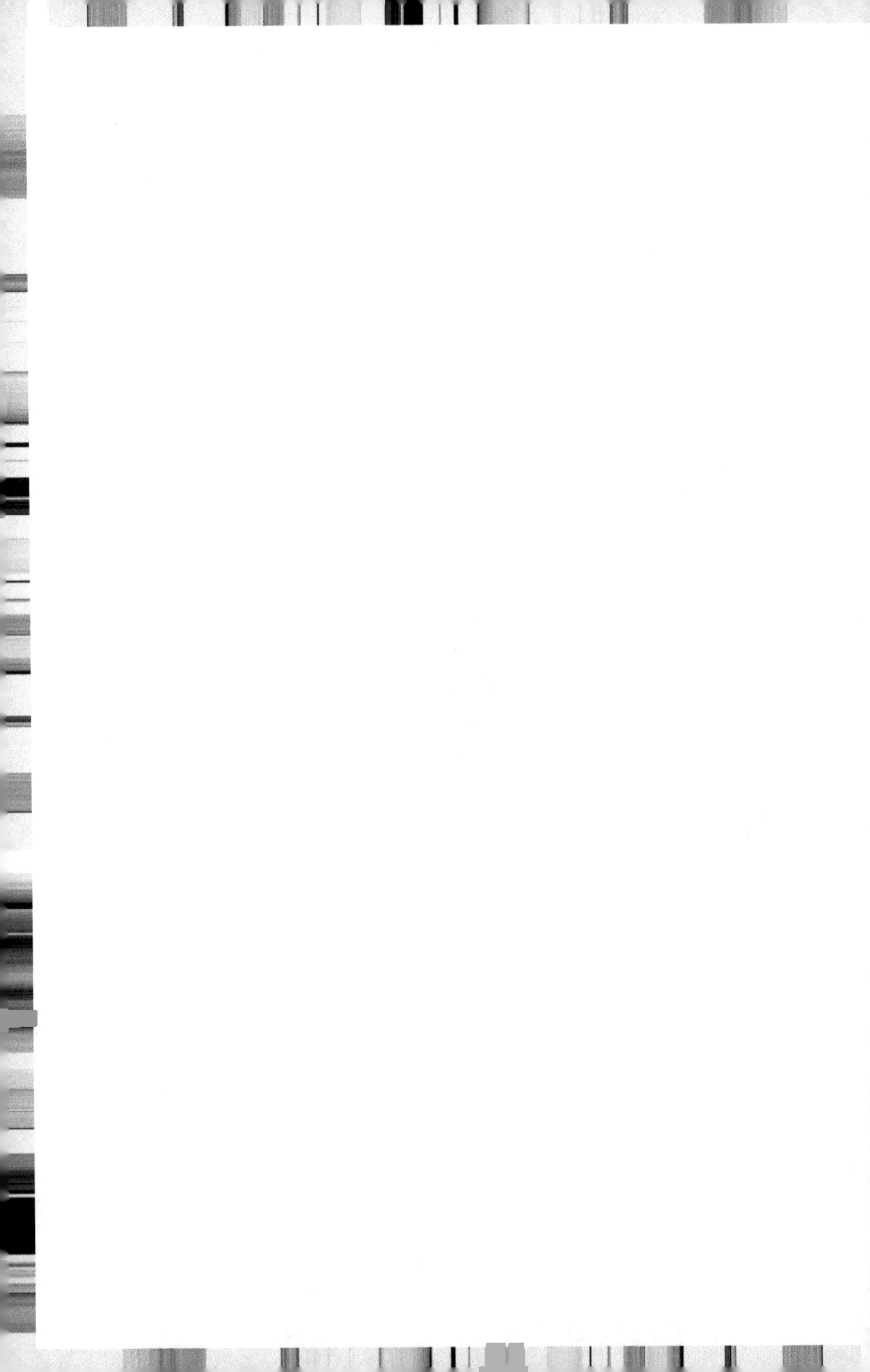

ABOUT THE PUBLISHER

City Owl Press is a cutting edge indie publishing company, bringing the world of romance and speculative fiction to discerning readers.

Escape Your World. Get Lost in Ours!

www.cityowlpress.com

facebook.com/CityOwlPress
x.com/cityowlpress
instagram.com/cityowlbooks
pinterest.com/cityowlpress
tiktok.com/@cityowlpress

www.ingramcontent.com/pod-product-compliance
Lightning Source LLC
LaVergne TN
LVHW020531100826
845148LV00010B/1413

* 9 7 8 1 6 4 8 9 8 4 6 9 3 *